GREAT SCIENCE FICTION
Stories by the World's Great Scientists

GREAT SCIENCE FICTION

Stories by the World's Great Scientists

Edited by Isaac Asimov, Martin H. Greenberg, and Charles G. Waugh

DONALD I. FINE, INC.
New York

Library of Congress Catalogue Card Number: 84-073519
ISBN: 0-917657-26-8
Manufactured in the United States of America
10 9 8 7 6 5 4 3 2 1

This book is printed on acid free paper. The paper in this book meets the guidelines for permanence and durability of the Committee on Production Guidelines for Book Longevity of the Council on Library Resources.

Acknowledgments, the following pages constitute an extension of the copyright page

White Creatures, by Gregory Benford, copyright © 1975 by Gregory Benford. Reprinted by permission of the author.

The Singing Diamond, by Robert L. Forward, copyright © 1979 by Robert L. Forward. Reprinted by permission of the author and the author's agent, the Scott Meredith Literary Agency, Inc., 845 Third Avenue, New York, NY 10022.

Publish and Perish, by Paul J. Nahin, copyright © 1978 by Condé Nast Publications, Inc. Reprinted by permission of the author.

Skystalk, by Charles Sheffield, copyright © 1979 by Charter Communications, Inc. Reprinted by permission of the author.

The Universal Library, by Kurd Lasswitz, translation copyrighted by Willy Ley. Reprinted by permission of Olga Ley.

Long Shot, by Vernor Vinge, copyright © 1972 by Condé Nast Publications, Inc. Reprinted by permission of the author.

Blackmail, by Fred Hoyle, copyright © 1967 by Fred Hoyle. Reprinted by permission of the author.

Jeannette's Hands, by Philip Latham, copyright © 1973 by Mercury Press, Inc. Reprinted by permission of the Scott Meredith Literary Agency, Inc., 845 Third Avenue, New York, NY 10022.

The Warm Space, by David Brin, copyright © 1985 by David Brin. Reprinted by permission of the author.

The Wind from the Sun, by Arthur C. Clarke, copyright © 1964 by Arthur C. Clarke. Reprinted by permission of the author and the author's agent, the Scott Meredith Literary Agency, Inc., 845 Third Avenue, New York, NY 10022.

Industrial Accident, by Lee Correy, copyright © 1980 by Davis Publications, Inc. Reprinted by permission of the author and the author's agent, the Scott Meredith Literary Agency, Inc., 845 Third Avenue, New York, NY 10022.

Choice, by J.R. Pierce, copyright © 1971 by Galaxy Publishing Corporation. Reprinted by permission of the author.

The Winnowing, by Isaac Asimov, copyright © 1976 by Condé Nast Publications, Inc. Reprinted by permission of the author.

Dr. Snow Maiden, by Larry Eisenberg, copyrighted © 1975 by Mercury Press, Inc. Reprinted by permission of the author.

On the Fourth Planet, by J.F. Bone, copyright © 1963 by Galaxy Publishing Corporation. Reprinted by permission of the author and the author's agent, the Scott Meredith Literary Agency, Inc., 845 Third Avenue, New York, NY 10022.

Acknowledgments continued on page 10.

Contents

INTRODUCTION

ONE OF THE great scientists in the days when modern science was beginning was the German astronomer and physicist, Johannes Kepler (1571–1630). His fascination with the heavenly bodies was such that he actually sat down and wrote a romance about someone who had flown to the Moon. He was cautious enough to keep it hidden during his lifetime. It was not published till 1634.

Interplanetary travel was not a totally original idea. The first fictional trip to the Moon, that still survives today, was written by Lucian of Samosata in Roman times, fifteen centuries before Kepler. Kepler, however, was the first scientist to write of such a trip. In fact, he was the first scientist who, as far as we know, wrote a story of any kind that was recognizable science fiction.

This created problems for Kepler. Earlier authors who wrote of flights to the Moon were romancers who did not trouble their heads with such matters as the distance to the Moon, which since the second century B.C. was known to be enormous. Lucian, for instance, had his travelers reach their goal by being lifted there by a waterspout.

Kepler was too knowledgeable to use such a device, but failing to think of a rational method, he had his hero carried to the Moon by spirits. Where earlier writers treated the Moon as just another country, not much different from such little-known regions as Africa or India, Kepler knew that the Moon was different, at least insofar as it had a day and a night that were each two weeks long. He therefore imagined it to be populated by strange plants and animals that grew madly during the day and died at nightfall.

7

Kepler's story was not followed immediately by a wealth of similar stories written by scientists. Science fiction grew and developed, but those writers who nurtured it, although usually quite knowledgeable in the science of the day (Edgar Allan Poe, Jules Verne, and H. G. Wells were all scientifically literate), were not professional scientists. Working scientists only occasionally tried their hands at writing science fiction, and when they did they usually didn't set the literary world on fire with their efforts. (This is not surprising. The craft of writing often requires a long and painstaking period of apprenticeship, and professional scientists who have arduous work of their own usually lack the time to develop literary polish.)

The French astronomer, Camille Flammarion (1842–1925), who was an ardent believer in life on other worlds—especially Mars—tried his hand at science fiction. The Russian physicist, Konstantin Tsiolkovsky (1857–1935), who was the first to deal with rocketry and space flight with mathematical rigor, also wrote a science fiction novel to illustrate his ideas for those who were not up to dealing with his equations.

Nowadays, however, it has become quite common for scientists to try their hands at science fiction. Why not? A surprising number of scientists found themselves fascinated by science fiction in their younger days and some were even lured into science this way. Why not, then, return the compliment, so to speak, and try to fascinate others in the same imaginative way that they themselves had been caught.

Not that it's easy to do this. On the contrary, it is very difficult, for to be a great scientist who writes great science fiction, one must have achieved an extraordinary balance, rather like a cone standing upright on its tip without falling over. To tell you the truth, I know some great scientists who write science fiction, and some great science fiction writers who are scientists, but, despite the title of this anthology, I don't know any *great* scientists who are *great* science fiction writers.

The trouble is that greatness in any direction doesn't usually catch a person by surprise. If, early on, a person realizes he is likely to become a great science fiction writer, he finds himself fascinated with his writing and, even though he may be on the road to science, will in all probability abandon that road.

Again, if, early on, a person realizes he has the capacity to be a great scientist, then even if he has the urge to write science fiction, chances are that he never will manage to find enough time to do much of it.

As a matter of fact, I myself came closer to the balance than most people. From my mid-teens, I was determined to be a science fiction writer, and I was also determined to be a scientist. I moved ahead in both directions with a kind of ferocious energy. I wrote more and more science fiction stories (some now recognized as classics) while at the same time obtaining my Ph.D. in chemistry from Columbia University and then joining the department of biochemistry at Boston University School of Medicine. By 1958, I was an associate professor, had written textbooks, and was at the same time in the first rank of S.F. writers. But by then, I had to choose. There was no time to do both properly. I chose writing. I still have my academic title, but I have been a full-time writer since 1958.

It is important, I think, to emphasize that there *are* people who try to do both, for too many scientists and too many science fiction readers think that there is some kind of peculiar dividing line between science and science fiction—that scientists must, of necessity, scorn science fiction, and that science fiction writers must, of equal necessity, be ignorant of science.

Not so! Not so!

So here we have a collection of a sizable number of science fiction stories of excellent quality that have been written by people who are either practicing scientists, or who obtained the education to become such, but drifted away from scientific disciplines because of their greater interest in writing. (We give the details in the headnotes.)

Wherever possible, we chose a story in which the writer dealt with his own field of expertise. Thus, my story "The Winnowing" is one of the few I have written that deals with biochemistry. Nor do we insist on the hard sciences only. Mario Pei (whom I knew when he was alive) has a story here that deals with linguistics in a thoroughly delightful and almost de Campian way.

So I wish you all joy in the reading.

—Isaac Asimov

Acknowledgements (continued)

Learning Theory, by James V. McConnell, copyright © 1957 by Galaxy Publishing Corporation. Reprinted by permission of the author.

Love is the Plan the Plan is Death, by James Tiptree, Jr., copyright © 1973 by James Tiptree, Jr. Reprinted by permission of the author and the author's agent, Virginia Kidd, 538 East Hartford Street, Milford, PA 18337.

Transfusion, by Chad Oliver copyright © 1959 by Street & Smith Publications, Inc. Reprinted by permission of the author.

In the Beginning, by Morton Klass, copyright © 1954 by Street & Smith Publications, Inc; copyright © renewed 1983 by Morton Klass. Reprinted by permission of the author.

Modulation in All Things, by Suzette Haden Elgin, copyright © 1980 by Suzette Haden Elgin. Reprinted by permission of the author.

The Bones of Charlemagne, by Mario A. Pei, copyright © 1958 by Mario A. Pei; copyright © renewed 1971 by Mario A. Pei. Reprinted by permission of Devin-Adair Publishers.

Gregory Benford

Born in Mobile, Alabama, both Gregory Benford (1941–)
and his twin brother James grew up to be physicists.

Gregory received a B.S. from the University of Oklahoma
(1963) and his M.S. (1965) and Ph.D. (1967) from the University of California, San Diego. He worked at the Lawrence
Radiation Laboratory in California as fellow and research
physicist (1967–1971) before accepting a faculty appointment at the University of California, Irvine (1971), where
he is currently employed.

A member of the American Physical Society and the
Royal Astronomical Society, he has been a Woodrow Wil-
son Fellow and a visiting fellow at Cambridge University,
and has also won the Nebula Award (1975) for "If the Stars
Are Gods," a novella he co-authored with Gordon Eklund.

He is the author or co-author of many scientific papers,
has contributed articles to popular magazines such as
Smithsonian and Natural History, and has had published
more than sixty science fiction novels and stories.

In addition to the story below, which concerns a scientist's view of an age-old subject, some of his best work
includes "Nobody Lives on Burton Street" (1971), "If the
Stars are Gods" (1974), "Knowing Her" (1977), and *Time-
scape* (1980).

WHITE CREATURES

by Gregory Benford

And after let me lie
On the breast of the darkening sky.

—JOAN ABBE

THE ALIENS STRAP him in. He cannot feel the bindings but he knows they must be there; he cannot move. Or perhaps it is the drug. They must have given him something, because his world is blurred, spongy. The white creatures are flowing shapes in watery light. He feels numb. The white creatures are moving about him, making high chittering noises. He tries to fix on them but they are vague formless shapes moving in and out of focus. They are cloudy, moving too fast to see, but he knows they are working on him. Something nudges his leg. For a moment something clicks at his side. Two white creatures make a dull drone and fade into the distance. All sensations are formless and cloudy; the air puckers with moisture. He tries to move, but his body is lethargic, painless, suspended. There is gravity; above, a pale glow illuminates the room. Yes, he is in a room. They have not brought him to their ship; they are using human buildings. He cannot remember being captured. How many people do they have? When he tries to focus on the memory it dissolves and slips away. He knows they are experi-

12

menting on him, probing for something. He tries to recall what happened but there are only scraps of memory and uncon- nected bunches of facts. He closes his eyes. Shutting out the murky light seems to clear his mind. Whatever they have given him still affects his body, but with concentration the vague- ness slips away. He is elated. Clarity returns; thoughts slide effortlessly in place. The textures of his inner mind are deep and strong.

Muddy sounds recede. If he can ignore the white creatures, things become sharp again. He knows he must get free of the white creatures and he can only do that if he can understand what is happening. He is absolutely alone and he must fight them. He must remember. He tries. The memories resolve slowly with a weight of their own. He tries.

He cut across the body of the wave, awash in churning foam. The clear Atlantic was startlingly cold. The waves were too small for boards but Merrick was able to body-surf on them easily. The momentum carried him almost to shore. He waded through the rippling currents and began jogging down the beach. After a moment his wind came to him and he ran faster. His long stride devoured the yards. He churned doggedly past forests of firm bodies; the beach was littered with Puerto Ricans. The tropical sun shimmered through a thin haze of sweat that trickled into his eyes. As his arms and legs grew leaden he diverted himself with glimpses of the figures and faces sliding by, moving stride by stride into his past. His mind wandered. Small families, leathery men, dogs and children—he made them all act out plays in his head, made them populate his preconceived universe. That was where he saw Erika Bascomb for the second time. He had met her at a reception some months before, known her only as the distant smiling wife of the Cyclops director. She sat on the sand, arms braced behind, and followed his progress. Her deliciously red lips parted in a smile more than mere welcoming and he slowed, stopped. His thickening waistline showed his age, thirty-eight, but his legs were as good as ever; strong, tanned, no stringy muscles or fine webbed nets of blue veins. Erika was a few years younger, heavily tanned from too much leisure time. So he stopped. He remembered that day better than any of the others. She was the first fresh element in his life for years, an antidote to the tedious hours of listening that filled his nights with Cyclops. He remembered her brown nipples pouting and the image dissolved into the green and brown swath of jungle that ringed the Cyclops project. The directional radio telescopes were each enormous, but ranked together in rigid lanes they added up to something somehow less massive. Each individual dish tipped soundlessly to cup an ear at the sky. The universe whispered, exciting a tremor of electrons in the metal lattice. He spent his days and nights trying to decipher those murmurs from eternity. Pens traced out the signals on graph paper and it was his lot to scan them for signs of order and intelligence. Bascomb was a pudgy radio astronomer intent on his work who tried to analyze each night's returns. Erika worked there as a linguist, a decoder for a message that never came. Merrick was merely a technician, a tracer of circuits. Project Cyclops had begun in earnest only the year before and he had landed a job with it after a decade of routine at NASA. When he came they were just beginning to search within a two-degree cone about the galactic center, looking for permanent beacons. If the galactic superculture was based in the hub, this was the most probable search technique. That was the Lederberg hypothesis, and as director Bascomb adopted it, supported it; and when it failed his stock in the project dropped somewhat. One saw him in the corridors late at night, gray slacks hanging from a protruding belly, the perpetual white shirt with its crescent of sweat at the armpits. Bascomb worked late, neglected his wife, and Erika drifted into Merrick's orbit. He remembered one night when they met at the very edge of the bowl valley and coupled smoothly beneath the giant webbing of the phased array. Bascomb was altering the bandwidth of the array, toying with the frequencies between the hydroxyl line and the twenty-one-centimeter hydrogen resonance. Merrick lay in the lush tropical grass with Erika and imagined he could hear the faint buzzing of hydrogen noise as it trickled from the sky into the Cyclops net, bearing random messages of the inert universe. Bascomb and his bandwidth, blind to the chemical surges of the body. Bascomb resisting the urgings of Drake, Bascomb checking only the conventional targets of Tau Ceti, Epsilon Eridani, the F and G and K stars within thirty light-years. Politics, a wilderness of competition and ideals and guesses. He tried to tell Erika of this but she knew it already, knew the facts anyway, and had tired of them. A linguist with nothing to translate. She waited for a mutter from the sky, but waiting dulled the mind and sharpened the senses. She shook her head when he spoke of it, fingers pale and white where she gripped the grass with compressed energy, head lowered as he took her from behind. Blonde strands hung free in the damp jungle twilight. Her eyelids flickered as his rhythm swelled up in her; she groaned with every stroke. The galaxy turned, a white swarm of bees.

The aliens seize him. He struggles against the padded ghost-like webbing. He moves his head a millimeter to see them but he cannot focus, cannot bring things to a point. The white creatures are patches of light. They make chittering shrieks to each other and move about him. Their images ripple and splinter; light cannot converge. They are performing experiments on humans. He tilts his head and sees a plastic tube snaking in from infinity. There is a fetid smell. The tube enters his nostril and penetrates his sinuses. Something flows into him or out of him—there seems little difference—and his perceptions shift and alter again. The white creatures make a nugget of pain within him. He tries to twist away but his cody is full of strange weaknesses, limbs slack. His face crinkles with pain. He feels delicate tremors, minute examinations at points along his legs and belly. He is an animal on the dissecting table and the white creatures are high above him, taller than men. Their rapid, insectlike gestures melt into the murky liquid light. They are cutting him open; he feels the sharp slitting in his calf. He opens his mouth to scream but nothing comes out. They will break him into parts; they will turn him inside out and spill his brains into a cup. His fluids will trickle onto cracked linoleum, be absorbed into the parched eternal earth. Do they know that he is male? Is this what they want to find out? Siphon away hormones, measure blood count, trace the twisted DNA helix, find the sense of rotation in body sugar?

15

What are they after? What could they use? He shuts them out, disconnects from the dense flooded universe outside his eyelids. He thinks.

Erika continued to meet him. There were sly deceptions, shopping expeditions in the town, Erika in a Peter Pan collar and cable-stitch cardigan; tan, arranged, intent, as much a monument to an America now vanished as a statue of Lincoln. Neat, making casual purchases, then into the back hotel room and coiled about him in sweaty ecstasy. She whispered things to him. That Bascomb was pale and soft underneath his clothes, a belly of suet, mind preoccupied with problems of planning, signal-to-noise ratios, search strategies. Listening to her secrets, Merrick thought uneasily that he was not that different from Bascomb, he believed the same things, but his body was hard and younger than the other man's. Erika had gradually drifted into the public relations office of Cyclops; as a linguist she had nothing to do. She escorted the oil-rich Arabs around the bowl-shaped valley, flattered the philanthropists who supported the project, wrote the press releases. She was good, she was clever, she made connections. And one day when Bascomb appeared suddenly in the hotel room, entering into the holy place of sighs and groans unannounced, she was ready. Merrick did not know what to do, saw himself in a comic role of fleeing adulterer, out the window with half his clothes and into the streets, running. But there was none of that. They were all very civilized. Erika said little, simply put on her clothes and left with Bascomb. The silence was unnerving. Merrick did not see her for two weeks and Bascomb never came into Merrick's part of the technical shop. A while later the rumor spread that Erika had left Bascomb, and before he could check it she was gone. She went to South America, they said, and he wondered why. But he knew quite well why he got the less desirable shifts now, why he was passed over for promotion, why he was transferred to the least likable foreman in the project. He knew.

The white creatures are gone for a while. Perhaps it is night. He lies with prickly points radiating in his body where they had cut him. He feels pierced and immobile, a butterfly pinned to a board. Blurred globs of cloudy sensation wash over him. Occasionally an alien passes through the murky light in the distance. The pale glow from the ceiling seems yellow. He wonders if he can deduce anything from this. He must try to gather scraps of information. Only through knowledge can he discover their weaknesses. Yellow light. A G-type star? The sun is a G-type and appears white in space. What would it look like beneath an atmosphere somewhat different from Earth's? It is impossible to say; there are so many kinds of stars: O and B and A and F and G and K and M. The O's are fierce and young; the M's red, aged, wise. O Be A Fine Girl, Kiss Me. He remembers Drake arguing that the search strategy should not include M-types because the volume around them supporting a ter-restrial-type planet would be so small. They would be locked by tides to their primary, said Dole. Merrick cannot follow the argument.

He left Puerto Rico after two years of gradual pressure from Bascomb. Erika severed her n-year marriage contract with Bascomb from Chile. Merrick was in Washington, D. C., doing routine work for NASA again, when he received her first letter. She had become a guide for the wealthy rising capitalists of Brazil, Chile, Argentina. She showed them the North American continent, carefully shepherding them around the polluted areas and the sprawling urban tangle. There was a market for that sort of talent; the insulation between social classes was breaking down in America. Erika could shuttle her group of rising capitalists from hotel to sea resort to imitation ranch, all the while preserving their serenity by taking care of all dealings with the natives. Her customers invariably spoke no English. She passed through Washington every few months and they began their affair again. He had other women, of course, but with Erika new doors of perception opened. Her steamy twists and slides never failed to wrap him in a timeless cloak. The dendrites demanded, the synapses chorused, ganglia murmured and the ligaments summoned; they danced the great dance. She forced him to cling to his youth. Between their rendings in the bedroom she would pace the floor energetically, generating piles of cigarette butts and speaking of everything, anything, nothing. He did not know if he ever really learned anything from her but that furious drive onward. She was no longer a girl: the slight slackening of age, the first bluntings of a world once sharp-edged, had begun. She could not deal with it. He saw the same beginnings in himself but ignored them, passed them over. Erika could not accept. The thought of juices souring within her made her pace furiously, smoke more, eat with a fierce energy. She knew what was coming. She saw. She had forgotten Alpha Centauri, Tau Ceti, the aching drifting silences.

The white creatures move in the watery light. He wonders suddenly if they swim in a liquid. He is in a bubble, moored to the bottom of a pool of ammonia, a plastic interface through which they study him. It explains much. But no, one brushes against his bed in passing and Merrick feels the reassuring vibration. They can breathe our atmosphere. They come from some place quite similar, perhaps guided by our UHF or VHF transmissions. He thinks this through. The North Canadian Defense Network is gone, victim of international treaties. There is cable television, satellite relay. Each no longer emits great bursts of power in those frequency bands. It has ceased to be a noisy signal in the universe. How did the white creatures find Earth? Why did Cyclops find nothing? We are not alone, the white creatures found us, but are all the other civilizations simply listening, can no one afford beacons? The white creatures do not say. Except for them is it a dead wheeling galaxy of blind matter? He cannot believe that.

He transferred to California in his late forties. There were still Mariners and Vikings, gravity-assisted flights to the outer planets, Mars burrowers and balloons for the clouds of Venus, sun skimmers and Earth measurers. He wanted that sort of work. It seemed to him as the years went on that it was the only thing worth doing. Cyclops was sputtering along, torn by factionalism and the eternal silence at twenty-one centimeters. He went to Los Angeles to do the work even though he hated the city; it was full of happy homogeneous people without

Table 2.

Comparison of Forecasts, 1964 and 1977 Developments

1964 STATEMENT	1977 STATEMENT	1964 MEDIAN	1977 MEDIAN	CORRELATION
Availability of a machine that comprehends standard IQ tests and scores above 150	Same; comprehend is understood as ability to respond to questions in English, accompanied by diagrams	1990	1992	About the same; larger deviation from median in 1977
Permanent base established on the Moon (ten men, indefinite stay)	Same	1982	1992	Later, a less optimistic forecast
Economic feasibility of commercial manufacture of many chemical elements from subatomic building blocks	Same	2100	2012	Earlier, a more optimistic forecast
Two-way communication with extraterrestrials	Discovery of information that proves the existence of intelligent beings beyond Earth (note change of wording; bias for earlier forecast)	2075	2025	Earlier, as expected
Commercial global ballistic transport (including boost-glide techniques)	Same	2000	2030	Later, though less deviation from median in 1977

structure or direction. While on the bus to work, it seemed to him Los Angeles went on long after it had already made its point. There were women there and people worth talking to, but nothing that drew him out of himself. Instead he concentrated on circuits and design work. Mazes of cold electrical logic had to be planted in delicate substrates. There were details of organization, of scheduling procedures, of signal strength and redundancy probability. To Erika all this was the same; she had lost interest in these matters when she left

19

Bascomb. Her business was thriving, however, and she had picked up a good series of contacts with China's subtle protectors of the people. These gentlemen were the new international rich who vacationed in the New World because the currency differential was favorable and, of course, increasing such contacts was good for the advancement of the ideas of Marx and Lenin and Mao. They came to see Disneyland, the beaches, the few tattered remnants of California history. But they remained in their hotels at night (even Los Angeles had muggers by then) and Erika could come to him whenever she chose. She was drinking more then and smoking one pack of cigarettes after another, choking the ashtray. The lines were lengthening around her eyes and on her forehead. Despite tanning and exercise and careful diet, age was catching her and in her business that was nearly fatal. She depended on her charm, gaiety, lightness; the South Americans and Chinese liked young Americans, blonde Americans. Erika was still witty and shrewd, sometimes warm, but her long legs, thin wrists, tight and sleek tanned skin were losing their allure. So she came to him frequently for solace and did not notice that he aged as well. She came to him again and again, whenever possible. He opened her. She stretched thin in the quilted shadows of his apartment, a layer one molecule thick that wrapped him in a river of musk. They made a thick animal pant fill the room until the sound became larger than they could control; they left it and went back to speaking with smoke fingers. He knew what to say. Erika moved under him. Above him. Through him. Some natural balance was lost in her, some sureness. He saw for a moment what it was and then she groaned and no longer did he know what he was about. O Be A Fine Girl, Open To Me.

They come to him in watery silence and slice him again. The smokelike strands keep him from struggling and needle points sting, cut, penetrate to marrow. These are no coded cries across hydrogen. These are real. The white creatures dart in and out of the mosaic around him. He looks beyond them and suddenly sees a cart go by with a body upon it. A human is trussed and bound, dead. The white creatures ignore the sight. They work upon him.

She began to lose patronage. The telephone rang less often and she made fewer trips to California. She began smoking more and picked at her food, afraid to ingest too many carbohydrates or fats that lengthen the lines and make the tissues sag. You have always lived in the future, she said. You love it, don't you. That's why you were at Cyclops and that's why you are with NASA. Yes, he said. Then what do you think of it now, she said. What do you think of your future? He shrugged. What do you think of mine, then? he said. A long slide down the back slope of the hill. It's harder for a woman, you know. I haven't got anyone. Bascomb is dead, you know. She snuffed out a cigarette. The failure of the project killed him, Merrick said. Erika studied the back of her hand. Her lips moved and she traced the fine webbing of lines with a fingernail. It's all downhill, she said absently. And then, abruptly: but not me. I'm not going to let it happen to me. He gave her a wry smile and lifted an eyebrow. She had drunk a lot of red wine and he attributed everything she said to that. No, I really mean it. She looked at him earnestly. I have some money now. I can do it now. What? he asked. The long sleep. He was shocked. He fumbled with his apartment keys and they made a hollow clanking sound in the sudden silence. You won't do that, he said. Of course I will. Her eyes blazed and she was suddenly filled with fire. Things will be different in the future, she said. We can't even get organ replacements without special approval now. I'm sure that will be different in a few decades and I know there will be some way to retard aging by that time. He frowned doubtfully. No, she went on, I'm sure of it. I'm going to have myself frozen. I would rather take the chance on that than live out my life the way it must be from now on. Merrick did not know how to deal with her. He took her home and saw her again the next day but she was an Erika changed now. In the long dry California night she sat astride him and rocked and wriggled her way to her own destination. Her breasts loomed over him like gravestones. Even when he was within

21

the sacred pocket of her she was an island bound for the frozen wastes. He did not let her see him cry.

Stephen Dole. Parameters for quasi-terrestrial planets.
    —surface gravity between 0.68 G and 1.5 G.
    —mean annual temperature of 10% of planetary surface between 0 and 30 degrees C. Seasonal variance not to exceed ± 10 degrees C.
    —atmospheric pressure between 0.15 and 3.4 Earth sea level. Partial pressure of oxygen between 107 and 400 Torr.
    —surface between 20% and 90% covered with water.
    —rainfall between 10 and 80 inches annually.
    —dust levels not to exceed 50 million particles per cubic foot. Winds and storms infrequent. Low seismic activity.
    —ionizing radiation must not exceed 0.02 Rem per week.
    —meteor infall rate comparable to Earth normal.
    —oxygen-producing life forms or suitable ammonia or methane-based biochemistry.
    —star on main sequence between types F_2 and K_1.
    —no nearby gas giant planets. Planet must not be tide-locked to primary star.
    —stable orbits within the ecosphere.
    —for habitation by men, eccentricity of planetary orbit must not exceed 0.2. Period of rotation between 2 and 96 hours. Axial tilt must be less than 80%.

Throughout the next year he tried to reason with her. There was so little hope of being revived. True, they were successfully bringing back people from nitrogen temperatures, 77 degrees Kelvin, but the cost was enormous. Even if she put her name on the public waiting list it could be decades before she was called, if ever. So she carefully took out the papers and documents and showed him the bank accounts in Mexico City, Panama, Melbourne, San Francisco. She had concealed it from him all the years, her steadily amassing assets that never showed in her style of living or her choice of friends. He began to realize that she was a marvelously controlled woman. She had leeched an Argentine businessman of hundreds of thousands while she was his mistress. She had made sound speculations in the land markets of rural Brazil. She withdrew from the stock market just before the catastrophe of '93. It seemed incredible but there it was. She had the money to ensure that she would be revived when something fundamental had been achieved in retarding aging. He realized he did not truly know her, yet he wanted to. There was a long silence between them and then she said, you know this feeling? She threw her head back. Her blonde hair swirled like a warm, dry fluid in the air. Yes, sure, Merrick said. She looked at him intensely. I've just begun to realize that isn't what you're about, she said. You're married to something else. But that instant of feeling and being alive is worth all your ideals and philosophies.

He mixed himself a drink. He saw he did not know her.

The white creatures come again. He is so small, compared to his scream.

He went with her to the center. There were formalities and forms to be signed, but they evaporated too soon and the attendant led her way. He waited in a small cold room until she reappeared wearing a paper smock. Erika smiled uncertainly. Without makeup she was somehow younger but he knew it would be useless to say so. The attendants left them alone and they talked for a while about inconsequential things, recalling Puerto Rico and Washington and California. He realized they were talking about his life instead of hers. Hers would go on. She had some other port of call beyond his horizon and she was already mentally going there, had already left him behind. After an hour their conversation dribbled away. She gave him a curiously virginal kiss and the attendants returned when she signaled. She passed through the beaded curtain. He heard their footsteps fade away. He tried to imagine where she was going, the infinite cold nitrogen bath in which she would swim. She drifted lazily, her hair swirling. He saw only her gravestone breasts.

Merrick worked into the small hours of the morning at the Image Processing Laboratory. The video monitor was returning data from the Viking craft that had landed on the surface of Titan the day before. Atmospheric pressure was 0.43 Earth sea level. The chemical processors reported methane, hydrogen, some traces of ammonia vapor. The astrophysicists were watching the telemetered returns from the onboard chemical laboratory and Merrick was alone as he watched the computer contrast-enhancement techniques fill in line by line the first photographic returns. Through his headphones he heard the bulletins about the chemical returns. There was some evidence of amino acids and long-chain polymers. The chemists thought there were signs of lipids and the few reporters present scurried over to that department to discuss the news. So it was that Merrick became the first man to see the face of Titan. The hills were rocky, with dark grainy dust embedded in ammonia ice. A low methane cloud clung to the narrow valley. Pools of methane lay scattered among boulders; the testing tendrils of the Viking were laced through several of the ponds. There was life. Scattered, rudimentary, but life. With aching slowness, some simple process of reproduction went on in the shallow pools at 167 degrees Kelvin. Merrick watched the screen for a long time before he went on with the technician's dry duties. It was the high point of his life. He had seen the face of the totally alien.

Some years later, seeking something, he visited the Krishna temple. There was a large room packed with saffron-robed figures being lectured on doctrine. Merrick could not quite tell them what he wanted. They nodded reassuringly and tried to draw him out but the words would not come. Finally they led him through a beaded curtain to the outside. They entered a small garden through a bamboo gate, noisily slipping the wooden latch. A small man sat in lotus position on a broad swath of green. As Merrick stood before him, the walnut-brown man studied him with quick, assessing yellow eyes. He gestured for Merrick to sit. They exhanged pleasantries. Merrick explained his feelings, his rational skepticism about religion in any form. He was a scientist. But perhaps there was more to these matters than met the eye, he said hopefully. The

24

teacher picked up a leaf, smiling, and asked why anyone should spend his life studying the makeup of this leaf. What could be gained from it? Any form of knowledge has a chance of resonating with other kinds, Merrick replied. So? the man countered. Suppose the universe is a parable, Merrick said haltingly. By studying part of it, or finding other intelligences in it and discovering their viewpoints, perhaps we could learn something of the design that was intended. Surely the laws of science, the origins of life, were no accident. The teacher pondered for a moment. No, he said, they are not accidents. There may be other creatures in this universe, too. But these laws, these beings, they are not important. The physical laws are the bars of a cage. The central point is not to study the bars, but to get out of the cage. Merrick could not follow this. It seemed to him that the act of discovering things, of reaching out, was everything. There was something immortal about it. The small man blinked and said, it is nothing. This world is an insane asylum for souls. Only the flawed remain here. Merrick began to talk about his work with NASA and Erika. The small man waved away these points and shook his head. No, he said. It is nothing.

On the way to the hospital he met a woman in the street. He glanced at her vaguely and then a chill shock ran through him, banishing all thoughts of the cancer within. She was Erika. No, she only looked like Erika. She could not be Erika, that was impossible. She was bundled up in a blue coat and she hurried through the crisp San Francisco afternoon. A half block away he could see she did not have the same facial lines, the same walk, the bearing of Erika. He felt an excitement nonetheless. The turbulence was totally intellectual, he realized. The familiar vague tension in him was gone, had faded without his noticing the loss. He felt no welling pressure. As she approached he thought perhaps she would look at him speculatively but her glance passed through him without seeing. He knew that it had been some time now since the random skitting images of women had crossed his mind involuntarily. No fleshy feast of thighs, hips, curving waists, no electric

25

flicker of eyelashes that ignited broiling warmth in his loins. He had not had a woman in years.

The hospital was only two blocks farther but he could not wait. Merrick found a public restroom and went in. He stood at the urinal feeling the faint tickling release and noticed that the word BOOK was gouged in square capitals in the wall before him. He leaned over and studied it. After a moment he noticed that this word had been laid over another. The F had been extended and closed to make a B, the U and C closed to O's, the K left as it was. He absorbed the fact, totally new to him, that every FUCK could be made into a BOOK. Who had done the carving? Was the whole transition a metaphysical joust? The entire episode, now fossilized, seemed fraught with interpretation. Distracted, he felt a warm trickle of urine running down his fingers. He fumbled at his pants and shuffled over to the washbasin. There was no soap but he ran water over his wrinkled fingers and shook them dry in the chill air. There was a faint sour tang of urine trapped in the room, mingling with the ammonia odor of disinfectant. Ammonia. Methane. Titan. His attention drifted away for a moment and suddenly he remembered Erika. That was her in the street, he was sure of it. He looked around, found the exit and slowly made his way up the steps to the sidewalk. He looked down the street but there was no sign of her. A car passed; she was not in it. He turned one way, then the other. He could not make up his mind. He had been going that way, toward the hospital. Carrying the dark heavy thing inside him, going to the hospital. That way. But this—he looked in the other direction. Erika had walked this way and was moving rather quickly. She could easily be out of sight by now. He turned again and his foot caught on something. He felt himself falling. There was a slow gliding feel to it as though the falling took forever and he gave himself over to the sensation without thought of correcting it. He was falling. It felt so good.

The aliens are upon him. They crowd around, gibbering. Blurred gestures in the liquid light. They crowd closer; he raises his arm to ward them off and in the act his vision clears. The damp air parts and he sees. His arm is a spindly thread of bone, the forearm showing strings of muscle under the skin. He does not understand. He moves his head. The upper arm is a sagging bag of fat, and white. The sliding marbled slabs of flesh tremble as he strains to hold up his arm. Small black hairs sprout from the gray skin. He tries to scream. Cords stand out on his neck but he can make no sound. The white creatures are drifting ghosts of white in the distance. Something has happened to him. He blinks and watches an alien seize his arm. The image ripples and he sees it is a woman, a nurse. He moves his arm weakly. O Be A Fine Girl, Help Me. The blur falls away and he sees the white creatures are men. They are men. Words slide by him; he cannot understand. His tongue is thick and heavy and damp. He twists his head. A latticework of glass tubes stands next to his bed. He sees his reflection in a stainless-steel instrument case; hollow pits of his eyes, slack jaw, wrinkled skin shiny with sweat. They speak to him. They want him to do something. They are running clean and cool. They want him to do something, to write something, to sign a form. He opens his mouth to ask why and his tongue runs over the smooth blunted edge of his gums. They have taken away his teeth, his bridge. He listens to their slurred words. Sign something. A release form, he was found in the street on his way to check in. The operation is tomorrow—a search, merely a search, exploratory . . . he wrenches away from them. He does not believe them. They are white creatures. Aliens from the great drifting silences between the stars. Cyclops. Titan. He has spent his life on the aliens and they are not here. They have come to nothing. They are speaking again but he does not want to listen. If it were possible to close his ears—

But why do they say I am old? I am still here. I am thinking, feeling. It cannot be like this. I am, I am . . . Why do they say I am old?

Robert L. Forward

Born in Geneva, New York, Robert L. Forward (1932–   ) seems to have made a habit of hopping from coast to coast.

After receiving his B.S. from the University of Maryland (1954), he served in the air force for two years, then acquired his M.S. from the University of California, Los Angeles (1958). He returned to Maryland for his Ph.D. in gravitational physics in 1965. Part of this last work involved the construction of the first gravitational radiation antenna for the detection of interstellar gravitational radiation, a device which is now on display at the Smithsonian Institution in Washington, D.C.

A senior scientist at the Hughes Research Laboratories in California, he is a member of the American Institute of Aeronautics and Astronautics, the American Astronautical Society, the Institute of Electrical and Electronic Engineers, the American Physical Society, the American Geophysical Union and the British Interplanetary Society.

The author or co-author of some sixty professional papers, he has received the Research Award from the Ventura Branch of the Scientific Research Society of America (1968) and the weighty Award for Outstanding Achievement in the Field of Gravity from the Gravity Research Foundation (1965).

To date he has written three science fiction novels (*Dragon's Egg*, 1980; *The Flight of The Dragonfly*, 1984; and *Starquake!*, in press) and several short stories, including the striking piece on alien contact that follows.

THE SINGING DIAMOND

BY *ROBERT L. FORWARD*

M Y ASTEROID WAS singing. Alone, but safe in my ship, I heard the multitude of voices coming through the rock. They were an angel chorus in a fluid tongue, strange but beautiful.

I followed the source of the sound, stereo headphones connected to a pair of sonar microphones buried in the crust. The voices were moving slowly through the solid stone. They suddenly stopped, cut off in the middle of a tremulous crescendo. I took off the earphones, looked up from the sonar screen, and peered out the port at the black void around me. I could see nothing. I would have thought my ears were playing tricks on me if I had not seen the unusual fuzzy ball on the three-dimensional display of the sonar mapper.

I stopped the pinger that was sending short bursts of sound down into the asteroid I had captured and waited while the last few pulses echoed back from within the body of almost pure metallic ore. This find would bring me a fortune once I surveyed it and got it back to the processing plant.

Most rock-hoppers are content to set up the sonar mapper on a potential claim and let the computer do the job of determining whether there is enough metal in the rock to justify dragging it in. But I always liked to work along with the computer, watching the reflections on the screen and listening to the quality of the echoes. By now my ears were so well trained I could almost tell the nickel content of an inclusion by the "accent" it put on the returning sound. But this time my ears had heard something coming from the solid rock that had not been put there by the pinger.

I had the computer play back its memory, and again I heard the eerie voices, like a chorus of sirens calling me to leave my ship and penetrate into their dense home. I was sure now that the music was real, since the computer had heard it too. I replayed the data again and found that the sound had started on one side of the asteroid, traveled right through the center in a straight line and then had gone out the other side. I had a hunch, and ninety minutes later was waiting, earphones on, when the singing started again. This time the voices started at a different position on the surface of the asteroid, but as before, they slowly traveled in a straight line, right through the exact center of the rock and out the other side. A quick session with the computer verified my hunch. Whatever was doing the singing was orbiting the asteroid, but instead of circling about it like a moon, the orbit went back and forth right through the dense nickel-iron core!

My first thought was that the weak gravity field of the asteroid had trapped a miniature black hole. The singing would be caused by stresses in the metal ore from the intense gravitational field of the moving point of warped space. But then I realized the asteroid was too tiny, only a few hundred meters across, to have captured a black hole.

The computer did more work. It determined the orbital parameters and predicted where the singers would next intersect the surface of my slowly revolving rock. I was outside, waiting at that point, when it came.

For a long time I could see nothing. Then, high above me, there was a cloud of little sun specks—falling toward me. The glittering spots in the cloud moved in rapid swirls that were too fast to follow, and the cloud seemed to pulsate, changing in size and shape. Sometimes it collapsed into an intense concentration that was almost too small to see, only to expand later into a glittering ball as big as my helmet. Inexorably, the gravity of the asteroid pulled the swarm of star-midges down toward me. They were getting close. I tried to move back out of their path, but in my excitement I had floated upward in the weak gravity, and my magnetic boots were useless. Twisting my body around, I tried to dodge, but the cloud of light spots expanded just as it passed me. I screamed and blanked out as my right leg burst into pain. I felt as if I had stepped into a swarm of army ants.

I awoke, the emergency beeper shouting in my ear. My leg ached, and my air was low. Detached, I looked down at the agony below my knee to see fine jets of vapor shooting out from hundreds of tiny holes in my boot. Fortunately, most of the holes seemed to be clogged with frozen balls of reddish stuff. My numbed brain refused to recognize the substance.

Using my hands, I dragged myself across the surface to my ship and carefully pulled my suit off. Insult was added to injury as the suit's sani-seal extracted a few red hairs as I peeled it off. I looked carefully at my leg. The tiny holes had stopped bleeding, so I was in no immediate danger. I just hurt a lot.

For the next few days I let my leg heal while I listened to the music. I know that I was imagining it, but the beautiful voices now seemed to have a tinge of menace to them. The computer carefully monitored the motion of the swarm. It returned every ninety-three minutes, the normal time of close orbit around an asteroid with such a high density. Once, I had to move the ship to keep it away from the singing swarm as it came up out of the rock underneath.

After I could move around again, I experimented. Tracking the swarm as it went upward away from the surface. I used the mass detector on it at the top of its trajectory. The collection of nearly invisible specks weighed eighty kilos—as much as I did in my space suit!

I put a thin sheet of foil underneath the swarm as it fell and later examined the myriad tiny holes under a microscope. The aluminum had been penetrated many hundreds of times by each of the specks as they swirled about in the slowly falling cloud. Whatever they were, they were about the size of a speck of dust. I finally counted the midges by tracing the streaks on a print made with my instacamera. There were over one thousand of them.

I was stumped. What was I going to do? No matter how valuable the asteroid was to me, I could not drag it back to the processing plant with its deadly hornet's nest swirling about it.

I thought about pushing the asteroid out from under the cloud, but my small ship was not going to move a twenty-million-ton chunk of rock at anything like the acceleration needed. I would have to get rid of the stinging swarm in some way, but how do you trap something that travels through solid iron like it isn't there? Besides, it could be that the tiny star specks themselves were worth more than the ball of ore that they orbited.

I finally gave up and called for help. "Belt Traffic Control, this is 'Red' Vengeance in The Billionaire. I have a problem. Would you please patch the following message to Belt Science Authority?" I then gave a detailed description of what I had been able to learn about my tiny pests. I signed off and started lunch. It was nearly twenty light-minutes to the Belt Traffic Control station.

In two weeks a few of the small cadre of scientists who were allowed to live out in the belt were there, cluttering up my rock with their instruments. They couldn't learn much more with their gadgets than I did with my camera and aluminum foil. The specks were tiny and very dense. No one could think of any way to trap them.

I was ready to abandon my claim and leave a fortune and its buzzing poltergeist to the scientists when I remembered the Belt Facility for Dangerous Experiments. The major activity was a high-current particle accelerator designed to produce the antihydrogen that filled the "water torch" engines used in deep space. At each refueling I would watch apprehensively as electric fields and laser beams carefully shepherded a few grams of

frozen antimatter into my engine room. There, each grain anni-
hilated would heat many tons of water into a blazing exhaust.

However, antimatter has other uses, and nearby a group
made exotic materials by explosive-forming. I went to them
with my problem. Soon I had a bemused entourage of high-
powered brains trying to think of ways to stop my irrestible
objects. We were relaxing with drink squeezers in the face-
tiously named Boom! room, which overlooked the distant explosive-forming test site. I dressed for the occasion in an
emerald-green bodysuit that I had chosen to match my eyes,
and a diaphanous skirt that required dexterity to keep it looking properly arranged in free fall. I wore my one luxury, an
uncirculated solid-gold Spanish doubloon.

While the discussions were going on, news arrived from the
contingent still observing my find. The specks were still moving too fast to take close-up pictures with the cameras available, but at least the size and density of the specks had been
determined. They were dense, but not of nuclear density, only
about a million times greater than the density of water.

"Our bodies are one thousand times more dense than air, and
we can move through that with ease," I said. "So, at a density
ratio of a million to one, my leg was like a vacuum to them!
No wonder they can go through solid iron like it isn't even
there! . . ."

"Although the asteroid's iron can't stop the swarm, its gravity does hold them," said one scientist. He pulled out a card
computer and started scratching with his fingernail on the plia-
ble input-output surface. We clustered around, holding position
by whatever handhold was available and watched as his crude
scratchings were replaced by a computer-generated picture of a
flat disk with curved arrows pointing smoothly in toward its
two faces.

"What is it?" I asked.

"Flypaper," he said, looking up at me floating above him.
"Or, for your problem, Red—gnat paper."

His thick fingers scratched some more calculations, this
time in pure math. I followed them without too much trouble.
There were no pictures to give me any clues, but it was obvious

from the symbols that he was merely applying Newton's Law of Gravity to a disk instead of to the usual sphere.

"We can make the flypaper with the explosive-forming techniques we have developed," he said, "but to keep it from decomposing, we are going to have to contain it in a pressure capsule."

The process looks deceptively simple when one looks out through the eyes of an auto-robot. You merely take a large rotating asteroid as big as an office building and hit it from all sides with a spray of antimatter. When the shock wave passes, you have a small, rapidly spinning plate of glowing decomposed matter that is trying desperately to regain its former bulk. Before it does, you hit it from twelve sides with a carefully arranged set of accurately cut chunks of nickel-iron lined with pure carbon. In the split nanosecond that the configuration is compressed together into an elastically rebounding supersolid, you coat it heavily with another layer of antimatter and let it cool for a week.

The auto-robots brought it to us—still warm. It was a diamond—with a flaw. Right in the center of the barrel-sized crystal was a thick sheet of highly reflecting metal.

"What is that?" I asked the one who had arranged the fireworks display.

"The original asteroid, Miss Vengeance," he replied. "All four million tons of it. It has been compressed into a thin disk of ultradense matter and surrounded by diamond to keep it from expanding back into normal matter. There is your flypaper; let's go use it."

The disk was thirty centimeters across and only a centimeter thick, but it took a large space tug to heave that ultraheavy pancake griddle into an orbit that would reach my claim and its singing hangers-on. Once it was there, it was delicate work getting the sluggish plate placed in the path of the glittering cloud that still bounced back and forth through my property every ninety-three minutes. Finally the task was accomplished. Passing slowly through the diamond casing as if it were not there, the scintillating sparks floated upward toward the metal disk—and stuck.

"They stopped!" I shouted in amazement.

"Of course," said a metallic voice over my suit speaker. "They ran into something that was denser than they are, and its gravitational field is strong enough to hold them on its surface."

"Something that dense must be a billion g's," I said.

"I wish it were," said the voice. "I would have liked to have made the gravity stronger so I could be sure we would hold on to the specks once we had stopped them. With the limited facilities we have at the test site, the most matter we can compress at one time is four million tons. That disk has a gravitational field of only one g on each side."

After watching for a while, I saw that the tiny specks were not going to be able to leave the surface of their flat-world prison. I conquered my fear and let my helmet rest against the outside of the diamond casing that encapsulated the shiny disk and its prisoners.

The diamond was singing.

The voices I remembered were there, but they were different from the wild, free-swirling chorus that still haunted me from our first meeting. The singing now seemed constrained and flat.

I laughed at my subconscious double pun and pulled back to let the scientists have their prize. They hauled the crystalline cask away with the space tug, and I returned to the difficult months-long task of getting my asteroid back to the processing station.

I made a fortune. Even my trained ear had underestimated the nickel content. When payoff time came, I knew that from then on every expedition I made out into the belt was for fun and gravy, for all the money I would ever need for a decent retirement nest egg was in solid credits in the Bank of Outer Belt.

With no more financial worries, I began to take an interest in my little beasties—for that is what they were. The high-speed cameras had been able to determine that their complex motion was not due to random natural laws but was caused by the deliberate motion of each of the spots with respect to the others. A few frames had even shown some of the tiny specks in the process of emitting a little jet of gamma-ray exhaust in order to change its course to meet with another speck for a fraction of a microsecond. Then, many revolutions and many milliseconds later, each of the two specks that had previously met would release another tiny speck, which joined the great swarm in its seemingly random motion.

The most significant frame from the high-speed cameras, however, is the one that I have blown up into a holopicture over the head of my bunk. I didn't think that you could create a decent three-dimensional likeness of someone using only a thousand points of light, but it is me, all right. Everyone recognizes it instantly—aristocratic nose, bobbed hair, helmet, mike, freckles, and all the rest.

But that is all the beasties have ever done in the way of communication. For years the scientists have tried to get some other response from them, but the specks just ignore their efforts. I guess that when you live a trillion times faster than someone else, even a short dialogue seems to drag on forever and just isn't worth the effort. The scientist even took the diamond down to Earth and tried to build a superfast robot as a translator. Now, after years of examination and fruitless attempts to communicate, we finally were able to place the diamond in the San-San Zoo.

The specks, which used to be plastered to one side of the dense disk, are free now that they are on Earth. The one-g upward pull of the underside of the disk is exactly canceled by the one-g downward pull of the Earth. The specks seem to be perfectly happy. They could easily leave the gravity-free region under the disk, but they don't seem to want to. Their cloud stays a compact sphere just below their antigravity ceiling. They continue with their complex intermingling, swirling behaviour, passing easily through the ultrahard diamond that holds up their four-million-ton roof.

When I was a young girl at Space Polytech, I dreamed that when I got rich I would spend my later years reveling in the vacation spots around the world and throughout the solar system, but now I don't want to. Sometimes I can stand it for a whole month—but then I just have to go back and hear my diamond song.

Paul J. Nahin

To Paul J. Nahin (1940–   ), associate professor of electrical and computer engineering at the University of New Hampshire, college life must seem familiar, having been born in Berkeley, California to a father attending graduate school there.

All three of his degrees are in electrical engineering, the B.S. obtained from Stanford (1962), the M.S. from the California Institute of Technology (1963), and the Ph.D.—an investigation of pattern recognition—from the University of California at Irvine (1972).

The author of about a dozen research papers, he received the Best Technical Paper Award from the Institute of Electrical and Electronic Engineers in 1979, and is currently writing the biography of Oliver Heavyside, a prominent early twentieth-century scientist.

Nahin says that he is a family man whose life is mostly bland and uneventful, the major spice being his science fiction short stories, which began attracting attention in 1977. So far, he has published more than a score. But the devastating satire of government-sponsored research that appears in the story below suggests that he will publish many more before his career is through.

PUBLISH AND PERISH

by Paul J. Nahin

March 17, 1977

Mr. Thomas W. Starr
3613 Laguna Avenue
La Mesa, California 92041

Dear Mr. Starr,

It is with pleasure that I welcome you to the faculty of the California Technological Institute. Dean Johnson has informed me that you have accepted the appointment of instructor in physics. Your title will change to assistant professor upon completion of your doctoral studies.

We look forward to seeing you in September.

Sincerely,

Dr. W. Alden Smith
Office of the President

May 3, 1977

Mr. Thomas W. Starr
3613 Laguna Avenue
La Mesa, California 92041

Dear Tom,

President Smith has asked me to write to you about an issue we wish to have clear before you arrive on campus in September. Your appointment is for two years (renewable), but you must receive your Ph.D. by December 1 of your second academic year with us. Otherwise, because of the institute's by-laws, we would be unable to recommend your reappointment to the trustees.

Sincerely,

Peter V. Johnson, Ph.D.
Office of the Dean

May 8, 1977

Dr. Peter V. Johnson
Dean of Engineering and Science
California Technological Institute
Claremont, California 91711

Dear Dean Johnson,

The completion of my doctorate by December 1, 1978, will be no problem. I have talked this matter over, at some length, with my dissertation adviser, Professor B. B. Abernathy, at San Diego Tech. He assures me there will be no difficulty. He is even joking about there being a Nobel Prize in it for the two of us!

Cordially,

Thomas W. Starr

September 9, 1977

Mr. Thomas W. Starr
1713 12th Street
Claremont, California 91711

Dear Tom,

Sorry we missed our regular meeting last week, but I couldn't skip the review briefing on my grant at the Pentagon (but the thought of the agony of the red-eye flight to D.C. almost made it worthwhile to cancel out). While losing my way wandering around the Puzzle Palace, I happened to mention some of your most recent results toward inducing nuclear fusion in water and it caused quite a stir. If you get tired of teaching in Claremont, give the Civil Service a thought—you can't believe some of the nitwits with GS-12 and -13 ratings they've got back there. A good man like you would get snapped right up, and it certainly beats what they pay young, new college teachers.

See you next week, and we will discuss the first draft of your thesis.

Regards,

Bertram B. Abernathy, Ph.D.
Professor of Physics

14 October 1977

Mr. Thomas W. Starr
Physics Department
California Technical Institute
Claremont, California 91711

Dear Mr. Starr,

It has recently come to our attention that you have been pursuing innovative concepts on the possibility of introducing nuclear fusion in water. Your doctoral research support is funded through an Army Office of Scientific Research grant to professor B. B. Abernathy, and as you know, we retain the right to request periodic reviews of research supported by us.

Professor Abernathy has informed us that you are now writing a thesis for open publication, based on your work. Please send three (3) copies of your draft to:

Colonel Andrew Bobble
Chief, Nuclear Security Review Office (Army)
The Pentagon
Washington, DC 20310

Sincerely,

Patricia Adams
Administrative Assistant
Nuclear Security Review Office (Army)

7 January 1978

Mr. Thomas W. Starr
Physics Department
California Technological Institute
Claremont, California 91711

Dear Mr. Starr,

After a careful study of the material you recently sent to us for a review, we have classified it. Please forward all additional copies of your thesis drafts, plus any other related documents, within ten days, by registered mail in a sealed envelope within a sealed envelope.

Sincerely,

Colonel Andrew Bobble
Chief, Nuclear Security Review Office (Army)

January 11, 1978

Colonel Andrew Bobble
Chief, Nuclear Security Review Office (Army)
The Pentagon
Washington, DC 20310

Dear Colonel Bobble,

I have read your letter to me of January 7, and I am at a loss to understand what you mean by "classifying" my Ph.D. dissertation. I have no security clearance, and at no time have I had access to classified information.

I am sure that any little details in my writing that might cause some concern by your office will be easy for me to work around. If you will send me a list of the particular issues in question, I will be glad to take them into consideration as I finish up my writing.

Sincerely,

Thomas W. Starr

20 January 1978

Mr. Thomas W. Starr
Physics Department
California Technological Institute
Claremont, California 91711

Dear Mr. Starr,

This letter is to inform you that there is no appeal from our decision to classify the draft material you recently sent to us. It is our final conclusion that there is no possible way to rewrite this material to eliminate the possibility of disclosing information vital to the national security of the United States. We cannot transmit the list requested in your letter because such a list would be classified, and you have no clearance.

To discuss this matter further, it will be necessary for you to obtain a clearance from the Defense Industrial Security Corporation (at your personal expense), and to travel to Washington to meet with our staff. Even if you decide to do this, we must receive all information still in your possession.

Sincerely,

Colonel Andrew Bobble
Chief, Nuclear Security Review Office (Army)

January 25, 1978

Colonel Andrew Bobble
Chief, Nuclear Security Review Office (Army)
The Pentagon
Washington, DC 20319

Dear Colonel Bobble,

I can't believe this! You are destroying my career with all this Catch-22 crap about national security leaks that you can't tell me about because I don't have a clearance.

I have looked into getting a clearance, too. The DISCO investigation fee is $4,000! I haven't got forty bucks.

How did you get to be a colonel? Thinking up stupid things like this? Well, you can go to hell! What I think up on my time, with my brain, is none of the Pentagon's damn business. I will finish my writing, publish it, and the army can go screw itself.

Sincerely,

Thomas W. Starr

Paul A. Nahin

February 1, 1978

Mr. Thomas W. Starr
Physics Department
California Technological Institute
Claremont, California 91711

Dear Mr. Starr,

In response to your letter of 25 January, enclosed is a copy of Title 18 of the United States Espionage and Sabotage Acts. Release of classified information is a felony offense, punishable by up to ten years in prison, or up to a $10,000 fine, or both.

We are instructing University Microfilms not to produce microfilm xerographic copies of any unauthorized thesis you attempt to submit. In addition, we have notified all domestic and international journals of physics and/or chemistry that publication of papers by you, without any prior release, may constitute a security violation.

Please submit all documents on your research to us, as requested earlier, postmarked no later than 15 February 1978.

Sincerely,

Colonel Andrew Bobble
Chief, Nuclear Security Review Office (Army)

February 10, 1978

Colonel Andrew Bobble
Chief, Nuclear Security Review Office (Army)
The Pentagon
Washington, DC 20310

Dear Andy,

Enclosed are all the documents you have requested from Tom Starr. I am taking care of all the details of tranferring the water fusion work to secure, classified areas as Tom is in no shape, emotionally, to do it himself.

I know you understand the reason for his recent intemperate letter to you. He has even cut off his contacts with me, but I think he will come around in time. I am confident of his ultimate discretion and loyalty.

I am pretty sure I can handle the new classified work on water fusion for your office, but we should discuss contract funding levels on my trip to Washington next month. Take me to lunch at the Sans Souci and tell me how much you can give me!

Regards,

Bert Abernathy

December 2, 1978

Mr. Thomas W. Starr
1713 12th Street
Claremont, California 91711

Dear Tom,

I write this letter with regret. You are a talented teacher, and I believe that with time you will become an outstanding member of the academic community. Still, though the circumstances of your doctoral dissertation difficulties were beyond your control, I cannot recommend the continuation of your contract with us beyond June 30, 1979. The institute bylaws are most specific, and the failure to obtain your Ph.D. by December 1 leaves no room for an exception or waiver.

I will, if you wish, do what I can to aid you in seeking a new position for next year.

Sincerely,

Peter V. Johnson, Ph.D.
Office of the Dean

Paul A. Nahin

July 15, 1979

Dr. Peter V. Johnson
Dean of Engineering and Science
California Technical Institute
Claremont, California 91711

Dear Dean Johnson,

I am writing to thank you for your help in getting me a teaching job for the coming semester. Teaching freshman physics and chemistry at Contra Costa J.C. is going to be a change for me, but without a doctorate I guess I am lucky to have that—at least I won't be pumping gas or hacking a cab. I hope I can find something for the second semester.

The nature of my work in water fusion is such that the lab facilities I saw on my interview at Contra Costa will let me continue. What the army doesn't know won't hurt me!

Thanks, again, for your help.

Regards,

Thomas W. Starr

December 13, 1979

Mr. Thomas W. Starr
Science Department
Contra Costa Junior College
Walnut Creek, California 94595

Dear Mr. Starr,

I am pleased to inform you of the acceptance of your paper "An Interesting Classroom Demonstration of Power from Water." It will appear in our issue of February 24, 1980.

Quite frankly, we were astounded when we duplicated the techniques described in your paper. We would be interested in seeing a second paper which elaborates, mathematically, on the specific chemical and physical processes of your demonstration, as we believe the present one will attract considerable attention.

We wish you well in your new post at the South Australian Boys' Military Prep School, and the galley proofs of the paper will be sent to you there.

Cordially,

Peterson S. Day
Editor, *Review of High School Experimental Science*

Charles Sheffield

Born in Hull, England, Charles Sheffield (1935–   )
moved to the United States in the middle 1960s and now
lives near Washington, D. C.

He holds a B.A. (1957) and M.A. (1960) in mathematics,
and a Ph.D. (1964) in theoretical physics (specialization:
general relativity and gravitation) from St. John's College,
Cambridge.

A past-president of the American Astronautical Society,
he is currently a vice-president of the Earth Satellite Corporation (where he specializes in computer image enhancing
systems) and president of the Science Fiction Writers of
America. His nonfiction includes more than fifty research
papers and the following books: *Algebraically Special
Space Times in Problems of General Relativity and Gravitation* (1964), *Algebraically Special Space Times in Relativity,
Black Holes, and Pulsar Models* (with Ron Adler, 1973),
Earthwatch: A Survey of the World From Space (1981), *Man
on Earth* (1983) and (along with Carol Rosin) *Space Careers*
(1984).

Sheffield began producing science fiction in the
mid-1970s. His work currently includes four novels (*Sight
of Proteus*, 1978, *The Web Between the Worlds*, 1979; *My
Brother's Keeper*, 1982; and *Between the Strokes of Night*,
1985); two fix-ups (*Eramus Magister*, 1982; and *The
McAndrew Chronicles*, 1983) and more than fifty short
stories—many of which are collected in *Vectors* (1979) and
Hidden Variables (1981). The story below is his initial attempt at describing how an elevator into space might be
built. Later, it was expanded into his second novel.

SKYSTALK

by Charles Sheffield

F INLAY'S LAW: TROUBLE comes at 3:00 A.M. That's always been my experience, and I've learned to dread the hand on my shoulder that shakes me to wakefulness. My dreams had been bad enough, blasting off into orbit on top of an old chemical rocket, riding the torch, up there on a couple of thousand tons of volatile explosives. I'll never understand the nerve of the old-timers, willing to sit up there on one of those monsters.

I shuddered, forced my eyes open, and looked up at Marston's anxious face. I was already sitting up.

"Trouble?" It was a stupid question, but you're allowed a couple of those when you first wake up.

His voice was shaky. "There's a bomb on the Beanstalk."

I was off the bunk, pulling on my undershirt and groping around for my shoes. Larry Marston's words pulled me bolt upright.

"What do you mean, *on* the Beanstalk?"

"That's what Velasquez told me. He won't say more until you get on the line. They're holding a coded circuit open to Earth."

I gave up my search for shoes and went barefoot after Marston. If Arnold Velasquez were right—and I didn't see how he could be—then one of my old horrors was coming true. The Beanstalk had been designed to withstand most natural events, but sabotage was one thing that could never be fully ruled out. At any moment, we had nearly four hundred buckets climbing the Stalk and the same number going down. With the best screening in the world, with hefty rewards for information even of *rumors* of sabotage, there was always the small chance that something could be sneaked through on an outbound bucket. I had less worries about the buckets that went down to Earth. Sabotage from the space end had little to offer its perpetrators, and the Colonies would provide an unpleasant form of death to anyone who tried it, with no questions asked.

Arnold Velasquez was sitting in front of his screen door at Tether Control in Quito. Next to him stood a man I recognized only from news pictures: Otto Panosky, a top aide to the president. Neither man seemed to be looking at the screen. I wondered what they were seeing on their inward eye.

"Jack Finlay here," I said. "What's the story, Arnold?"

There was a perceptible lag before his head came up to stare at the screen, the quarter of a second that it took the video signal to go down to Earth, then back up to synchronous orbit.

"It's best if I read it to you, Jack," he said. At least his voice was under control, even though I could see his hands shaking as they held the paper. "The president's office got this in over the telecopier about twenty minutes ago."

He rubbed at the side of his face, in the nervous gesture that I had seen during most major stages of the Beanstalk's construction. "It's addressed to us, here in Sky Stalk Control. It's quite short. 'To the head of Space Transportation Systems. A fusion bomb has been placed in one of the outgoing buckets. It is of four megaton capacity, and was armed prior to placement. The secondary activation command can be given at any time by a coded radio signal. Unless terms are met by the president and

53

World Congress on or before 02:00 U.T., seventy-two hours from now, we will give the command to explode the device. Our terms are set out in the following four paragraphs. One—'"

Never mind those, Arnold." I waved my hand, impatient at the signal delay. "Just tell me one thing. Will Congress meet their demands?"

He shook his head. "They can't. What's being asked for is preposterous in the time available. You know how much red tape there is in the intergovernmental relationships."

"You told them that?"

"Of course. We sent out a general broadcast." He shrugged. "It was no good. We're dealing with fanatics, with madmen. I need to know what you can do at your end."

"How much time do we have now?"

He looked at his watch. "Seventy-one and a half hours, if they mean what they say. You understand that we have no idea which bucket might be carrying the bomb. It could have been planted there days ago, and still be on the way up."

He was right. The buckets—there were three hundred and eighty-four of them each way—moved at a steady five kilometers a minute, up or down. That's a respectable speed, but it still took almost five days for each one of them to climb the cable of the Beanstalk out to our position in synchronous orbit.

Then I thought a bit more, and decided he wasn't quite right.

"It's not that vague, Arnold. You can bet the bomb wasn't placed on a bucket that started out more than two days ago. Otherwise, we could wait for it to get here and disarm it, and still be inside their deadline. It must still be fairly close to Earth, I'd guess."

"Well, even if you're right, that deduction doesn't help us." He was chewing a pen to bits between sentences. "We don't have anything here that could be ready in time to fly out and take a look, even if it's only a couple of thousand kilometers. Even if we did, and even if we could spot the bomb, we couldn't rendezvous with a bucket on the Stalk. That's why I need to know what you can do from your end. Can you handle it from there?"

I took a deep breath and swung my chair to face Larry Marston.

"Larry, four megatons would vaporize a few kilometers of the main cable. How hard would it be for us to release ballast at the top end of the cable, above us here, enough to leave this station in position?"

"Well . . ." He hesitated. "We could do that, Jack. But then we'd lose the power satellite. It's right out at the end there, by the ballast. Without it, we'd lose all the power at the station here, and all the buckets too—there isn't enough reserve power to keep the magnetic fields going. We'd need all our spare power to keep the recycling going here."

That was the moment when I finally came fully awake. I realized the implications of what he was saying, and was nodding before he'd finished speaking. Without adequate power, we'd be looking at a very messy situation.

"And it wouldn't only be us," I said to Velasquez and Panosky, sitting there tense in front of their screen. "Everybody on the Colonies will run low on air and water if the supply through the Stalk breaks down. Damnit, we've been warning Congress how vulnerable we are for years. All the time, there've been fewer and fewer rocket launches, and nothing but foot-dragging on getting the second Stalk started with a Kenya tether. Now you want miracles from us at short notice."

If I sounded bitter, that's because I *was* bitter. Panosky was nodding his head in a conciliatory way.

"We know, Jack. And if you can pull us through this one, I think you'll see changes in the future. But right now, we can't debate that. We have to know what you can do for us *now*, this minute."

I couldn't argue with that. I swung my chair again to face Larry Marston.

"Get Hasse and Kano over here to the Control Room as soon as you can." I turned back to Velasquez. "Give us a few minutes here, while we get organized. I'm bringing in the rest of my top engineering staff."

While Larry was rounding up the others, I sat back and let the full dimensions of the problem sink in. Sure, if we had to we could release the ballast at the outward end of the Stalk. If the Beanstalk below us were severed we'd have to do that, or be whipped out past the Moon like a stone from a slingshot, as the tension in the cable suddenly dropped.

But if we did that, what would happen to the piece of the Beanstalk that was still tethered to Earth, anchored down there in Quito? There might be as much as thirty thousand kilometers of it, and as soon as the break occurred it would begin to fall. Not in a straight line. That wasn't the way that the dynamics went. It would begin to curl around the Earth, accelerating as it went, cracking into the atmosphere along the equator like a billion-ton whip stretching halfway around the planet. Forget the carrier buckets, and the superconducting cables that carried electricity down to the drive train from the solar power satellite seventy thousand kilometers above us. The piece that would do the real damage would be the central, load-bearing cable itself. It was only a couple of meters across at the bottom end, but it widened steadily as it went up. Made of bonded and doped silicon whiskers, with a tensile strength of two hundred million Newtons per square centimeter, it could handle an incredible load—almost two-thirds of a billion tons at its thinnest point. When that stored energy hit that atmosphere, there was going to be a fair amount of excitement down there on the surface. Not that we'd be watching it—the loss of the power satellite would make us look at our own survival problems; and as for the Colonies, a century of development would be ended.

By the time that Larry Marston came back with Jen Hasse and Alicia Kano, I doubt if I looked any more cheerful than Arnold Velasquez down there at Tether Control. I sketched out the problem to the two newcomers; we had what looked like a hopeless situation on our hands.

"We have seventy-one hours," I concluded. "The only question we need to answer is, what will we be doing at this end during that time? Tether Control can coordinate disaster planning for the position on Earth. Arnold has already ruled out the possibility of any actual *help* from Earth—there are no rockets there that could be ready in time."

"What about the repair robots that you have on the cable?" asked Panosky, jumping into the conversation. "I thought they were all the way along its length."

"They are," said Jen Hasse. "But they're special purpose, not general purpose. We couldn't use one to look for a radioactive signal on a bucket, if that's what you're thinking of. Even if they had the right sensors for it, we'd need a week to reprogram them for the job."

"We don't have a week," said Alicia quietly. "We have seventy-one hours." She was small and dark haired, and never raised her voice much above the minimum level needed to reach her audience—but I had grown to rely on her brains more than anything else on the station.

"Seventy-one hours, if we act *now*," I said. "We've already agreed that we don't have time to sit here and wait for that bucket with the bomb to arrive—the terrorists must have planned it that way."

"I know." Alicia did not raise her voice. "Sitting and waiting won't do it. But the total travel time of a carrier from the surface up to synchronous orbit, or back down again, is a little less than a hundred and twenty hours. That means that the bucket carrying the bomb will be at least *halfway* here in sixty hours. And a bucket that started down from here in the next few hours—"

"—would have to pass the bucket with the bomb on the way up, before the deadline," broke in Hasse. He was already over at the control board, looking at the carrier schedule. He shook his head. "There's nothing scheduled for a passenger bucket in the next twenty-four hours. It's all cargo going down."

"We're not looking for luxury." I went across to look at the schedule. "There are a couple of ore buckets with heavy metals scheduled for the next three hours. They'll have plenty of space in the top of them, and they're just forty minutes apart from each other. We could squeeze somebody in one or both of them, provided they were properly suited up. It wouldn't be a picnic, sitting in suits for three days, but we could do it."

"So how would we get at the bomb, even if we did that?" asked Larry. "It would be on the other side of the Beanstalk from us, passing at a relative velocity of six hundred kilometers an hour. We couldn't do more than wave to it as it went by, even if we knew just which bucket was carrying the bomb."

"That's the tricky piece." I looked at Jen Hasse. "Do you have enough control over the mass driver system to slow everything almost to a halt whenever an inbound and an outbound bucket pass each other?"

He was looking doubtful, rubbing his nose thoughtfully. "Maybe. Trouble is, I'd have to do it nearly a hundred times, if you want to slow down for every pass. And it would take me twenty minutes to stop and start each one. I don't think we have that much time. What do you have in mind?"

I went across to the model of the Beanstalk that we kept on the control room table. We often found that we could illustrate things with it in a minute that would have taken thousands of words to describe.

"Suppose we were here, starting down in a bucket," I said. I put my hand on the model of the station, thirty-five thousand kilometers above the surface of the Earth in synchronous orbit. "And suppose that the bucket we want to get to, the one with the bomb, is here, on the way up. We put somebody in the inbound bucket, and it starts on down."

I began to turn the drive train, so that the buckets began to move up and down along the length of the Beanstalk.

"The people in the inbound bucket carry a radiation counter," I went on. "We'd have to put it on a long arm, so that it cleared all the other stuff on the Stalk, and reached around to get near the upbound buckets. We can do that, I'm sure—if we can't, we don't deserve to call ourselves engineers. We stop at each outbound carrier, and test for radioactivity. There should be enough of that from the fission trigger of the bomb, so that we'll easily pick up a count when we reach the right bucket. Then you, Jan, hold the drive train in the halt position. We leave the inbound bucket, swing around the Stalk, and get into the other carrier. Then we try and disarm the bomb. I've had some experience with that."

"You mean we get out and actually *climb* around the Beanstalk?" asked Larry. He didn't sound pleased at the prospect.

"Right. It shouldn't be too bad," I said. "We can anchor ourselves with lines to the ore bucket, so we can't fall."

Even as I was speaking, I realized that it didn't sound too plausible. Climbing around the outside of the Beanstalk in a space suit, twenty thousand kilometers or more up, dangling

58

on a line connected to an ore bucket—and then trying to take apart a fusion bomb wearing gloves. No wonder Larry didn't like the sound of that assignment. I wasn't surprised when Arnold Velasquez chipped in over the circuit connecting us to Tether Control.

"Sorry, Jack, but that won't work—even if you could do it. You didn't let me read the full message from the terrorists. One of their conditions is that we mustn't stop the bucket train on the Stalk in the next three days. I think they were afraid that we would reverse the direction of the buckets, and bring the bomb back down to Earth to disarm it. I guess they don't realize that the Stalk wasn't designed to run in reverse."

"Damnation. What else do they have in that message?" I asked. "What can they do if we decide to stop the bucket drive anyway? How can they even tell that we're doing it?"

"We have to assume that they have a plant in here at Tether Control," replied Velasquez. "After all, they managed to get a bomb onto the Stalk in spite of all our security. They say they'll explode the bomb if we make any attempt to slow up or stop the bucket train, and we simply can't afford to take the risk of doing that. We have to assume they can monitor what's going on with the Stalk drive train."

There was a long, dismal silence, which Alicia finally broke.

"So that seems to leave us with only one alternative," she said thoughtfully. Then she grimaced and pouted her mouth. "It's a two-bucket operation, and I don't even like to think about it—even though I had a grandmother who was a circus trapeze artiste."

She was leading in to something, and it wasn't like her to make a big buildup.

"That bad, eh?" I said.

"That bad, if we're lucky," she said. "If we're unlucky, I guess we'd all be dead in a month or two anyway, as the recycling runs down. For this to work, we need a good way of dissipating a lot of kinetic energy—something like a damped mechanical spring would do it. And we need a good way of sticking to the side of the Beanstalk. Then, we use *two* ore buckets—forty minutes apart would be all right—like this . . ."

She went over to the model of the Beanstalk. We watched her with mounting uneasiness as she outlined her idea. It sounded crazy. The only trouble was, it was that or nothing. Making choices in those circumstances is not difficult.

One good thing about space maintenance work—you develop versatility. If you can't wait to locate something down on Earth, then waste another week or so to have it shipped up to you, you get into the habit of making it for yourself. In an hour or so, we had a sensitive detector ready, welded on to a long extensible arm on the side of a bucket. When it was deployed, it would reach clear around the Beanstalk, missing all the drive train and repair station fittings, and hang in close to the outbound buckets. Jen had fitted it with a gadget that moved the detector rapidly upward at the moment of closest approach of an upbound carrier, to increase the length of time available for getting a measurement of radio activity. He swore that it would work on the fly, and have a better than 99 percent chance of telling us which outbound bucket contained the bomb—even with a relative fly-by speed of six hundred kilometers an hour.

I didn't have time to argue the point, and in any case Jen was the expert. I also couldn't dispute his claim that he was easily the best-qualified person to operate the gadget. He and Larry Marston, both fully suited up, climbed into the ore bucket. We had to leave the ore in there, because the mass balance between ingoing and outbound buckets was closely calculated to give good stability to the Beanstalk. It made for a lumpy seat, but no one complained. Alicia and I watched as the bucket was moved into the feeder system, accelerated up to the correct speed, attached to the drive train, and dropped rapidly out of sight down the side of the Beanstalk.

"That's the easy part," she said. "They drop with the bucket, checking the upbound ones as they come by for radioactivity, and that's all they have to do."

"Unless they can't detect any signal," I said. "Then the bomb goes off, and they have the world's biggest roller coaster ride. Twenty thousand kilometers of it, with the big thrill at the end."

"They'd never reach the surface," replied Alicia absentmind-edly. "They'll frizzle up in the atmosphere long before they get there. Or maybe they won't. I wonder what the terminal velocity would be if you hung on to the Stalk cable?"

As she spoke, she was calmly examining an odd device that had been produced with impossible haste in the machine shop on the station's outer rim. It looked like an old-fashioned para-chute harness, but instead of the main chute the lines led to a wheel about a meter across. From the opposite edge of the wheel, a doped silicon rope led to a hefty magnetic grapnel. Another similar arrangement was by her side.

"Here," she said to me. "Get yours on over your suit, and let's make sure we both know how to handle them. If you miss with the grapnel, it'll be messy."

I looked at my watch. "We don't have time for any dry run. In the next fifteen minutes we have to get our suits on, over to the ore buckets, and into these harnesses. Anyway, I don't think rehearsals here inside the station mean too much when we get to the real thing."

We looked at each other for a moment, then began to suit up. It's not easy to estimate odds for something that has never been done before, but I didn't give us more than one chance in a hundred of coming out of it safely. Suits and harnesses on, we went and sat without speaking in the ore bucket.

I saw that we were sitting on a high-value shipment—silver and platinum, from one of the belt mining operations. It wasn't comfortable, but we were certainly traveling in expensive com-pany. Was it King Midas who complained that a golden throne is not right for restful sitting?

No matter what the final outcome, we were in for an un-pleasant trip. Our suits had barely enough capacity for a six-day journey. They had no recycling capacity, and if we had to go all the way to the halfway point we would be descending for almost sixty hours. We had used up three hours to the dead-line, getting ready to go, so that would leave us only nine hours to do something about the bomb when we reached it. I suppose that it was just as bad or worse for Hasse and Marston. After they'd done their bit with the detector, there wasn't a thing they could do except sit in their bucket and wait, either for a message from us or an explosion far above them.

"Everything all right down there, Larry?" I asked, testing the radio link with them for the umpteenth time.

"Can't tell." He sounded strained. "We've passed three buckets so far, outbound ones, and we've had no signal from the detector. I guess that's as planned, but it would be nice to know it's working all right."

"You shouldn't expect anything for at least thirty-six hours," said Alicia.

"I know that. But it's impossible for us *not* to look at the detector whenever we pass an outbound bucket. Logically, we should be sleeping now and saving our attention for the most likely time of encounter—but neither one of us seems able to do it."

"Don't assume that the terrorists are all that logical, either," I said. "Remember, we are the ones who decided that they must have started the bomb on its way only a few hours ago. It's possible they put it into a bucket three or four days ago, and made up the deadline for some other reason. We think we can disarm that bomb, but they may not agree—and they may be right. All we may manage to do is advance the time of the explosion when we try and open up the casing."

As I spoke, I felt our bucket begin to accelerate. We were heading along the feeder and approaching the bucket drive train. After a few seconds, we were outside the station, dropping down the Beanstalk after Jen and Larry.

We sat there in silence for a while. I'd been up and down the Stalk many times, and so had Alicia, but always in passenger modules. The psychologists had decided that people rode those a lot better when they were windowless. The cargo bucket had no windows either, but we had left the hatch open to simplify communications with the other bucket and to enable us to climb out if and when the time came. We would have to close it when we were outside, or the aerodynamic pressures would spoil bucket stability when it finally entered the atmosphere— three hundred kilometers an hour isn't that fast, but it's a respectable speed for travel at full atmospheric pressure.

Our bucket was about four meters wide and three deep. It carried a load of seven hundred tons, so our extra mass was negligible. I stood at its edge and looked up, then down. The pscyhologists were quite right. Windows were a bad idea.

Above us, the Beanstalk rose up and up, occulting the backdrop of stars. It went past the synchronous station, which was still clearly visible as a blob on the stalk, then went on further up, invisible, to the solar power satellite and the great ballast weight, a hundred and five thousand kilometers above the surface of the Earth. On the Stalk itself I could see the shielded superconductors that ran its full length, from the power satellite down to Tether Control in Quito. We were falling steadily, our rate precisely controlled by the linear synchronous motors that set the accelerations through pulsed magnetic fields. The power for that was drawn from the same superconducting cables. In the event of an electrical power failure, the buckets were designed to "freeze" to the side of the Stalk with mechanical coupling. We had to build the system that way, because about once a year we had some kind of power interruption—usually from small meteorites, not big enough to trigger the main detector system, but large enough to penetrate the shields and mess up the power transmission.

It was looking down, though, that produced the real effect. I felt my heart begin to pump harder, and I was gripping at the side of the bucket with my space suit gloves. When you are in a rocket-propelled ship, you don't get any real feeling of height. Earth is another part of the universe, something independent of you. But from our position, moving along the side of the Beanstalk, I had quite a different feeling. We were *connected* to the planet. I could see the Stalk, dwindling smaller and smaller down to the Earth below. I had a very clear feeling that I could fall all the way down it, down to the big blue-white glove at its foot. Although I had lived up at the station quite happily for over five years, I suddenly began to worry about the strength of the main cable. It was a ridiculous concern. There was a safety factor of ten built into its design, far more than a rational engineer would use for anything. It was more likely that the bottom would fall out of our ore bucket, than that the support cable for the Beanstalk would break. I was kicking myself for my illogical fears, until I noticed Alicia also peering out at the Beanstalk, as though trying to see past the clutter of equipment there to the cable itself. I wasn't the only one thinking wild thoughts.

"You certainly get a different look at things from here," I said, trying to change the mood. "Did you ever see anything like that before?"

She shook her head ponderously—the suits weren't made for agility of movement.

"Not up here, I haven't," she replied. "But I once went up to the top of the towers of the Golden Gate Bridge in San Francisco, and looked at the support cables for that. It was the same sort of feeling. I began to wonder if they could take the strain. That was just for a bridge, not even a big one. What will happen if we don't make it, and they blow up the Beanstalk?"

I shrugged inside my suit, then realized that she couldn't see the movement. "This is the only bridge to space that we've got. We'll be out of the bridge business and back in the ferryboat business. They'll have to start sending stuff up by rockets again. Shipments won't be a thousandth of what they are now, until another Stalk can be built. That will take thirty years, starting without this one to help us—even if the Colonies survive all right and work on nothing else. We don't have to worry about that, though. We won't be there to hassle with it."

She nodded. "We were in such a hurry to get away it never occurred to me that we'd be sitting here for a couple of days with nothing to do but worry. Any ideas?"

"Yes. While you were making the reel and grapnel, I thought about that. The only thing that's worth our attention right now is a better understanding of the geometry of the Stalk. We need to know exactly where to position ourselves, where we'll set the grapnels, and what our dynamics will be as we move. I've asked Ricardo to send us schematics and layouts over the suit videos. He's picking out ones that show the drive train, the placing of the superconductors, and the unmanned repair stations. I've also asked him to deactivate all the repair robots. It's better for us to risk a failure on the maintenance side than have

64

one of the monitoring robots wandering along the Stalk and mixing in with what we're trying to do."

"I heard what you said to Panosky, but it still seems to me that the robots ought to be useful."

"I'd hoped so, too. I checked again with Jen, and he agrees we'd have to reprogram them, and we don't have the time for it. It would take weeks. Jen said having them around would be like taking along a half-trained dog, bumbling about while we work. Forget that one."

As we talked, we kept our eyes open for the outbound buckets, passing us on the other side of the Beanstalk. We were only about ten meters from them at closest approach and they seemed to hurtle past us at an impossible speed. The idea of hitching on to one of them began to seem more and more preposterous. We settled down to look in more detail at the configuration of cables, drive train, repair stations and buckets that was being flashed to us over the suit videos.

It was a weary time, an awful combination of boredom and tension. The video images were good, but there is a limit to what you can learn from diagrams and simulations. About once an hour, Jen Hasse and Larry Marston called in from the lower bucket beneath us, reporting on the news—or lack of it— regarding the bomb detection efforts. A message relayed from Panosky at Tether Control reported no progress in negotiations with the terrorists. The fanatics simply didn't believe their terms couldn't be met. That was proof of their naïveté, but didn't make them any less dangerous.

It was impossible to get comfortable in our suits. The ore buckets had never been designed for a human occupant, and we couldn't find a level spot to stretch out. Alicia and I passed into a half-awake trance, still watching the images that flashed onto the suit videos, but not taking in much of anything. Given that we couldn't sleep, we were probably in the closest thing we could get to a resting state. I hoped that Jen and Larry would keep their attention up, watching an endless succession of buckets flash past them and checking each one for radioactivity count.

The break came after fifty-four hours in the bucket. We didn't need to hear the details from the carrier below us to know they had it—Larry's voice crackled with excitement.

"Got it," he said. "Jen picked up a strong signal from the bucket we just passed. If you leave the ore carrier within thirty-four seconds, you'll have thirty-eight minutes to get ready for it to come past you. It will be the second one to reach you. For God's sake don't try for the wrong one."

There was a pause, then Larry said something I would never have expected from him. "We'll lose radio contact with you in a while, as we move farther along the Stalk. Good luck, both of you—and look after him, Alicia."

I didn't have time to think that one through—but shouldn't he be telling *me* to look after *her?* It was no time for puzzling. We were up on top of our bucket in a second, adrenaline moving through our veins like an electric current. The cable was whipping past us at a great rate; the idea of forsaking the relative safety of the ore bucket for the naked wall of the Beanstalk seemed like insanity. We watched as one of the repair stations, sticking out from the cable into open space, flashed past.

"There'll be another one of those coming by in thirty-five seconds," I said. "We've got to get the grapnels onto it, and we'll be casting blind. I'll throw first, and you follow a second later. Don't panic if I miss—remember, we only have to get one good hook there."

"Count us down, Jack," said Alicia. She wasn't one to waste words in a tight spot.

I pressed the digital readout in my suit, and watched the count move from thirty-five down to zero.

"Countdown display on channel six," I said, and picked up the rope and grapnel. I looked doubtfully at the wheel that was set in the middle of the thin rope, then even looked suspiciously at the rope itself, wondering if it would take the strain. That shows how the brain works in a crisis—that rope would have held a herd of elephants with no trouble at all.

I cast the grapnel as the count touched to zero, and Alicia threw a fraction later. Both ropes were spliced onto both suits, so it was never clear which grapnel took hold. Our bucket continued to drop rapidly toward Earth, but we were jerked off the top of it and went zipping on downward fractionally slower as the friction reel in the middle of the rope unwound, slowing our motion.

We came to a halt about fifty meters down the Beanstalk from the grapnel, after a rough ride in which our deceleration must have averaged over seven g's. Without that reel to slow us down gradually, the jerk of the grapnel as it caught the repair station wall would have snapped our spines when we were lifted from the ore bucket.

We hung there, swinging free, suspended from the wall of the Stalk. As the reel began to take up the line that had been paid out, I made the mistake of looking down. We dangled over an awful void, with nothing between us and that vast drop to the Earth below but the thin line above us. When we came closer to the point of attachment to the Beanstalk wall, I saw just how lucky we had been. One grapnel had missed completely, and the second one had caught the very lip of the repair station platform. Another foot to the left and we would have missed it altogether.

We clawed our way up to the station rim—easy enough to do, because the gravity at that height was only a fraction of a g, less than a tenth. But a fall from there would be inexorable, and we would have fallen away from the Beanstalk, with no chance to reconnect to it. Working together, we freed the grapnel and readied both lines and grapnels for reuse. After that there was nothing to do but cling to the side of the Beanstalk, watch the sweep of the heavens above us, and wait for the outbound ore buckets to come past us.

The first one came by after seventeen minutes. I had the clock readout to prove it, otherwise I would have solemnly sworn that we had waited there for more than an hour, holding to our precarious perch. Alicia seemed more at home there than I was. I watched her moving the grapnel to the best position for casting it, then settle down patiently to wait.

It is hard to describe my own feelings in that period. I watched the movement of the stars above us, in their great circle, and wondered if we would be alive in another twenty minutes. I felt a strong communion with the old sailors of Earth's seas, up in their crow's nest in a howling gale, sensing nothing but darkness, high-blown spindrift, perilous breakers ahead, and the dipping, rolling stars above.

Alicia kept her gaze steadily downward, something that I found hard to do. She had inherited a good head for heights from her circus-performer grandmother.

"I can see it," she said at last. "All ready for a repeat performance?"

"Right." I swung the grapnel experimentally. "Since we can see it this time, we may as well throw together."

I concentrated on the bucket sweeping steadily up toward us, trying to estimate the distance and the time that it would take before it reached us. We both drew back our arms at the same moment and lobbed the grapnels toward the center of the bucket.

It came past us with a monstrous, silent rush. Again we felt the fierce accelerations as we were jerked away from the Beanstalk wall and shot upward after the carrier. Again, I realized that we couldn't have done it without Alicia's friction reel, smoothing the motion for us. This time, it was more dangerous than when we had left the downbound bucket. Instead of trying to reach the stationary wall of the Stalk, we were now hooked on to the moving bucket. We swung wildly beneath it in its upward flight, narrowly missing contact with elements of the drive train, and then with another repair station that flashed past a couple of meters to our right.

Finally, somehow, we damped our motion, reeled in the line, slid back the cover to the ore bucket and fell safely forward inside it. I was completely drained. It must have been all nervous stress—we hadn't expended a significant amount of physical energy. I know that Alicia felt the same way as I did, because after we plumped over the rim of the carrier we both fell to the floor and lay there without speaking for several minutes. It gives some idea of our state of mind when I say that the bucket we had reached, with a four-megaton bomb inside it that might go off at any moment, seemed like a haven of safety.

We finally found the energy to get up and look around us. The bucket was loaded with manufactured goods, and I thought for a sickening moment that the bomb was not there. We found it after five minutes of frantic searching. It was a compact blue cylinder, a meter long and fifty centimeters wide, and it had been cold-welded to the wall of the bucket. I knew the design.

"There it is," I said to Alicia. Then I didn't know what to say next. It was the most advanced design, not the big, old one that I had been hoping for.

"Can you disarm it?" asked Alicia.

"In principle. There's only one problem. I know how it's put together—but I'll never be able to get it apart wearing a suit. The fingerwork I'd need is just too fine for gloves. We seem to be no better off than we were before."

We sat there side by side, looking at the bomb. The irony of the situation was sinking in. We had reached it, just as we hoped we could. Now, it seemed we might as well have been still back in the station.

"Any chance that we could get it free and dump it overboard?" asked Alicia. "You know, just chuck the thing away from the bucket."

I shook my head, aware again of how much my suit impeded freedom of movement. "It's spot welded. We couldn't shift it. Anyway, free fall from here would give it an impact orbit, and a lot of people might be killed if it went off inside the atmosphere. If we were five thousand kilometers higher, perigee would be at a safe height above the surface—but we can't afford to wait for another sixteen hours until the bucket gets up that high. Look, I've got another idea, but it will mean that we'll lose radio contact with the station."

"So what?" said Alicia. Her voice was weary. "There's not a thing they can do to help us anyway."

"They'll go out of their minds with worry down on Earth, if they don't know what's happening here."

"I don't see why we should keep all of it for ourselves. What's your idea, Jack?"

"All right." I summoned my reserves of energy. "We're in vacuum now, but this bucket would be airtight if we were to close the top hatch again. I have enough air in my suit to make a breathable atmosphere in this enclosed space, at least for long enough to let me have a go at the bomb. We've got nearly twelve hours to the deadline, and if I can't disarm it in that time I can't do it at all."

Alicia looked at her air reserve indicator and nodded. "I can spare you some air, too, if I open up my suit."

"No. We daren't do that. We have one other big problem—the temperature. It's going to feel really cold in here, once I'm outside my suit. I'll put my heaters on to maximum, and leave the suit open, but I'm still not sure I can get much done before I begin to freeze up. If I begin to lose feeling in my fingers, I'll need your help to get me back inside. So you have to stay in your suit. Once I'm warmed up, I can try again."

She was silent for a few moments, repeating the calculations that I had just done myself.

"You'll only have enough air to try it twice," she said at last. "If you can't do it in one shot, you'll have to let me have a go. You can direct me on what has to be done."

There was no point in hanging around. We sent a brief message to the station, telling them what we were going to do, then closed the hatch and began to bleed air out of my suit and into the interior of the bucket. We used the light from Alicia's suit, which had ample power to last for several days.

When the air pressure inside the bucket was high enough for me to breathe, I peeled out of my suit. It was as cold as charity in that metal box, but I ignored that and crouched down alongside the bomb in my underwear and bare feet.

I had eleven hours at the most. Inside my head, I fancied that I could hear a clock ticking. That must have been only my fancy. Modern bombs have no place for clockwork timers.

By placing my suit directly beneath my hands, I found that I could get enough heat from the thermal units to let me keep on working without a break. The clock inside my head went on ticking, also without a break.

On and on and on.

They say that I was delirious when we reached the station. That's the only way the press could reconcile my status as public hero with the things that I said to the president when he called up to congratulate us.

I suppose I could claim delirium if I wanted to—five days without sleep, two without food, oxygen starvation, and frostbite of the toes and ears, that might add up to delirium. I had received enough warmth from the suit to keep my hands going, because it was very close to them, but that had been at the expense of some of my other extremities. If it hadn't been for Alicia, cramming me somehow back into the suit after I had disarmed the bomb, I would have frozen to death in a couple of hours.

As it was, I smelled ripe and revolting when they unpacked us from the bucket and winkled me out of my suit—Alicia hadn't been able to reconnect me with the plumbing arrangements.

So I told the president that the World Congress was composed of a giggling bunch of witless turds, who couldn't sense a global need for more bridges to space if a Beanstalk were pushed up their backsides—which was where I thought they kept their brains. Not quite the speech that we used to get from the old-time returning astronauts, but I must admit it's one that I'd wanted to give for some time. The audience was there this time, with the whole world hanging on my words over live TV.

We've finally started construction on the second Beanstalk. I don't know if my words had anything to do with it, but there was a lot of public pressure after I said my piece, and I like to think that I had some effect.

And me? I'm designing the third Beanstalk; what else? But I don't think I'll hold my breath waiting for a congressional vote of thanks for my efforts saving the first one.

Kurd Lasswitz

Born in Breslau, Kurd Lasswitz (1848–1910) was Germany's first major S.F. writer.

He was trained in math and physics at Breslau and Berlin and received his doctorate in 1873. After a year teaching at the Royal College of Ratibor (1875) he accepted a professorship at the Gymnasium Ernestinsium (sort of a cross between a high school and a university) in Gotha. There he spent the rest of his career.

His professional writings were mainly in the area of philosophy and physics and strongly influenced by Fechner and Kant. They include a biography of Gustav Theodor Fechner, *The Theory of the Ideality of Space and Time of Kant* (1883), and *The History of Atomic Theory from the Middle Ages to Newton* (1890).

Throughout his career he wrote many works of science fiction and fantasy to amuse himself and promote his ideas. Indeed, his magnum opus, the utopian novel of a Martian occupation of Earth, *Two Planets* (1897), is reported to have exerted a profound influence on many of the Peenemünde rocket scientists such as Wernher von Braun. Within ten years it had sold several hundred thousand copies and been translated into Swedish, Norwegian, Danish, Dutch, Spanish, Italian, Czech, Polish, and Hungarian.

However, much of his fiction remains unfamiliar to English speaking audiences. From the few stories Willy Ley translated from *Images of the Future* (1878), *Soap Bubbles* (1890), and *Never, Ever* (1902), we have selected the remarkably clever tale below.

THE UNIVERSAL LIBRARY

by *Kurd Lasswitz*

"COME AND SIT down over here, Max," said Professor Wallhausen, "and stop digging around on my desk. I assure you there is nothing there which you could use for your magazine."

Max Burkel walked over to the living room table, sat down slowly and reached for his beer glass. "Well, *prosit,* old boy. Nice to be here again. But no matter what you say, you've got to write something for me."

"Unfortunately, I don't have any good ideas right now. Besides, so much superfluous stuff is being written and, unfortunately, printed too."

"You don't have to tell that to a harassed editor like yours truly. The question is, however, just what is superfluous stuff? The authors and their public completely fail to agree about that. Same for editors and reviewers. Well, my three weeks' vacation is just beginning. In the meantime my assistant can do the worrying."

"I have sometimes wondered," said Mrs. Wallhausen, "that you can still find something new for the printer. I should think that by now practically everything that can be expressed with letters has been tried."

"One would think so, but the human mind seems to be inexhaustible."

"In repetitions, you mean."

"Well, yes," Burkel admitted, "but also when it comes to new ideas and expressions."

"Just the same," mused Professor Wallhausen, "one could express in print everything that can ever be given to humanity, be it historical information, scientific understanding of the laws of nature, poetic imagination and power of expression or even the teachings of wisdom. Provided, of course, that it can be expressed in words. After all, our books conserve and disseminate the results of thought. But the number of the possible combinations of a given number of letters is limited. Therefore, all possible literature must be printable in a finite number of volumes."

"Dear friend," said Burkel, "now you are talking as a mathematician rather than as a philosopher. How can all possible literature, including that of the future, make a finite number of books?"

"I'll figure out in a moment how many volumes would be required to make a Universal Library. Will you"—he turned to his daughter—"hand me a sheet of paper and a pencil from my desk?"

"Bring the logarithm table too," Burkel added dryly.

"Not necessary, not necessary at all," the professor declared. "But now our literary friend has the first word. I ask: If we are frugal and do away with various fonts of type, writing only for a hypothetical reader who is willing to put up with some typographical inconveniences and who is only interested in the meaning—"

"There is no such reader," Burkel said firmly.

"I said 'hypothetical reader.' How many different characters would one need for printing general literature?"

"Well," said Burkel, "let's just stick to the upper- and lower-case letters of the Latin alphabet, the customary punctuation marks and the space that keeps the words apart. That wouldn't be too much. But for scientific works, that's another story. Especially you mathematicians have an enormous number of symbols."

"Which could be replaced by an agreement with small indices like a_1, a_2, a_3 and a^1, a^2 and a^3, adding just twice ten characters. One could even use this system to write words from languages which do not use the Latin alphabet."

"All right. Maybe your hypothetical, or better, your ideal reader will put up with that too. Under these conditions we could probably express everything with, say one hundred different characters."

"Well, well. Now how big do you want each volume?"

"I should think that one can exhaust a theme pretty well with five hundred book pages. Let's say that there are forty lines per page and fifty characters per line, we'll have forty times fifty times five hundred characters per volume, which is—you calculate it."

"One million," said the professor. "Therefore, if we take our one hundred characters, repeat them in any order often enough to fill a volume that has room for one million characters, we'll get a piece of literature of some kind. Now if we produce all possible combinations mechanically we'll ultimately get all the works that ever have been written in the past or can be written in the future."

Burkel slapped his friend's shoulder. "You know, I'm going to subscribe right now. I won't have to read manuscripts any more. This is wonderful for both editor and publisher: the elimination of the author from the literary business! The replacement of the writer by the automatic printing press! A triumph of technology!"

"What?" said Mrs. Wallhausen. "You say everything will be in that library? The complete works of Goethe? The Bible? The works of all the classical philosophers?"

"Yes, and with all the variations of wording nobody has thought up yet. You'll find the lost works of Tacitus and their translations into all living and dead languages. Furthermore, all of my and friend Burkel's future works, all forgotten and still undelivered speeches in all parliaments, the official version of the Universal Declaration of Peace, the history of the subsequent wars, all the compositions all of us wrote in school and college—"

"I wish I had had this volume when I was in college," Mrs. Wallhausen said. "Or would it be volumes?"

"Volumes, probably. Don't forget that the space between words is a typographical character too. A book may contain a single line; everything else might be empty. On the other hand, even the longest works could be accommodated because if they don't fit into one volume they could be continued through several."

"No, thanks. Finding something must be a chore."

"Yes, this is *one* of the difficulties," Professor Wallhausen said with a pleased smile, looking after the smoke from his cigar. "At first glance one should think that this would be simplified by the fact that the library must contain its own catalogue and index."

"Good!"

"The problem would be to find that one. Moreover, if you had found an index volume it wouldn't help you any because the contents of the Universal Library are not only indexed correctly, but also in every possible incorrect and misleading manner."

"The devil! But unfortunately true."

"Yes, there would be quite a number of difficulties. Let's say we take the first volume of the Universal Library. Its first page is empty, so is the second and the third and so forth through all five hundred pages. This is the volume in which the 'space' has been repeated one million times."

"At least that volume can't contain any nonsense," Mrs. Wallhausen observed.

"Hardly a consolation. But we'll take the second volume. Also empty until, on page 500, line 40 at the extreme end, there is a lonely little *a*. Same thing in the third volume, but the *a* has moved up one place. And then the *a* slowly moves up, place by place, through the first million volumes until it reaches the first place on page 1, line 1 of the first volume of the second million. Things continue that way through the first hundred million volumes until each of the hundred characters has made its lonely way from last to first place in the books. The same then happens with *aa* or with any other two characters. One volume could contain one million period marks and another one million question marks."

"Well," said Burkel, "it should be simple to recognize and discard those volumes."

"Maybe, but the worst is yet to come. It happens when you have found a volume that seems to make sense. Say you want to refresh your memory about a passage in Goethe's *Faust* and you manage to locate a volume with the right beginning. But when you have progressed for a page or two it goes on *aaaaaa* and that is the only thing in the remaining pages of the book. Or you find a table of logarithms, but you can't tell whether it is correct. Remember, the Universal Library contains everything that is correct, but also everything that is not. You can't trust the chapter headings either. A volume may begin with the words 'History of the Thirty Years War' and then say: 'After the nuptials of Prince Blücher and the Queen of Dahomey had been celebrated at Thermopylae'—you see what I mean. Of course, nobody would ever be embarrassed. If an author has written the most incredible nonsense it will, of course, be in the Universal Library. It will be under his byline. But it will also be under the byline of William Shakespeare and under any other possible byline. He will find one of his books where it is asserted after every sentence that all this is nonsense and another one where it is stated after the selfsame sentences that they are the purest wisdom."

"I have enough," said Burkel. "I knew as soon as you started that this was going to be a tall tale. I won't subscribe to your Universal Library. It would be impossible to sift truth from falsehood, sense from nonsense. If I find several million volumes all claiming to be the true history of Germany during the twentieth century and all contradicting each other, I would do much better by reading the original works of the historians."

"Very clever! Otherwise you would have taken on an impossible burden. But I wasn't telling a tall tale in your sense. I did not claim that you could *use* the Universal Library, I merely said that it is possible to tell exactly how many volumes would be required for a Universal Library containing all possible literature."

"Go ahead and calculate," said Mrs. Wallhausen. "It is easy to see that this blank sheet of paper bothers you."

"Not needed," said the professor. "*That* I can do in my head. All we have to do is to realize very clearly how that library is going to be produced. First we put down each one of our hundred characters. Then we add to each, every one of our hundred characters, so that we have one hundred times one hundred groups of two characters each. Adding the third set of our hundred characters we get $100 \times 100 \times 100$ groups of three characters each and so forth. Since we have one million possible positions per volume, the total number of volumes is 100 raised to the millionth power. Now since 100 is the square of 10, we obtain the same figure if we write a 10 with two million as the power. This is simply a 1 followed by two million zeroes. Here it is: $10^{2,000,000}$."

"You make your life easy," remarked Mrs. Wallhausen. "Why don't you write it down in the normal manner?"

"Not me. This would take me at least two weeks, without time out for food and sleep. If you printed that figure, it would be a little over two miles long."

"What is the name of that figure?" the daughter wanted to know.

"It has no name. There isn't even a way in which we could hope to grasp that figure, it is so colossal, even though it is finite."

"How about expressing it in trillions?" asked Burkel.

"A mathematical trillion is a nice big figure, a 1 followed by 18 zeros. But if you express the number of volumes in trillions, you get a figure with 1,999,982 zeros instead of two million zeros. It's no help; one is as ungraspable as the other. But, just wait a moment." The professor scribbled a few figures on the sheet of paper.

"I *knew* it would come to that!" Mrs. Wallhausen said with much satisfaction.

"All done," her husband announced. "I assumed that each volume is two centimeters thick and that the whole library is arranged in one long row. How long do you think this row would be?"

"I know," said the daughter. "You want me to say it?"

"Go ahead."

"Twice as many centimeters as the number of volumes."

"Bravo, my dear. Absolutely correct. Now let's look at this more closely. You know that the speed of light, expressed in metric units, is 300,000 kilometers per second, which for a year amounts to about 10,000 million kilometers, which equals 1,000,000,000,000,000,000 centimeters, your mathematical trillion, Burkel. If our librarian can move with the speed of light it will still take him two years to pass a trillion volumes. To go from one end of the library to the other with the speed of light will take twice as many years as there are trillions of volumes in the library. We had that figure before, and I feel that nothing shows more clearly how impossible it is to grasp the meaning of this $10^{2,000,000}$ even though, as I have said repeatedly, it is a finite figure."

"If the ladies will permit, I have one more question," said Burkel. "I suspect that you have calculated a library for which there is no room in the universe."

"We'll see in a moment," the professor answered, reaching for the pencil. "Well, I assumed you packed the library in 1,000-volume boxes, each box having a capacity of precisely one cubic meter. All space to the farthest known spiral galaxies would not hold the Universal Library. In fact, you would need this volume of space so often that the number of packed universes would be a figure with only some 60 zeros less than the figure for the number of volumes. No matter how we try to visualize it, we are bound to fail."

"I thought all along that it was infinite," said Burkel.

"No, that's just the point. The figure is not infinite, it is a finite figure. The mathematics of it are flawless. What is surprising is that we can write down on a very small piece of paper the number of volumes comprising all possible literature, something which at first glance seems to be infinite. But if we then try to visualize it—for example, try to find a specific volume—we realize that we cannot grasp what is otherwise a very clear and logical thought that we evolved ourselves."

"Well," concluded Burkel, "coincidence plays, but reason creates. And for this reason you'll write down tomorrow what amused us tonight. That way I'll get an article for my magazine that I can carry with me."

"All right. I'll write it down for you. But I'm telling you right now that your readers will conclude that this is an excerpt from one of the superfluous volumes of the Universal Library."

Vernor Vinge

Born in Waukesha, Wisconsin, Vernor Vinge (1944–   )
is a second generation professor who has been publishing
science fiction for over twenty years.

A Ph.D. in mathematics, he earned his B.S. from Michigan State University (1966) and his M.A. (1968) and doctorate (1971) from that hotbed—it must be something in the
water—of science fiction scientists, the University of California, San Diego. Since 1972 he has been employed by San
Diego State University, currently holding the rank of associate professor. Though his dissertation dealt with func-
tional analysis and geometric function theory, he reports
devoting most of his current time to the field of computer
science.

A former holder of a NASA traineeship (1970), Vinge has
written a half dozen professional papers, the most clever of
which is the one explaining how our space probe might
have been stopped at Saturn without using retro rockets.
His fiction consists of four S.F. novels (*Grimm's World*,
1976; *The Witling*; 1976; *The Peace War*, 1984; and *True
Names*, 1985) and about fifteen shorter S.F. stories.

The work chosen for this book appeared in two "Best of
the Year" anthologies. It provides a good synthesis of
Vinge's interests and is an excellent example of the op-
timistic, high-tech type of story most readers seem to
prefer.

LONG SHOT

by *Vernor Vinge*

THEY NAMED HER Ilse, and of all Earth's creatures, she was to be the longest lived—and perhaps the last. A prudent tortoise might survive three hundred years and a bristlecone pine six thousand, but Ilse's designed span exceeded one hundred centuries. And though her brain was iron and germanium doped with arsenic, and her heart was a tiny cloud of hydrogen plasma, Ilse *was*—in the beginning—one of Earth's creatures: she could feel, she could question, and—as she discovered during the dark centuries before her fiery end—she could also forget.

Ilse's earliest memory was a fragment, amounting to less than fifteen seconds. Someone, perhaps inadvertently, brought her to consciousness as she sat atop her S-5N booster. It was night, but their launch was imminent and the booster stood white and silver in the light of a dozen spotlights. Ilse's sharp eye scanned rapidly around the horizon, untroubled by the glare from below. Stretching away from her to the north was a line of thirty launch pads. Several had their own boosters, though none were lit up as Ilse's was. Three thousand meters to the west were more lights, and the occasional sparkle of an automatic rifle. To the east, surf marched in phosphorescent ranks against the Merritt Island shore.

There the fragment ended: she was not conscious during the launch. But that scene remained forever her most vivid and incomprehensible memory.

When next she woke, Ilse was in low Earth orbit. Her single eye had been fitted to a one hundred fifty centimeter reflecting telescope so that now she could distinguish stars set less than a tenth of a second apart, or, if she looked straight down, count the birds in a flock of geese two hundred kilometers below. For more than a year Ilse remained in this same orbit. She was not idle. Her makers had allotted this period for testing. A small manned station orbited with her, and from it came an endless sequence of radioed instructions and exercises.

Most of the problems were ballistic: hyperbolic encounters, transfer ellipses and the like. But it was often required that Ilse use her own telescope and spectrometer to discover the parameters of the problems. A typical exercise: determine the orbits of Venus and Mercury; compute a minimum energy flyby of both planets. Another: determine the orbit of Mars; analyze its atmosphere; plan a hyperbolic entry subject to constraints. Many observational problems dealt with Earth: determine atmospheric pressure and composition; perform multispectrum analysis of vegetation. Usually she was required to solve organic analysis problems in less than thirty seconds. And in these last problems, the rules were often changed even while the game was played. Her orientation jets would be caused to malfunction. Critical portions of her mind and senses would be degraded.

One of the first things Ilse learned was that in addition to her private memories, she had a programmed memory, a "library" of procedures and facts. As with most libraries, the programmed memory was not as accessible as Ilse's own recollections, but the information contained there was much more complete and precise. The solution program for almost any ballistic, or chemical, problem could be lifted from this "library," used for seconds, or hours, as an integral part of Ilse's mind, and then returned to the "library." The real trick was to select the proper program on the basis of incomplete information, and then to modify that program to meet various combinations of power and equipment failure. Though she did poorly at first, Ilse eventually surpassed her design specifications. At this point her training stopped and for the first—but not the last—time, Ilse was left to her own devices.

Though she had yet to wonder on her ultimate purpose, still she wanted to see as much of her world as possible. She spent most of each daylight pass looking straight down, trying to see some order in the jumble of blue and green and white. She could easily follow the supply rockets as they climbed up from Merritt Island and Baikonur to rendezvous with her. In the end, more than a hundred of the rockets were floating about her. As the weeks passed, the squat white cylinders were fitted together on a spidery frame.

Now her ten-meter-long body was lost in the web-work of cylinders and girders that stretched out two hundred meters behind her. Her programmed memory told her that the entire assembly massed 22,563.901 tons—more than most ocean-going ships—and a little experimenting with her attitude-control jets convinced her that this figure was correct.

Soon her makers connected Ilse's senses to the mammoth's control mechanisms. It was as if she had been given a new body, for she could feel, and see, and use each of the hundred propellant tanks and each of the fifteen fusion reactors that made up the assembly. She realized that now she had the power to perform some of the maneuvers she had planned during her training.

Finally the great moment arrived. Course directions came over the maser link with the manned satellite. Ilse quickly computed the trajectory that would result from these directions. The answer she obtained was correct, but it revealed only the smallest part of what was in store for her.

In her orbit two hundred kilometers up, Ilse coasted smoothly toward high noon over the Pacific. Her eye was pointed forward, so that on the fuzzy blue horizon she could see the edge of the North American continent. Nearer, the granulated cloud cover obscured the ocean itself. The command to begin the burn came from the manned satellite, but Ilse was following the clock herself, and she had determined to take over the launch if any mistakes were made. Two hundred meters behind her, deep in the maze of tanks and beryllium girders, Ilse felt magnetic fields establish themselves, felt hydrogen plasma form, felt fusion commence. Another signal from the station, and propellant flowed around each of ten reactors.

Ilse and her twenty-thousand-ton booster were on their way.

Acceleration rose smoothly to one gravity. Behind her, vidicons on the booster's superstructure showed the Earth shrinking. For half an hour the burn continued, monitored by Ilse, and the manned station now fallen far behind. Then Ilse was alone with her booster, coasting away from Earth and her creators at better than twenty kilometers a second.

So Ilse began her fall toward the sun. For eleven weeks she fell. During this time, there was little to do: monitor the propellants, keep the booster's sunshade properly oriented, relay data to Earth. Compared to much of her later life, however, it was a time of hectic activity.

A fall of eleven weeks toward a body as massive as the sun can result in only one thing: speed. In those last hours, Ilse hurtled downward at better than two hundred and fifty kilometers per second—an Earth to Moon distance every half hour. Forty-five minutes before her closest approach to the sun— perihelion—Ilse jettisoned the empty first stage and its sunshade. Now she was left with the two-thousand-ton second stage, whose insulation consisted of a bright coat of white paint. She felt the pressure in the propellant tanks begin to rise.

Though her telescope was pointed directly away from the sun, the vidicons on the second stage gave her an awesome view of the solar fireball. She was moving so fast now that the sun's incandescent prominences changed perspective even as she watched.

Seventeen minutes to perihelion. From somewhere beyond the flames, Ilse got the expected maser communication. She pitched herself and her booster over so that she looked along the line of her trajectory. Now her own body was exposed to the direct glare of the sun. Through her telescope she could see luminous tracery within the solar corona. The booster's fuel tanks were perilously close to bursting, and Ilse was having trouble keeping her own body at its proper temperature.

Fifteen minutes to perihelion. The command came from Earth to begin the burn. Ilse considered her own trajectory data, and concluded that the command was thirteen seconds premature. Consultation with Earth would cost at least sixteen minutes, and her decision must be made in the next four seconds. Any of man's earlier, less sophisticated creations would have accepted the error and taken the mission on to catastrophe, but independence was the essence of Ilse's nature: she overrode the maser command, and delayed ignition till the instant she thought correct.

The sun's northern hemisphere passed below her, less than three solar diameters away.

Ignition, and Ilse was accelerated at nearly two gravities. As she swung toward what was to have been perihelion, her booster lifted her out of elliptic orbit and into a hyperbolic one. Half an hour later she shot out from the sun into the spaces south of the ecliptic at three hundred and twenty kilometers per second—about one solar diameter every hour. The booster's now empty propellant tanks were between her and the sun, and her body slowly cooled.

Shortly after burnout, Earth offhandedly acknowledged the navigation error. This is not to say that Ilse's makers were without contrition for their mistake, or without praise for Ilse. In fact, several men lost what little there remained to confiscate for jeopardizing this mission, and Man's last hope. It was simply that Ilse's makers did not believe that she could appreciate apologies or praise.

Now Ilse fled up out of the solar gravity well. It had taken her eleven weeks to fall from Earth to Sol, but in less than two weeks she had regained this altitude, and still she plunged outward at more than one hundred kilometers per second. That velocity remained her inheritance from the sun. Without the gravity well maneuver, her booster would have had to be five hundred times as large, or her voyage three times as long. It had

been the very best that men could do for her, considering the
time remaining to them.

So began the voyage of one hundred centuries. Ilse parted
with the empty booster and floated on alone: a squat cylinder,
twelve meters wide, five meters long, with a large telescope
sticking from one end. Four light-years below her in the well of
the night she saw Alpha Centauri, her destination. To the
naked human eye, it appears a single bright star, but with her
telescope Ilse could clearly see two stars, one slightly fainter
and redder than the other. She carefully measured their position and her own, and concluded that her aim had been so
perfect that a midcourse correction would not be necessary for
a thousand years.

For many months, Earth maintained maser contact—to pose
problems and ask after her health. It was almost pathetic, for if
anything went wrong now, or in the centuries to follow, there
was very little Earth could do to help. The problems were interesting, though. Ilse was asked to chart the nonluminous bodies
in the solar system. She became quite skilled at this and eventually discovered all nine planets, most of their moons, and
several asteroids and comets.

In less than two years, Ilse was farther from the sun than any
known planet, than any previous terrestrial probe. The sun
itself was no more than a very bright star behind her, and Ilse
had no trouble keeping her frigid innards at their proper temperature. But now it took sixteen hours to ask a question of
Earth and obtain an answer.

A strange thing happened. Over a period of three weeks, the
sun became steadily brighter until it gleamed ten times as
luminously as before. The change was not really a great one. It
was far short of what Earth's astronomers would have called a
nova. Nevertheless, Ilse puzzled over the event, in her own
way, for many months, since it was at this time that she lost
maser contact with Earth. That contact was never regained.

Now Ilse changed herself to meet the empty centuries. As
her designers had planned, she split her mind into three co-
equal entities. Theoretically each of these minds could handle
the entire mission alone, but for any important decision, Ilse

required the agreement of at least two of the minds. In this fractionated state, Ilse was neither as bright nor as quick-thinking as she had been at launch. But scarcely anything happened in interstellar space, the chief danger being senile decay. Her three minds spent as much time checking each other as they did overseeing the various subsystems.

The one thing they did not regularly check was the programmed memory, since Ilse's designers had—mistakenly—judged that such checks were a greater danger to the memories than the passage of time.

Even with her mentality diminished, and in spite of the caretaker tasks assigned her, Ilse spent much of her time contemplating the universe that spread out forever around her. She discovered binary star systems, then watched the tiny lights swing back and forth around each other as the decades and centuries passed. To her the universe became a moving, almost a living, thing. Several of the nearer stars drifted almost a degree every century, while the great galaxy in Andromeda shifted less than a second of arc in a thousand years.

Occasionally, she turned about to look at Sol. Even ten centuries out she could still distinguish Jupiter and Saturn. These were auspicious observations.

Finally it was time for the midcourse correction. She had spent the preceding century refining her alignment and her navigational observations. The burn was to be only one hundred meters per second, so accurate had been her perihelion impulse. Nevertheless, without that correction she would miss the Centauran system entirely. When the second arrived and her alignment was perfect, Ilse lit her tiny rocket—and discovered that she could obtain at most only three quarters of the rated thrust. She had to make two burns before she was satisfied with the new course.

For the next fifty years, Ilse studied the problem. She tested the rocket's electrical system hundreds of times, and even fired the rocket in microsecond bursts. She never discovered how the centuries had robbed her, but extrapolating from her observations, Ilse realized that by the time she entered the Centauran system, she would have only a thousand meters per second left in her rocket—less than half its designed capability.

90

Even so it was possible that, without further complications, she would be able to survey the planets of both stars in the system.

But before she finished her study of the propulsion problem, Ilse discovered another breakdown—the most serious she was to face.

She had forgotten her mission. Over the centuries the pattern of magnetic fields on her programmed memory had slowly disappeared—the least used programs going first. When Ilse recalled those programs to discover how her reduced maneuverability affected the mission, she discovered that she no longer had any record of her ultimate purpose. The memories ended with badly faded programs for biochemical reconnaissance and planetary entry, and Ilse guessed that there was something crucial left to do after a successful landing on a suitable planet.

Ilse was a patient sort—especially in her cruise configuration—and she didn't worry about her ultimate purpose, so far away in the future. But she did do her best to preserve what programs were left. She played each program into her own memory and then back to the programmed memory. If the process were repeated every seventy years, she found that she could keep the programmed memories from fading. On the other hand, she had no way of knowing how many errors this endless repetition was introducing. For this reason she had each of her subminds perform the process separately, and she frequently checked the ballistic and astronomical programs by doing problems with them.

Ilse went further: she studied her own body for clues as to its purpose. Much of her body was filled with a substance she must keep within a few degrees of absolute zero. Several leads disappeared into this mass. Except for her thermometers, however, she had no feeling in this part of her body. Now she raised the temperature in this section a few thousandths of a degree, a change well within design specifications, but large enough for her to sense. Comparing her observations and the section's mass with her chemical analysis programs, Ilse concluded that the mysterious area was a relatively homogeneous body of frozen water, doped with various impurities. It was interesting information, but no matter how she compared it with her memories she could not see any significance to it.

Ilse floated on—and on. The period of time between the midcourse maneuver and the next important event on her schedule was longer than man's experience with agriculture had been on Earth.

As the centuries passed, the two closely set stars that were her destination became brighter until, a thousand years from Alpha Centauri, she decided to begin her search for planets in the system. Ilse turned her telescope on the brighter of the two stars . . . call it Able. She was still thirty-five thousand times as far from Able—and the smaller star . . . call it Baker—as Earth is from Sol. Even to her sharp eye, Able didn't show as a disk but rather as a diffraction pattern: a round blob of light—many times larger than the star's true disk—surrounded by a ring of light. The faint gleam of any planets would be lost in that diffraction pattern. For five years Ilse watched the pattern, analyzed it with one of her most subtle programs. Occasionally she slid occulting plates into the telescope and studied the resulting, distorted, pattern. After five years she had found suggestive anomalies in the diffraction pattern, but no definite signs of planets.

No matter. Patient Ilse turned her telescope a tiny fraction of a degree, and during the next five years she watched Baker. Then she switched back to Able. Fifteen times Ilse repeated this cycle. While she watched, Baker completed two revolutions about Able, and the stars' maximum mutual separation increased to nearly a tenth of a degree. Finally Ilse was certain: she had discovered a planet orbiting Baker, and perhaps another orbiting Able. Most likely they were both gas giants. No matter: she knew that any small, inner planets would still be lost in the glare of Able and Baker.

There remained less than nine hundred years before she coasted through the Centauran system.

Ilse persisted in her observations. Eventually she could see the gas giants as tiny spots of light—not merely as statistical correlations in her carefully collected diffraction data. Four hundred years out, she decided that the remaining anomalies in Able's diffraction pattern must be another planet, this one at about the same distance from Able as Earth is from Sol. Fifteen years later she made a smiliar discovery for Baker.

If she were to investigate both of these planets she would have to plan very carefully. According to her design specifications, she had scarcely the maneuvering capability left to investigate one system. But Ilse's navigation system had survived the centuries better than expected, and she estimated that a survey of both planets might still be possible.

Three hundred and fifty years out, Ilse made a relatively large course correction, better than two hundred meters per second. This change was essentially a matter of pacing: it would delay her arrival by four months. Thus she would pass near the planet she wished to investigate and, if no landing were attempted, her path would be precisely bent by Able's gravitational field and she would be cast into Baker's planetary system.

Now Ilse had less than eight hundred meters per second left in her rocket—less than 1 percent of her velocity relative to Able and Baker. If she could be at the right place at the right time, that would be enough, but otherwise . . .

Ilse plotted the orbits of the bodies she had detected more and more accurately. Eventually she discovered several more planets: a total of three for Able, and four for Baker. But only her two prime candidates—call them Able II and Baker II— were at the proper distance from their suns.

Eighteen months out, Ilse sighted moons around Able II. This was good news. Now she could accurately determine the planet's mass, and so refine her course even more. Ilse was now less than fifty astronomical units from Able, and eighty from Baker. She had no trouble making spectroscopic observations of the planets. Her prime candidates had plenty of oxygen in their atmospheres—though the farther one, Baker II, seemed deficient in water vapor. On the other hand, Able II had complex carbon compounds in its atmosphere, and its net color was blue-green. According to Ilse's damaged memory, these last were desirable features.

The centuries had shrunk to decades, then to years, and finally to days. Ilse was within the orbit of Able's gas giant. Ten million kilometers ahead her target swept along a nearly circular path about its sun, Able. Twenty-seven astronomical units beyond Able gleamed Baker.

But Ilse kept her attention on that target, Able II. Now she could make out its gross continental outlines. She selected a landing site, and performed a two-hundred-meter-per-second burn. If she chose to land, she would come down in a greenish, beclouded area.

Twelve hours to contact, Ilse checked each of her subminds one last time. She deleted all malfunctioning circuits, and reassembled herself as a single mind out of what remained. Over the centuries, one third of all her electrical components had failed, so that besides her lost memories, she was not nearly as bright as she had been when launched. Nevertheless, with her subminds combined she was much cleverer than she had been during the cruise. She needed this greater alertness, because in the hours and minutes preceding her encounter with Able II, she would do more analysis and make more decisions than ever before.

One hour to contact. Ilse was within the orbit of her target's outer moon. Ahead loomed the tentative destination, a blue and white crescent two degrees across. Her landing area was around the planet's horizon. No matter. The important task for these last moments was a biochemical survey—at least that's what her surviving programs told her. She scanned the crescent, looking for traces of green through the clouds. She found a large island in a Pacific-sized ocean, and began the exquisitely complex analysis necessary to determine the orientation of amino acids. Every fifth second, she took one second to reestimate the atmospheric densities. The problem seemed even more complicated than her training exercises back in Earth orbit.

Five minutes to contact. She was less than forty thousand kilometers out, and the planet's hazy limb filled her sky. In the next ten seconds she must decide whether or not to land on Able II. Her ten-thousand-year mission was at stake here. For once Ilse landed, she knew that she would never fly again. Without the immense booster that had pushed her out along this journey, she was nothing but a brain and an entry shield

94

and a chunk of frozen water. If she decided to bypass Able II, she must now use a large portion of her remaining propellants to accelerate at right angles to her trajectory. This would cause her to miss the upper edge of the planet's atmospere, and she would go hurtling out of Able's planetary system. Thirteen months later she would arrive in the vicinity of Baker, perhaps with enough left in her rocket to guide herself into Baker II's atmosphere. But, if that planet should be inhospitable, there would be no turning back: she would have to land there, or else coast on into interstellar darkness.

Ilse weighed the matter for three seconds and concluded that Able II satisfied every criterion she could recall, while Baker II seemed a bit too yellow, a bit too dry.

Ilse turned ninety degrees and jettisoned the small rocket that had given her so much trouble. At the same time she ejected the telescope that had served her so well. She floated indivisible, a white biconvex disk, twelve meters in diameter, fifteen tons in mass.

She turned ninety degrees more to look directly back along her trajectory. There was not much to see now that she had lost her scope, but she recognized the point of light that was Earth's sun and wondered again what had been on all those programs that she had forgotten.

Five seconds. Ilse closed her eye and waited.

Contact began as a barely perceptible acceleration. In less than two seconds that acceleration built to two hundred and fifty gravities. This was beyond Ilse's experience, but she was built to take it: her body contained no moving parts and— except for her fusion reactor—no empty spaces. The really difficult thing was to keep her body from turning edgewise and burning up. Though she didn't know it, Ilse was repeating—on a grand scale—the landing technique that men had used so long ago. But Ilse had to dissipate more than eight hundred times the kinetic energy of any returning Apollo capsule. Her maneuver was correspondingly more dangerous, but since her designers could not equip her with a rocket powerful enough to decelerate her, it was the only option.

Now Ilse used her wits and every dyne in her tiny electric thrusters to arc herself about Able II at the proper attitude and altitude. The acceleration rose steadily toward five hundred gravities, or almost five kilometers per second in velocity lost every second. Beyond that Ilse knew that she would lose consciousness. Just centimeters away from her body the air glowed at fifty thousand degrees. The fireball that surrounded her lit the ocean seventy kilometers below as with daylight.

Four hundred and fifty gravities. She felt a cryostat shatter, and one branch of. her brain short through. Still Ilse worked patiently and blindly to keep her body properly oriented. If she had calculated correctly, there were less than five seconds to go now.

She came within sixty kilometers of the surface, then rose steadily back into space. But now her velocity was only seven kilometers per second. The acceleration fell to a mere fifteen gravities, then to zero. She coasted back through a long ellipse to plunge, almost gently, into the depths of Able II's atmosphere.

At twenty thousand meters altitude, Ilse opened her eye and scanned the world below. Her lens had been cracked, and several of her gestalt programs damaged, but she saw green and knew her navigation hadn't been too bad.

It would have been a triumphant moment if only she could have remembered what she was supposed to do *after* she landed.

At ten thousand meters, Ilse popped her paraglider from the hull behind her eye. The tough plastic blossomed out above her, and her fall became a shallow glide. Ilse saw that she was flying over a prairie spotted here and there by forest. It was near sunset and the long shadows cast by trees and hills made it easy for her to gauge the topography.

Two thousand meters. With a glide ratio of one to four, she couldn't expect to fly more than another eight kilometers. Ilse looked ahead, saw a tiny forest, and a stream glinting through the trees. Then she saw a glade just inside the forest, and some vagrant memory told her this was an appropriate spot. She pulled in the paraglider's forward lines and slid more steeply downward. As she passed three or four meters over the trees surrounding the glade, Ilse pulled in the rear lines, stalled her glider, and fell into the deep, moist grass. Her dun and green paraglider collapsed over her charred body so that she might be mistaken for a large black boulder covered with vegetation.

The voyage that had crossed one hundred centuries and four light-years was ended.

Ilse sat in the gathering twilight and listened. Sound was an undreamed-of dimension to her: tiny things burrowing in their holes, the stream gurgling nearby, a faint chirping in the distance. Twilight ended and a shallow fog rose in the dark glade. Ilse knew her voyaging was over. She would never move again. No matter. That had been planned, she was sure. She knew that much of her computing machinery—her mind—had been destroyed in the landing. She would not survive as a conscious being for more than another century or two. No matter.

What did matter was that she knew that her mission was not completed, and that the most important part remained, else the immense gamble her makers had undertaken would finally come to nothing. That possibility was the only thing that could frighten Ilse. It was part of her design.

She reviewed all the programmed memories that had survived the centuries and the planetary entry, but discovered nothing new. She investigated the rest of her body, testing her parts in a thorough, almost destructive, way she never would have dared while still centuries from her destination. She discovered nothing new. Finally she came to that load of ice she had carried so far. With one of her cryostats broken, she couldn't keep it at its proper temperature for more than a few years. She recalled the apparently useless leads that disappeared into that mass. There was only one thing left to try.

Ilse turned down her cryostats, and waited as the temperature within her climbed. The ice near her small fusion reactor warmed first. Somewhere in the frozen mass a tiny piece of metal expanded just far enough to complete a circuit, and Ilse discovered that her makers had taken one last precaution to ensure her reliability. At the base of the icy hulk, next to the reactor, they had placed an auxiliary memory unit, and now Ilse had access to it. Her designers had realized that no matter what dangers they imagined, there would be others, and so they had decided to leave this backup cold and inactive till the very end. And the new memory unit was quite different from her old ones, Ilse vaguely realized. It used optical rather than magnetic storage.

Now Ilse knew what she must do. She warmed a cylindrical tank filled with frozen amniotic fluid to thirty-seven degrees centigrade. From the store next to the cylinder, she injected a single microorganism into the tank. In a few minutes she would begin to suffuse blood through the tank.

It was early morning now and the darkness was moist and cool. Ilse tried to probe her new memory further, but was balked. Apparently the instructions were delivered according to some schedule to avoid unnecessary use of the memory. Ilse reviewed what she had learned, and decided that she would know more in another nine months.

Sir Fred Hoyle

One of the world's most famous astronomers, Sir Fred Hoyle (1915–   ) was born in Bingley, Yorkshire, England.

After receiving an M.A. from Emmanuel College, Cambridge (1939), he began his long association with Cambridge University as a research fellow of St. John's College. Later titles included lecturer in mathematics (1945–1958), Plumian professor of theoretical astronomy and experimental philosophy (1958–1973), and director of the Institute of Theoretical Astronomy (1966–1972). In addition, he has held several visiting positions at other universities and institutes.

He has authored or co-authored approximately twenty-five nonfiction books such as *The Nature of The Universe* (1951); *Frontiers of Astronomy* (1955); *Galaxies, Nuclei, and Quasars* (1965); *From Stonehenge to Modern Cosmology* (1972); and *The Physics-Astronomy Frontier* (1980).

His most prominent honor was his knighting in 1972, but he has also been given several honorary doctorate of science degrees, and has earned such prestigious awards as the Royal Astronomical Society's Gold Medal (1968) and UNESCO's Kalinga Prize (1968).

Much of his science fiction is co-authored with his son, and most consists of novels such as *The Black Cloud* (1957), *Ossian's Ride* (1959) and *The Inferno* (1973). Those few short pieces he has written are collected in *Element 79* (1967). From there we have chosen the following hilarious story, which might have been called "Paws for Thought."

BLACKMAIL

by Fred Hoyle

A NGUS CARRUTHERS WAS a wayward, impish genius. Genius is not the same thing as high ability. Men of great talent commonly spread their efforts, often very effectively, over a wide front. The true genius devotes the whole of his skill, his energies, his intelligence, to a particular objective, which he pursues unrelentingly.

Early in life, Carruthers became skeptical of human superiority over other animals. Already in his early teens, he understood exactly where the difference lies—it lies in the ability of humans to pool their knowledge through speech, in the ability through speech to educate the young. The challenging problem to his keen mind was to find a system of communication every bit as powerful as language that could be made available to others of the higher animals. The basic idea was not original, it was the determination to carry the idea through to its conclusion that was new. Carruthers pursued his objective inflexibly down the years.

Gussie had no patience with people who talked and chattered to animals. If animals had the capacity to understand language, wouldn't they have done it already, he said, thousands of years ago? Talk was utterly and completely pointless. You were just damned stupid if you thought you were going to teach English to your pet dog or cat. The thing to do was to understand the world from the point of view of the dog or cat. Once you'd got yourself into *their* system, it would be time enough to think about trying to get them into *your* system.

Gussie had no close friends. I suppose I was about as near to being a friend as anyone, yet even I would see him only perhaps once in six months. There was always something refreshingly different when you happened to run into him. He might have grown a black spade beard, or he might just have had a crew cut. He might be wearing a flowing cape, or he might be neatly tailored in a Bond Street suit. He always trusted me well enough to show off his latest experiments. At the least they were remarkable, at the best they went far beyond anything I had heard of, or read about. To my repeated suggestions that he simply must "publish," he always responded with a long, wheezy laugh. To me it seemed just plain common sense to publish, if only to raise money for the experiments, but Gussie obviously didn't see it this way. How he managed for money I could never discover. I supposed him to have a private income, which was very likely correct.

One day I received a note asking me to proceed to such-and-such an address, sometime near four P.M. on a certain Saturday. There was nothing unusual in my receiving a note, for Carruthers had got in touch with me several times before in this way. It was the address which came as the surprise, a house in a Croydon suburb. On previous occasions, I had always gone out to some decrepit barn of a place in remotest Hertfordshire. The idea of Gussie in Croydon somehow didn't fit. I was sufficiently intrigued to put off a previous appointment and to hie myself along at the appropriate hour.

My wild notion that Carruthers might have got himself well and truly wed, that he might have settled down in a nine-to-five job, turned out to be quite wrong. The big tortoiseshell spectacles he had sported at our previous meeting were gone, replaced by plain steel rims. His lank black hair was medium-long this time. He had a lugubrious look about him, as if he had just been rehearsing the part of Quince in *A Midsummer Night's Dream.*

"Come in," he wheezed.

"What's the idea, living in these parts?" I asked as I slipped off my overcoat. For answer, he broke into a whistling, croaking laugh. "Better take a look, in there."

The door to which Gussie pointed was closed. I was pretty sure I would find animals "in there," and so it proved. Although the room was darkened by a drawn curtain, there was sufficient light for me to see three creatures crouched around a television set. They were intently watching the second half of a game of Rugby League football. There was a cat with a big rust-red patch on the top of its head. There was a poodle, which cocked an eye at me for a fleeting second as I went in, and there was a furry animal sprawled in a big armchair. As I went in, I had the the odd impression of the animal lifting a paw, as if by way of greeting. Then I realized it was a small brown bear.

I had known Gussie long enough now, I had seen enough of his work, to realize that any comment in words would be ridiculous and superfluous. I had long ago learned the right procedure, to do exactly the same thing as the animals themselves were doing. Since I have always been partial to rugby, I was able to settle down quite naturally to watch the game in company with this amazing trio. Every so often I found myself catching the bright, alert eyes of the bear. I soon realized that, whereas I was mainly interested in the run of the ball, the animals were mainly interested in the tackling, qua tackling. Once, when a player was brought down particular heavily, there was a muffled yap from the poodle, instantly answered by a grunt from the bear.

After perhaps twenty minutes, I was startled by a really loud bark from the dog, there being nothing at all in the game to warrant such an outburst. Evidently, the dog wanted to attract the attention of the engrossed bear, for when the bear looked up quizzically, the dog pointed a dramatic paw toward a clock standing a couple of yards to the left of the television set. Immediately the bear lumbered from its chair to the set. It fumbled with the controls. There was a click, and to my astonishment we were on another channel. A wrestling bout had just begun.

The bear rolled back to its chair. It stretched itself, resting lazily on the base of its spine, arms raised with the claws cupped behind the head. One of the wrestlers spun the other violently. There was a loud thwack as the unfortunate fellow cracked his head on a ring post. At this, the cat let out the strangest animal noise I had ever heard. Then it settled down into a deep, powerful purr.

I had seen and heard enough. As I quitted the room the bear waved me out, much in the style of royalty and visiting heads of state. I found Gussie placidly drinking tea in what was evidently the main sitting room of the house. To my frenzied requests to be told exactly what it meant, Gussie responded with his usual asthmatic laugh. Instead of answering my questions, he asked some of his own. "I want your advice, professionally, as a lawyer. There's nothing illegal in the animals watching television, is there? Or in the bear switching the programs?"

"How could there be?"

"The situation's a bit complicated. Here, take a look at this."

Carruthers handed me a typewritten list. It covered a week of television programs. If this represented viewing by the animals, the set must have been switched on more or less continuously. The programs were all of one type, sports, westerns, suspense plays, films of violence.

"What they love," said Gussie by way of explanation, "is the sight of humans bashing themselves to pieces. Really, of course, it's more or less the usual popular taste, only a bit more so."

I noticed the name of a well-known rating firm on the letterhead.

"What's this heading here? I mean, what's all this to do with the TV ratings?"

Gussie fizzed and crackled like a soda siphon. "That's exactly the point. This house here is one of the odd few hundreds used in compiling the weekly ratings. That's why I asked if there was anything wrong in Bingo doing the switching."

103

"You don't mean viewing by those animals is going into the ratings?"

"Not only here, but in three other houses I've bought. I've got a team of chaps in each of them. Bears take quite naturally to the switching business."

"There'll be merry hell to pay if it comes out. Can't you see what the papers will make of it?"

"Very clearly, indeed."

The point hit me at last. Gussie could hardly have come on four houses by chance, all of which just happened to be hooked up to the TV rating system. As far as I could see, there wasn't anything illegal in what he'd done, so long as he didn't make any threats or demands. As if he read my thoughts, he pushed a slip of paper under my nose. It was a check for fifty thousand pounds.

"Unsolicited," he wheezed, "came out of the blue. From somebody in the advertising game, I suppose. Hush money. The problem is, do I put myself in the wrong if I cash it?"

Before I could form an opinion on this tricky question, there came a tinkling of breaking glass. "Another one gone," Gussie muttered. "I haven't been able to teach Bingo to use the vertical or horizontal holds. Whenever anything goes wrong, or the program goes off for a minute, he hammers away at the thing. It's always the tube that goes."

"It must be a costly business."

"Averages about a dozen a week. I always keep a spare set ready. Be a good fellow and give me a hand with it. They'll get pretty shirty if we don't move smartly."

We lifted what seemed like a brand-new set from out of a cupboard. Each gripping an end of it, we edged our way to the television snuggery. From inside, I was now aware of a strident uproar, compounded from the bark of a dog, the grunt of a bear, and the shrill moan of a redheaded cat. It was the uproar of animals suddenly denied their intellectual pabulum.

R. S. Richardson

Born in Kokomo, Indiana, R(obert) S(hirley) Richardson (1902–   ) has published much of his science fiction under the Philip Latham pseudonym.

Most of his career was spent as a working astronomer. After obtaining a B.A. from the University of California at Los Angeles (1926) and a Ph.D. from the University of California at Berkeley (1931), he joined the staff of Mount Palomar Observatory and remained until 1958. He subsequently became associate director of Griffith Observatory, staying there until 1964 when he decided to become a full-time writer.

He is author or co-author of more than a dozen nonfiction books, including *Astronomy* (1947); *Sun, Moon and Stars* (1959); *Getting Acquainted With Comets* (1967); and *The Stars and Serendipity* (1971), which won him the New York Academy of Sciences Children's Science Book Award.

In science fiction, he has written three novels *(Five Against Venus* (1952), *Missing Men of Saturn* (1953) and *Second Satellite* (1956), a number of "Captain Video" television plays and a score of short stories. Most of these shorter works involve astronomical themes and, like the selection below, offer rich insights into astronomers' working habits and lifestyles.

JEANNETTE'S HANDS

by *Philip Latham*
(Robert S. Richardson)

AGNY WAS IN bed when Bob came up with the breakfast
tray and paper. He had started serving his wife's breakfast
in bed when she became ill shortly after their marriage five
years ago and had continued the custom as a once-a-week
ritual. It was nearly eleven, late for the Archers even for Sunday. Dagny lay back on her pillow, her face still pale and lan-
guid from sleep.

"Ready for coffee?" he inquired.

"Please."

Bob had his usual trouble clearing a place for the tray. He
didn't mind the lotion, lipstick, tampon boxes, nail scissors
and other toilet articles that littered the dressing table. You
expected such junk on a woman's dressing table. What aroused
his ire were those damn hands.

Originally the "hands" had been part of Jeannette, a manne-
quin in an exclusive boutique over in Beverly Hills. Jeannette's
hands were among Dagny's most prized possessions. (It was
not until Jeannette's forepaws had entered their household that

Bob had learned that mannequins have proper names the same as people.) The hands and forearms, alas, were all that remained of Jeannette's anatomy after the 6.7 magnitude California earthquake of memorable date. Whereas her head and torso were shattered beyond repair, by some strange quirk of fate her hands had gone unscathed. The proprietress, a close friend of Dagny's, had bestowed them upon her as a precious keepsake. The hands not only looked real but felt real. Unlike most mannequins, the fingers were flexible, made of some rubber-and-fiberglass composition, a closely guarded secret of the manufacturer.*

Dagny had put the hands to effective use when playing the Snow Queen in the annual Christmas show of the Women's Assistance League. She kept the hands concealed in a refrigerator. Then with the forearms shrouded under her robe, she elicited delighted squeals from the kids at the icy impact of their touch. In fact, Jeannette's hands, together with Dagny's dramatic experience, had made the Snow Queen the hit of the show.

"Couldn't find anyplace else for these hands, could you?" Bob said, maneuvering for space on the dresser top.

"I don't see why you're continually complaining about those hands," Dagny murmured.

"They bug me, that's why."

"'Bug' you?"

Dagny still occasionally had trouble with her husband's Americanisms. Although a native Russian, she had lived mostly in Paris, until she met Bob and moved to Pasadena. Only to her he was never "Bob" but "Robert."

"Simply the pontifical symbol of blessing." Dagny said, "It means you're in a state of grace."

"Like hell I am."

"I promise to move them," Dagny said.

"Needn't bother. Got room now," Bob told her.

For several minutes they sat in silence, sipping coffee, and perusing the paper. It appeared from the headlines that unless

---

* The mannequins you see displayed in the best dress shops are not exactly cheap. Their price starts at about $200.

immediate remedial measures were taken, the world was doomed to imminent extinction.

After a hasty glance through the sports section Bob tossed his paper aside.

"End of fiscal year. Notice from Great White Father at Washington came this week. No raise as usual."

Dagny continued with the comic section.

"We'll manage somehow," Dagny told him. "I was casting our horoscope yesterday. Our future looks quite promising."

Dagny's preoccupation with astrology, sorcery, witchcraft and other assorted nonsense had been a source of bitter contention in their premarriage period. Society today will tolerate practically anything: interracial marriage or no marriage at all provoke scarcely the lift of an eyebrow. But an astronomer tied up with an astrologer . . . well, that's going a bit too far. With the passage of time, however, Bob had come to accept his wife's interest in the occult with the same resignation with which most husbands eventually learn to live with their wives' various and sundry foibles. Also, in Bob's particular case, submission to Dagny's faith in the supernatural was more readily understandable than most. His wife had other things going for her besides her horoscope.

Dagny handed him a sheet from the *Times.*

"Some more about your friend Dr. Thornton."

"Again!"

The page featured a photograph of a man of middle age, with strong well-defined features, a straight-stemmed briar pipe clenched in his teeth. He was standing by a measuring machine examining a picture of some celestial object.

"Good looking, isn't he?" said Dagny.

"You think so?"

"Very."

Bob gave the photo and story a quick once-over.

"Only half a dozen errors," he commented. "Photographer shot him from below 'stead of topside so his bald spot doesn't show. He's forty-two, not thirty-nine. And that's M-33 in Triangulum he's got there, not M-31 in Andromeda.

"'Dr. Thornton, noted astronomer at the world-famous Mt. Elsinore Observatory, will be in London this September when he receives the gold medal of the Royal Astronomical Society, one of the highest honors—'"

Bob snorted.

"Best thing astronomical societies do—hand out gold medals.

"'—Dr. Thornton's researches indicate a value for the age of the universe some ten times the previously accepted value—' There's some of us don't agree."

"Anyone I know?"

"Your husband, for one."

Dagny's gaze remained fixed on Thornton's profile.

"If you are right and he is wrong," she said, "then why doesn't the Royal Society give their gold medal to you?"

"Well, it's kind of hard to explain," Bob said, after a pause. "Personality enters into these things more'n you might think. Thornton's the masterful, dominating type. People read what he writes. Nobody pays attention to my stuff. He's a lucky observer. He proceeds as if it were impossible to fail. I'm always afraid of failing—so I generally fail. The farther you get from Thornton the bigger he looms. You either worship him from afar or hate him from the sidelines."

"Where is it you disagree?" Dagny inquired.

"That's a rather tough question . . ."

"Oh, well, if it's so top secret . . ."

Bob hesitated.

"Promise you won't breathe a word?"

Dagny shrugged. "I promise."

"Well, you see, I've gone over some of Thornton's stuff myself. Used the same measures and the same techniques. And our results don't agree. I just can't make 'em agree."

"You scientists never agree."

"Well, not exactly," Bob admitted. "You don't expect *exact* agreement. But in this case disagreement is way beyond the normal limits of error. It's my considered opinion"—his voice fell—"that Thornton's results are deliberately rigged."

"'Rigged'?"

"Changed just enough to give results exceeding other observers. With the largest telescope in the world at his command he's pretty safe. Who can check him?"

Dagny received this astounding communication with comparative calm.

"Darling, I thought you were going to tell me of Thornton doing something serious. Like stealing the *Blue Boy* at the Huntington or uprooting Christmas Tree Lane. After all, it's only the universe."

"Deliberate scientific deception *is* something pretty serious," Bob declared. "Understand—I can't prove a thing. He's rigged his results to give the cosmologists a real jolt. So now they're talking about the 'Thornton Universe.' Hence . . . the gold medal."

Dagny contemplated her husband long and thoughtfully. Her violet eyes narrowed.

"Darling Robert," she said, "you know what I think?"

"Precious angel, I wouldn't have the faintest notion what's going through that lovely blonde head of yours."

"I think you're jealous."

"What's so wrong with a man wanting a little recognition for his work?"

"And you're hurt—really hurt."

Bob did not respond.

Dagny squeezed his hand.

"Your turn is coming, Robert. I *know* it's coming. Any time . . . any moment."

Bob shook his head.

"Sorry . . . 'fraid I'm just not the gold medal type."

"But I *know*!"

Their remarks were interrupted by a peal from the doorbell.

"You see!" Dagny cried. "The good news—right on cue. *La pièce bien faite!*"

Dagny, in moments of stress, had a disconcerting way of lapsing into French.

"More likely the Girl Scouts selling peanuts," Bob muttered. He hesitated, then at the second peal, rose reluctantly and shuffled down the stairs. He returned after a moment with a long thin envelope bearing an impressive wax seal.

"Special delivery," he said, handing Dagny the missive. "For you."

Dagny paled. Her eyes darkened. She reached for the envelope hesitantly, almost fearfully, as if it were some relic sacred to the touch. Then with a sudden convulsive motion she tore open the envelope from which she extracted a stiff parchmentlike sheet of paper, upon which was inscribed a single handwritten line. For what must have been a full minute she lay staring at it, her lips moving perceptibly, as if savoring every word. Then she sank back upon the pillow, the parchment clutched to her breast, her fingers trembling.

Bob was not so alarmed by this emotional upheaval as one might have supposed. His wife was a good actress. So good he could never be sure whether her histrionics were for real or just pretend.

"Bad news?" he inquired.

"Wonderful news," said Dagny in a barely audible whisper.

"We're a long time overdue."

"It's like a dream."

"Must be a real REM blockbuster."*

"I've been appointed."

Bob regarded his wife with a sense of vague foreboding. "Appointed? Appointed to what?"

"Official witch! Official witch of California!"

Bob's reaction might be compared with that of a patient just informed he is the victim of inoperable lung cancer.

"I knew California's got an official poet laureate. I knew we've got more crackpots per square centimeter than any other state in the Union. But I'll be damned if I knew we had an official witch."

"Robert, darling, there are so many things you don't know."

"You mean really *official*? Like the governor or treasurer?"

"Well, not exactly . . ."

"God!" he cried. "To think we've come down to *that*!"

"Come *down*!" Dagny said. "Think of the honor. Think what it *means*."

"I'll tell you what it means," Bob roared, rising and pacing the floor. "It means the end of my career. Before—well, dabbling in astrology and that junk wasn't so bad. People just shrugged it off. But *now*! Who'll have any use for an astronomer whose wife goes in for witchcraft . . . black magic . . . satanism?"

---

* Strong REMs, or rapid eye movements, generally indicate a person is experiencing a vivid dream.

But he had lost his audience. Dagny was in a trance. Lady Macbeth sleepwalking in a twin bed.

"Theodoris of Lemnos . . . Madeleine de Bovan of France . . . Medea of Colchis. And now"—she hugged herself ecstatically—"Dagny Archer of Pasadena. I'll outdo them all!"

Dagny's apotheosis to official state witchdom was announced in the Los Angeles *Times* of the following Tuesday morning. Bob had cherished some faint hope of its being buried in an obscure paragraph among the vital statistics. Instead he found it spread all over the front page of the second section. At the top was a close-up of Dagny gazing fondly at her ginger cat Margarita. The young fellow who did the write-up took special pains to emphasize the unusual nature of the Golden State's new sorceress. Instead of the stereotyped witch of old, she was a young and beautiful suburban housewife, a far cry from the secret, black and midnight hags that had wrought such havoc in the Macbeth household.

Yes, Mrs. Archer said, she had been fascinated by the occult since earliest childhood. She deplored the widespread misconceptions concerning witchcraft. Witches inflict injury? In the Middle Ages they called it, "casting an evil spell." Today to the psychoanalysts it was the "id impulse." Withdrawing the sins you had committed in the external world and turning them upon yourself. The witch served merely as the scapegoat for one's own evil impulses.

How about those so-called "love philtres"?

Mrs. Archer could not refrain from laughter. Without going into detail, she intimated there were other means of arousing a man's desire available to a woman far more potent than any brew in the pharmacopoeia of witchcraft.

As to hobbies, her chief interest outside the occult was in the theater. Although a native Russian, she had spent her youth in France and played professionally upon the stage in Paris.

"My best role was Laura in Strindberg's *The Father.* Laura, you know, was Strindberg's surrogate for his first wife. [*Surrogate*, Bob told himself. Make mental note to look it up.] A fascinating part that must be played with the greatest restraint.

A woman smoldering inside before she becomes demoniacal in her rage to destroy her enemy."

Bob had to admit the part about Dagny was pretty good. It was the part about himself that rankled.

Yes, her husband was an astronomer on the staff of the Mt. Elsinore Observatory.

What was his opinion of astrology?

His opinion on that subject, she feared, would not be printable in a family paper like the *Times*. To put it mildly, he was rather skeptical on the subject. Fortunately the part about himself came at the end, where few people were likely to see it.

Upon arrival at the office, however, it was quite plain that everybody in the entire institution had seen it. Not that anybody said anything. Oh, a few close friends made quips about their whoreoscopes, when Venus would be at the ascending node of Jupiter and similar bits of scintillating humor. Otherwise he was not merely left alone. He was virtually shunned.

Bob made straight for his office,* shut the door and began sweating over some calculations on the Hyades cluster.† But try as he would, inevitably, his thoughts kept straying from Ambrosia, Eudora, Pedile, Coronis, Polyxo, Phyto and Thyene, to another nymph some one hundred thirty-five light-years closer by the name of Dagny Archer. *Official witch!* He must declare—nay, demand—that forthwith she resign this odious appointment that would soon render his professional position intolerable. He rehearsed his speech all the way home.

But when he stalked into the house, he found Dagny on the telephone, talking long distance to some warlock or werewolf, and could not be interrupted under any circumstances. He hung around the phone for a while, but when it became apparent that members of the occult had as much difficulty communicating as ordinary mortals, he wandered out to the kitchen to seek solace in the liquor cabinet. First he took a long pull straight out of the bottle, then mixed a whiskey and soda and

---

* Astronomers spend most of their time in their offices in town.

† Besides those visible to the eye, some 200 stars have been identified within the Hyades cluster. Our scale of the universe depends in a critical way upon the distance assigned this cluster.

retired to the patio to drink like a gentleman. Margarita, dozing on the chair opposite, regarded him with that introspective expression characteristic of felines in repose.

At length Dagny joined him with her glass of tomato juice. She neither smoked nor drank; in fact, she regarded any drug that might impair the acuity of her senses as shocking.

"This revival of interest in the occult," she enthused. "It's positively sweeping the country. You know, so much of your science doesn't sound a bit different to me from occultism. All this talk about quarks and leptons and these new things . . . black holes?"

"Nothing new to me," Bob said. "Been groping around in some black hole all my life."

Dagny sensed his mood in an instant.

"Oh, Robert, don't be so stuffy. So I'm official witch. Does that mean the end of the world? 'What is truth?' Who can say? There are two sides to every question."

"Not to this one there isn't."

"You're not being fair."

"Dagny, darling, *think*!" Bob cried. "How can some miserable chunk of matter like Uranus, three billion miles away, conceivably influence our lives here on Earth?"

Dagny's fingers wandered to Margarita.

"You said yourself the discovery of radio waves had revolutionized astronomy. May not other waves be reaching us too? Waves as yet unknown?"

"Probably are," Bob agreed.

"I *know* they are. I can feel them."

Bob was also beginning to feel certain vibrations stirring within him, albeit noncosmic in origin. He was drunk and he knew it. Tomorrow he would feel like the devil.

He crossed the patio a bit unsteadily, enfolded Dagny in his arms, his fingers groping for her breasts. She drew his face down to hers. The violet tints of her veins were as delicate as those of an angel.

Or a witch.

He didn't know. At the moment he didn't care.

He was right about the hangover. But it was a hangover of a special type, one not accompanied by the usual depression of the higher nerve centers. Some of the buoyancy of the previous evening still lingered. Of one thing Bob was sure. Dagny, if she cared to make the effort, could get any man she wanted to do anything she wanted.

He pitched into the Hyades with renewed zeal. Once he had gotten discouraged and chucked the girls in the wastebasket. Today they were more encouraging. He drove himself relentlessly. Long after the building was quiet and the parking lot emptied, he was still pounding away.

Someone knocked.

He turned sharply, genuinely startled. A dark figure loomed in the opal glass of the doorway.

"Come in."

To his relief it was MacGuire. MacGuire was one of the few members of the staff he really liked.

To MacGuire, as secretary of the institution, fell the unenviable task of making out the observing program for the telescopes on the mountain. Professional astronomers bear scant resemblance to their popular image: lofty-minded, idealistic souls, with their heads among the stars. For the most part they are cranky antisocial characters, absorbed in their own narrow field of investigation, and little else. Thus, making out an observing program acceptable to all was fraught with difficulties. The astronomers seldom got the nights they wanted, at the times they wanted, or as many as they felt they deserved.

MacGuire's expression was solemn as befits a man laden with heavy responsibilities. He laid several long sheets on the desk headed *250-Inch, Schmidt, 60-Inch,* and so forth. The papers were marked into columns and squares. At the top of each column was a date. About half the squares were filled with various observers' initials. He indicated the sheet headed *250-Inch.*

"I got you down for July twenty-ninth, thirtieth and thirty-first. Okay?"

"Okay," Bob told him, jotting the dates on his desk pad. "Now how about the others?"

"That's all."

"That's all?" Bob regarded him incredulously. "What d'you mean—that's all? You know I want to do some more photometry on M-110."

"Bob, I'm sorry as hell. But the schedule's all balled up this run."

"It's all balled up every run."

"Yeah, but it's worse this time. On account of Thornton going to Hawaii, you know."

"No, I didn't know."

"Neither did I till he sprung it on me last week."

"What's so big with Hawaii?"

"Jupiter's occulting a sixth-magnitude star morning of the thirty-first. BO. Thornton wants to try for it with that new telescope he designed for Mauna Kea. Best chance to get molecular abundance of Jupiter's atmosphere in years."

"Screw Jupiter's atmosphere. Let him observe it here."

"Can't. Doesn't begin on Pacific Coast till sunrise."

"What's that got to do with me?"

MacGuire's expression was not altogether happy.

"He needs more spectra on that new cluster of his. Only got one good one so far. But if the others bear it out, it'll prove up his model universe for sure."

"I still don't see—"

"So Thornton, as chairman of the program committee, thought maybe you—"

"Maybe *me*!"

"Bob, it's just on account of this damn occultation."

"You mean I'm to work as . . . Thornton's *assistant*?"

There was a long silence. MacGuire stirred uneasily.

"I guess there's something else we ought to talk about, too."

Bob remained staring straight ahead.

"You know they're pretty lenient around here some ways," McGuire said. "Like getting drunk or taking a woman up on the mountain. But there's absolutely one thing you can't do in a serious scientific institution like this place. You can't mix astronomy and astrology."

"Are you by any chance referring to my wife?"

MacGuire nodded reluctantly.

"But, damnit, Mac, it's not *my* doing," Bob protested. "I'm just as set against it—"

"Sure, Bob, that's what I told the committee. It'd been all right except for Thornton."

"Thornton?"

"You know how he's been pressuring the Astronomy Missions Board to get a couple of million for that gravitational wave detector. AMB's getting tougher every year. But Thornton's got lots of pull. Almost had 'em convinced. Then this story about Dagny's being official witch broke.

"Well . . . that killed it. Legislators just laughed. Claimed we're no different from those other quacks and screwballs."

Bob turned slowly.

"Mac, tell me, did Thornton mention Dagny by name?"

"Well, it's kind of hard to remember—"

"Did he?"

"Guess he might have—"

Bob was on his feet in an instant.

"The son of a bitch! I'll knock his head off!"

MacGuire shoved him back in his seat.

"Now you listen to me," he said sternly. "You think a long time before you go taking a swing at anybody around here."

Suddenly Bob's hangover hit him like a wave. His hands, his arms, began trembling. He couldn't keep them from trembling.

"I'm resigning," he said dully.

MacGuire patted his shoulder.

"Don't do anything now. Go home. Have a drink. I'd say you could use one."

Bob didn't answer.

Dagny and Margarita were in the patio when Bob joined them with his drink. Dagny was sipping iced tomato juice. Margarita, curled on her lap, scrutinized him briefly and resumed her slumbers.

"So things didn't go so well at the office?" said Dagny.

Bob wished he could make out her face, but the shadows were too deep.

"I believe you are a witch," he muttered.

Dagny laughed.

"There are things one need not be a witch to know. Being a wife is quite sufficient."

Bob poured out the whole story. Dagny heard him through without comment.

117

"Well, that's it," he concluded. "Thornton'll be in Hawaii observing Jupiter while I'm slaving away on his stuff."

"Is that then so bad?"

"Bad? It's a disgrace."

"Why not see Dr. Thornton? Talk things over."

"You don't talk things over with a guy like Thornton."

"He is such a monster?"

"No. Some ways he's not so bad. Just inhuman, that's all."

"*Non, non. C'est incroyable.* Impossible."

"Oh, guess he's got a few human traits. Heard he hits the bottle occasionally." He stared at his empty glass.

Several minutes must have passed.

"You're not a big psychic, are you, Robert?" said Dagny.

"Nope. Never had a psychic experience in my life. All lot of bunk."

"That is unfortunate, for then you would see your Dr. Thornton is not what he appears. His desire for dominance is—what you call?—a mere cover-up. Underneath, believe me, he is *un homme mal assuré.*"

Bob could follow his wife's French. It was her Russian that left him lost.

"You are a witch, aren't you?" he mused.

Dagny did not respond.

"And you've still got Thornton's picture?"

She waved one hand in a careless gesture. "Somewhere."

"Then what are we waiting for?" Bob demanded. "Let's get busy with some witchcraft."

"What would you suggest?"

"Hell, that's your business," Bob exclaimed impatiently. "Hex him. put the old curse on him."

"*Je ne com—*"

"Always heard there's a regular routine in these things. There's a guy you don't like. You get his picture. You stick a needle . . ."

He hurried on enthusiastically, so enthusiastically that he failed to notice his wife's face buried in her hands. Oh, lord, he'd done it now.

He rushed to her side, tore aside her hands. She was sobbing . . . really sobbing. This was not pretend. He could feel the tears streaming down her cheeks.

"Honey . . . darling. I was only kidding. Honest. I supposed you knew."

This woman in his arms wasn't the official witch of California. She was Dagny, his wife, the one person in the world he loved the most.

"You go right ahead with your witchcraft," he told her. There was a grim note in his voice. "Why, you're lots better in witchcraft than me in astronomy."

Tenderly he kissed away the tears.

"I tell you what let's do," he exclaimed. "Let's spend my three days on the mountain together. I'll reserve a cottage at the inn tonight. Working on Thornton's stuff won't seem so bad—if you're there."

He waited anxiously. "All right?"

She nodded.

"Wonderful!"

Dagny retired early. Bob wandered into the library, where he sat down by the table lamp, trying to put his world together. Perhaps another drink—no, better not. Maybe something to read.

He took down one of Dagny's books on witchcraft and began turning through it at random, pausing at some passage that caught his attention.

"'Astral Flight.' The puzzling thing about astral flight is that, although rejected intuitively by a mind accustomed to scientific habits of thought, there is nevertheless a great weight of evidence in favor of its occurrence. Indeed, the evidence would be regarded as overwhelming were the phenomenon not so intrinsically unlikely."

How could anyone as intelligent as Dagny believe in such crap?

His eyes strayed from the book to last Sunday's *Times* spread on the table bearing Thornton's picture. Thornton's face was half covered by shadow, an odd double-pronged shadow.

There was something familiar . . . where . . .?

Jeannette's hands! Dagny had promised she would move them. And so she had. There they stood by the lamp with unpraised fingers.

He caught an entry in the book.

". . . the position of the hand, with the second and third fingers raised, symbolizes God and Perfected Man, pouring out their blessing. Yet like all forces in the physical world, this blessing may also become a curse. For if the hand be so lifted that the shadow of the two fingers resembles the head and horns of the Goat Baphhomet, the fate of the person upon which their shadow falls is terrible indeed."

To Bob the trip up the winding road to the observatory was just a part of his job. The first sight of the white domes perched on the mountaintop ceasd to thrill. But going with Dagny was something special. She seldom accompanied him on his observing assignments. Astronomy to her was not a science but a *mystique.* Owing to her interest in astrology, however, she had of necessity acquired a considerable knowledge of practical astronomy. Not merely a superficial acquaintance with the stars, planets and constellations, but the ability to comprehend such terms as hour angle and sidereal time, declination and right ascension.

The air cooled rapidly with altitude. At the five-thousand-foot level they began encountering wisps of fog, and at seven thousand feet the fog had thickened until Bob was forced to reduce their progress to a bare creep. Dagny was enraptured. Buried in the fog, they seemed isolated from the world of reality. Once they spied a white squirrel peering at them from the limb of a tree.

After a leisurely lunch at the inn, Bob announced his intention of going over to the observatory, where the other astronomers who happened to be on the mountain were staying, as well as the engineers and assistants who made the mountain their permanent home.

"Why bother?" said Dagny, unpacking their luggage. "The fog's so thick you can hardly see our car outside the window?"

"Matter of principle," Bob told her, changing into his old observing clothes. "An astronomer prepares his work regardless of the weather. This fog might clear up in a minute. Then where'd I be? Standing around with nothing done?"

"Embarrassing," Dagny murmured.

Bob laughed reminiscently.

"Remember solar eclipse expedition I was on in New Guinea. Just a graduate student then. Morning of eclipse, clouds were so thick couldn't even find the sun. I was all for packing up. Director gave me hell. So we went ahead as per schedule. Then, few minutes before totality, just like a miracle. Clouds broke away. Corona blazed out. Got everything we came for."

He hesitated awkwardly at the door.

"Remember other night, told you I'd never had a psychic experience? Well, came pretty close at that eclipse. Just before totality when the moon's about cut off last bit of sun, you get the funniest feeling. Darkness comes on fast. Landscape changes color—kind of pale-green tint. It's as if the light of the world was going out. The moon's shadow comes rushing at you like a pillar of doom. You get scared—really scared. All your old supernatural fears come back." He laughed sheepishly. "Funniest feeling."

Dagny was surveying their clothes and toilet articles strewn over the bed.

"I forgot the toothpaste," she exclaimed.

Bob felt humiliated and degraded at the thought of being reduced to working on Thornton's program. Once having committed himself, however, personalities ceased to matter. He would exert himself to secure the best observations possible, just as a surgeon would operate with the same care on an enemy as a friend. Naturally, if the weather prevented observations, that was not his fault.

At sunset the fog suddenly cleared away leaving the sky washed crystal clear. Bob waited a while, then telephoned his night assistant at the 250-inch to go ahead and open the dome. But he had hardly covered the half mile to the dome when the fog was back again. And so it went the whole night, alternately clearing up and clouding over, so that Bob got nothing, and returned to their cottage at dawn feeling more tired and frustrated than if he had put in a solid night's work.

He stole into the cottage as quietly as possible to keep from waking Dagny. Ever since midnight he had been anticipating that wonderful moment when he could crawl into his twin bed and forget the stars. But as so often happens on an astronomer's first night, the moment his head hit the pillow found him wide-eyed and staring. Sometimes he felt like two persons: one fully conscious lying beside another in a dream. Eventually he dropped into a restless sleep from which he awoke about noon. Dagny was gone. And the landscape looked as dismal as ever.

Dagny came in while he was shaving, bright and cheerful, smelling of pine and the fresh outdoors. She had bought some postcards at the inn.

"I got some pictures," she said, displaying the cards. "Deer, squirrels, flowers."

"So I see."

"Bad night?"

He nodded.

"Terrible night. No luck at all."

The second night was a repetition of the first. Bob put on a suitably doleful face and commiserated with his fellow observers at the Schmidt and 60-inch. Secretly he could hardlly conceal his exultation. Just let it stick around one more night. Thornton's stuff would go down the drain, and he could pull out with a clear conscience. Moreover, he slept well the second night and at mealtime was all animation. (Breakfast for Bob; lunch for Dagny).

After dinner on the evening of the thirty-first he gave the 250-inch dome a ring. "We'll stay up till two," he told his night assistant. "Then unless it looks real good, we'll call it a night."

After dinner he and Dagny changed into lounging robes and settled down for a grim session with the ancient TV set provided by the management. To their delight they discovered an old movie was on dating back to their honeymoon days. Soon they were holding hands and feeling very nostalgic. Even the commercials were welcome, as they gave Bob a chance to duck outside to check on the weather. And always he was gratified by confrontation with a solid wall of fog.

At the final fade-out at eleven, however, he found the world transformed: the lights of the valley visible clear to the horizon, and the stars of Cygnus and Lyra glittering overhead.

"Jupiter," Dagny whispered, gazing in awe at a huge yellow star in the east.

"Yep. Jupiter rising in Capricornus," said Bob.

"I wonder what Dr. Thornton's doing in Hawaii?"

Bob laughed.

"Probably not much of anything right now. Occultation won't start till around dawn here."

Suddenly the lights of the valley dimmed. Jupiter vanished. And in a matter of moments the world was its old dreary self again.

They scurried back to the warmth of the cottage. Bob glanced at the clock. Midnight. Two more hours till freedom.

Bob turned out the lights except for the shaded lamp by the clock. Dagny laid aside her robe and stretched out on her bed. For a while they sat in the semidarkness exchanging desultory remarks. Conversation dwindled . . . faded into silence.

Dagny removed her thin nightdress. Bob began caressing her, gently at first, then almost fiercely. Already he could feel her responding, straining closer . . .

It was going to be a good night, Bob reflected, fog or no fog.

Bob came struggling up into consciousness through some vast gray distance measurable only in megaparsecs. There was a ringing noise. For what seemed a long time he thought it part of some dream. Suddenly it got through to him. The telephone.

He groped for the instrument.

"Opening up, Dr. Archer?" It was the night assistant at the 250-inch.

"Thought it'd fogged over."

"Cleared up an hour ago."

"Go ahead and set up. Be right over."

This last was a slight exaggeration. Bob had not anticipated getting dressed in such a hurry, and his observing clothes were scattered all over the place. Another handicap was trying to get dressed without awakening Dagny. Her face was nearly covered by her hair, leaving only her profile exposed against the pillow. How still she lay. Her long dark lashes as imobile of those of a doll's. Not the slightest perceptible motion of the coverlet to betray her breathing.

He decided to walk instead of taking the car. Trying to start their old car would make an awful racket. Walking would be just about as quick anyway. With his flashlight he could take the little trail to the dome they called the Lucky Strike.

But he had reckoned without the altitude. By the time he reached the dome and climbed the long flight of stairs to the control board, he was panting and speechless. He hung draped over the iron railing encircling the telescope like a beaten fighter dangling on the ropes.

The dome was open, but the telescope was in its usual upright position.

"How come you didn't make the setting?" Bob gasped when he was able to speak.

The night assistant knocked the ashes from his pipe. "Didn't have the position."

"Left it right here on the desk."

"Didn't see it."

Followed a frantic session in which they searched the desk, the floor around the desk, the drawers, the record book, even the darkroom and toilet. But the vital information necessary to pinpoint the tiny spot of light far beyond the range of vision remained obstinately missing. The conclusion was inescapable. In his haste to get away, Bob had left the setting and identification chart back at the cottage.

What to do?

The time needed for Bob to make the round-trip to the cottage, get the telescope set and start the exposure could easily take an hour, probably longer since he was unfamiliar with the star field and might have trouble identifying his object. Dawn comes on early in July. He could, of course, call the cottage and get the object's right ascension and declination from Dagny. But the position of the star field would be no good without the identification chart. The object might be any one of a dozen stars.*

---

* The 250-inch reflector on Mount Elsinore is unique among large telescopes in having an alta-azimuth instead of the usual equatorial mounting. An equatorially mounted telescope driven at the sidereal rate will track a star automatically. The alta-azimuth type mounting is simpler but will not track the stars. To overcome this disadvantage an elaborate computer system is necessary.

Bob was going through his pockets for the third time when he stopped, frozen by the clang from the iron door at the foot of the stairs. A moment's silence. Then the sound of footsteps slowly mounting the stairs. He and the night assistant exchanged glances.

"Somebody from the Schmidt or sixty-inch?" said Bob.

The assistant shook his head emphatically. "Couldn't be. They closed up for good at eleven."

"Must be a staff member. Who else'd have a key?"

"Don't know," the assistant muttered. "But I mean to find out."

He touched a button killing the dome lights, leaving them in darkness except for the faint red glow of the dials on the instrument panel. Bob heard him hurrying down the winding stairs to the landing by the coudé room. Followed the sound of low voices, then soft footsteps receding down the stairs. The assistant emerged from the darkness, hit the dome lights. He handed Bob an envelope.

"These the papers you wanted?"

Bob made a quick inspection.

"The works!" he cried. "But who—"

"Dunno. Lady gave 'em to me."

Undoubtedly Dagny. She must have awakened, noticed the papers on the dresser, and realizing his predicament brought them over in the car. She had a key to the dome.

He glanced at the sidereal clock. Nearly 23 hours. They'd have to work fast.

"Well, here you are," he said, handing the assistant the position.

"Stephan's quintet, eh?" the assistant remarked.

"Stephan's quintet? No. This object's way farther north in Pegasus."

"Position sure looks like Stephan's quintet to me," the night assistant declared. "Set on it too many times before."

Bob examined the figures written on the slip of paper. "That's Thornton's handwriting, isn't it?"

The assistant began leafing through the record book.

"Soon find out."

He stopped at some entries under Thornton's initials.

125

"Thornton's handwriting all right," he said. "Notice way he makes his figure fours. Always writes a four closed at the top. Everybody else leaves it open.

"Well, I got this setting straight from MacGuire, and Mac-Guire got it straight from Thornton," Bob said. "So . . . must be Stephan's quintet."

Once decided, they went ahead in record time. In a few minutes Bob was comparing the stars in the field of view of the telescope with those of his negative print. Fortunately the object was easily identified. He maneuvered it onto the slit of the spectrograph, picked up a guide star, and managed to get two full-length exposures just as dawn was showing.

"Got 'em," Bob called triumphantly to his assistant. "You can close 'er up and go home."

Bob stayed behind in the darkroom to develop and process his plates. That way they should be dry by noon, so he and Dagny could leave for home directly after lunch. One glance at the dark streaks on the slivers of glass showed he had hit the exposure time and focus just right.

Bob took Dagny home, changed his clothes, and started back to the office.

"Don't expect me till late," he told Dagny. "I want to take a good look at these plates."

It was fortunate he warned her, for it was deep twilight when he returned. After the cool of the mountain the valley was like an oven. Bob's clean shirt was soaked through. Dagny, clad in a thin transparent Empire-style gown, was as cool and serene as a goddess.

They sat in the patio for several minutes without speaking, Bob sipping his whiskey and soda, Dagny her iced tomato juice.

Bob was the first to speak.

"Quite a bit's happened in the last three days."

"Oh?" said Dagny, her fingertips lightly brushing Margarita's silken hair.

"You heard about Thornton yet?"

Dagny shook her head.

"Thornton never got that occultation."

126

"No? He, too, then, had clouds?"

"Thornton's dead."

Dagny continued stroking Margarita.

"How . . . dead?"

Bob hesitated.

"Don't know for sure yet. Seems Thornton was relaxing in the observatory library. Had everything ready to roll. Immersion still couple of hours off. Night assistant in galley thought he heard voices . . . then a shot. Rushed in. Found Thornton dead with revolver nearby."

Bob wished he could see Dagny's face, but it was full night now.

"Apparently Thornton wasn't alone," Bob continued. "There were two glasses on the table, both of which showed fingerprints. One set was identified with Thornton's. The other also showed prints of fingers."

"These fingerprints . . . they have been identified?"

Bob shook his head.

"I didn't say *fingerprints*. I said *prints of fingers*. No whorls or ridge structure. Just blank impressions."

"Probably gloves."

"Police don't think so. It seems they have ways of checking these things. Right now police don't know what to think. Could be most anything. Accident . . . suicide . . . murder."

"*Dlia menia eto boodet camoubistvo,*" said Dagny.

"What was that?"

"*Moi, je crois qu'il s'est tué.*"

"You believe. . . ."

"I believe it was suicide," said Dagny. "I told you he was *un homme mal assuré* — very insecure."

"That's right—so you did."

Neither spoke for several minutes.

"Maybe it was just as well," Bob mused. "Those observations I got were . . . well, very peculiar. MacGuire and I both agreed. Put an awful dent in Thornton's theory. He probably suspicioned something of the sort. In any case, after seeing them, he couldn't possibly have accepted that award from the Royal Society. Upset our whole conception of the universe."

Dagny's gaze wandered upward to the stars. "To me . . . the stars look just the same."

Bob dismissed the visible stars with a contemptuous wave of his hand.

"Oh, those stars don't count. I'm talking about way-out objects. The invisible universe."

"What invisible universe?" Dagny cried. "Time and distance—for me they do not exist.

"Those witches of old!" She laughed. "Their powers were so limited. Medea—she scarcely spanned the Aegean Sea. But for Dagny, her power extends to the farthest star. To the outermost bounds of creation."

Bob lingered till long after midnight in the library. The events of the last twenty-four hours had left him completely unstrung.

Again he began leafing through Dagny's book on the occult.

"'It is a mistake to think that witches are invariably old and haglike. Many are beautiful young women and often married. They flee home by enchanting their husbands and escape detection by means of a surrogate.'"

"Surrogate." There was that word again. He turned to the glossary.

"'Surrogate. As ordinarily used, an agent or deputy representing another. In witchcraft, a phantom image left behind to deceive another.'"

The paper with Thornton's picture was still there on the table. But different now. Where were the two forked shadows of Jeannette's fingers that had fallen across it? Jeannette's hands with the smooth velvety fingers? Gone . . . gone . . .

Bob felt fear stealing over him. Fear buried below his thin veneer of scientific learning. The same primitive fear he had experienced at the total eclipse of the sun.

And just as impossible to resist.

David Brin

The third of four "San Diego" graduates we will encounter in this book, David Brin (1950–   ) was born in Glendale, California. He earned a B.S. from the California Institute of Technology (1972) and an M.S. (1980) and Ph.D. (1981) in astronomy from the University of California, San Diego.

He has worked as an electrical engineer in semiconductor device development for Hughes Aircraft Research Laboratories (1973–1977), as a lecturer at San Diego State University (1981–1982) and as a book reviewer and science editor for Heritage Press.

The author of some twelve research papers, and editor of the *Journal of the Laboratory of Comparative Human Cognition*, he is currently preparing a book for Cambridge University Press entitled *The Great Silence: The Scientific Questions Behind the Search for Extraterrestrial Intelligence*.

In addition to a post-doctoral fellowship at the California Space Institute, he has won both Hugo and Nebula Awards for *Star Tide Rising* (1983). Other science fiction works include *Sundiver* (1980), *The Practice Effect* (1984) and *The Postman* (in press), as well as about a dozen short stories such as the one below, which might have been called "Glaring Error."

THE WARM SPACE

by *David Brin*

1.

JASON FORBS(S-62B/129876Rd (bio-human): REPORT AT
ONCE TO PROJECT LIGHTPROBE FOR IMMEDIATE
ASSUMPTION OF DUTIES AS "DESIGNATED ORAL WITNESS
ENGINEER."

—BY ORDER OF DIRECTOR

JASON LET THE flimsy message slip from his fingers, fluttering in the gentle, centrifugal pseudo-gravity of the station apartment. Coriolis force—or perhaps the soft breeze from the wall vents—caused it to drift past the edge of the table and land on the floor of the small dining nook.

"Are you going to go?" Elaine asked nervously from Jesse's crib, where she had just put the baby down for a nap. Wide eyes made plain her fear.

"What choice do I have?" Jason shrugged. "My number was drawn. I can't disobey. Not the way the Utilitarian Party has been pushing its weight around. Under the Required Services Act, I'm just another motile, sentient unit, of some small use to the state."

That was true, as far as it went. Jason did not feel it necessary to add that he had actually volunteered for this mission. There was no point. Elaine would never understand.

A woman with a child doesn't need to look for justifications for her existence, Jason thought as he gathered what he would need from the closet.

But I'm tired of being an obsolete, token representative of the Old Race, looked down upon by all the sleek new types. At least this way my kid may be able to say his old man had been good for something, once. It might help Jesse hold his head up in the years to come . . . years sure to be hard for the old style of human being.

He zipped up his travel suit, making sure of the vac-tight ankle and wrist fastenings. Elaine came to him and slipped into his arms.

"You could try to delay them," she suggested without conviction. "System-wide elections are next month. The Ethicalists and the Naturalists have declared a united campaign. . . ."

Jason stroked her hair, shaking his head. Hope was deadly. They could not afford it.

"It's no use, Elaine. The Utilitarians are completely in charge out here at the station, as well as nearly everywhere else in the solar system. Anyway, everyone knows the election is a foregone conclusion."

The words stung, but they were truthful. On paper, it would seem there was still a chance for a change. Biological humans still outnumbered the mechanical and cyborg citizen types, and even a large minority of the latter had misgivings about the brutally logical policies of the Utilitarian Party.

But only one biological human in twenty bothered to vote any more.

There were still many areas of creativity and skill in which mechano-cryo citizens were no better than organics, but a depressing conviction weighed heavily upon the old type. They knew they had no place in the future. The stars belonged to the other varieties, not to them.

"I've got to go." Gently, Jason peeled free of Elaine's arms. He took her face in his hands and kissed her one last time, then picked up his small travel bag and helmet. Stepping out into the corridor, he did not look back to see the tears that he knew were there, laying soft, saltwater history down her face.

2.

The quarters for biological human beings lay in the Old Wheel . . . a part of the research station that had grown ever shabbier as old style scientists and technicians lost their places to models better suited to the harsh environment of space.

Once, back in the days when mechano-cryo citizens were rare, the Old Wheel had been the center of excited activity here beyond the orbit of Neptune. The first starships had been constructed by clouds of space-suited humans, like tethered bees swarming over mammoth hives. Giant "slowboats," restricted to speeds far below that of light, had ventured forth from here, into the interstellar night.

That had been long ago, when organic people had still been important. But even then there were those who had foreseen what was to come.

Nowhere were the changes of the last century more apparent than here at Project Lightprobe. The old type now only served in support roles, few contributing directly to the investigations . . . perhaps the most important in human history.

Jason's vac-sled was stored in the Old Wheel's north hub airlock. Both sled and suit checked out well, but the creaking outer doors stuck halfway open when he tried to leave. He had to leap over with a spanner and pound the great hinges several times to get them unfrozen. The airlock finally opened in fits and starts.

Frowning, he remounted the sled and took off again.

The Old Wheel gets only scraps for maintenance, he thought glumly. Soon there'll be an accident, and the Utilitarians will use it as an excuse to ban organic humans from every research station in the solar system.

The Old Wheel fell behind as short puffs of gas sent his sled toward the heart of the research complex. For a long time he seemed to ride the slowly rotating wheel's shadow, eclipsing the dim glow of the distant sun.

From here, Earth-home was an invisible speck. Few ever focused telescopes on the old world. Everyone knew that the future wasn't back there but out here and beyond, with the innumerable stars covering the sky.

Gliding slowly across the gulf between the Old Wheel and the Complex, Jason had plenty of time to think.

Back when the old slowboats had set forth from here to explore the nearest systems, it had soon became apparent that only mechanicals and cyborgs were suited for interstellar voyages. Asteroid-sized arks—artificial worldlets capable of carrying entire ecospheres—remained a dream out of science fiction, economically beyond reach. Exploration ships could be sent much farther and faster if they did not have to carry the complex artificial environments required by old style human beings.

By now ten nearby stellar systems had been explored, all by crews consisting of "robo-humans." There were no plans to send any other kind, even if, or when, Earthlike planets were discovered. It just wouldn't be worth the staggering investment required.

That fact, more than anything else, had struck at the morale of biological people in the solar system. The stars, they realized, were not for them. Resignation led to a turning away from science and the future. Earth and the "dirt" colonies were apathetic places, these days. Utilitariansism was the guiding philosophy of the times.

Jason hadn't told his wife his biggest reason for volunteering for this mission. He was still uncertain he understood it very well himself. Perhaps he wanted to show people that a biological citizen could still be useful, and contribute to the advance of knowledge.

Even if it were by a task so humble as a suicide mission.

He saw the lightship ahead, just below the shining spark of Sirius, a jet-black pearl half a kilometer across. Already he could make out the shimmering of its fields as its mighty engines were tuned for the experiment ahead.

The technicians were hoping that this time it would work. But even if it failed again, they were determined to go on trying. Faster-than-light travel was not something anyone gave up on easily, even a robot with a life span of five hundred years. The dream, and the obstinacy to pursue it, was a strong inheritance from the parent race.

Next to the black experimental probe, with its derricks and workshops, was the towering bulk of the central cooling plant, by far the largest object in the Complex. The cooling plant made even the Old Wheel look like a child's toy hoop. Jason's rickety vac-sled puffed beneath the majestic globe, shining in the sky like a great silvery planet.

On this, the side facing the sun, the cooling globe's reflective surface was nearly perfect. On the other side, a giant array of fluid-filled radiators stared out on to intergalactic space, chilling liquid helium down to the basic temperature of the universe—a few degrees above absolute zero.

The array had to stare at the blackness between the galaxies. Faint sunlight—even starlight—would heat the cooling fluid too much. That was the reason for the silvery reflective backing. The amount of infrared radiation leaving the finned coolers had to exceed the few photons coming in in order for the temperature of the helium to drop far enough.

The new types of citizens might be faster and tougher, and in some ways smarter, than old style humans. They might need neither food nor sleep. But they did require a lot of liquid helium to keep their supercooled, superconducting brains humming. The shining, well-maintained cooling plant was a reminder of the priorities of the times.

Some years back, an erratic bio-human had botched an attempt to sabotage the cooling plant. All it accomplished was to have the old style banished from that part of the station. And some mechano-cryo staff members who had previously been sympathetic with the Ethicalist cause switched to Utilitarianism as a result.

The mammoth sphere passed over and behind Jason. In moments there was only the lightship ahead, shimmering within its cradle of spotlit gantries. A voice cut in over his helmet speaker in a sharp monotone.

"Attention approaching biological . . . you are entering a restricted zone. Identify yourself at once."

Jason grimaced. The station director had ordered all mechano personnel—meaning just about everybody left—to reprogram their voice functions along "more logical tonal lines." That meant they no longer mimicked natural human intonations, but spoke in a new, shrill whine.

Jason's few android and cyborg friends—colleagues on the support staff—had whispered their regrets. But these days it was dangerous to be in the minority. All soon adjusted to the new order.

"Jason Forbs, identifying self." He spoke as crisply as possible, mimicking the toneless Utilitarian dialect. He spelled his name and gave his ident code. "Oral witness engineer for Project Lightprobe, reporting for duty."

There was a pause, then the unseen security overseer spoke again.

"Cleared and identified, Jason Forbs. Proceed directly to slip nine, scaffold B. Escorts await your arrival."

Jason blinked. Had the voice softened perceptibly? A closet Ethicalist, perhaps, out here in this Utilitarian stronghold.

"Success, and an operative return are approved outcomes," the voice added, hesitantly, with just a hint of tonality.

Jason understood Utilitarian dialect well enough to interpret the simple good luck wish. He didn't dare thank the fellow, whoever he might be, whatever his body form. But he appreciated the gesture.

"Acknowledged," he said, and switched off. Ahead, under stark shadows cast by spotlights girdling the starship, Jason saw at least a dozen scientists and technicians, waiting for him by a docking slip. One or two of the escorts actually appeared to be fidgeting as he made his final maneuvers into the slot.

They came in all shapes and sizes. Several wore little globe-bot bodies. Spider forms were also prominent. Jason hurriedly tied the sled down, almost slipping as he secured his magnetic boots to the platform.

He knew his humaniform shape looked gawky and unsuited to this environment. But he was determined to maintain some degree of dignity. Your ancestors *made* these guys, he re-

135

minded himself. And old style people built this very station. We're all citizens under the law, from the director down to the janitor-bot, all the way down to me.

Still, he felt awkward under their glistening camera eyes.

"Come quickly, Jason Forbs." His helmet speaker whined and a large mechanical form gestured with one slender, articulated arm. "There is little time before the test begins. We must instruct you in your duties."

Jason recognized the favorite body-form of the director, an antibiological Utilitarian of the worst sort. The machine-scientist swiveled at the hips and rolled up the gangplank. Steam-like vapor puffed from vents in the official's plasteel carapace. It was an ostentatious display, to release evaporated helium that way. It demonstrated that the assistant director could keep his circuits as comfortably cool as anybody's, and hang the expense.

An awkward human in the midst of smoothly gliding machines, Jason glanced backward for what he felt sure would be his last direct view of the universe. He had hoped to catch a final glimpse of the Old Wheel, or at least the sun. But all he could see was the great hulk of the cooling plant, staring out into the space between the galaxies, keeping cool the lifeblood of the apparent inheritors of the solar system.

The director called again, impatiently. Jason turned and stepped through the hatch to be shown his station and his job.

3.

"You will remember not to touch any of the controls at any time. The ship's operation is automatic. Your function is purely to observe and maintain a running oral monologue into the tape recorder."

The director sounded disgusted. "I will not pretend that I agreed with the decision to include a biological entity in this experiment. Perhaps it was because you are expendable, and we have already lost too many valuable mechano-persons in these tests. In any event, the reasons are not of your concern. You are to remain at your station, leaving only to take care of"—the voice lowered in distaste and the shining cells of the official's eyes looked away—"to take care of bodily functions. A refresher unit has been installed behind that hatchway."

Jason shrugged. He was getting sick of the pretense.

"Wasn't that a lot of expense to go to? I mean, whatever's been killing the silicon and cyborg techs who rode the other ships is hardly likely to leave me alive long enough to get hungry or go to the bathroom."

The official nodded, a gesture so commonly used that it had been retained even in Utilitarian fashion.

"We share an opinion, then. Nevertheless, it is not known at what point in the mission the . . . malfunctions occur. The minimum duration in hyperspace is fifteen days, the engines cannot cut the span any shorter. After that time the ship emerges at a site at least five light-years away. It will take another two weeks to return to the solar system. You will continue your running commentary throughout that period, if necessary, to supplement what the instruments tell us."

Jason almost laughed at the ludicrous order. Of course he would be dead long before his voice gave out. The techs and scientists who went out on the earlier tests had all been made of tougher stuff than he, and none of them had survived.

Until a year ago, none of the faster-than-light starships had even returned. Some scientists had even contended that the theory behind their construction was in error, somehow.

At last, simple mechanical auto-pilots were installed, in case the problem had to do with the crews themselves. The gamble paid off. After that the ships returned . . . filled with corpses.

Jason had only a rough impression of what had happened to the other expeditions, all from unreliable scuttlebutt. The official story was still a state secret. But rumor had it the prior crews had all died of horrible violence.

Some said they had apparently gone mad and turned on each other. Others suggested that the fields that drove the ship through that strange realm known as hyperspace twisted the shapes of things within the ship—not sufficiently to affect the cruder machines, but enough to cause the subtle, cryogenic circuitry of the scientists and techs to go haywire.

One thing Jason was sure of: anything that could harm mechano-cryos would easily suffice to do in a biological. He was resigned, but all the same determined to do his part. If some small thing he noticed, and commented on into the tape machine, led to a solution—maybe some little thing missed by all the recording devices—then Terran civilization would have the stars.

That would be something for his son to remember, even if the true inheritors would be "human" machines.

"All right," he told the director. "Take this bunch of gawkers with you and let's go on with it."

He strapped himself into the observer's chair, behind the empty pilot's seat. He did not even look up as the technicians and officials filed out and closed the hatch behind them.

4.

In the instant after launching, the lightship made an eerie trail across the sky. Cylindrical streaks of pseudo-Cerenkov radiation lingered long after the black globe had disappeared, bolting faster and faster toward its rendezvous with hyperspace.

The director turned to the emissary from Earth.

"It is gone. Now we wait. One Earth-style month. "I will state, one more time, that I did not approve willingly of the inclusion of the organic form aboard the ship. I object to the inelegant modifications required in order to suit the ship to . . . to biological functions. Also, old style humans are three times as often subject to irrational impulses than more modern forms. This one may take it into its head to try to change the ship's controls when the fatal stress begins."

Unlike the director, the visiting councilor wore a humaniform body, with legs, arms, torso and head. He expressed his opinion with a shrug of his subtly articulated shoulders.

"You exaggerate the danger, Director. Don't you think I know that the controls Jason Forbs sees in front of him are only dummies?"

The director swiveled quickly to stare at the councilor. *How—?*

He made himself calm down. *It—doesn't—matter.* So what if he knew that fact? Even the sole Ethicalist member of the Solar System Council could not make much propaganda of it. It was only a logical precaution to take, under the circumstances.

"The designated oral witness engineer should spend his living moments performing his function," the director said coolly. "Recording his subjective impressions as long as he is able. It is the role you commanded we open up for an old style human, using your peremptory authority as a member of the council."

The other's humaniform face flexed in a traditional, pseudo-organic smile, archaic in its mimicry of the Old Race. And yet the director, schooled in Utilitarian belief, felt uneasy under the councilor's gaze.

"I had a peremptory commandment left to use up before the elections," the councilor said smoothly in old-fashioned, modulated tones. "I judged that this would be an appropriate way to use it."

He did not explain further. The director quashed an urge to push the question. What was the Ethicalist up to? Why waste a peremptory command on such a minor, futile thing as this? How could he gain anything by sending an old style human out to his certain death!

Was it to be some sort of gesture? Something aimed at getting out the biological vote for the upcoming elections?

If so, it was doomed to failure. In-depth psychological studies had indicated that the level of resignation and apathy among organic citizens was too high to ever be overcome by anything so simple.

Perhaps, though, it might be enough to save the seat of the one Ethicalist on the council . . .

The director felt warm. He knew that it was partly subjective—resentment of this invasion of his domain by a ridiculous sentimentalist. Most of all, the director resented the feelings he felt boiling within himself.

Why, *why* do we modern forms have to be cursed with this burden of emotionalism and uncertainty! I hate it!

Of course he knew the reasons. Back in ancient times, fictional "robots" had been depicted as caricatures of jerky motion and rigid, formal thinking. The writers of those precryo

days had not realized that complexity commanded flexibility
. . . even fallibility. The laws of physics were adamant on this.
Uncertainty accompanied subtlety. An advanced mind had to
have the ability to question itself, or creativity was lost.

The director loathed the fact, but he understood it.

Still, he suspected that the biologists had played a trick on
his kind, long ago. He and other Utilitarians had an idea that
there had been some deep programming, below anything nowadays accessed, to make mechano-people as much like the old
style as possible.

If I ever had proof it was true . . . he thought, gloweringly,
threateningly.

Ah, but it doesn't matter. The biologicals will be extinct in a
few generations, anyway. They're dying of a sense of their own
uselessness.

Good riddance!

"I will leave you now, Councilor. Unless you wish to accom-
pany me to recharge on refrigerants?"

The Ethicalist bowed slightly, ironically, aware, of course,
that the director could not return the gesture. "No, thank you,
Director. I shall wait here and contemplate for a while.

"Before you go, however, please let me make one thing clear.
It may seem, at times, as if I am not sympathetic with your
work here. But that is not true. After all, we're all humans, all
citizens. Everybody wants Project Lightprobe to succeed. The
dream is one we inherit from our makers . . . to go out and live
among the stars.

"I am only acting to help bring that about—for *all* of our
people."

The director felt unaccountabaly warmer. He could not
think of an answer. "I require helium," he said, curtly, and
swiveled to leave. "Good bye, Councilor."

The director felt as if eyes were watching his armored back as
he sped down the hallway.

Damn the biologicals and their allies! he cursed within.
Damn them for making us so insidiously like them . . . emotional, fallible and, worst of all, uncertain!

Wishing the last of the old style were already dust on their
dirty, wet little planet, the director hurried away to find himself a long, cold drink.

5.

"Six hours and ten minutes into the mission, four minutes since breakover into hyperspace . . ." Jason breathed into the microphone. "So far so good. I'm a little thirsty, but I believe it's just a typical adrenaline fear reaction. Allowing for expected tension, I feel fine."

Jason went on to describe everything he could see, the lights, the controls, the readings on the computer displays, his physical feelings . . . he went on until his throat felt dry and he found he was repeating himself.

"I'm getting up out of the observer's seat, now, to go get a drink." He slipped the recorder strap over his shoulder and unbuckled from the flight chair. There was a feeling of weight, as the techs had told him to expect. About a tenth of a g. It was enough to make walking possible. He flexed his legs and moved about the control room, describing every aspect of the experience. Then he went to the refrigerator and took out a squeeze-tube of lemonade.

Jason was frankly surprised to be alive. He knew the previous voyagers had lived several days before their unknown catastrophe struck. But they had been a lot tougher than he. Perhaps the mysterious lethal agency had taken nearly all the fifteen days of the minimum first leg of the round trip to do them in.

If so, he wondered, how long will it take to get me?

A few hours later, the failure of anything to happen was starting to make him nervous. He cut down the rate of his running commentary in order to save his voice. Besides, nothing much seemed to be changing. The ship was cruising, now. All the dials and indicators were green and steady.

During sleep period he tossed in the sleeping hammock, sharing it with disturbed dreams. He awakened several times impelled by a sense of duty and imminent danger, clutching his recorder tightly. But when he stared about the control room he could find nothing amiss.

By the third day he had had enough.

"I'm going to poke around in the instruments," he spoke into the microphone. "I know I was told not to. And I'll certainly not touch anything having to do with the functioning of the ship. But I figure I deserve a chance to see what I'm traveling through. Nobody's ever looked out on hyperspace. I'm going to take a look."

Jason set about the task with a feeling of exultation. What he was doing wouldn't hurt anything, just alter a few of the sensors.

Sure, it was against orders, but if he got back alive he would be famous, too important to bother with charges over such a minor infraction.

Not that he believed, for even a moment, that he was coming home alive.

It was a fairly intricate task, rearranging a few of the ship's programs so the external cameras—meant to be used at the destination star only—would work in hyperspace. He wondered if it had been some sort of Utilitarian gesture not to include viewing ports, or to do the small modifications of scanning electronics necessary to make the cameras work here. There was no obvious scientific reason to "look at" hyperspace, so perhaps the Utilitarian technicians rejected it as an atavistic desire.

Jason finished all but the last adjustments, then took a break to fix himself a meal before turning on the cameras. While he ate he made another recorder entry; there was little to report. A little trouble with the cryogen cooling units; they were laboring a bit. But the efficiency loss didn't seem to be anything critical, yet.

After dinner he sat cross-legged on the floor in front of the screen he had commandeered. "Well, now, let's see what this famous hyperspace looks like," he said. "At least the folks back home will know that it was an old style man who first looked out on . . ."

The screen rippled, then suddenly came alight.

Light! Jason had to shield his eyes. Hyperspace was ablaze with light!

His thoughts whirled. Could this have something to do with the threat? The unknown, malign force that had killed all the previous crews?

Jason cracked an eyelid and lowered his arm slightly. The screen was bright, but now that his eyes had adapted, it wasn't painful to look at. He gazed in fascination on a scene of whirling pink and white, as if the ship was hurtling through an endless sky of bright, pastel clouds.

It looked rather pleasant, in fact.

This is a threat? He wondered, dazedly. How could this soft brillance kill?

Jason's jaw opened as a relay seemed to close in his mind. He stared at the screen for a long moment, wondering if his growing suspicion could be true.

He laughed out loud—a hard, ironic laugh, as yet more tense than hopeful. He set to work finding out if his suspicion was right, after all.

6.

The lightship cruised on autopilot until at last it came to rest not far from its launching point. Little tugs approached gently and grappled with the black globe, pulling it toward the derricks where the inspection crew waited to swarm aboard. In the station control center, technicians monitored the activity outside.

"I am proceeding with routine hailing call," the communications technician announced, sending a metal tentacle toward the transmit switch.

"Why bother?" another mechano-cryo tech asked. "There certainly isn't anyone aboard that death ship to hear it."

The comm officer did not bother answering. He pressed the send switch. "This is Lightprobe Central to Lightprobe Nine. Do you read, Lightprobe Nine?"

The other tech turned away in disgust. He had already suspected the comm officer of being a closet Ethicalist. Imagine, wasting energy trying to talk to a month-dead organic corpse!

"Lightprobe Nine, come in. This is . . ."

"Lightprobe Nine to Lightprobe Central. This is Oral Witness Engineer Jason Forbs, ready to relinquish command to inspection crew."

The control room was suddenly silent. All the techs stared at the wall speaker. The comm officer hovered, too stunned to reply.

"Would you let my wife know I'm all right?" the voice continued. *"And please have station services bring over something cool to drink!"*

The tableau held for another long moment. At last, the comm officer moved to reply, a an undisciplined tone of excitement betrayed in his voice.

"Right away, Witness Engineer Forbs. And welcome home!"

At the back of the control room a tech wearing a globe-form body hurried off to tell the director.

7.

A crowd of metal, ceramic, and cyborg-flesh surrounded a single, pale old-style human, floating stripped to his shorts, sipping a frosted squeeze-tube of amber liquid.

"Actually, it's not too unpleasant a place," he told those gathered around in the conference room. "But it's a good thing I violated orders and looked outside when I did. I was able to turn off all unnecessary power and lighting in time to slow the heat buildup. "As it was, it got pretty hot toward the end of the fifteen days."

The director was still obviously in a state of shock. The globular-form bureaucrat had lapsed from Utilitarian dialect, and spoke in the quasi-human tones he had grown up with.

"But . . . but the ship's interior should not have heated up so! The vessel was equipped with the best and most durable refrigerators and radiators we could make! Similar models have operated in the solar system and on slowboat starships for hundreds of years!"

Jason nodded. He sipped from his tube of iced lemonade and grinned.

"Oh yeah, the refrigerators and radiators worked just fine . . . just like the cooling plant." He gestured out the window, where the huge radiator globe could be seen drifting slowly across the sky.

"But there was one problem. Just like the cooling plant, the shipboard refrigeration system was designed to work in normal space!"

He gestured at the blackness outside, punctuated here and there by pinpoint stars.

"Out there, the ambient temperature is less than three degrees, absolute. Point your radiators into intergalactic space and virtually no radiation hits them from the sky. Even the small amount of heat in supercooled helium can escape. One doesn't need compressors and all that complicated gear they had to use in order to make cryogens on Earth. You hardly have to do more than point shielded pipes out at the blackness and send the stuff through 'em. You mechanical types get the cheap cryogens you need. But in hyperspace it's different!

"I didn't have the right instruments, so I couldn't give you a precise figure, but I'd guess the ambient temperature on that plane is above the melting point of water ice! Of course, in an environment like that the ship's radiators were horribly inefficient . . . barely good enough to get rid of the heat from the cabin and engines, and certainly not efficient enough—in their present design—to cool cryogens!"

The director stared, unwilling to believe what he was hearing. One of the senior scientists rolled forward.

"Then the previous crews . . ."

"All went mad or died when the cryo-helium evaporated! Their superconducting brains overheated! It's the one mode of mortality that is hard to detect, because it's gradual. The first effect is a deterioration of mental function, followed by insanity and violence. No wonder the previous crews came back all torn up! And autopsies showed nothing since everything heats up after death, anyway!"

Another tech sighed. "Hyperspace seemed so harmless! The theory and the first automated probes . . . we looked for complicated dangers. We never thought to . . ."

"To take its temperature?" Jason suggested wryly.

"But why look so glum!" He grinned. "You all should be delighted! We've found out the problem, and it turns out to be nothing at all."

The director spun on him. *"Nothing?* You insipid biological, can't you see? This is a disaster! We counted on hyperspace to open the stars for us. But it is infernally expensive to use unless we keep the ships small.

145

"And how can we keep them small if we must build huge, intricate cooling systems that must look out into that boiling hell you found? With the trickle of cryogens we'll be able to maintain during those weeks in hyperspace, it will be nearly impossible to maintain life aboard!

"You say our problems are solved," the director spoke acidly. "But you miss one point, Witness Engineer Forbs! How will we ever find crews to man those ships?"

The director hummed with barely suppressed anger, his eye-cells glowing.

Jason rubbed his chin and pursed his lips sympathetically. "Well, I don't know. But I'd bet with a few minor improvements something could be arranged. Why don't you try recruiting crews from another 'boiling hell' . . . one where water ice is already melted?"

There was silence for a moment. Then, from the back of the room, came laughter. A mechano with a seal of office hanging from its humaniform neck clapped its hands together and grinned. "Oh, wait till they hear of this on Earth! *Now* we'll see how the voting goes!" He grinned at Jason and laughed in rich, human tones. "When the biologists find out about this, they'll rise up like the very tide! And so will every closet Ethicalist in the system!"

Jason smiled, but right now his mind was far from politics. All he knew was that his wife and son would not live in shame. His boy would be a starship rider, and inherit the galaxy.

"You won't have any trouble recruiting crews, sir," he told the director. "I'm ready to go back any time. Hyperspace isn't all that bad a place. "Would you care to come along?"

Super-cold steam vented from the director's carapace, a loud hiss of indignation. The Utilitarian bureaucrat ground out something too low for Jason to overhear, even though he leaned forward politely.

The laughter from the back of the room rose in peals of hilarity. Jason sipped his lemonade and waited.

Arthur C. Clarke

Born in Minehead, Somersetshire, England, Arthur C. Clarke (1917–   ) has been for many years a resident of Sri Lanka.

In scientific circles he is most noted for originating the concept of fixed orbit communication satellites, an idea which came to him during World War II while a radar instructor for the Royal Air Force.

After obtaining a B.Sc. (first class honors) from King's College (1948), he served briefly as an editor of Science Abstracts, but from 1951, with the exception of a couple of brief academic appointments, he has worked primarily as a free-lance writer. Like Asimov, his forte is popularizing science, and like Asimov, he has achieved great success. For his work he has been presented the Kalinga Prize for science writing (1961), the Aviation Space Writers Association's Robert Ball Award (1965) for best aerospace reporting, the Westinghouse Science Writing Award (1969), the Aerospace Communiations Award from the American Institute of Aeronautics and Astronautics (1974), The International Fantasy Award (1952), the Hugo Award (1956,1974) and the Nebula Award (1972, 1973, 1980).

Classic novels include *Childhood's End* (1953), *The City and the Stars* (1956), *2001: A Space Odyssey* (1968) and *Rendezvous With Rama* (1973). Classic stories are too numerous to mention, but for this volume, we have chosen a soaring tale of clipper ships in space.

THE WIND FROM THE SUN

by *Arthur C. Clarke*

T HE ENORMOUS DISK of sail strained at its rigging, already filled with the wind that blew between the worlds. In three minutes the race would begin, yet now John Merton felt more relaxed, more at peace, than at any time for the past year. Whatever happened when the commodore gave the starting signal, whether *Diana* carried him to victory or defeat, he had achieved his ambition. After a lifetime spent designing ships for others, now he would sail his own.

"T minus two minutes," said the cabin radio. "Please confirm your readiness."

One by one, the other skippers answered. Merton recognized all the voices—some tense, some calm—for they were the voices of his friends and rivals. On the four inhabited worlds, there were scarcely twenty men who could sail a sun yacht; and they were all here, on the starting line or aboard the escort vessels, orbiting twenty-two thousand miles above the equator.

"Number one—*Gossamer*—ready to go."

"Number two—*Santa Maria*—all okay."

"Number three—*Sunbeam*—okay."

"Number four—*Woomera*—all systems go."

Merton smiled at that last echo from the early, primitive days of astronautics. But it had become part of the tradition of space; and there were times when a man needed to evoke the shades of those who had gone before him to the stars.

"Number five—*Lebedev*—we're ready."

"Number six—*Arachne*—okay."

Now it was his turn, at the end of the line; strange to think that the words he was speaking in this tiny cabin were being heard by at least five billion people.

"Number seven—*Diana*—ready to start."

"One through seven acknowledged," answered that impersonal voice from the judge's launch. "Now T minus one minute."

Merton scarcely heard it. For the last time, he was checking the tension in the rigging. The needles of all the dynamometers were steady; the immense sail was taut, its mirror surface sparkling and glittering gloriously in the sun.

To Merton, floating weightless at the periscope, it seemed to fill the sky. As well it might—for out there were fifty million square feet of sail, linked to his capsule by almost a hundred miles of rigging. All the canvas of all the tea clippers that had once raced like clouds across the China seas, sewn into one gigantic sheet, could not match the single sail that *Diana* had spread beneath the sun. Yet it was little more substantial than a soap bubble; that two square miles of aluminized plastic was only a few millionths of an inch thick.

"T minus ten seconds. All recording cameras on."

Something so huge, yet so frail, was hard for the mind to grasp. And it was harder still to realize that this fragile mirror could tow him free of Earth merely by the power of the sunlight it would trap.

". . . five, four, three, two, one, cut!"

Seven knife blades sliced through seven thin lines tethering the yachts to the mother ships that had assembled and serviced them. Until this moment, all had been circling Earth together in a rigidly held formation, but now the yachts would begin to disperse, like dandelion seeds drifting before the breeze. And the winner would be the one that first drifted past the Moon.

Aboard *Diana*, nothing seemed to be happening. But Merton knew better. Though his body could feel no thrust, the instrument board told him that he was now accelerating at almost one thousandth of a gravity. For a rocket, that figure would have been ludicrous—but this was the first time any solar yacht had ever attained it. *Diana's* design was sound; the vast sail was living up to his calculations. At this rate, two circuits of the Earth would build up his speed to escape velocity, and then he could head out for the Moon, with the full force of the sun behind him.

The full force of the sun. . . . He smiled wryly, remembering all his attempts to explain solar sailing to those lecture audiences back on Earth. That had been the only way he could raise money, in those early days. He might be chief designer of Cosmodyne Corporation, with a whole string of successful spaceships to his credit, but his firm had not been exactly enthusiastic about his hobby.

"Hold your hands out to the sun," he'd said. "What do you feel? Heat, of course. But there's pressure as well—though you've never noticed it, because it's so tiny. Over the area of your hands, it comes to only about a millionth of an ounce.

"But out in space, even a pressure as small as that can be important, for it's acting all the time, hour after hour, day after day. Unlike rocket fuel, it's free and unlimited. If we want to, we can use it. We can build sails to catch the radiation blowing from the sun."

At that point, he would pull out a few square yards of sail material and toss it toward the audience. The silvery film would coil and twist like smoke, then drift slowly to the ceiling in the hot-air currents.

"You can see how light it is," he'd continue. "A square mile weighs only a ton, and can collect five pounds of radiation pressure. So it will start moving—and we can let it tow us along, if we attach rigging to it.

"Of course, its acceleration will be tiny—about a thousandth of a g. That doesn't seem much, but let's see what it means.

"It means that in the first second, we'll move about a fifth of an inch. I suppose a healthy snail could do better than that. But after a minute, we've covered sixty feet, and will be doing just over a mile an hour. That's not bad, for something driven by pure sunlight! After an hour, we're forty miles from our starting point, and will be moving at eighty miles an hour. Please remember that in space there's no friction, so once you start anything moving, it will keep going forever. You'll be surprised when I tell you what our thousandth-of-a-g sailboat will be doing at the end of a day's run: *almost two thousand miles an hour!* If it starts from orbit—as it has to, of course—it can reach escape velocity in a couple of days. And all without burning a single drop of fuel!"

Well, he'd convinced them, and in the end he'd even convinced Cosmodyne. Over the last twenty years, a new sport had come into being. It had been called the sport of billionaires, and that was true. But it was beginning to pay for itself in terms of publicity and TV coverage. The prestige of four continents and two worlds was riding on this race, and it had the biggest audience in history.

Diana had made a good start; time to take a look at the opposition. Moving very gently—though there were shock absorbers between the control capsule and the delicate rigging, he was determined to run no risks—Merton stationed himself at the periscope.

There they were, looking like strange silver flowers planted in the dark fields of space. The nearest, South America's *Santa Maria,* was only fifty miles way; it bore a close resemblance to a boy's kite, but a kite more than a mile on a side. Farther away, the University of Astrograd's *Lebedev* looked like a Maltese cross; the sails that formed the four arms could apparently be tilted for steering purposes. In contrast, the Federation of Australasia's *Woomera* was a simple parachute, four miles in circumference. General Spacecraft's *Arachne,* as its name suggested, looked like a spiderweb, and had been built on the same principles, by robot shuttles spiraling out from a central point. Eurospace Corporation's *Gossamer* was an identical design, on a slightly smaller scale. And the Republic of Mars's *Sunbeam* was a flat ring, with a half-mile-wide hole in the center, spinning slowly, so that centrifugal force gave it stiffness. That was an old idea, but no one had ever made it work; and Merton was fairly sure that the colonials would be in trouble when they started to turn.

That would not be for another six hours, when the yachts had moved along the first quarter of their slow and stately twenty-four-hour orbit. Here at the beginning of the race, they were all heading directly away from the sun—running, as it were, before the solar wind. One had to make the most of this lap, before the boats swung around to the other side of Earth and then started to head back into the sun.

Time, Merton told himself, for the first check, while he had no navigational worries. With the periscope, he made a careful examination of the sail, concentrating on the points where the rigging was attached to it. The shroud lines—narrow bands of unsilvered plastic film—would have been completely invisible had they not been coated with fluorescent paint. Now they were taut lines of colored light, dwindling away for hundreds of yards toward that gigantic sail. Each had its own electric windlass, not much bigger than a game fisherman's reel. The little windlasses were continually turning, playing lines in or out as the autopilot kept the sail trimmed at the correct angle to the sun.

The play of sunlight on the great flexible mirror was beautiful to watch. The sail was undulating in slow, stately oscillations, sending multiple images of the sun marching across it, until they faded away at its edges. Such leisurely vibrations were to be expected in this vast and flimsy structure. They were usually quite harmless, but Merton watched them carefully. Sometimes they could build up to the catastrophic undulations known as the "wriggles," which could tear a sail to pieces.

When he was satisfied that everything was shipshape, he swept the periscope around the sky, rechecking the positions of his rivals. It was as he had hoped: the weeding-out process had begun, as the less efficient boats fell astern. But the real test would come when they passed into the shadow of Earth. Then, maneuverability would count as much as speed.

It seemed a strange thing to do, what with the race having just started, but he thought it might be a good idea to get some sleep. The two-man crews on the other boats could take it in turns, but Merton had no one to relieve him. He must rely on his own physical resources, like that other solitary seaman, Joshua Slocum, in his tiny *Spray*. The American skipper had sailed *Spray* single-handed around the world; he could never have dreamed that, two centuries later, a man would be sailing single-handed from Earth to Moon—inspired, at least partly, by his example.

Merton snapped the elastic bands of the cabin seat around his waist and legs, then placed the electrodes of the sleep-inducer on his forehead. He set the timer for three hours, and relaxed. Very gently, hypnotically, the electronic pulses throbbed in the frontal lobes of his brain. Colored spirals of light expanded beneath his closed eyelids, widening outward to infinity. Then nothing . . .

The brazen clamor of the alarm dragged him back from his dreamless sleep. He was instantly awake, his eyes scanning the instrument panel. Only two hours had passed—but above the accelerometer, a red light was flashing. Thrust was falling; *Diana* was losing power.

Merton's first thought was that something had happened to the sail; perhaps the antispin devices had failed, and the rigging had become twisted. Swiftly, he checked the meters that showed the tension of the shroud lines. Strange—on one side of the sail they were reading normally, but on the other the pull was dropping slowly, even as he watched.

In sudden understanding, Merton grabbed the periscope, switched to wide-angle vision, and started to scan the edge of the sail. Yes—there was the trouble, and it could have only one cause.

A huge, sharp-edged shadow had begun to slide across the gleaming silver of the sail. Darkness was falling upon *Diana*, as if a cloud had passed between her and the sun. And in the dark, robbed of the rays that drove her, she would lose all thrust and drift helplessly through space.

But, of course, there were no clouds here, more than twenty thousand miles above the Earth. If there was a shadow, it must be made by man.

Merton grinned as he swung the periscope toward the sun, switching in the filters that would allow him to look full into its blazing face without being blinded.

153

"Maneuver 4a," he muttered to himself. "We'll see who can play best at *that* game."

It looked as if a giant planet was crossing the face of the sun; a great black disk had bitten deep into its edge. Twenty miles astern, *Gossamer* was trying to arrange an artificial eclipse, specially for *Diana's* benefit.

The maneuver was a perfectly legitimate one. Back in the days of ocean racing, skippers had often tried to rob each other of the wind. With any luck, you could leave your rival becalmed, with his sails collapsing around him—and be well ahead before he could undo the damage.

Merton had no intention of being caught so easily. There was plenty of time to take evasive action; things happened very slowly when you were running a solar sailboat. It would be at least twenty minutes before *Gossamer* could slide completely across the face of the sun, and leave him in darkness.

Diana's tiny computer—the size of a matchbox, but the equivalent of a thousand human mathematicians—considered the problem for a full second and then flashed the answer. He'd have to open control panels three and four, until the sail had developed an extra twenty degrees of tilt; then the radiation pressure would blow him out of *Gossamer's* dangerous shadow, back into the full blast of the sun. It was a pity to interfere with the autopilot, which had been carefully programmed to give the fastest possible run—but that, after all, was why he was here. This was what made solar yachting a sport, rather than a battle between computers.

Out went control lines 1 and 6, slowly undulating like sleepy snakes as they momentarily lost their tension. Two miles away, the triangular panels began to open lazily, spilling sunlight through the sail. Yet, for a long time, nothing seemed to happen. It was hard to grow accustomed to this slow-motion world, where it took minutes for the effects of any action to become visible to the eye. Then Merton saw that the sail was indeed tipping toward the sun—and that *Gossamer's* shadow was sliding harmlessly away, its cone of darkness lost in the deeper night of space.

Long before the shadow had vanished, and the disk of the sun had cleared again, he reversed the tilt and brought *Diana* back on course. Her new momentum would carry her clear of the danger; no need to overdo it, and upset his calculations by sidestepping too far. That was another rule that was hard to learn: the very moment you had started something happening in space, it was already time to think about stopping it.

He reset the alarm, ready for the next natural or man-made emergency. Perhaps *Gossamer*, or one of the other contestants, would try the same trick again. Meanwhile, it was time to eat, though he did not feel particularly hungry. One used little physical energy in space, and it was easy to forget about food. Easy—and dangerous; for when an emergency arose, you might not have the reserves needed to deal with it.

He broke open the first of the meal packets, and inspected it without enthusiasm. The name on the label—Spacetasties— was enough to put him off. And he had grave doubts about the promise printed underneath: Guaranteed crumbless. It had been said that crumbs were a greater danger to space vehicles than meteorites; they could drift into the most unlikely places, causing short circuits, blocking vital jets and getting into instruments that were supposed to be hermetically sealed.

Still, the liverwurst went down pleasantly enough; so did the chocolate and the pineapple puree. The plastic coffee bulb was warming on the electric heater when the outside world broke in upon his solitude, as the radio operator on the commodore's launch routed a call to him.

"Dr. Merton? If you can spare the time, Jeremy Blair would like a few words with you." Blair was one of the more responsible news commentators, and Merton had been on his program many times. He could refuse to be interviewed, of course, but he liked Blair, and at the moment he could certainly not claim to be too busy. "I'll take it," he answered.

"Hello, Dr. Merton," said the commentator immediately. "Glad you can spare a few minutes. And congratulations—you seem to be ahead of the field."

"Too early in the game to be sure of *that*," Merton answered cautiously.

155

"Tell me, Doctor, why did you decide to sail *Diana* by yourself? Just because it's never been done before?"

"Well, isn't that a good reason? But it wasn't the only one, of course." He paused, choosing his words carefully. "You know how critically the performance of a sun yacht depends on its mass. A second man, with all his supplies, would mean another five hundred pounds. That could easily be the difference between winning and losing."

"And you're quite certain that you can handle *Diana* alone?"

"Reasonably sure, thanks to the automatic controls I've designed. My main job is to supervise and make decisions."

"But—two square miles of sail! It just doesn't seem possible for one man to cope with all that."

Merton laughed. "Why not? Those two square miles produce a maximum pull of just ten pounds. I can exert more force with my little finger."

"Well, thank you, Doctor. And good luck. I'll be calling you again."

As the commentator signed off, Merton felt a little ashamed of himself. For his answer had been only part of the truth; and he was sure that Blair was shrewd enough to know it.

There was just one reason why he was here, alone in space. For almost forty years he had worked with teams of hundreds or even thousands of men, helping to design the most complex vehicles that the world had ever seen. For the last twenty years he had led one of those teams, and watched his creations go soaring to the stars. (Sometimes . . . there *were* failures, which he could never forget, even though the fault had not been his.) He was famous, with a successful career behind him. Yet he had never done anything by himself; always he had been one of an army.

This was his last chance to try for individual achievement, and he would share it with no one. There would be no more solar yachting for at least five years, as the period of the Quiet Sun ended and the cycle of bad weather began, with radiation storms bursting through the solar system. When it was safe again for these frail, unshielded craft to venture aloft, he would be too old. If, indeed, he was not too old already . . .

He dropped the empty food containers into the waste disposal and turned once more to the periscope. At first he could find only five of the other yachts; there was no sign of *Woomera*. It took him several minutes to locate her—a dim, star-eclipsing phantom, neatly caught in the shadow of *Lebedev*. He could imagine the frantic efforts the Australasians were making to extricate themselves, and wondered how they had fallen into the trap. It suggested that *Lebedev* was unusually maneuverable. She would bear watching, though she was too far away to menace *Diana* at the moment.

Now the Earth had almost vanished; it had waned to a narrow, brilliant bow of light that was moving steadily toward the sun. Dimly outlined within that burning bow was the night side of the planet, with the phosphorescent gleams of great cities showing here and there through gaps in the clouds. The disk of darkness had already blanked out a huge section of the Milky Way. In a few minutes, it would start to encroach upon the sun.

The light was fading; a purple, twilight hue—the glow of many sunsets, thousands of miles below—was falling across the sail as *Diana* slipped silently into the shadow of Earth. The sun plummeted below that invisible horizon; within minutes, it was night.

Merton looked back along the orbit he had traced, now a quarter of the way around the world. One by one he saw the brilliant stars of the other yachts wink out, as they joined him in the brief night. It would be an hour before the sun emerged from that enormous black shield, and through all that time they would be completely helpless, coasting without power.

He switched on the external spotlight, and started to search the now-darkened sail with its beam. Already the thousands of acres of film were beginning to wrinkle and become flaccid. The shroud lines were slackening, and must be wound in lest they become entangled. But all this was expected; everything was going as planned.

Fifty miles astern, *Arachne* and *Santa Maria* were not so lucky. Merton learned of their troubles when the radio burst into life on the emergency circuit.

"Number two and Number six, this is Control. You are on a collision course; your orbits will intersect in sixty-five minutes! Do you require assistance?"

There was a long pause while the two skippers digested this bad news. Merton wondered who was to blame. Perhaps one yacht had been trying to shadow the other, and had not completed the maneuver before they were both caught in darkness. Now there was nothing that either could do. They were slowly but inexorably converging, unable to change course by a fraction of a degree.

Yet—sixty-five minutes! That would just bring them out into sunlight again, as they emerged from the shadow of the Earth. They had a slim chance, if their sails could snatch enough power to avoid a crash. There must be some frantic calculations going on aboard *Arachne* and *Santa Maria*.

Arachne answered first. Her reply was just what Merton had expected.

"Number six calling Control. We don't need assistance, thank you. We'll work this out for ourselves."

I wonder, thought Merton; but at least it will be interesting to watch. The first real drama of the race was approaching, exactly above the line of midnight on the sleeping Earth.

For the next hour, Merton's own sail kept him too busy to worry about *Arachne* and *Santa Maria*. It was hard to keep a good watch on that fifty million square feet of dim plastic out there in the darkness, illuminated only by his narrow spotlight and the rays of the still-distant Moon. From now on, for almost half his orbit around the Earth, he must keep the whole of this immense area edge-on to the sun. During the next twelve or fourteen hours, the sail would be a useless encumbrance; for he would be heading *into* the sun, and its rays could only drive him backward along his orbit. It was a pity that he could not furl the sail completely, until he was ready to use it again; but no one had yet found a practical way of doing this.

Far below, there was the first hint of dawn along the edge of the Earth. In ten minutes the sun would emerge from its eclipse. The coasting yachts would come to life again as the blast of radiation struck their sails. That would be the moment of crisis for *Arachne* and *Santa Maria*—and, indeed, for all of them.

Merton swung the periscope until he found the two dark shadows drifting against the stars. They were very close together—perhaps less than three miles apart. They might, he decided, just be able to make it. . . .

Dawn flashed like an explosion along the rim of Earth as the sun rose out of the Pacific. The sail and shroud lines glowed a brief crimson, then gold, then blazed with the pure white light of day. The needles of the dynamometers began to lift from their zeros—but only just. *Diana* was still almost completely weightless, for with the sail pointing toward the sun, her acceleration was now only a few millionths of a gravity.

But *Arachne* and *Santa Maria* were crowding on all the sail that they could manage, in their desperate attempt to keep apart. Now, while there were less than two miles between them, their glittering plastic clouds were unfurling and expanding with agonizing slowness as they felt the first delicate push of the sun's rays. Almost every TV screen on Earth would be mirroring this protracted drama; and even now, at this last minute, it was impossible to tell what the outcome would be.

The two skippers were stubborn men. Either could have cut his sail and fallen back to give the other a chance; but neither would do so. Too much prestige, too many millions, too many reputations were at stake. And so, silently and softly as snowflakes falling on a winter night, *Arachne* and *Santa Maria* collided.

The square kite crawled almost imperceptibly into the circular spiderweb. The long ribbons of the shroud lines twisted and tangled together with dreamlike slowness. Even aboard *Diana*, Merton, busy with his own rigging, could scarcely tear his eyes away from this silent, long-drawn-out disaster.

For more than ten minutes the billowing, shining clouds continued to merge into one inextricable mass. Then the crew capsules tore loose and went their separate ways, missing each other by hundreds of yards. With a flare of rockets, the safety launches hurried to pick them up.

That leaves five of us, thought Merton. He felt sorry for the skippers who had so thoroughly eliminated each other only a few hours after the start of the race, but they were young men and would have another chance.

Within minutes, the five had dropped to four. From the beginning, Merton had had doubts about the slowly rotating *Sunbeam*; now he saw them justified.

The Martian ship had failed to tack properly. Her spin had given her too much stability. Her great ring of a sail was turning to face the sun, instead of being edge-on to it. She was being blown back along her course at almost her maximum acceleration.

That was about the most maddening thing that could happen to a skipper—even worse than a collision, for he could blame only himself. But no one would feel much sympathy for the frustrated colonials, as they dwindled slowly astern. They had made too many brash boasts before the race, and what had happened to them was poetic justice.

Yet it would not do to write off *Sunbeam* completely; with almost half a million miles still to go, she might yet pull ahead. Indeed, if there were a few more casualties, she might be the only one to complete the race. It had happened before.

The next twelve hours were uneventful, as the Earth waxed in the sky from new to full. There was little to do while the fleet drifted around the unpowered half of its orbit, but Merton did not find the time hanging heavily on his hands. He caught a few hours of sleep, ate two meals, wrote his log, and became involved in several more radio interviews. Sometimes, though rarely, he talked to the other skippers, exchanging greetings and friendly taunts. But most of the time he was content to float in weightless relaxation, beyond all the cares of Earth, happier than he had been for many years. He was—as far as any man could be in space—master of his own fate, sailing the ship upon which he had lavished so much skill, so much love, that it had become part of his very being.

The next casualty came when they were passing the line between Earth and sun, and were just beginning the powered half of the orbit. Aboard *Diana*, Merton saw the great sail stiffen as it tilted from the microgravities, though it would be hours yet before it would reach its maximum value.

It would never reach it for *Gossamer*. The moment when power came on again was always critical, and she failed to survive it.

Blair's radio commentary, which Merton had left running at low volume, alerted him with the news: "Hello, *Gossamer* has the wriggles!" He hurried to the periscope, but at first could see nothing wrong with the great circular disk of *Gossamer's* sail. It was difficult to study it because it was almost edge-on to him and so appeared as a thin ellipse; but presently he saw that it was twisting back and forth in slow, irresistible oscillations. Unless the crew could damp out these waves by properly timed but gentle tugs on the shroud lines, the sail would tear itself to pieces.

They did their best, and after twenty minutes it seemed that they had succeeded. Then, somewhere near the center of the sail, the plastic film began to rip. It was slowly driven outward by the radiation pressure, like smoke coiling upward from a fire. Within a quarter of an hour, nothing was left but the delicate tracery of the radial spars that had supported the great web. Once again there was a flare of rockets, as a launch moved in to retrieve the *Gossamer's* capsule and her dejected crew.

"Getting rather lonely up here, isn't it?" said a conversational voice over the ship-to-ship radio.

"Not for you, Dimitri," retorted Merton. "You've still got company back there at the end of the field. I'm the one who's lonely, up here in front." It was not an idle boast; by this time *Diana* was three hundred miles ahead of the next competitor, and her lead should increase still more rapidly in the hours to come.

Aboard *Lebedev*, Dimitri Markoff gave a good-natured chuckle. He did not sound, Merton thought, at all like a man who had resigned himself to defeat.

"Remember the legend of the tortoise and the hare," answered the Russian. "A lot can happen in the next quarter-million miles."

It happened much sooner than that, when they had completed their first orbit of Earth and were passing the starting line again—though thousands of miles higher, thanks to the extra energy the sun's rays had given them. Merton had taken careful sights on the other yachts, and had fed the figures into the computer. The answer it gave for *Woomera* was so absurd that he immediately did a recheck.

There was no doubt of it—the Australasians were catching up at a completely fantastic rate. No solar yacht could possibly have such an acceleration, unless . . .

A swift look through the periscope gave the answer. *Woomera's* rigging, pared back to the very minimum of mass, had given way. It was her sail alone, still maintaining its shape, that was racing up behind him like a handkerchief blown before the wind. Two hours later it fluttered past, less than twenty miles away; but long before that, the Australasians had joined the growing crowd aboard the commodore's launch.

So now it was a straight fight between *Diana* and *Lebedev*—for though the Martians had not given up, they were a thousand miles astern and no longer counted as a serious threat. For that matter, it was hard to see what *Lebedev* could do to overtake *Diana's* lead; but all the way around the second lap, through eclipse again and the long, slow drift against the sun, Merton felt a growing unease.

He knew the Russian pilots and designers. They had been trying to win this race for twenty years—and, after all, it was only fair that they should, for had not Pyotr Nikolaevich Lebedev been the first man to detect the pressure of sunlight, back at the very beginning of the twentieth century? But they had never succeeded.

And they would never stop trying. Dimitri was up to something—and it would be spectacular.

Aboard the official launch, a thousand miles behind the racing yachts, Commodore van Stratten looked at the radiogram with angry dismay. It had traveled more than a hundred million miles, from the chain of solar observatories swinging high above the blazing surface of the sun; and it brought the worst possible news.

The commodore—his title was purely honorary, of course; back on Earth he was professor of astrophysics at Harvard—had been half expecting it. Never before had the race been arranged so late in the season. There had been many delays; they had gambled—and now, it seemed, they might all lose.

Deep beneath the surface of the sun, enormous forces were gathering. At any moment the energies of a million hydrogen bombs might burst forth in the awesome explosion known as a solar flare. Climbing at millions of miles an hour, an invisible fireball many times the size of Earth would leap from the sun and head out across space.

The cloud of electrified gas would probably miss the Earth completely. But if it did not, it would arrive in just over a day. Spaceships could protect themselves, with their shielding and their powerful magnetic screens; but the lightly built solar yachts, with their paper-thin walls, were defenseless against such a menace. The crews would have to be taken off, and the race abandoned.

John Merton knew nothing of this as he brought *Diana* around the Earth for the second time. If all went well, this would be the last circuit, both for him and for the Russians. They had spiraled upward by thousands of miles, gaining energy from the sun's rays. On this lap, they should escape from Earth completely, and head outward on the long run to the Moon. It was a straight race now; *Sunbeam's* crew had finally withdrawn exhausted, after battling valiantly with their spinning sail for more than a hundred thousand miles.

Merton did not feel tired; he had eaten and slept well, and *Diana* was behaving herself admirably. The autopilot, tensioning the rigging like a busy little spider, kept the great sail trimmed to the sun more accurately than any human skipper could have. Though by this time the two square miles of plastic sheet must have been riddled by hundreds of micrometeorites, the pinhead-sized punctures had produced no falling off of thrust.

He had only two worries. The first was shroud line number 8, which could no longer be adjusted properly. Without any warning, the reel had jammed; even after all these years of astronautical engineering, bearings sometimes seized up in vacuum. He could neither lengthen nor shorten the line, and would have to navigate as best he could with the others. Luckily, the most difficult maneuvers were over; from now on, *Diana* would have the sun behind her as she sailed straight down the solar wind. And as the old-time sailors had often said, it was easy to handle a boat when the wind was blowing over your shoulder.

His other worry was *Lebedev,* still dogging his heels three hundred miles astern. The Russian yacht had shown remarkable maneuverability, thanks to the four great panels that could be tilted around the central sail. Her flipovers as she rounded the Earth had been carried out with superb precision. But to gain maneuverability she must have sacrificed speed. You could not have it both ways; in the long, straight haul ahead, Merton should be able to hold his own. Yet he could not be certain of victory until, three or four days from now, *Diana* went flashing past the far side of the Moon.

And then, in the fiftieth hour of the race, just after the end of the second orbit around Earth, Markoff sprang his little surprise.

"Hello, John," he said casually over the ship-to-ship circuit. "I'd like you to watch this. It should be interesting."

Merton drew himself across to the periscope and turned up the magnification to the limit. There in the field of view, a most improbable sight against the background of the stars, was the glittering Maltese cross of *Lebedev,* very small but very clear. As he watched, the four arms of the cross slowly detached themselves from the central square, and went drifting away, with all their spars and rigging, into space.

Markoff had jettisoned all unnecessary mass, now that he was coming up to escape velocity and need no longer plod patiently around the Earth, gaining momentum on each circuit. From now on, *Lebedev* would be almost unsteerable—but that did not matter; all the tricky navigation lay behind her. It was as if an old-time yachtsman had deliberately thrown away his rudder and heavy keel, knowing that the rest of the race would be straight downwind over a calm sea.

"Congratulations, Dimitri," Merton radioed. "It's a neat trick. But it's not good enough. You can't catch up with me now."

"I've not finished yet," the Russian answered. "There's an old winter's tale in my country about a sleigh being chased by wolves. To save himself, the driver has to throw off the passengers one by one. Do you see the analogy?"

Merton did, all too well. On this final straight lap, Dimitri no longer needed his copilot. *Lebedev* could really be stripped down for action.

"Alexis won't be very happy about this," Merton replied. "Besides, it's against the rules."

"Alexis isn't happy, but I'm the captain. He'll just have to wait around for ten minutes until the commodore picks him up. And the regulations say nothing about the size of the crew—*you* should know that."

Merton did not answer; he was too busy doing some hurried calculations, based on what he knew of *Lebedev's* design. By the time he had finished, he knew that the race was still in doubt. *Lebedev* would be catching up with him at just about the time he hoped to pass the Moon.

But the outcome of the race was already being decided, ninety-two million miles away.

On Solar Observatory 3, far inside the orbit of Mercury, the automatic instruments recorded the whole history of the flare. A hundred million square miles of the sun's surface exploded in such blue-white fury that, by comparison, the rest of the disk paled to a dull glow. Out of that seething inferno, twisting and turning like a living creature in the magnetic fields of its own creation, soared the electrified plasma of the great flare. Ahead of it, moving at the speed of light, went the warning flash of ultraviolet and X rays. That would reach Earth in eight minutes, and was relatively harmless. Not so the charged atoms that were following behind at their leisurely four million miles an hour—and which, in just over a day, would engulf *Diana, Lebedev* and their accompanying little fleet in a cloud of lethal radiation.

The commodore left his decision to the last possible minute. Even when the jet of plasma had been tracked past the orbit of Venus, there was a chance that it might miss the Earth. But when it was less than four hours away, and had already been picked up by the Moon-based radar network, he knew that there was no hope. All solar sailing was over, for the next five or six years—until the sun was quiet again.

A great sigh of disappointment swept across the solar system. *Diana* and *Lebedev* were halfway between Earth and Moon, running neck and neck—and now no one would ever know which was the better boat. The enthusiasts would argue the result for years; history would merely record: "Race canceled owing to solar storm."

When John Merton received the order, he felt a bitterness he had not known since childhood. Across the years, sharp and clear, came the memory of his tenth birthday. He had been promised an exact scale model of the famous spaceship *Morning Star,* and for weeks had been planning how he would assemble it, where he would hang it in his bedroom. And then, at the last moment, his father had broken the news. "I'm sorry, John—it cost too much money. Maybe next year . . ."

Half a century and a successful lifetime later, he was a heartbroken boy again.

For a moment, he thought of disobeying the commodore. Suppose he sailed on, ignoring the warning? Even if the race was abandoned, he could make a crossing to the Moon that would stand in the record books for generations.

But that would be worse than stupidity; it would be suicide—and a very unpleasant form of suicide. He had seen men die of radiation poisoning, when the magnetic shielding of their ships had failed in deep space. No—nothing was worth that . . .

He felt as sorry for Dimitri Markoff as for himself. They had both deserved to win, and now victory would go to neither. No man could argue with the sun in one of its rages, even though he might ride upon its beams to the edge of space.

Only fifty miles astern now, the commodore's launch was drawing alongside *Lebedev,* preparing to take off her skipper. There went the silver sail, as Dimitri—with feelings that he would share—cut the rigging. The tiny capsule would be taken back to Earth, perhaps to be used again; but a sail was spread for one voyage only.

He could press the jettison button now, and save his rescuers a few minutes of time. But he could not do it; he wanted to stay aboard to the very end, on the little boat that had been for so long a part of his dreams and his life. The great sail was spread now at right angles to the sun, exerting its utmost thrust. Long ago it had torn him clear of Earth, and *Diana* was still gaining speed.

Then, out of nowhere, beyond all doubt or hestitation, he knew what must be done. For the last time, he sat down before the computer that had navigated him halfway to the Moon.

When he had finished, he packed the log and his few personal belongings. Clumsily, for he was out of practice, and it was not an easy job to do by oneself, he climbed into the emergency survival suit. He was just sealing the helmet when the commodore's voice called over the radio.

"We'll be alongside in five minutes, Captain. Please cut your sail, so we won't foul it."

John Merton, first and last skipper of the sun yacht *Diana*, hesitated a moment. He looked for the last time around the tiny cabin, with its shining instruments and its neatly arranged controls, now all locked in their final positions. Then he said into the microphone: "I'm abandoning ship. Take your time to pick me up. *Diana* can look after herself."

There was no reply from the commodore, and for that he was grateful. Professor van Stratten would have guessed what was happening—and would know that, in these final moments, he wished to be left alone.

He did not bother to exhaust the air lock, and the rush of escaping gas blew him gently out into space. The thrust he gave her then was his last gift to *Diana*. She dwindled away from him, sail glittering splendidly in the sunlight that would be hers for centuries to come. Two days from now she would flash past the Moon; but the Moon, like the Earth, could never catch her. Without his mass to slow her down, she would gain two thousand miles an hour in every day of sailing. In a month, she would be traveling faster than any ship that man had ever built.

As the sun's rays weakened with distance, so her acceleration would fall. But even at the orbit of Mars, she would be gaining a thousand miles an hour in every day. Long before then, she would be moving too swiftly for the sun itself to hold her. Faster than a comet had ever streaked in from the stars, she would be heading out into the abyss.

The glare of rockets, only a few miles away, caught Merton's eye. The launch was approaching to pick him up—at thousands of times the acceleration that could ever attain. But its engines could burn for a few minutes only, before they exhausted their fuel—while *Diana* would still be gaining speed, driven outward by the sun's eternal fires, for ages yet to come.

"Good-bye, little ship," said John Merton. "I wonder what eyes will see you next, how many thousand years from now?"

At last he felt at peace, as the blunt torpedo of the launch nosed up beside him. He would never win the race to the Moon; but his would be the first of all man's ships to set sail on the long journey to the stars.

G. Harry Stine

Born in Philadelphia, Pennsylvania, G(eorge) Harry Stine (1928–   ) is a rocket propulsion scientist who has written much of his science fiction under the "Lee Correy" pseudonym.

After obtaining a B.A. in physics from Colorado College in 1952, Stine took a job at the White Sands Proving Ground as chief of the controls and instruments section of the propulsion branch, rising to chief of the range operations division before leaving in disgust over the Sputnik fiasco. Since then he has held several jobs in the aerospace industry and headed his own firm. He turned to full-time writing in 1976.

He is a member of several professional organizations and has won many awards, including the Special Award of the American Rocket Society (1957), the Bendix Trophy of the National Association of Rocketry (1964, 1965, 1967, 1968) and the U.S. Army Association's American Space Pioneer Silver Medal.

The author of more than a dozen books of nonfiction, such as *Rocket Power and Space Flight* (1957), *Earth Satellites and the Race for Space Superiority* (1957), *The Handbook of Model Rocketry* (1965), *The Third Industrial Revolution* (1975) and *Space Power* (1981), he has also written approximately ten science-fiction novels and more than twenty shorter works.

The following story is a passionate plea for a space-based guardian system to protect earth from the type of cosmic collision that may have killed the dinosaurs.

INDUSTRIAL ACCIDENT

by *Lee Correy*
(G. Harry Stine)

IT WAS INEVITABLE that it would happen someday.
And it did happen . . . and nobody will ever know why.

Perhaps an electron did not move from one crystal lattice to another because of a solar X-ray photon or a high-energy cosmic ray, in spite of shielding. Regardless of cause, the effect was known. The book-sized package of nucleide electronics of the autopilot and guidance system did not send the command signal to the fusion-powered pulsed plasma space drive. As a result, the space drive did not swivel, causing TriPlanet Transport's load SLZ-420 to perform the required end-over-end skew flip to begin deceleration for eventual Earth-orbit insertion. Instead, the glitch locked out the command receiver.

SLZ-420 had boosted away from the planetoid Pallas at a constant acceleration of one-tenth standard gravity. This doesn't sound like much acceleration. But, at the programmed turnover point, the SLZ-420 was moving at a sun-referenced velocity of more than six hundred kilometers per second.

Now, instead of starting to slow down on its journey to the space factories in orbit around the Earth, SLZ-420 kept on accelerating.

For centuries, people had been afraid of things falling on them from the sky—early airplanes, meteors, comets and even small planetoids. The doomsday literature of the early space age was full of such scenarios because geological evidence pointed to the fact that large celestial bodies had collided with the Earth in the distant past. And there was abundant visible evidence of such celestial bombardment on the Moon, Mercury and Mars. Scientists and engineers pooh-poohed these fears as they learned that the solar system had swept itself clean of the debris of its birth.

Man-made meteors were rarely considered as one of the hazards of the Third Industrial Revolution.

SLZ-420 had become such a man-made meteor. It was nothing more than a solid cylinder of planetoid iron fifteen meters in diameter and twenty-three meters long, weighing a mere thirty-five thousand tons . . . a grain of celestial sand on the beach of the solar system.

The glitch in the electronic guidance system had not affected the instructions to "go to Earth" that had been implanted in its memory on Pallas. Faithfully, it continued to do its job . . . except for that one little program step. Faithfully, the reliable constant-boost space drive continued to work, adding one meter per second to the velocity every second . . . in the wrong direction. Toward Earth. Toward eight billion people aboard a giant spaceship living in an ecology that was vulnerable to the man-made meteor. Toward people who were ignorant of SLZ-420 and who did not understand the consequences of what could and would happen. But, also, toward people who had not ignored the possibility that it would indeed happen someday.

The House committee hearing room had not changed in nearly a hundred years. Established behind his elevated desk with the status symbols of the microphones before him sat a man who was almost indistinguishable from most of his predecessors. Representative Claypool Evans Perrin had served the people of his district for nearly a quarter of a century . . . or so they believed. However, he knew full well that politics was simply the interaction of various power groups . . . and thus he had remained in office through twelve election battles. He scorned implant lenses, preferring old rimless eyeglasses. He felt that they lent a distinctive touch to his craggy face topped by its famous shock of unruly hair, hair that was now pure white and worn long in the romantic fashion of the ancient seventies. Perrin believed it helped maintain his image as a young-thinking firebrand radical, the image that had served him well for all those years and all those elections.

He peered now through those spectacles and fixed his stare on the man behind the witness table below him. "Please let me get this absolutely clear in my mind, Mr. Armitage." He spoke in the measured cadence of his rasping voice. "The Control and Inspection Division of the Department of Space Commerce is requesting a budget line item of 4.7 billion dollars for something you term an 'emergency accident system.' If I understand this correctly, it's for the development and deployment of interceptor-type space vehicles based at L-5."

Chuck Armitage was quick to attempt a reply. "Yes, sir, we—"

But Perrin wasn't about to let the witness speak yet. "Under the terms of various United Nations treaties, some of them more than fifty years old, no nation is permitted to maintain any sort of deep-space military system beyond that necessary to police its own space operations . . . sort of the equivalent of the old Coast Guard, if you will. We've spent billions of dollars to ensure that the Space Watch can defend our national airspace up to a hundred kilometers, as we are permitted to do under international agreement." He paused and shook his long white hair out of his face. "Mr. Armitage, isn't the Department of Space Commerce asking Congress to let you build an armed force based in space and capable of carrying out offensive military acts against space facilities as well as against Earth?"

It was a loaded question, and Chuck Armitage knew it. Hunching forward over the witness table, he looked intently back at Congressman Perrin while he collected his thoughts and tried to choose his words very carefully. His thinking processes were quite rapid in this environment because he had fought his way through many congressional appropriations hearings in the past.

"Mr. Chairman, the department can't do what you are claiming, as Secretary Seton has said many times. The intent of the budget line item request is quite different, and this is why Secretary Seton has asked me to speak for it in her stead. As head of the Control and Inspection Division, I am the policeman of our space commerce activities and—"

"I have read your vitae, sir—" Perrin broke in, apparently with impatience. It was, however, a technique that he used very effectively with witnesses. But it didn't work with Chuck Armitage.

"Then you know what sort of situation I am faced with on a daily basis," Armitage broke in himself. "In fact, for the past twenty-two years we have lived with the situation since the Whitney Drive was first used for constant-boost spaceflight . . . "

"Ah, yes, but for those twenty-two years, there have been no problems that space crews have not been able to solve."

"Those were manned vehicles, Congressman," Armitage pointed out. The exchange was becoming rapid-fire as both men tried to gain and maintain control of the situation.

"What possible difference does that make?"

"Problems could be solved in transit. But things have changed. The majority of cargo vehicles today are unmanned because of various governmental restrictions—not in our department, by the way—that prevent the necessary capital accumulation required to finance manned ships."

"Well, such rules pertaining to the regulation of space commerce are not the province of this committee!"

"No, sir, but the unmanned cargo ship is a consequence that we must deal with here. The solar system is full of unmanned ships right this instant, some of them boosting at more than a standard g. I am responsible for the safe operation of those ships of United States registry. And I am especially worried about the unmanned, automated vehicles. There is a finite chance that something could go wrong with an unmanned ship . . . and we would be faced with the prospect of a very large

173

mass coming at us with terminal velocity approaching a thousand kilometers per second. . . .In effect, man-made meteors."

Perrin waved his hand. "That seems to be a rather remote possibility. Meteors have been hitting the Earth for millions of years. The government of the United States has never had to concern itself with any problems of protecting its citizens against falling meteors!" A titter of laughter ran around the hearing room. Perrin felt that he had counted coup on that one.

"We are not talking about natural meteors, Mr. Chairman! Most of the natural meteorite material out there is no bigger than a pebble . . . or somebody would be mining it right now! We are concerned with a recent man-made phenomenon: unmanned constant-boost cargo ships. There are more than a hundred of them boosting toward the Earth–Moon system right now. We need only one failure—*one failure*—to have a worldwide catastrophe on our hands."

"Come, come! I have never known you to exaggerate in your testimony before, Mr. Armitage. Worldwide catastrophe? Really!"

"I wish it were not possible, Congressman. We estimate that the impact of a thirty-thousand-ton planetoid ore carrier at five hundred kilometers per second would produce an effect equivalent to several hundred megatons of TNT. But the scaling laws break down because we cannot extrapolate from the results of early thermonuclear warhead testing. The United States set off a ten-megaton thermonuclear device in 1952, and the Soviets blew off a fifty-megaton nuke shortly thereafter. We are not sure that—"

Perrin cut in again. "We're not discussing military warheads, Mr. Armitage!"

"No, sir, but we are discussing the rapid release of large amounts of energy—and the only difference between a large nuke and a fast-moving rock is the lack of radiation from the rock impact. In addition, when a large unmanned ship hits, it will be moving many times faster than a natural meteor, and its kinetic energy increases as the square of —"

"Mr. Armitage, isn't your division responsible for seeing to it that a runaway spaceship could never occur? Aren't we discussing something so highly hypothetical as to be ridiculous? Aren't your people on top of the safety aspect?"

"Yes, sir, they are. Our specifications and technical directives must be followed by all manufacturers and users of equipment licensed or registered by the United States. By international agreements, all other spacefaring nations either adopt our rules or have rules that are compatible. Our field representatives inspect and sign-off all new equipment as it comes out of the factory door. They do the same for all routine maintenance, overhauls, and even for preboost checks."

"Then what is it that could possibly go wrong, Mr. Armitage?"

"Mr. Chairman, no technology is ever perfect. We are not gods; we are people with a very incomplete understanding of the way the universe works. Sooner or later, no matter how diligent we are and no matter how exhaustive our tests, something will misbehave. Let me state categorically—and I'll back it up with numbers at a later time if you wish—that there is a statistically valid possibility that the Earth will be impacted by an unmanned multithousand-ton cargo ship within the next ten years. We *must* have an emergency system of long-range deep-space interceptors . . . a dozen is all that we are asking for. They would be based at our L-5 facility. They have to be because of the negligible gravity well there and because of the fact that it is easier to intercept a runaway ship as far out as possible . . . and not even very easy under those conditions."

Perrin leaned back and made a steeple of his fingertips.

"Isn't the Space Watch prepared to take care of such matters?"

"Ask the Space Watch."

"But I am asking you, Mr. Armitage."

"The Space Watch interceptor force is Earth-based by treaty. The beam weapons at L-5 have limited power under the SWAP agreements with the Soviet Union, whose L-4 beam weapons are also limited. Ask the Space Watch, sir, because they are well equipped to handle defense against Earth-launched missiles or against anything the Soviets might try to do from L-4."

"You haven't answered my question, have you?"

175

"I cannot answer it in open session, nor am I privileged to know all of the sensitive details of the Space Watch systems." Chuck Armitage *did* know these details. He wasn't supposed to. He wasn't cleared for that information, but he had his channels of information that were zealously protected. He had known for five years that the Space Watch did not have the capability to even deflect the course of an unmanned runaway. "This is why I suggested, Mr. Chairman, that you might ask the Space Watch to . . . "

An aide leaned over Perrin's shoulder and whispered something into the congressman's right ear. Perrin nodded and glanced at his old-fashioned digital wristwatch. He turned his attention again to Armitage. "We have an important roll-call vote coming up in a few minutes. So we'll not have time to discuss this further today. We may have a duplication of effort conflict arising between DSC and the Space Watch. The fine line of division between military and civilian utilization of space has been a major problem for nearly sixty years, and I doubt that we will find the solution to it today." Perrin decided that he would mention the matter to the presidents of Tri-Planet Spaceways and TransWorld Transit at dinner that evening to find out if there was any support for this program from the space transportation lobby.

The session adjourned for the day. Armitage inwardly chewed his fingernails as he gathered up his papers and stalked out of the hearing room with his deputy, George Bonnieul.

"Wait until some nonsked Zaire registry load slams into his constituency!" Chuck growled so that only George could hear.

"No reason to be upset, Chuck," Bonnieul remarked smoothly. "Perrin was Perrin today, as usual but more so. He's up for reelection and he's got some hot young competition. He wants political advantage out of this." He looked over at Armitage.

"Too damned many things in space operations have been determined by political compromise rather than by technical or economic realities," Armitage continued to mutter. "I once thought that when private enterprise became involved, it would be the end of the political football game . . . but they just started playing again with new rules . . . "

"So what else is new?" George wanted to know. "Let's say to hell with it. You-know-who called from Singapore this morning. Says the offer is still open for all of us."

"And turn the division over to The Slob?" Chuck was referring to the civil service hack who would most probably be promoted into Chuck's position from a nonoperating division of the department because there just wasn't anybody to take it if Chuck and his colleagues left. If the deal had just been for Chuck alone, he might have given it more consideration because George would have then been in line for division chief.

"You have a disturbing habit of bringing up unsavory matters," George told him as they descended the long stairway to reach the elevators going to the roof. Only in a government building would one have to walk down stairs to get an elevator going up. The two men were quiet in the elevator because there were others present, although they were the only ones going all the way to the roof.

An agency aircar was waiting for them, manned and running.

Chuck sensed that something was wrong. "Didn't you park that heap in the transient area over there?"

George nodded.

The two of them walked normally over to the waiting aircar. If there was something wrong somewhere, this was not the place to indicate it by unusual action because there were, as always, news media crews standing by on the roof to interview important witnesses and newsworthy congressmen.

Immediately the door was closed, the driver put the air to the Coanda wings and went straight up to transition altitude. Only then did Chuck remark, "Howdy, Jed. How did you get here?"

The wiry little pilot, another of Armitage's assistants, replied without turning his head. "Pete brought me over and dropped me off. We didn't dare call you out of the hearing, and we wanted to make sure that you got back to the center as quickly as possible once it was over." He paused, listened to the radio loudspeaker, replied into a microphone, then continued his monologue. "Thirty minutes ago, we got the data

177

that cargo load SLZ-420 out of Pallas at one-tenth g missed turnover a little over three hours ago."

There was not a trace of emotion on the faces or in the actions of either man, but this belied the inner feelings that each of them had at the moment. But they were professionals in a high-tech area and were trained not to display their emotions. George took out his pocket computer, pulled out the antenna, and put it near the south window of the aircar so that it could communicate with the geosynchronous data transfer satellite that was linked to the computers at the center and with the internationally maintained master unit at Singapore. "A little more than sixty-six hours to arrival here," George announced.

"Any telemetry indication of the malfunction?" Chuck then asked the driver.

"I've told you all I know. I left the center just after the alert sounded," Jed remarked. "Please let me handle this rush hour traffic so that I can get you to center as quickly as possible without arousing interest."

"The sheer coincidence of this amazes me," George said in deliberate understatement, looking at Chuck.

"History is a record of coincidental happenings and the people who managed to take opportune advantage of them," Armitage observed quietly. "I will not relish what I will have to do in the next few hours."

The traffic room of the Control and Inspection Center was large. It was quiet, but it was busy. The several dozen people hardly moved, but the data presentations on the walls were active. Chuck Armitage slumped in a chair behind one of the supervisory desks in the glassed-off gallery. He contemplated the data on the CRT display before him and on the walls of the traffic room. It had been a very busy several hours since he had walked in. Several telephone calls had been made. Hot lines between national traffic control centers had been activated on a permanent basis. Tacit agreements had been reached with Chuck's counterparts around the world. Some traffic in the Earth–Moon system had been rerouted or rescheduled; the department's public affairs people kept their cool and announced that the traffic changes were probably caused by the detection of a close-approach planetoid that might be moving near the Earth–Moon system. Traffic centers were normally closed to the news media, and they remained sealed off. Some of the news media were enraged; others decided to play it cool and wait for the inevitable leaks or further developments. However, news of wars, revolutions, murders, looting, rapes, invasions, famines and other commonplace, everyday happenings around the planet continued to occupy the major news slots; after all, those stories were about people, and very few media persons could get very excited about a rock in space.

Chuck Armitage had a decision to make, and he waited until the very last moment to make it. In one smooth motion, he reached out and picked a telephone handset out of its cradle. When he punched the call buttons, his motions were sharp, rapid and almost vicious. "Tom, Chuck Armitage. It's a 'go' situation, my friend. Let me know whether you or Kim decide to be number one. . . . Yes, it will be messy . . . I'll take care of that. . . . Good luck, Tom . . . and *arigato*." He put the handset back in its cradle softly. For minutes, he stared straight ahead at nothing.

The telephone blinked at him. He lifted it from its cradle again. "Armitage here. . . . Good, bring them up, George. . . . Yes, everything's going as planned. . . . Well, I'm glad you were able to find him. When will he get here? . . . Too bad. No latecomers, George. He'll just have to read about it later." After hanging up, he rose and walked slowly to the rear of the room where the bar and the buffet were stocked and ready. He couldn't eat; he didn't have any appetite just then. He wanted a drink, but he didn't dare. He didn't even want the stimulant of coffee.

Over the next thirty minutes, his guests arrived. Some were indignant. Some were quizzical. Some were somber. None of them knew the full story, some of them had snatches of data that they had agreed would not be discussed until Chuck had given them a full briefing, but almost all of them sensed that there was an aura of quiet, controlled, constrained terror in the air.

It had taken the full power of the president's office plus that of Secretary Seton to convene every one of the people who arrived. Chuck could not make small talk with any of them; it was impossible for him to do so. He fretted inwardly until the final group of three people came in. The younger of the three came up and shook hands with Chuck.

"Good to see you, Senator," Chuck remarked. "I'm glad you were able to locate Congressman Perrin and bring him with you."

"It wasn't easy," Senator Davidoff replied. "Thanks to Tri-Planet, I located Clay with Jeremiah at the Cosmos Club."

Chuck greeted Jeremiah Morris, the scarecrowlike ruler of TriPlanet Spaceways, who said nothing in return. Jeremiah knew the score. A quick telephone call from the Cosmos Club to his operations office did it, and he had passed the information along to Perrin in the aircar en route to the center. He didn't need to say anything to Chuck at this time; later, when liability had been established, he might make a statement. In any event, a Lloyd's associate would do the sweating. Or so he thought.

"I'm sorry I interrupted your dinner, Congressman," Chuck tried to apologize to Perrin.

Perrin's reply was a growl from an important man who has had his arm twisted. "If it hadn't been for Senator Davidoff, I would have considered this whole matter as a grandstand play resulting from the hearings. I'm still not certain that I . . ."

"Chuck Armitage does not make grandstand plays," the young senator cut in. "I've known him too long to . . ."

"How do we know this isn't a dry run?" Perrin wanted to know.

"I wish to God it were a dry run," was Chuck's reply. Raising his voice above the conversational hubbub of the room, he announced. "Please take a seat, everyone. I want to tell everyone what's going on here."

Most of the people in the room knew one another . . . Star Admiral Jacobs, top man of the Space Watch; Joseph Hirschfeld of TransWorld; Andrew Watermann of Terra-Luna Transport; Jeremiah Morris of TriPlanet; foreign liaison professionals from Europe, Japan and the Soviet Union; and Secretary Helen Seton, secretary of the Department of Space Commerce with the gleaming Distinguished Space Star pinned like a brooch to her high-necked tunic covering the scars and prosthetics from the power satellite accident.

"Ladies and gentlemen, you are here at the request of the president of the United States, who is fully aware of the crisis that now exists," Chuck began. "George, please get the rest of the teleconference on the line. Now, to anticipate some objections concerning national security, I wish to further tell you that I am acting with the full authority and approval of the president in establishing this hologram teleconference with our compatriots in Europe, Singapore and the Soviet Union. Please stand by until George completes the circuits."

The side wall of the room disappeared, revealing three more rooms similar to the one they were in. In each of the shimmering three rooms, the holographic projections from Europe, Singapore and the Soviet Union flickered into being as the circuits through the geosynchronous comsat platforms were given a final tuning. Brief greetings were exchanged, but they were short. The holographic participants seemed to know what the situation was, and they were all business.

"We have a crisis on our hands with worldwide implications," Chuck announced. "Our colleagues elsewhere must participate on a real-time basis. A space vehicle of United States' registry has become a runaway, and it may impact Earth . . ."

The room exploded with voices.

"Gospodin Armitage," the Soviet hologram spoke, causing the room to become quiet, "is it as bad as our information indicates to us?"

Chuck nodded. "Here are the full details. TriPlanet cargo load SLZ-420 running in from Pallas at thirty-five thousand tons gross weight did not execute turnover at 17:10 Universal Time today. Because of the distance involved, our tracking net did not learn about this for almost two hours. Neither we nor the people at TriPlanet know what is wrong. Telemetry indicated that everything aboard SLZ-420 is operating normally, but the autopilot will not acknowledge nor execute commands. This should not happen with triple-redundant circuits, but it has."

Luxemburg wanted to know, "What is the inspection history?"

"Our records and those of TriPlanet indicate that all systems have undergone periodic inspections as required and that all spaceworthiness directives have been complied with. Our Pallas field office gave clearance to boost based on an affirmative preboost check."

"Can we compare computer data?" the Soviet asked.

"Of course," Chuck said and noticed that Star Admiral Jacobs flinched slightly. "Call it up on our standard data transfer net. You can also get the graphic presentation we have on the walls here at center. At turnover, velocity was 612 kilometers per second, and it is still boosting toward us at one-tenth standard g. That doesn't sound like much, but it is adding one kilometer per second to its velocity every sixteen minutes and forty seconds."

A few people in the room were rapidly keying display consoles, calling up additional data. But most did not know how. They sat there, responsible for the use of the technology, but unable to manipulate it.

Senator Davidoff broke the silence. "But it doesn't seem to be boosting wild. According to the shape of the trajectories you're plotting on the walls out here, its guidance system seems to be working."

"Working perfectly and homing on Earth," Chuck told him.

"Have you alerted the Space Watch?" It was the first time Perrin had spoken since the briefing began. "Can they stop it?"

Chuck indicated the star admiral.

Jacobs was young, but he was both a competent engineer and an experienced leader. He first looked directly at the hologram of his Soviet counterpart. Then he turned to Perrin. "No," came the flat answer.

"But you've got an interceptor force!" Perrin complained.

Jacobs glanced at the Soviet hologram. "I am not free to discuss it."

Chuck picked up a telephone. "As Secretary Seton can verify, the president has authorized complete cooperation and the total lifting of security restrictions. Shall I call him to satisfy you?"

Jacobs hesitated.

"Since we began this teleconference, SLZ-420 has added one-hundred-fifty meters per second to its velocity, Admiral," Chuck pointed out, holding up the telephone. "Do you want me to get the president on the line for you, or are you willing to accept what I tell you?"

Jacobs looked at Secretary Seton. "I spoke with the president," she said quietly. "Speak freely, there is no security barrier."

"Our interceptors are Earth-based according to treaty. We've built some slight excess performance into them so that we could operate them de-rated," Jacobs rationalized. "With a very great deal of very good luck and everything working perfectly, we might intercept with a nuke at a range of three hundred kilometers from Earth. But at that point, the SLZ-420 is moving at eight hundred kilometers per second. . . . and those rates are beyond . . . are beyond the capabilities of . . . of our intercept system."

"You have exceeded SWAP treaty limitations!" the Soviet hologram objected strongly.

"Gospodin!" Chuck snapped. "I would be very happy now if you had exceeded them to a greater extent!"

"Burn it with your beam weapons at L-5!" Perrin suggested.

"Congressman," Jacobs told him, "those beam weapons won't make a dent in thirty-five thousand tons of iron! By treaty, they're defocused beyond four hundred thousand kilometers. We can refocus them in about four days' time . . . which is several days faster than I know my Soviet counterpart can manage. But even if we could refocus, we haven't got enough time to input enough energy into the target. At the velocity it will be moving, it will take only seven minutes from time of crossing the lunar orbit until it impacts."

"Mein Herr, do you have an impact prediction yet?" was the question from Luxemburg Center.

Chuck paused to key a terminal. "Here's the latest update, Fritz. Barring any malfunction of the SLZ-420's guidance system, which is unlikely, the ship will impact near Genk, Belgium, in fifty-nine hours and approximately ten minutes from now. Entry velocity is estimated to be 867 kilometers per second, which means that the Earth's atmosphere will have negligible effect on its mass from ablation or on its impact velocity. The impact will release kinetic energy equivalent to a 284-megaton bomb . . . and we do not know what the effects will be. The atmospheric shock wave will rebound around the planet several times, and the ground shock will certainly go off the top end of the Richter Scale. Some of the thirty-five thousand tons of iron will vaporize on impact, and some of it will get tossed clear around the planet as secondaries . . . some of which may pose a problem to near-Earth orbital facilities. Other than the brief burst of hard X rays from the atmospheric entry plasma sheath, there will be no radiation other than heat . . . and the fireball of impact will probably rise to the top of the stratosphere and squat there, radiating most of its heat to space. The meteor experts at Flagstaff couldn't even guess the effects on the planetary weather . . ."

"Is there any chance it may go into the Atlantic Ocean instead?" the hologram that was Fritz in Luxemburg asked.

"That just makes it worse," Chuck pointed out. "The impact might vaporize enough sea water to create a worldwide cloud layer . . . which in turn could raise the world temperatures by several degrees by virtue of greenhouse effect. . . . Look, all of you, I just don't know everything that could happen because we have never experienced anything like this in all recorded history! We can't even extrapolate from fairly recent strikes such as the Barringer Crater in Arizona . . . which was made by a small slowpoke in comparison to SLZ-420. . . ."

There was complete silence for moments as the full import of the information sunk in. It was Claypool Perrin who lost his cool. "We've got to start evacuation of the impact area!"

"Clay," Davidoff said, "an announcement would start a panic."

"But millions of people will die! How can you just sit here and let the sky literally fall on those millions in Europe without telling them?"

"Congressman, will you provide me with some guidelines on how to evacuate a *whole continent*?" Chuck said.

"But *you've got to do something!*" Perrin exploded. "How can you sit here and watch blinking lights and program computers and let the world come to an end? This is madness! *You've* got to do something!"

The people in the room, including the holographic projections, were now looking at one another, often with quick glances, sometimes with long eye contacts. Nobody said a word. Most were afraid to say anything.

Slowly and softly, Chuck broke the heavy silence. "I have already done something about it."

The room exploded again in voices. Chuck merely held up his hand, and the room fell silent again. Of all the powerful people in the room, Chuck Armitage was now the most powerful. He turned around and pointed to a screen in the traffic room. Two green triangles were now leaving a green trail on the near-Earth display. One of them appeared to be accelerating rapidly. The display had been up for several minutes, but only Chuck had noticed. The others had been far too engrossed in the problem or did not understand the display.

"Madame Secretary," Chuck addressed his boss who, because of her astronaut training, had maintained her cool consideration of the affair. "You know nothing of what I have done. I haven't told you about its planning. I initiated its implementation without your knowledge or approval. I utilized funds from several parts of the budget in such a way that the expenditures wouldn't be noticed until GAO audits us. I'm sorry that I had to do it this way, but I had to protect you and the department from the storm that is to follow. I accept full and complete responsibility."

"You still haven't told me what you've done, Chuck," Helen Seton pointed out with no trace of emotion.

"First off, here is my resignation, effective immediately." Chuck withdrew an envelope from his jacket pocket and proffered it to his boss.

"We'll discuss it at a later time when things are not so critical," she replied with a wave of her hand, refusing to accept the envelope. "What is going on now?" she asked quietly.

"My grandstand play. Senator Davidoff said a few minutes ago that I don't make them. That is not precisely true. I don't make them until it counts. If I had yelled and made a bloody nuisance of myself over the runaway possibility when I took over here seven years ago, I would not have remained in the position for more than six weeks . . ."

"That's a very astute observation, Chuck," Davidoff told him.

"I know. Jeremiah, your people, combined with those from TransWorld and Terra-Luna, would never live with any system that could reach into deep space. Neither would the League of Free Traders—"

"Don't try to put the blame for all of this on us, Armitage," Jeremiah Morris growled. "Because of your unreasonable regulations, we've had to put safety devices on the safety devices . . . and something was bound to go wrong sooner or—"

"Gentlemen!" Helen Seton's voice was still quiet, but it carried both leadership and authority in its tone. "Please! There will be ample time for bickering later . . . if we survive. Let Chuck explain what it is that he has done behind the scenes."

"Thank you. I did a bootleg engineering job that is something far less than perfect with high risk involved and exorbitant ultimate cost . . . hoping that I would never have to use it because others might be convinced to give us the means to do it right. Well, SLZ-420 forced the issue and pushed me into using my Plan B which is one-shot. We can never use it again, so we've got to get our heads together even while it is probably saving our necks . . . which is why the president acceded to my requests to bring you together here."

Perrin was on his feet, using his full-volumed House speaking voice. "I will not permit myself to be pressured in this manner. . . . Please excuse me!"

"You will have some trouble getting out of here," Chuck Armitage pointed out. "Madame Secretary, do I not have the authority to seal off the center in an emergency?"

"You do, and I will not countermand your order. But I would really like to know what you are doing, Chuck. All of this preamble obviously seems important, and it probably is. But SLZ-420 is coming down our throats, and that is Priority Number One. *Will everybody please be quiet and listen?*" When she raised her voice with emotion in it, the shock rippled through the room, which instantly became silent.

Chuck spun a chair around and literally fell into it. Fatigue was beginning to get to him, and there was a long time yet to go. "Those two green triangles boosting hard away from Earth are two of our deep-space inspection cutters from Hilo Base, Hawaii. They have been highly modified and each is manned only by a single pilot."

"Manned? Why manned?" Star Admiral Jacobs wanted to know.

"Because we had neither the time nor the money to develop the necessary long-range active guidance and homing systems that are required for an interceptor that can handle high closure rates at distances far beyond lunar orbit," Chuck explained. "I had to use a guidance system that was already available: a human being. The first triangle represents the cutter *Toryu,* which is boosting at four standard g's, the limit of sustained human endurance, under the control of Tomio Hattori. The second triangle represents the *Shoki,* boosting at two standard g under the control of Kimsuki Kusabake. In approximately twenty-five hours, the *Toryu* will intercept the SLZ-420. If Tom Hattori does the kind of job I know he can do, the impact of that two-thousand-ton cutter will do one or both of two jobs: deflect the SLZ-420 from its present trajectory and/or disable its constant-boost drive. If Tom doesn't do the complete job, we have the *Shoki* following with Kim to finish it off . . . but that will be a tough one because of the increased closure rate . . ."

Again, it was Congressman Claypool Perrin, the reelected romantic of the let-it-all-hang-out seventies, who broke in almost hysterically, "Do you mean to tell us that you have deliberately sent at least one person to a certain death? How can you possibly do this . . . this *inhumane* thing?"

"I know of no other way to do it at this time with the tools that you have permitted me," Chuck fired back. "And spare me the outrage. Ain't nobody here but us chickens, fellas . . . and that is an American folk saying for the benefit of our teleconferencing guests. Every one of us in this room, including the teleconferencing guests, has contributed to this situation in his own unique way."

"Now, that certainly isn't true, Chuck! This should have been a Space Watch job—" Star Admiral Jacobs started to say.

"See what I mean?" Chuck said. "The Watch fought us tooth and nail when we instituted orbital sweeping for the thousands of dead satellites up there. No, they wanted high-power beam weapons installed in L-5 to do the job. . . . And I know that your intelligence people knew that, Dimitri!"

"That's not a fair assessment!" Jacobs tried to break in. "The State Department didn't—"

"I don't care who tries to put the blame on who!" Chuck said in exasperation. "Governments, private enterprise, everyone involved in space commerce is right here, right now! Reading it on the news tube wouldn't have helped toward a solution; you had to be here right in the middle of it living with the consequences of your actions. You had to see and experience it, and it is a very difficult thing to do. And please don't think that taking care of this industrial accident was an easy thing for me to do, either!" He sighed deeply and rubbed his eyes. "But it *will* be an easy thing for Tom and Kim."

"What do you mean, Chuck?" Senator Davidoff asked.

"Admiral Jacobs knows what I mean. There are always people who are willing to sacrifice themselves for the greater good. Some people seek self-destruction for a cause in order to give meaning to their lives. Our psychologists can spot them. And sometimes it is a cultural trait. . . ."

"Kamikazes," Jacob muttered.

"Over two thousand pilots of World War II, and several thousand from time to time since then in suicide missions in brushfire wars for a glorious cause greater than they believe themselves to be." Chuck noticed that Perrin was now shaking his head in total disbelief. "No, Congressman Perrin, this job isn't all technology. It deals with people because technical problems are rarely unsolved due to technical factors. In this case, I am giving two people the opportunity to fulfill themselves. Tom and Kim are out there by their own free choice. I have been the only one who did not have a real choice."

Most of the people present in the room sat aghast, with three exceptions—the hologram from Singapore whose Japanese features indicated full understanding, Secretary Helen Seton, whose own sacrifice on PowerSat One had made her life as a woman and mother impossible, and Star Admiral Jacobs, who nodded as though he had discovered in Chuck Armitage a man he could fully understand. "We have them in the Space Watch, too. No military establishment could exist without them," he said, with pride.

It was now very quiet in the room again. Armitage looked around. "We have twenty-five hours before we know if Tom Hattori succeeds. In the meantime, we have placed the tightest possible worldwide news lid on this. There will be no leaks from Singapore or from the centers. Food and beverages will be available here, and there are secure rooms down the hall if anyone needs to rest. Your respective organizations have been notified that you are in a special international conference, which is no lie. We have all seen the consequences of our past activities. We now have the unique opportunity to work out an arrangement so that this sort of thing can never happen again. Madame Secretary, you are the logical one to chair this *ad hoc* conference. Would you care for some coffee?"

Tom Hattori and the *Toryu* did the job. The haggard group in the gallery of the center watched the displays as what was left careered around the Earth and plunged outward forever into deep space with a velocity that would take it to the stars. There were no cheers. The conference group was far too exhausted physically and emotionally. New agreements had been hammered out. A joint communiqué had been written and released to the news media.

Both in space and in the center, the solutions were compromises . . . but workable compromises.

Chuck Armitage was the first to leave the center.

He discovered Senator Davidoff and Secretary Seton walking on either side of him.

"Where are you going, Chuck?" Helen Seton asked.

"Home. To stay."

"Take a few days' rest. Then come and see me. There's work to be done . . . lots of work."

"Madame Secretary . . . Helen . . . my resignation holds. It has to."

"Chuck, you're a good man," Senator Davidoff put in. "We've always needed good men. Why do you think you're finished in your present position? With the new agreements, we need you more than ever. You were the spark plug that got it all together for us."

"Ah, my dear colleague from the good old days of the Shuttle missions!" Chuck Armitage replied. "Perhaps you and Helen can handle the political aspects of this and swing enough clout with GAO so that Justice does not indict me for misappropriation of funds . . ."

"But you saved the whole damned world!" Davidoff pointed out.

"Temporarily . . . until the next crisis in an era of crises."

"I can't be as dramatic as the senator," the petite secretary of space commerce remarked, "but he's right. We need you more than ever. When forced to make a decision, you didn't waffle . . . and it was a very tough decision. Both the senator and I know such a thing is rare among people today, but absolutely necessary in space. Chuck, your career and job are not in jeopardy. I'll stick by you, whatever happens . . ."

"And I will do the same," Davidoff added quickly, earnestly.

Chuck stopped walking so suddenly that his two companions went two steps beyond him, then turned to face where he stood. "No. For several reasons. You're on top of the hill, and I am down on a ridge. I see some things differently. I pushed around a lot of internationally powerful and influential people. I rubbed their noses in their own accumulated folly and made them admit to it by forcing them to come up with a new set of rules. I'll never be one of them and I'll no longer be able to work for them because I have proved that I am willing to rock the boat and make big waves. I am no longer to be trusted . . ."

"Nonsense!" Davidoff snorted.

"You know it isn't. I cannot ask you to risk your own careers. I've already sent one man to his willing destruction; I cannot ask anyone else to even risk it. In fact, my own personal values are making it very difficult for me to rationalize Tomio Hattori. In my own case, it doesn't count. When I spoke of people willing to sacrifice themselves for a greater cause, I knew exactly what I was talking about. . . . Now, please excuse me. I'm very tired . . ."

He turned and took a side path, walking away from them. In the star-specked evening, the ex-astronaut senator and the ex-astronaut minister watched him go. There wasn't anything either of them could say.

J. R. Pierce

J(ohn) R(obinson) Pierce (1910–   ) was born in Des Moines, Iowa, and has published some of his science fiction stories under the name of J. J. Coupling.

Obtaining three engineering degrees (B.S., 1933, M.S., 1934, and Ph.D., 1936) from the California Institute of Technology, he subsequently joined Bell Telephone Laboratories and rose from a simple member of the technical staff to director of electronics research (1952–1955), director of research communications principles (1958–1962), executive director of the research-communications principles and communications systems divisions (1962–1965) and executive director of the research-communications sciences division (1965–1971). Since then he has held academic positions.

Among the notable books he has authored are *Theory and Design of Electronic Beams* (1949); *Traveling Wave Tubes* (1950); *Electrons, Waves and Messages* (1956); *Symbols, Signals and Noise* (1961); *Science, Art and Communication* (1968); and *The Beginnings of Satellite Communications* (1968). His awards and honors are simply too numerous to mention.

Of the score of science fiction stories he has written thus far, the most popular are "Invariant" and "Period Piece," but for this volume we have chosen the first of two—the other is "The Exorcism"—all but forgotten speculations about computer simulations and their future potentialities.

CHOICE

by J. R. Pierce

WHEN, AFTER DINNER, Harvey Adam sat down before the communication alcove and keyed Myra's number, the puzzle and excitement of his unusual day dropped away from him. As the alcove glowed with the light of Myra's room he experienced that part of his life which, now old, was yet ever fresh and new. He saw her in profile, seated at her dressing table. She wore a soft, thin gown that hung in gentle folds about her body. She was looking at herself in the mirror, her head tilted back a little. The outlines of her forehead, nose, mouth and chin had the classic regularity he admired so much but could never quite recollect except in seeing her. The slight and unusual rounding of her features saved their perfection from severity and made him feel ever protective. The dressing table was littered with bottles and a tissue had fallen to the floor. It lay incongruously on the soft, deep-pile rug at her right.

Myra ignored the calling signal for a moment, continuing her examination. Then she turned slowly and smiled at him.

"Harvey," she said in her soft, warm voice. "I was expecting you." The tissue on the floor caught her eye. With a slightly vexed expression she leaned over to pick it up. The loose, low-cut bodice of the gown fell away from her body, revealing a perfect breast. With her hand on the tissue she looked up and smiled for a moment. "I'm messy," she said. She quickly stuffed the tissue in the disposal and sat up, touching her blonde hair lightly with her hands. The gesture showed her arms to perfection.

"And did you have a good day, dear?" Myra asked.

"Good but exciting," he replied. "I don't want to talk shop tonight, Myra. Just talk. And just see you. What did you do today?"

"Oh, nothing that would interest a historian," she replied.

"You must have done something," he coaxed.

"All right, then, I bought this gown," she told him, standing and walking toward him. The filmy material fell sheer and straight, outlining her figure wherever it touched—the points of her breasts, the roundness of her belly. He could see the rest of her body dimly through the fabric, more teasing and tantalizing than bare flesh. She turned around once, then faced him and asked anxiously, "Do you like it?"

"Immensely," he said. "Every woman should have one."

She looked a little hurt.

"But it especially suits you."

She smiled in mock relief. She moved the soft, light, comfortable chair from the dressing table to face him and sat down, her legs outlined by the translucent gown.

"Where did you find it?" he asked.

The conversation turned to shopping and to the trivialities of the day, which Myra seemed to find of consuming interest. Harvey found this very touching and amusing. But gradually, their interest returned to the gown. Harvey remarked on the texture.

"Would you like to feel it?" Myra asked. Harvey did, putting his hand through the filmy barrier at the face of the communication booth. As the barrier that gave him access to Myra's communication booth gave way his hand obscured his view of Myra where it passed through the film. But he felt the material of the gown between his fingers. Then he felt Myra's softness through the gown. The slithery softness of the fabric added a sensation all its own. Myra's hand came toward him, a shapely gray ghost emerging from the film. His vision clouded as the shimmering hand pushed him on the chest.

"Go away," Myra said. "I thought you wanted to talk."

Harvey grabbed the hand and pulled their bodies together. "I do," he said in a whisper, pressing his face through the film toward an unseen ear.

"Don't muss the gown," Myra said in alarm (simulated, he thought).

"Then take it off," he told her as she drew back. He could see her again.

"Really?" she asked, smiling.

He nodded solemnly. "Really."

Bending toward him, she took the hem of the gown lightly in both hands and slowly raised it, gathering folds of cloth into her hands. She smiled and raised the gown over her head; her face emerged and she stood with arms upthrust, naked.

"You and me," he said with a chuckle. Quickly he stepped through the film of the communication cubicle to put his arms about Myra. All sight was gone now but he could feel whatever his hands and body sought.

Later that night, after he and Myra had rung off, he lay in bed and thought of the goodness of life. Satisfaction was dearly bought. There had been the years of childhood, the peer group, the computer tutoring, the minors who tended one by assignment, not from choice. There had been the troubled time of adolescence: intellectual yearning without the intellectual discipline necessary for fulfillment; and physical yearning that dissolved into frankly curious explorations and selfish conflicts of personality.

Mating and parenthood were touching for those who were chosen (he had been). But each knew that he had *been* chosen. Mating was a rite, a duty. It could be moving; it could be exasperating. It could be frantic. But one was chosen; one did not do his own choosing. Only in adulthood did one have the competence and ability to select the work one was able to pursue with confidence of success. Only in adulthood could one search the whole world for friends like his—Harvey's—friends, Myra and Donald. The computer had been an aid in finding them—but the choice had been his own.

In his euphoria of self-congratulation Harvey Adam forgot the challenge and excitement of a day that had put him off his schedule for a whole hour. He sank into restful, blissful sleep.

To have missed schedule by an hour was an anomaly in his life. A modestly self-acknowledged genius, he prided himself on order as well as achievement. There was a time and a place for everything—for work, for sport, for friends. For calm enjoyment, each had its—his, her—place.

Ordinarily he left the library at five o'clock, stepping from his anachronistic office into the transportation cubicle to which his merit entitled him. In less than a minute he was at the athletic club, delivered directly to the locker room. There he stripped and zipped his spare but handsome body into his clinging sports suit. Cords gathered up and goggles in hand, he went through the door marked skiing. He stepped on the platform, placed his feet in the sockets and touched a button. The rockets gripped his feet and ankles firmly. He plugged in the cords. After a moment's thought, he typed ALTA on the keyboard. He put his hands through the dangling leather loops. Standing upright, knees slightly bent, he pulled the goggles over his noble features.

Simulation was different from communication with another human being. Sight and touch went together. There was no barrier between himself and the world in which he found himself. To all his senses to all at once—Harvey was standing on sun-drenched snow. He looked admiringly down familiar slopes, up at the sparkling mountains, the clear horizon and the deep blue of the cloudless sky. The air was almost still. The dry, new-fallen snow was scarcely touched. He could see two tiny skiers far below, sweeping slowly into and out of sight as they turned and twisted. Grasping the poles that hung from his wrists, he pushed himself forward, enchanted by the effortless glide of the skis on the snow. The cold air blew keenly against his cheeks, contrasting pleasantly with the warmth of the sun. He made a long, swift traverse and, turning in a flurry of powder, was away down a familiar and favorite course.

But many courses are familiar. He could have chosen the narrow, windy, changing trails of Stowe or Sugarbush in the east. He could have skied Zermatt in the Alps—or down the valley under the cable railway spanning the glacier of Mont Blanc—or in the mountains of South America or New Zealand. Tens of skiing sites were stored in the club's computer, complete in every geographical detail, each programmed for a variety of weather and for every possible choice and motion of the skier. Each user had the run to himself, save for distant phantoms who added interest. All depended on skill, on his skill at testing himself against the mountain and the snow. It was not as good as the real thing—it was better.

Once Harvey had gone all the way to Zermatt to make sure, despite the danger of injury in case of a fall. He had had to be fitted with ski boots by a grumpy, substandard human attendant. He had had to lace them up, an onerous and unfamiliar task. A chair lift had taken him uncomfortably to the top of the slope. The weather had been dull, the snow tracked by too many others. The trip had been instructive but the day had been wasted as sport.

So, at five o'clock of every day, Harvey enjoyed better-than-real skiing at the athletic club. Or, for variety, it might be better-than-real surfing on the most magnificent rollers in the world. Or out of it. It might be superb sailing across sparkling seas in an eighteen-footer. Then Harvey sailed against phantom boats with phantom yachtsmen, subject to the same wind and currents. The phantoms sailed as well as a partition of the computer could sail them, not knowing what gusts another partition would subject them to. Sailing is chancy. Harvey frequently beat the phantoms.

Some men played tennis, squash or even soccer against phantom opponents; Harvey regarded this as beneath human dignity. One used machines. One had dealings with people.

But today at five-thirty o'clock, Harvey had not been zipped into his sports suit, experiencing the ski slopes of Alta, or the rollers of Oahu, or sailing off the coast of Maine. He had been at his anachronistic wooden desk in his anachronistic office at the library, holding an anachronistic book in his hand and reading it avidly. The book was *Recognizing Patterns*, edited by P. A. Kolers and M. Eden, MIT Press, 1968. One chapter of the book had put him on a new trail.

Over some hundreds of years, computers had supplied man's goods and implemented man's services with admirable efficiency. They flexibly embodied all man's discoveries and inventions and wholly automated the routines of production and service, including the teaching of such intellectual skills as languages and mathematics. Computers also accumulated, cross-indexed, abstracted and reproduced on demand all of man's recorded knowledge, wisdom, speculations, art and his everything else, with an antlike energy and a pack-rat thoroughness that were less and more than human.

Agronomists, surgeons, physicists continually edited their current files. These were used in the teaching and practicing of their arts. Good or bad, that which was eliminated from the current files was not lost; it was retained in secondary storage, where it was mechanically related to an accumulation of centuries in an increasingly inaccessible jumble of data about what the world was and was not like, about events that had or had not taken place, about men who had or had not lived.

In the age of the flowering of the computer, men had been so relieved, surprised and enchanted with human progress that they took the old for granted while demanding the new. Some successul part of that new was then added to the taken-for-granted old. No one asked when or how the world of now had come to be. The past became buried in a mountain of uncritically accumulated detail. All this was instantly accessible electronically, but it far outweighed human ability to comprehend or verify. It became a junk pile of data, inaccessible to the human mind.

Or was it inaccessible? A few men were interested in that problem. A very few, like Harvey, tried to turn the computer on itself in ferreting out a track through the past. Formidable obstacles lay in the way. Harvey had had to learn how the computers and the machines they controlled really worked. He had traveled strange byways.

Many men could feed new locations or games into the sports simulators. Harvey was one of the very few who really knew how the simulators simulated. He could have programmed into them (as had been done ages ago) the complex shifts of point of view that accompanied a rapid turn or a tumble into the snow. It had been gratifying to him to notice for the first time the slight graininess that accompanied processor overload during such sequences.

Harvey's studies took him to things less familiar than the sports simulators. Behind the electronic records, he had found, were early microfiche cards. These he located in a library building, where he then made his office. After sending little servodriven constructs through passages inaccessible to human beings, he had at last held a microfiche card triumphantly in his hand. Behind microfiche, he had discovered printed books. Those that seemed relevant to the trail he sought now lined the shelves above and beside his desk. His latest find, the Kolers–Eden collaboration, contained a chapter by J. Weizenbaum, called "Contextual Understanding by Computers."

The chapter described a trivial twentieth-century computer program which "conversed" by teletypewriter as unintelligibly as a twentieth-century psychiatrist, giving trite and ambiguous but leading responses to human questions or statements. The program worked through key words and a superficial analysis of punctuation and grammatical structure. All of this was small and dull. But, there were two astonishing and exciting points.

Unexpectedly, many who had participated in the experiment had persisted in believing that there was a human being at the other end of the teletypewriter link, even when told otherwise. The ambiguous responses seemed pertinent. With the conversation went a sense of communion. Whence? Harvey wondered. Self-communion it must have been, born of wish, not fact. But, he reflected, all men were given to self-communion, to recollection, fantasy and imaginary conversations with others. In self-communion, things always turned out the way one wished. Self-communion was empty.

The second, more exciting point was that in that dim and distant day some men had believed that computers could think even as men do. A logician named Turing had put it very well in a paper in a journal called *Mind*. If in conversation you could not distinguish a computer from a human being, could you say that the computer did not think? Harvey had touched the keyboard in inquiry and had found *Mind* hopelessly obscured in lists of references. Tomorrow, he had thought. For he had suddenly realized that he had overstayed his usual time of departure by an hour. He had left directly for his apartment, his mind churning with a new thought, his senses on a new track.

At the beginning of an era, he had reflected, man had misjudged the most powerful force in his hands. Computers as thinking beings, indeed? And men who could not distinguish a machine from another human being? These thoughts, and what part they had or had not played in man's past, had distracted him through an unsatisfactory dinner. Finally his good sense, his value of order, had reasserted itself. Everything to its place. Work and sport. Inquiry and friendship. Too much of one spoiled the other. Harvey had dismissed his speculations and, with familiar and pleasant anticipation, had called Myra and passed the pleasant evening already recounted. At the end of it, he had fallen into blissful sleep. He awoke refreshed and ready to meet the day's new challenge.

Some men work best in the morning, sinking into confused fatigue as the day passes. Others do not really wake up until the evening advances. Harvey despised both failings. He was always ready for the task at hand. He awoke clear-eyed, stepped into the fresher, and emerged clean-bodied. Dressing in the clothing his dispenser provided, eating his usual spare breakfast—these took little time. Shortly he stepped into the transportation cubicle and thence into his office, exactly on schedule.

Harvey faced an untidy desk, but that was soon set in order. With the book in front of him, his fingers on the console, he made and edited a very brief list. Locate the article by Turing. Trace it backward if possible, forward certainly. He pondered a few moments. That was all he could think of as a start.

He located the article in a quarter of an hour and skimmed through it with interest. He admired Turing's examples and thought his exact phrasing of the problem fitting:

> The new form of the problem can be described in terms of a game we call the "imitation game." It is played with three people, a man (A), a woman (B) and an interrogator (C) who may be of either sex. The interrogator stays in a room apart from the other two. The object of the game for the interrogator is to determine which of the other two is the man and which the woman.
>
> We now ask the question, "What will happen when a machine takes the part of A in this game?"

Backward tracing from Turing's paper proved a sterile task. With their mechanical thoroughness of cross-referencing by associated words and descriptors the computers had provided countless trails into the past, all of them false or profitless.

The tracing into the future was bewildering. It led him into a strange field called *artificial intelligence,* an agglomeration of unproductive work in which it was hard to find any unifying or identifying principles except confusion and enthusiasm. Of course, computers could prove theorems—but left to themselves they did not create new mathematics interesting or useful to men. Rather, they endlessly elaborated, as they had in burying man's past in meaningless detail. Computers could play games, could pile up blocks like a child, could perform some recognition tasks.

Harvey already knew this. Those who worked on artificial intelligence must have known it. What they, like their machines, had lacked was human purpose. The sports simulators that he enjoyed, the computers he was using in finding a track through the past, were admirable because man had adapted them to human need, not because they aped nature or human function. Who would admire an airplane that aped a bird, landing in a tree and clinging to a limb? Who would admire a second-rate copy of a human being? Especially when computers could do so many things that unaided man could not do?

In this morass Harvey found little that informed him, but a few things that amused him. One was an actual record of an engineer maliciously badgering Weizenbaum's "doctor" program. The computer wrote in capitals, the man in lowercase letters. Part of the printout ran:

I'M A DOCTOR AND I'D LIKE VERY MUCH TO HELP YOU IF
I CAN. PLEASE TELL ME WHAT YOUR PROBLEM IS
i want to write music
WHAT WOULD IT MEAN TO YOU IF YOU GOT TO WRITE
MUSIC
i would be happy
YOU SAY YOU WOULD BE HAPPY
yes
YOU SEEM QUITE SURE
yes
LET'S CONTINUE
okay, okay
I AM NOT SURE I UNDERSTAND YOU FULLY
i hate my dog
YOUR DOG
he loves somebody else
BUT YOUR DOG
he loves my cat
WHY DO YOU SAY YOUR CAT
my mother loves my cat
TELL ME MORE ABOUT YOUR FAMILY
WHY HAVEN'T YOU SPOKEN ABOUT YOUR FATHER, FOR
EXAMPLE
he's dead
DOES ANY PART OF YOUR BODY HURT YOU
yes . . . my nose
DOES THAT SUGGEST ANYTHING ELSE THAT BELONGS
TO YOU
my ears
IS IT IMPORTANT TO YOU THAT YOUR EARS
you're a stupid doctor
WHAT MAKES YOU THINK I AM A STUPID DOCTOR

you don't know anything
WE WERE DISCUSSING YOU NOT ME
uggle wuggle love you
PERHAPS IN YOUR FANTASY WE LOVE TOGETHER

It was a strange document. Such behavior toward a human being might have indicated grievance or cruelty, Harvey thought—but directed toward whom? At Weizenbaum rather than at the insensate machine? Or, self-directed?

The other thing that amused Harvey he found in a letter on speech recognition, in the *Journal of the Acoustical Society of America*, October, 1969. He read:

> It is reasonable to believe that Turing's game may best be approached with the sort of artful deceit that men use in conversation when they want to hide their ignorance and make the most of their knowledge. It would perhaps be easier for a speaking computer to convince the listener that it was so deep as to be unintelligible, and had a cold or spoke with a Merovingian accent, than it would be for a speaking computer to understand what was said and re-play sensibly in good, lifelike general American.

Harvey sat back and thought. What strange goings-on at the beginning of the computer age. Kepler, he had read, was fascinated by astrology and a sort of numerology; he had believed in an arithmetical order of the solar system and in the music of the spheres. With the future in their hands, these early computer men had turned their gaze—whither?

And yet, he thought, there was an insidious plausibility about this. He himself had been taught many things by computer programs. He still used some occasionally. He had never thought of them as humanlike, but rather, as fascinating mechanical games, with a reward of understanding for success. How easily it might have been otherwise.

When a query went outside the content of a program the machine would respond, for example: "The answer lies in the fields of rings and lattices. If you want instruction, please key

547-3750." But what if the machine had responded: "That was a clever question, Harvey, one that I can't answer. But I have a very good friend who knows, and he would be glad to tell you. Would you like me to introduce you to him?"

That, and some of the features of the sports simulator, might have fooled even me, Harvey thought, when I was a child at least . . .

The day before Harvey had been so absorbed that he had not noticed the passage of time. This afternoon he kept his eye on the clock during musings which had, for some reason, become disturbing to him. He left promptly at five. At the athletic club he skied down the twisting trails at Stowe. The day's speculations recurred to him at inopportune moments and he fell twice, without injury, of course. He would have been infuriated if he allowed himself such an indulgence, but he had to admit to disquiet.

At home, he ate his dinner without the usual enjoyment. When he called his friend Donald he felt that he really needed human companionship. Was he perhaps dependent, he wondered. Did he need more than human companionship? Did he need someone's help?

The very sight of Donald inspired trust. Solid, gray, with a lined but strong face, he was seated in a shapeless but comfortable chair before a wood fire, smoking his briar pipe. Harvey had often wondered whether the fire were real or simulated. Donald had only smiled when he had asked.

The silky black cocker spaniel at Donald's feet stirred uneasily, its right hind leg twitching, then settled again into quiet contentment. Donald turned slowly toward Harvey, took the pipe from his mouth and smiled slightly.

"Smoky has dreams, too, Harvey," he said. "What are your dreams tonight?"

Harvey felt the wonderful calm that Donald's presence always brought. But he still experienced a trace of the undiagnosable unease that his discoveries and reflections had brought him.

"It isn't dreams tonight, Donald," he replied. "It's my work and what I think about it."

Donald nodded seriously and attentively. "Do you want to tell me about your work and your thoughts?" he asked.

Harvey launched into his explanation: Turing's assertion that a machine that could not be distinguished from a human being could not be said to think. The artificial-intelligence cultists who had wanted to use the computer, not for what it was, but to imitate human functions. Weizenbaum's simple-minded computer program that fooled some simpleminded people into believing that they were communicating with a human being. The assertion that Turing's test could be met by clever deceit and fraud rather than by objective performance. How successful a fraud might be if one used today's computers and today's simulation.

Donald listened, attentive and sympathetic, puffing on his pipe, nodding at Harvey's assertions, looking expectant during pauses and urging, "Go on, man," or, "I see," when the pause was long.

Finally Harvey ran down. Like most men who have something to say, he was forced to stop when he had said it. Donald stared at the fire, pulling occasionally at his pipe.

"What do you make of it, Donald?" Harvey demanded impatiently.

Donald looked up.

"Does it bother you, Harvey?" he asked seriously.

"It bothers me very much," Harvey answered almost rudely.

"I can see that it does," Donald said sadly and gravely. "I can see that it does."

Harvey felt contrite. Donald had been his friend, his confessor, his comforter for so long. And now he had troubled Donald.

"What should I do?" he asked.

Donald knocked the dottle from his pipe on the fender.

"You should play a game of chess with me," he said, kindly but decisively.

That was always Donald's remedy, Harvey thought. And a good one, too. It always worked. It a-l-w-a-y-s w-o-r-k-e-d— A horrid thought struck Harvey. Sounds came from his mouth without willing or thinking.

"Bumpfun sun billig fenter bright today."

"It was a fine day, Harvey," Donald said without surprise, pulling his chair around and taking the chessboard and pieces from a drawer in the table beside him.

"Blemp spelkins, morter hark," Harvey announced.

Donald looked up as if he hadn't caught the sense of the words. Harvey remained grimly silent. Donald looked as if he were thinking.

"I wouldn't say that, Harvey," Donald finally asserted, looking troubled.

"Why shouldn't I say it?" Harvey demanded.

"It isn't like you, Harvey," Donald told him.

"Why isn't it like me?" Harvey asked.

"Come on, man, let's start the game," it urged.

The program that is Donald has come to the end of one subroutine, Harvey thought icily, and the best it can do is to try another. Calmly he turned the communicator off while Donald was putting the pieces on the board. Or—while what was happening? Presumably a simple simulator program was generating a new visual aspect of objects whose descriptions were stored in memory.

Harvey's icy, analytical calm persisted for a few minutes more. Was the entire world a toy for his amusement or instruction? No, his childhood peer group had been real enough. He had seen and touched its members without simulator or computer. Ultimately he had lain with some of them. He could almost feel the reality now, the awkward conflict of will and interest; the imperfections in the body of Mary, mother of his last child. Mary of the slightly fallen breasts, hips too broad and knobby knees.

But then, was the communicator a communicator at all or only a simulator that presented what a deluded Harvey really wanted: faint echoes of his thoughts and desires in Donald, the companion in chess. And in Myra—what?

He remembered Mary's number. He keyed it into the communicator. From off-screen he heard a faint: "Damn thing—I thought I'd turned it off."

The voice sounded like Mary's. Mary was the early-awake, early-tired, early-dozing-off kind.

A bleary-eyed woman stumbled naked into sight, squinting with sleepy eyes into the screen. The body was heavier than he remembered Mary's to be, the breasts droopier, the hips wider and the knees the same.

"Harvey," she said, "What on earth are you calling for, damn you?"

Harvey turned off the communicator. He had seen all he needed to see and heard all he needed to hear. That was Mary. How well he knew her. Unreal as Donald might be, the communicator *was* a communicator. With a growing hope, he keyed Myra's number, Myra whom he had chosen, Myra whom he had grown to love. On whom he—depended even more than on Donald.

And he saw Myra sitting on the deep-pile rug, her legs folded over one another. A scissors and nail file lay beside her. She held her left foot in her right hand and was examining it intently. The graceful curve of her back and neck were perfection. She looked up and smiled.

"Hello, Harvey," she said and started to rise. As she leaned over slightly, he could see perfect breasts through the low-cut neck of her gown. He spoke in cold despair.

"Uggle wuggle love you," he asserted.

Myra's eyes grew misty and she smiled tremulously.

"And I love you, too, Harvey," she said. "We love together."

Harvey turned off the communicator.

Isaac Asimov

Born in Petrovichi, U.S.S.R., Isaac Asimov (1920–   )
was brought to the United States in 1923 and became a
naturalized citizen in 1928.

After receiving a B.S. (1939) and M.A. (1941) from Columbia University, he spent the bulk of the war years (1942–
1945) as a research chemist at the U.S. Navy Air Experimental Station in Philadelphia. Returning to Columbia, he
completed his Ph.D. in chemistry in 1948, then taught
biochemistry at Boston University's School of Medicine
(where he is still listed as a professor), becoming a full-time
writer in 1958.

Perhaps the world's greatest explainer of science, he has
written more than three hundred books on subjects as
diverse as chemistry, biology, physics, mathematics, astronomy, earth sciences, general science, history, literary
studies, humor, mysteries, and of course, science fiction.
For his efforts he has received numerous awards, such as the
James T. Grady Award from the American Chemical Society (1965), the American Association for the Advancement
of Science Westinghouse Award for science writing (1967),
the Hugo Award (1963, 1966, 1973, 1977, 1983) and the
Nebula Award (1972, 1976).

The following story, a tough look at overpopulation, il-
lustrates Asimov's ability to sandwich in message as well
as entertainment.

THE WINNOWING

by Isaac Asimov

F IVE YEARS HAD passed since the steadily thickening wall of
secrecy had been clamped down about the work of Dr.
Aaron Rodman.

"For your own protection—" they had warned him.

"In the hands of the wrong people—" they had explained.

In the right hands, of course (his own, for instance, Dr. Rodman thought rather despairingly), the discovery was clearly the
greatest boon to human health since Pasteur's working out of
the germ theory, and the greatest key to the understanding of
the mechanism of life, ever.

Yet, after his talk at the New York Academy of Medicine
soon after his fiftieth birthday, and on the first day of
the twenty-first century (there had been a certain fitness to
that) the silence had been imposed, and he could talk no
more, except to certain officials. He certainly could not
publish.

The government supported him, however. He had all the money he needed, and the computers were his to do with as he wished. His work advanced rapidly and government men came to him to be instructed, to be made to understand.

"Dr. Rodman," they would ask, "how can a virus be spread from cell to cell within an organism and yet not be infectious from one organism to the next?"

It wearied Rodman to have to say over and over that he did not have all the answers. It wearied him to have to use the term "virus." He said, "It's not a virus because it isn't a nucleic acid molecule. It is something else altogether—a lipoprotein."

It was better when his questioners were not themselves medical men. He could then try to explain in generalities instead of forever bogging down on the fine points. He would say, "Every living cell, and every small structure within the cell is surrounded by a membrane. The workings of each cell depend on what molecules can pass through the membrane in either direction and at what rates. A slight change in the membrane will alter the nature of the flow enormously, and with that, the nature of the cell chemistry and the nature of its activity.

"All disease may rest on alterations in membrane activity. All mutations may be carried through by way of such alterations. Any technique that controls the membranes controls life. Hormones control the body by their effect on membranes and my lipoprotein is an artificial hormone rather than a virus. The LP incorporates itself into the membrane and in the process induces the manufacture of more molecules like itself—and that's the part I don't understand myself.

"But the fine structures of the membranes are not quite identical everywhere. They are, in fact, different in all living things—not quite the same in any two organisms. An LP will affect no two individual organisms alike. What will open the cells of one organism to glucose and relieve the effects of diabetes, will close the cells of another organism to lysine and kill it."

That was what seemed to interest them most; that it was a poison.

"A selective poison," Rodman would say. "You couldn't tell, in advance, without the closest computer-aided studies of the membrane biochemistry of a particular individual, what a particular LP would do to him."

With time, the noose grew tighter around him, inhibiting his freedom, yet leaving him comfortable—in a world in which freedom and comfort alike were vanishing everywhere, and the jaws of hell were opening before a despairing humanity.

It was 2005 and Earth's population was six billion. But for the famines it would have been seven billion. A billion human beings had starved in the past generation, and more would yet starve.

Peter Affare, chairman of the World Food Organization, came frequently to Rodman's laboratories for chess and conversation. It was he, he said, who had first grasped the significance of Rodman's talk at the academy; and that had helped make him chairman. Rodman thought the significance was easy to grasp, but said nothing about that.

Affare was ten years younger than Rodman, and the red was darkening out of his hair. He smiled frequently although the subject of the conversation rarely gave cause for smiling, since any chairman of an organization dealing with world food was bound to talk about world famine.

Affare said, "If the food supply were evenly distributed among all the world's inhabitants, all would starve to death."

"If it were evenly distributed," said Rodman, "the example of justice in the world might lead at last to a sane world policy. As it is, there is world despair and fury over the selfish fortune of a few, and all behave irrationally in revenge."

"You do not volunteer to give up your own oversupply of food," said Affare.

"I am human and selfish, and my own action would mean little. I should not be asked to volunteer. I should be given no choice in the matter."

"You are a romantic," said Affare. "Do you fail to see that the Earth is a lifeboat? If the food store is divided equally among all, then all will die. If some are cast out of the lifeboat, the remainder will survive. The question is not whether some will die, for some *must* die; the question is whether some will live."

"Are you advocating triage—this sacrifice of some for the rest—officially?"

"We can't. The people in the lifeboat are armed. Several regions threaten openly to use nuclear weapons if more food is not forthcoming."

Rodman said, sardonically, "You mean the answer to 'You die that I may live' is 'If I die, you die'—an impasse?"

"Not quite," said Affare. "There are places on Earth where the people cannot be saved. They have overweighted their land hopelessly with hordes of starving humanity. Suppose they are sent food, and suppose the food kills them so that the land requires no further shipments."

Rodman felt the first twinge of realization. "Kills them how?" he asked.

"The average structural properties of the cellular membranes of a particular population can be worked out. An LP particularly designed to take advantage of those properties could be incorporated into the food supply, which would then be fatal," said Affare.

"Unthinkable," said Rodman, astounded.

"Think again. There would be no pain. The membranes would slowly close off and the affected person would fall asleep and not wake up—an infinitely better death than that of starvation which is otherwise inevitable—or nuclear annihilation. Nor would it be for everyone, for any population varies in its membranal properties. At worst, seventy percent will die. The winnowing out will be done precisely where overpopulation and hopelessness is worst and enough will be left to preserve each nation, each ethnic group, each culture."

"To deliberately kill billions—"

"We would not be killing. We would merely supply the opportunity for people to die. Which particular individuals would die would depend on the particular biochemistry of those individuals. It would be the finger of God."

"And when the world discovers what has been done?"

"That will be after our time," said Affare. "And by then, a flourishing world with limited population will thank us for our heroic action in choosing the death of some to avoid the death of all."

Dr. Rodman felt himself flushing, and found he had difficulty speaking. "The Earth," he said, "is a large and very complex

213

lifeboat. We still do not know what can or can't be done with a proper distribution of resources and it is notorious that to this very day we have not really made an effort to distribute them. In many places on Earth, food is wasted daily, and it is that knowledge that drives hungry men mad."

"I agree with you," said Affare, coolly, "but we cannot have the world as we want it to be. We must deal with it as it is."

"Then deal with me as I am. You will want me to supply the necessary LP molecules—and I will not do so. I will not lift a finger in that direction."

"Then," said Affare, "you will be a greater mass-murderer than you are accusing me of being. And I think you will change your mind when you have thought it through."

He was visited nearly daily, by one official or another, all of them well fed. Rodman was becoming very sensitive to the way in which all those who discussed the need for killing the hungry were themselves well fed.

The national secretary of agriculture said to him, insinuatingly, on one of these occasions, "Would you not favor killing a herd of cattle infected with hoof-and-mouth disease or with anthrax in order to avoid the spread of infection to healthy herds?"

"Human beings are not cattle," said Rodman, "and famine is not contagious."

"But it is," said the secretary. "That is precisely the point. If we don't winnow the overcrowded masses of humanity, their famine will spread to as-yet-unaffected areas. You must not refuse to help us."

"How can you make me? Torture?"

"We wouldn't harm a hair on your body. Your skill in this matter is too precious to us. Food stamps can be withdrawn, however."

"Starvation would harm me, surely."

"Not you. But if we are prepared to kill several billion people for the sake of the human race, then surely we are ready for the much less difficult task of withdrawing food stamps from your daughter, her husband and her baby."

Rodman was silent, and the secretary said, "We'll give you

time to think. We don't want to take action against your family, but we will if we have to. Take a week to think about it and next Thursday, the entire committee will be on hand. You will then be committed to our project and there must be no further delay."

Security was redoubled and Rodman was openly and completely a prisoner. A week later, all fifteen members of the World Food Council, together with the national secretary of agriculture and a few members of the National Legislature arrived at his laboratory. They sat about the long table in the conference room of the lavish research building that had been built out of public funds.

For hours they talked and planned, incorporating those answers that Rodman gave to specific questions. No one asked Rodman if he would cooperate; there seemed no thought that he could do anything else.

Finally, Rodman said, "Your project cannot, in any case, work. Shortly after a shipment of grain arrives in some particular region of the world, people will die by the hundreds of millions. Do you suppose those who survive will not make the connection and that you will not risk the desperate retaliation of nuclear bombs?"

Affare, who sat directly opposite Rodman, across the short axis of the table, said, "We are aware of that possibility. Do you think we have spent years determining a course of action and have not considered the possible reaction of those regions chosen for winnowing."

"Do you expect them to be thankful?" asked Rodman, bitterly.

"They will not know they are being singled out. Not all shipments of grain will be LP-infected. No one place will be concentrated on. We will see to it that locally-grown grain supplies are infected here and there. In addition, not everyone will die and only a few will die at once. Some who eat much of the grain will not die at all, and some who eat only a small amount, will die quickly—depending on their membranes. It will seem like a plague, like the Black Death returned."

Rodman said, "Have you thought of the effect of the Black Death returned? Have you thought of the panic?"

"It will do them good," growled the secretary from one end of the table. "It might teach them a lesson."

"We will announce the discovery of an antitoxin," said Affare, shrugging. "There will be wholesale inoculations in regions we know will not be affected. Dr. Rodman, the world is desperately ill, and must have a desperate remedy. Mankind is on the brink of a horrible death, so please do not quarrel with the only course that can save it."

"That's the point. *Is* it the only course or are you just taking an easy way out that will not ask any sacrifices of you—merely of billions of others?"

Rodman broke off as a food trolley was brought in. He muttered, "I have arranged for some refreshments. May we have a few moments of truce while we eat?"

He reached for a sandwich and then, after a while, said between sips of coffee, "We eat well, at least, as we discuss the greatest mass-murder in history."

Affare looked critically at his own half-eaten sandwich. "This is not eating *well*. Egg salad on white bread of indifferent freshness is not eating well, and I would change whatever coffee shop supplied this, if I were you." He sighed, "Well, in a world of famine, one should not waste food," and he finished.

Rodman watched the others and then reached for the last remaining sandwich on the tray. "I thought," he said, "that perhaps some of you might suffer a loss of appetite in view of the subject matter of discussion, but I see none of you did. Each one of you has eaten."

"As did you," said Affare, impatiently. "You are still eating."

"Yes, I am," said Rodman, chewing slowly. "And I apologize for the lack of freshness in the bread. I made the sandwiches myself last night and they are fifteen hours old."

"You made them yourself?" said Affare.

"I had to, since I could in no other way be certain of introducing the proper LP."

"What are you talking about?"

"Gentlemen, you tell me it is necessary to kill some to save others. Perhaps you are right. You have convinced me. But in order to know exactly what it is we are doing we should perhaps experience it ourselves. I have engaged in a little triage on my own, and the sandwiches you have all just eaten are an experiment in that direction."

Some of the officials were rising to their feet. "We're poisoned?" gasped the secretary.

Rodman said, "Not very effectively. Unfortunately, I don't know your biochemistries thoroughly so I can't guarantee the seventy percent death rate you would like."

They were staring at him in frozen horror, and Dr. Rodman's eyelids drooped. "Still it's likely that two or three of you will die within the next week or so, and you need only wait to see who it will be. There's no cure or antidote but don't worry. It's quite a painless death, and it will be the finger of God, as one of you told me. It's a good lesson, as another of you said. For those of you who survive, there may be new views on triage."

Affare said, "This is a bluff. You've eaten the sandwiches yourself."

Rodman said, "I know. I matched the LP to my own biochemistry so I will go fast." His eyes closed. "You'll have to carry on without me—those of you who survive."

Larry Eisenberg

Larry Eisenberg (1919–   ) was born in New York City and has spent almost all of his life there.

He received a B.E.E. (electrical engineering) from the College of the City of New York in 1944, then after military service in the U.S. Air Force returned to school at the Polytechnic Institute of Brooklyn to obtain an M.E.E. in 1952 and a Ph.D. in biomedical electronics in 1966. Part of this last work involved the construction of a special purpose computer to enable neurophysiologists to measure the absolute thresholds of neurons.

In 1958 Rockefeller University offered him a job as an assistant professor of electronics. By the time of his retirement in 1984, he had become head of the electronic and microprocessor laboratory, and even today remains affiliated with Rockefeller University as adjunct professor.

The author of some twenty-five research papers, he is perhaps most noted for having designed the first totally implanted cardiac pacemaker, a modification of which is currently being used in pain suppression research.

He has written more than one hundred short science fiction stories and expects that his first novel, *The Conquerors*, will soon be completed. Like the story below, much of his work is set in futuristic academic environments and filled with infectious humor.

DR. SNOW MAIDEN

by *Larry Eisenberg*

I CAN STILL recall most vividly the first time I saw her. We were all in the faculty dining room, an oak-paneled vault replete with oil portraits of the academic dead, where luncheons were served to the accompaniment of hushed voices. The same five or six of us tended to meet daily at the same table, chaps who were involved in tracing out the diverse networks of the central nervous system.

She appeared in the doorway, and I can't say that her loveliness hit me like the opening of a Bach toccata and fugue. Still, she was strikingly beautiful. Her smile was as cool and noncommittal as that of a psychiatrist's receptionist. The soft cheeks were round and plump, the forehead smooth, the eyebrows very dark, the eyes a bright china blue, and absolutely no makeup at all.

"Don't be obvious about it," I said, poking Sam Danby, who sat at my immediate right. "Doesn't that girl in the doorway have an unusually pretty face?"

Sam stole a look and blushed. I wondered why. But then I saw that she was coming directly to our table, directly that is to the one vacant seat, which was at my left. She sat down and flashed a five-second smile at the group.

"Do you gentlemen mind if I join you?"

"Not at all," I said.

I went about the table and made the introductions.

"I'm Marilyn Ross," she said by way of acknowledgment. "I'm a postdoc in genetics in the lab of Professor Heminway."

"You're very lucky," I said. "Heminway is not only a great scientist, but he's got the most marvelous sense of humor."

It was Heminway, a Nobel laureate, who had arranged with our instrument makers to fashion a replica of his gold medal with a nail welded to the bottom. Just prior to a faculty-student ball, he had nailed this pseudomedal to the floor and then watched President Hinkle struggle to lift it from the highly polished floor.

I tried to involve our guest in conversation, but she answered monosyllabically. After a bit, all of us resumed our in-group dialogue. There was a brief scratching of a chair later on, and when I looked about, she was gone.

"Not very friendly, is she?" asked Danby.

"I suppose she's shy. It's not easy to join a table of total strangers."

I'd forgotten about her when, one day, as I descended to the fourth-sublevel floor of the university library, I almost stumbled over a dark mass in an unlit recess of the stacks. There was a scraping of feet, and then the mass turned into two people. One was Tom Shelby, a mustachioed student who was darkly handsome; the other was Marilyn Ross.

I reached out blindly and took a book from the shelves, any book. There was dust on the binding. I felt a hand on my wrist and half turned.

"Hello," she said.

Tom Shelby had gone.

"Hello," I replied, happy that the lights were off because I could feel the flush that had radiated upward from my neck to my ears.

"How's your work going?" she asked.

"Well," I mumbled. "And yours?"

"I'm doing exciting things," she said. "You must come and visit me one time."

"I'll do that," I said.

I didn't tell anyone of what I had seen. Ordinarily I'm not that close-mouthed and I've done my share of gossiping. But I didn't want to mention this episode. In some way that I couldn't fathom, it had upset me.

The shock wore off fairly rapidly. I was immersed in preparing a seminar on some work I had done on snail brain. There were over twenty people at my seminar, an unusually large turnout, and Marilyn was one of them. She came in to the lecture hall halfway through my talk but stayed afterward.

"That was fascinating," she said. "I admire the kind of skills you needed to dissect your preparation."

"It was hard to do," I acknowledged, flattered that she had stayed to talk to me.

"I think you'd admire my work, too," she said. "If you have time, why not come by tomorrow."

"I'd be delighted to."

Actually I had arranged to meet with the budget director to talk over my next year's budget. But I put that off to visit with Marilyn. And she was right. Her skills were fascinating.

"Most of my work is with fruit flies," she said. "*Drosophila melanogaster.*"

I smiled.

"I'd hate to do anatomical work with those tiny fellows."

"But that's just the point," she said. "Watch this."

She had deftly fixed one of the flies to her dissecting board and flipped her scalpel.

"You've just witnessed a total hysterectomy," she said.

"Fantastic," I admitted. "What's more, your patient seems to be up and about."

The amazing thing was that the fly had darted off upon its release and seemd to show no ill effects.

Marilyn seemed quite pleased at my remarks. She even smiled one of her rare smiles.

"It's nice to be appreciated by one's peers," she said. "You see, I'm searching for agents that will sterilize these flies, *naturally.*"

"Something besides radiation, I take it?"

"Exactly. It could make my fortune."

I was puzzled.

"Fortune?"

"There's a bushel of money waiting for the scientist who can wipe out flies and other pestilential insects. You have no idea of how much money."

I shrugged.

"I didn't expect you to be focused on money. After all, why go into research if it's wealth that you want?"

"I like both," said Marilyn.

I thought about her remarks, after, and decided that we were poles apart in our values. I would keep away from Marilyn Ross thereafter. Occasionally we passed in the hallways. I'd usually nod and sometimes she acknowledged it. She ignored my colleagues totally. Danby was quite angered at her snubs.

"She's a distant bitch, isn't she?" he remarked one day.

"Not really," I said. "I think she's just totally involved in her work."

"*Too* involved," said Danby. "There's nothing of the woman about her. Dr. Snow Maiden, if you ask me."

"Dr. Snow Maiden?"

I shook my head ruefully, remembering that day in the library stacks.

"You may be wrong," I said.

"I doubt it," said Danby.

She stopped me one afternoon.

"Would you like to see something really exciting?" she asked.

"Well, I don't know. I was just about to begin a critical experiment."

"Let it wait for ten minutes," she said. "I think you'll find it worthwhile."

I went with her to her laboratory. She picked out a fruit fly and fixed it to her dissecting stand with a bit of gel.

"Another female?" I asked.

"No," she said, frowning in concentration. "This one is male."

Her scalpel flashed.

"I've got his testes, now," she said.

I felt little beads of sweat pop out on my brow. Why had she dragged me over to witness this castration?

She took her sample over to a microtome and sliced several sections, which she stained and mounted for viewing. Later, we examined them under an electron microscope.

"Do you see those darker bodies?" she asked. "It's a virus I introduced into the fly's circulatory system."

"What of it?"

"Don't you see?" she cried, exultant. "It went right to the testes of the fly. The virus goes to a *specific* location!"

"That's all very interesting. But after it gets there, what happens?"

Her fingers began to tremble as she turned away from the microscope. She looked at me and the dark eyebrows arched.

"It doesn't do a thing to the female, but it does make the male fly sterile," she said.

"Indeed," I said. "That is a great discovery."

The funny thing was that I didn't really feel that way at all. My sympathies lay with the goddamned fly, although I knew that the identification was ridiculous.

I laughed to relieve the tension.

"I hope you haven't found a similar virus for men," I said in a bantering tone.

She meditated for a moment.

"Don't you think it's possible?"

"My God!" I cried. "Have you made headway in *that* direction, too?"

She smiled.

"Not yet, but I have some ideas."

"Well, anyway," I said, "this all calls for a celebration. May I buy you a drink?"

She shrugged and went back to the eyepiece of the microscope.

"Why not?" she asked. "I'll meet you at the faculty bar at six."

She was prompt. She also put away five stiff drinks as though they were water.

"You were impressed this afternoon, weren't you?" she asked.

"And also puzzled. I can understand your pursuit of the virus for the fruit fly. But why for men? Is there any glory in it, or money?"

"All of the birth control devices you see about relate to women. And all of them have their dangers. I think it's time to put the shoe on the other foot."

"Maybe so. What does Professor Heminway think about all of this?"

"I haven't told him yet. I don't want to jolt him off his male pedestal."

"Are you implying that he's biased?"

"Don't you think he is?"

I ordered another round of drinks.

"I don't think so," I said after fishing out my olive and munching on it. "I know that there's some discrimination against women at the university, but I don't support it."

"*Some* discrimination? Only one woman appointed as full professor and she's an emeritus? And have you compared our salary levels to those of the men? It's sickening."

"I agree. I've heard senior faculty people maintain that women are not primarily focused on science but on a husband and children. They use that pretext to deny women tenured positions. But I think that Heminway will be genuinely pleased by your discovery."

"Were you?"

I was jolted by the unexpectedness of the question.

"Well, I don't know. But really, it's not because you're a woman. I just feel some kind of personal upset over what took place. An idiosyncrasy of mine."

"The hysterectomy didn't bother you, did it?"

"No," I admitted.

Before we left the bar, I had begun to feel the effects of the liquor. Marilyn seemed her usual self. But there was one striking exception. She asked me if I would like to see her room.

"Where is it?" I asked.

"In the student dormitory," she said. "But it's quite private."

I sought her out the following afternoon, but she was distant again, even cold.

"I'm too busy," she said.

I was hurt and I suppose my face showed it as I turned away. But she didn't seem to care. Still, when I came out of my laboratory at six to have a look into my files, she was sitting at my desk. I walked past her and pulled out one of the file drawers.

"You're angry at me," she said.

"Shouldn't I be?"

"You make too much out of a single night," she said.

I looked away.

"You know," she said, "before I knew you better, I thought of you as stodgy and Victorian."

"And now?"

"Now I'm certain that you're stodgy and Victorian."

"It's an accurate appraisal," I admitted. "My reading ended with Tennyson's *Idylls of the King.*"

"Probably true," she said. "You're an incurable romantic. But I didn't come here to exchange boy-girl banter with you. I wanted to tell you something really important."

I winced.

"Go ahead," I said. "What do you want to say?"

"That you were right yesterday. I lied to you. I think I've already isolated the viral agent that sterilizes men."

I felt my jaw sagging.

"That isn't what I expected to hear. Yesterday you demonstrated your discovery on a fly. Today, you announce you may have its human counterpart."

"I could have told you yesterday," she said. "But I thought it

226

might be more expedient to wait. You see, even now I still don't know if it works."

"I appreciate your consideration," I said. Then I drew a deep breath. "Now tell me how it is transmitted."

"Through the female," she said.

She was smiling at me. I can still remember that smile because it was only an instant later that I hit her.

J. F. Bone

The son of a U. S. Senator, J(esse) F. Bone (1916–   ) was born in Tacoma, Washington.

He received a B.A. degree from Washington State University (1937); then after serving as an officer in the Pacific theater during World War II, returned to complete a B.S. degree in 1949 and a D.V.M. in 1950.

Hired in 1950 as an instructor of veterinary medicine at Oregon State University, he picked up an M.S. from that school in 1953 and gradually worked his way up to full professor, a position he has held since 1965.

A very active professional, he is a member of the American Veterinary Medical Association, the American Association for Laboratory Animal Science, the Royal Society of Health and the American College of Veterinary Toxicologists. A columnist for, and editor of, Modern Veterinary Practice, he has also prepared numerous papers and texts on the subject, such as *Canine Medicine* (1959), *Animal Anatomy and Physiology* (1961) and *Equine Medicine and Surgery* (1963).

His honors include Washington State University's Veterinarian of the Year Award (1959) and Fulbright lectureships to Egypt (1965–1966) and Kenya (1980–1981).

Though the following tale of alien life is just one of more than thirty-five science fiction stories and novels he has written, it may be his most charming and successful.

ON THE FOURTH PLANET

by J. F. Bone

THE UL KWORN paused in his search for food, extended his eye and considered the thing that blocked his path.

He hadn't noticed the obstacle until he had almost touched it. His attention had been focused upon gleaning every feeder large enough to be edible from the lichens that covered his feeding strip. But the unexpected warmth radiating from the object had startled him. Sundown was at hand. There should be nothing living or nonliving that radiated a fraction of the heat that was coming from the gleaming metal wall which lay before him. He expanded his mantle to trap the warmth as he pushed his eye upward to look over the top. It wasn't high, just high enough to be a nuisance. It curved away from him toward the boundaries of his strip, extending completely across the width of his land.

A dim racial memory told him that this was an artifact, a product of the days when the Folk had leisure to dream and time to build. It had probably been built by his remote ancestors millennia ago and had just recently been uncovered from its hiding place beneath the sand. These metal objects kept appearing and disappearing as the sands shifted to the force of the wind. He had seen them before, but never a piece so large or so well preserved. It shone as though it had been made yesterday, gleaming with a soft silvery luster against the blue-black darkness of the sky.

As his eye cleared the top of the wall, he quivered with shock and astonishment. For it was not a wall as he had thought. Instead, it was the edge of a huge metal disk fifty raads in diameter. And that wasn't all of it. Three thick columns of metal extended upward from the disk, leaning inward as they rose into the sky. High overhead, almost beyond the range of accurate vision, they converged to support an immense cylinder set vertically to the ground. The cylinder was almost as great in diameter as the disk upon which his eye first rested. It loomed overhead, and he had a queasy feeling that it was about to fall and crush him. Strange jointed excrescences studded its surface, and in its side, some two thirds of the way up, two smaller cylinders projected from the bigger one. They were set a little distance apart, divided by a vertical row of four black designs, and pointed straight down his feeding strip.

The Ul Kworn eyed the giant structure with disgust and puzzlement. The storm that had uncovered it must have been a great one to have blown so much sand away. It was just his fortune to have the thing squatting in his path! His mantle darkened with anger. Why was it that everything happened to him? Why couldn't it have lain in someone else's way, upon the land of one of his neighbors? It blocked him from nearly three thousand square raads of life-sustaining soil. To cross it would require energy he could not spare. Why couldn't it have been on the Ul Caada's or the Ul Varsi's strip—or any other of the numberless Folk? Why did he have to be faced with this roadblock?

He couldn't go around it since it extended beyond his territory and, therefore, he'd have to waste precious energy propelling his mass up the wall and across the smooth shining surface of the disk—all of which would have to be done without food, since his eye could see no lichen growing upon the shiny metal surface.

The chill of evening had settled on the land. Most of the Folk were already wrapped in their mantles, conserving their energy until the dawn would warm them into life. But Kworn felt no need to estivate. It was warm enough beside the wall.

The air shimmered as it cooled. Microcrystals of ice formed upon the legs of the structure, outlining them in shimmering contrast to the drab shadowy landscape, with its gray-green cover of lichens stippled with the purple balls of the lichen feeders that clung to them. Beyond Kworn and his neighbors, spaced twenty raads apart, the mantled bodies of the Folk stretched in a long single line acros the rolling landscape, vanishing into the darkness. Behind this line, a day's travel to the rear, another line of the Folk was following. Behind them was yet another. There were none ahead, for the Ul Kworn and the other Ul were the elders of the Folk and moved along in the first rank where their maturity and ability to reproduce had placed them according to the Law.

Caada and Varsi stirred restlessly, stimulated to movement by the heat radiating from the obstacle, but compelled by the Law to hold their place in the ranks until the sun's return would stimulate the others. Their dark crimson mantles rippled over the soil as they sent restless pseudopods to the boundaries of their strips.

They were anxious in their attempt to communicate with the Ul Kworn.

But Kworn wasn't ready to communicate. He held aloof as he sent a thin pseudopod out toward the gleaming wall in front of him. He was squandering energy; but he reasoned that he had better learn all he could about this thing before he attempted to cross it tomorrow, regardless of what it cost.

It was obvious that he would have to cross it, for the Law was specific about encroachment upon a neighbor's territory. *No member of the Folk shall trespass the feeding land of another during the Time of Travel except with published permission. Trespass shall be punished by the ejection of the offender from his place in rank.*

And that was equivalent to a death sentence.

He could ask Caada or Varsi for permission, but he was virtually certain that he wouldn't get it. He wasn't on particularly good terms with his neighbors. Caada was querulous, old and selfish. He had not reproduced this season and his vitality was low. He was forever hungry and not averse to slipping a sly pseudopod across the boundaries of his land to poach upon that of his neighbor. Kworn had warned him some time ago that he would not tolerate encroachment and would call for a group judgment if there was any poaching. And since the Folk were physically incapable of lying to one another, Caada would be banished. After that Caada kept his peace, but his dislike for Kworn was always evident.

But Varsi, who held the land on Kworn's right, was worse. He had advanced to Ul status only a year ago. At that time there had been rumors among the Folk about illicit feeding and stealing of germ plasm from the smaller and weaker members of the race. But that could not be proved, and many young Folk died in the grim process of growing to maturity. Kworn shrugged. If Varsi was an example of the younger generation, society was heading hell-bent toward Emptiness. He had no love for the pushing, aggressive youngster who crowded out to the very borders of his domain, pressing against his neighbors, alert and aggressive toward the slightest accidental spillover into his territory. What was worse, Varsi had reproduced successfully this year and thus had rejuvenated. Kworn's own attempt had been only partially successful. His energy reserves hadn't been great enough to produce a viable offspring, and the rejuvenation process in his body had only gone to partial completion. It would be enough to get him to the winter feeding grounds. But as insurance he had taken a place beside Caada, who was certain to go into Emptiness if the feeding en route was bad.

Still, he hadn't figured that he would have Varsi beside him.

He consoled himself with the thought that others might have as bad neighbors as he. But he would never make the ultimate mistake of exchanging germ plasm with either of his neighbors, not even if his fertility and his position depended on it. Cells like theirs would do nothing to improve the sense of discipline and order he had so carefully developed in his own. His offspring were courteous and honorable, a credit to the Folk and to the name of Kworn. A father should be proud of his offspring, so that when they developed to the point where they could have descendants, he would not be ashamed of what they would produce. An Ul, Kworn thought grimly, should have some sense of responsibility toward the all-important future of the race.

His anger died as he exerted synergic control. Anger was a waster of energy, a luxury he couldn't afford. He had little enough as it was. It had been a bad year. Spring was late, and winter had come early. The summer had been dry and the lichens in the feeding grounds had grown poorly. The tiny, bulbous lichen feeders, the main source of food for the Folk, had failed to ripen to their usual succulent fullness. They had been poor, shrunken things, hardly worth ingesting. And those along the route to the winter feeding grounds were no better.

Glumly he touched the wall before him with a tactile filament. It was uncomfortably warm, smooth and slippery to the touch. He felt it delicately, noting the almost microscopic horizontal ridges on the wall's surface. He palpated with relief. The thing was climbable. But even as he relaxed, he recoiled, the filament writhing in agony! The wall had burned his flesh! Faint threads of vapor rose from where he had touched the metal, freezing instantly in the chill air. He pinched off the filament in an automatic protective constriction of his cells. The pain ceased instantly but the burning memory was so poignant that his mantle twitched and shuddered convulsively for some time before the reflexes died.

Thoughtfully he ingested his severed member. With a sense of numbing shock he realized that he would be unable to pass across the disk. The implications chilled him. If he could not pass, his land beyond the roadblock would be vacant and open to preemption by his neighbors. Nor could he wait until they had passed and rejoin them later. The Law was specific on that point. *If one of the Folk lags behind in his rank, his land becomes vacant and open to his neighbors. Nor can one who has lagged behind reclaim his land by moving forward. He who abandons his position, abandons it permanently.*

Wryly, he reflected that it was this very Law that had impelled him to take a position beside the Ul Caada. And, of course, his neighbors knew the Law as well as he. It was a part of them, a part of their cells even before they split off from their parent. It would be the acme of folly to expect that neighbors like Varsi or Caada would allow him to pass over their land and hold his place in rank.

Bitterness flooded him with a stimulation so piercing that Caada extended a communication filament to project a question. "What is this thing which lies upon your land and mine?" Caada asked. His projection was weak and feeble. It was obvious that he would not last for many more days unless feeding improved.

"I do not know. It is something of metal, and it bars my land. I cannot cross it. It burns me when I touch it."

A quick twinge of excitement rushed along Caada's filament. The old Ul broke the connection instantly, but not before Kworn read the flash of hope that Kworn had kindled. There was no help in this quarter, and the wild greed of Varsi was so well known that there was no sense even trying that side.

A surge of hopelessness swept through him. Unless he could find some way to pass this barrier he was doomed.

He didn't want to pass into Emptiness. He had seen too many others go that way to want to follow them. For a moment he thought desperately of begging Caada and Varsi for permission to cross into their land for the short time that would be necessary to pass the barrier, but reason asserted itself. Such an act was certain to draw a flat refusal and, after all, he was the Ul Kworn and he had his pride. He would not beg when begging was useless.

And there was a bare possibility that he might survive if he closed his mantle tightly about him and waited until all the ranks had passed. He could then bring up the rear ... and, possibly, just possibly, there would be sufficient food left to enable him to reach the winter feeding grounds.

And it might still be possible to cross the disk. There was enough warmth in it to keep him active. By working all night he might be able to build a path of sand across its surface and thus keep his tissues from being seared by the metal. He would be technically violating the law by moving ahead of the others, but if he did not feed ahead, no harm would be done.

He moved closer to the barrier and began to pile sand against its base, sloping it to make a broad ramp to the top of the disk. The work was slow and the sand was slippery. The polished grains slipped away and the ramp crumbled time after time. But he worked on, piling up sand until it reached the top of the disk. He looked across the flat surface that stretched before him.

Fifty raads!

It might as well be fifty zets. He couldn't do it. Already his energy level was so low that he could hardly move, and to build a raad-wide path across this expanse of metal was a task beyond his strength. He drooped across the ramp, utterly exhausted. It was no use. What he ought to do was open his mantle to Emptiness.

He hadn't felt the communication filaments of Caada and Varsi touch him. He had been too busy, but now with Caada's burst of glee, and Varsi's cynical, "A noble decision, Ul Kworn. You should be commended," he realized that they knew everything.

His body rippled hopelessly. He was tired, too tired for anger. His energy was low. He contemplated Emptinesss impassively. Sooner or later it came to all Folk. He had lived longer than most, and perhaps it was his time to go. He was finished. He accepted the fact with a cold fatalism that he never dreamed he possessed. Lying there on the sand, his mantle spread wide, he waited for the end to come.

It wouldn't come quickly, he thought. He was still far from the cellular disorganization that preceded extinction. He was merely exhausted, and in need of food to restore his energy.

With food he might still have an outside chance of building the path in time. But there was no food. He had gleaned his area completely before he had ever reached the roadblock.

Lying limp and relaxed on the ramp beside the barrier, he slowly became conscious that the metal wasn't dead. It was alive! Rhythmic vibrations passed through it and were transmitted to his body by the sand.

A wild hope stirred within him. If the metal were alive it might hear him if he tried to communicate. He concentrated his remaining reserves of energy, steeled himself against the pain and pressed a communication filament against the metal.

"Help me!" he projected desperately. "You're blocking my strip! I can't pass!"

Off to one side he sensed Varsi's laughter and on the other felt Caada's gloating greed.

"I cannot wake this metal," he thought hopelessly as he tried again, harder than before, ignoring the pain of his burning flesh.

Something clicked sharply within the metal, and the tempo of the sounds changed.

"It's waking!" Kworn thought wildly.

There was a creaking noise from above. A rod moved out from the cylinder and twisted into the ground in Varsi's territory, to the accompaniment of clicking, grinding noises. A square grid lifted from the top of the cylinder and began rotating. And Kworn shivered and jerked to the tremendous power of the words that flowed through him. They were words, but they had no meaning, waves of sound that hammered at his receptors in an unknown tongue he could not understand. The language of the Folk had changed since the days of the ancients, he thought despairingly.

And then, with a mantle-shattering roar, the cylinders jutting overhead spouted flame and smoke. Two silvery balls trailing thin, dark filaments shot out of the great cylinder and buried themselves in the sand behind him. The filaments lay motionless in the sand as Kworn, wrapped defensively in his mantle, rolled off the ramp to the ground below.

The silence that followed was so deep that it seemed like Emptiness had taken the entire land.

Slowly Kworn loosened his mantle. "In the name of my first ancestor," he murmured shakily, "what was that?" His senses were shocked and disorganized by the violence of the sound. It was worse even than the roar and scream of the samshin that occasionally blew from the south, carrying dust, lichens, feeders, and even Folk who had been too slow or too foolish to hide from the fury of the wind.

Gingerly, Kworn inspected the damage to his mantle. It was minor. A tiny rip that could easily be repaired, a few grains of sand that could be extruded. He drew himself together to perform the repairs with the least possible loss of energy, and as he did, he was conscious of an emanation coming from the filaments that had been hurled from the cylinder.

Food!

And such food!

It was the distilled quintessence of a thousand purple feeders! It came to his senses in a shimmering wave of ecstasy so great that his mantle glowed a bright crimson. He stretched a pseudopod toward its source, and as he touched the filament his whole body quivered with anticipation. The barrier was blotted from his thoughts by an orgy of shuddering delight almost too great for flesh to endure. Waves of pleasure ran through his body as he swiftly extended to cover the filament. It could be a trap, he thought, but it made no difference. The demands of his depleted body and the sheer vacuole-constricting delight of this incredible foodstuff made a combination too potent for his will to resist, even if it had desired to do so. Waves of pleasure rippled through him as more of his absorptive surface contacted the filament. He snuggled against it, enfolding it completely, letting the peristaltic rushes sweep through him. He had never fed like this as long as he could recall. His energy levels swelled and pulsed as he sucked the last delight from the cord, and contemplated the further pleasure waiting for him in that other one lying scarcely twenty raads away.

Sensuously, he extended a pseudopod from his upper surface and probed for the other filament. He was filled to the top of his primary vacuole but the desire for more was stronger than ever—despite the fact that he knew the food in the other filament would bring him to critical level, would force him to reproduce. The thought amused him. As far back as he could remember, no member of the Folk had ever budded an offspring during the Time of Travel. It would be unheard of, something that would go down through the years in the annals of the Folk, and perhaps even cause a change in the Law.

The pseudopod probed, reached and stopped short of its goal. There was nothing around it but empty air.

Fear drove the slow orgasmic thoughts from his mind. Absorbed in gluttony, he hadn't noticed that the filament had tightened and was slowly drawing back into the cylinder from whence it came. And now it was too late! He was already over the rim of the metal disk.

Feverishly, he tried to disengage his absorptive surfaces from the filament and crawl down its length to safety, but he couldn't move. He was stuck to the dark cord by some strange adhesive that cemented his cells firmly to the cord. He could not break free.

The line moved steadily upward, dragging him inexorably toward a dark opening in the cylinder overhead. Panic filled him! Desperately he tried to loosen his trapped surfaces. His pseudopod lashed futilely in the air, searching with panic for something to grip, something to clutch that would stop this slow movement to the hell of pain that waited for him in the metal high overhead.

His searching flesh struck another's, and into his mind flooded the Ul Caada's terrified thought. The old one had reacted quicker than he, perhaps because he was poaching, but like himself he was attached and could not break free.

"Serves you right," Kworn projected grimly. "The thing was on my land. You had no right to feed upon it."

"Get me loose!" Caada screamed. His body flopped at the end of a thick mass of digestive tissue, dangling from the line, writhing and struggling in mindless terror. It was strange, Kworn thought, that fear should be so much stronger in the old than in the young.

"Cut loose, you fool," Kworn projected. "There isn't enough of you adhered to hurt if it were lost. A little body substance isn't worth your life. Hurry! You'll be too late if you don't. That metal is poisonous to our flesh."

"But it will be pain to cut my absorbing surface," Caada protested.

"It will be death if you don't."

"Then why don't you?"

"I can't," Kworn said hopelessly. "All my surface is stuck to the filament. I can't cut free." He was calm now, resigned to the inevitable. His greed had brought him to this. Perhaps it was a fitting punishment. But Caada need not die if he would show courage.

He rotated his eye to watch his struggling neighbor. Apparently Caada was going to take his advice. The tissue below the part of him stuck to the filament began to thin. His pseudopod broke contact. But his movements were slow and hesitant. Already his body mass was rising above the edge of the disk.

"Quick, you fool!" Kworn projected. "Another moment and you're dead!"

But Caada couldn't hear. Slowly his tissues separated as he reluctantly abandoned his absorptive surface. But he was already over the disk. The last cells pinched off and he fell, mantle flapping, full on the surface of the disc. For a moment he lay there quivering, and then his body was blotted from sight by a cloud of frozen steam, and his essence vanished screaming into Emptiness.

Kworn shuddered. It was a terrible way to die. But his own fate would be no better. He wrapped his mantle tightly around him as his leading parts vanished into the dark hole in the cylinder. In a moment he would be following Caada on the journey from which no member of the Folk had ever returned. His body disappeared into the hole.

—and was plunged into paradise!

His foreparts slipped into a warm, thick liquid that loosened the adhesive that bound him to the cord. As he slipped free, he slowly realized that he was not to die. He was bathed in liquid food! He was swimming in it! He was surrounded on all sides by incredible flavors so strange and delicious that his mind could not classify them! The filament had been good, but this—this was indescribable! He relaxed, his mantle spreading through the food, savoring, absorbing, digesting, metabolizing, excreting. His energy levels peaked. The nuclei of his germ plasm swelled, their chromosomes split, and a great bud formed and separated from his body. He had reproduced!

Through a deadening fog of somatic sensation, he realized dully that this was wrong, that the time wasn't right, that the space was limited, and that the natural reaction to abundant food supply was wrong. But for the moment he didn't care.

For thousands of seasons he had traveled the paths between equator and pole in a ceaseless hunt for good, growing and rejuvenating in good seasons, shrinking and aging in bad. He had been bound to the soil, a slave to the harsh demands of life and Nature. And now the routine was broken.

He luxuriated in his freedom. It must have been like this in the old days, when the waters were plentiful and things grew in them that could be eaten, and the Folk had time to dream young dreams and think young thoughts, and build their thoughts and dreams into the gleaming realities of cities and machines. Those were the days when the mind went above the soil into the air and beyond it to the moons, the sun and the evening stars.

But that was long ago.

He lay quietly, conscious of the change within him as his cells multiplied to replace those he had lost, and his body grew in weight and size. He was rejuvenated. The cells of his growing body, stimulated by the abundance of food, released memories he had forgotten he had ever possessed. His past ran in direct cellular continuity to the dawn of his race, and in him was every memory he had experienced since the beginning. Some were weak, others were stronger, but all were there awaiting an effort of recall. All that was required was enough stimulation to bring them out of hiding.

And for the first time in millennia the stimulus was available. The stimulus was growth, the rapid growth that only an abundant food supply could give, the sort of growth that the shrunken environment outside could not supply. With sudden clarity he saw how the Folk had shrunk in mind and body as they slowly adapted to the ever-increasing rigor of life. The rushing torrent of memory and sensation that swept through him gave him a new awareness of what he had been once and what he had become. His eye was lifted from the dirt and lichens.

What he saw filled him with pity and contempt. Pity for what the Folk had become; contempt for their failure to recognize it. Yet he had been no better than the others. It was only through the accident of this artifact that he had learned. The Folk *couldn't* know what the slow dwindling of their food supply had done to them. Over the millennia they had adapted, changing to fit the changing conditions, surviving only because they were more intelligent and more tenacious than the other forms of life that had become extinct. A thousand thousand seasons had passed since the great war that had devastated the world. A million years of slow adaptation to the barren waste that had been formed when the ultimate products of Folk technology were loosed on their creators had created a race tied to a subsistence level of existence, incapable of thinking beyond the basic necessities of life.

The Ul Kworn sighed. It would be better if he would not remember so much. But he could suppress neither the knowledge nor the memories. They crowded in upon him, stimulated by the food in which he floated.

Beside him, his offspring was growing. A bud always grew rapidly in a favorable environment, and this one was ideal. Soon it would be as large as himself. Yet it would never develop beyond an infant. It could not mature without a transfer of germ plasm from other infants of the Folk. And there were no infants.

It would grow and keep on growing because there would be no check of maturity upon its cells. It would remain a partly sentient lump of flesh that would never be complete. And in time it would be dangerous. When it had depleted the food supply it would turn on him in mindless hunger. It wouldn't ralize that the Ul Kworn was its father, or if it did, it wouldn't care. An infant is ultimately selfish, and its desires are the most important thing in its restricted universe.

Kworn considered his situation dispassionately.

It was obvious that he must escape from this trap before his offspring destroyed him. Yet he could think of no way to avoid the poison metal. He recognized it now, the element was the twelve protons in its nucleus, a light metal seldom used by the Folk even in the days of their greatness because of its ability to rapidly oxidize and its propensity to burst into brilliant flame when heated. With sudden shock he realized that the artifact was nothing less than a gigantic torch!

Why had it been built like this? What was its function? Where had it come from? Why hadn't it spoken since it had released that flood of unintelligible gibberish before it had drawn him inside? Ever since he had entered this food tank it had been quiet except for a clicking, chattering whir that came from somewhere above him. He had the odd impression that it was storing information about him and the way he reacted in the tank.

And then, abruptly, it broke into voice. Cryptic words poured from it, piercing him with tiny knives of sound. The intensity and rapidity of the projections shocked him, left him quivering and shaking when they stopped as abruptly as they had begun.

In the quiet that followed, Kworn tried to recall the sequence of the noise. The words were like nothing he had ever heard. They were not the language of the Folk either past or present. And they had a flow and sequence that was not organic. They were mechanical, the product of a metal intelligence that recorded and spoke but did not think. The Folk had had machines like that once.

How had it begun? There had been a faint preliminary, an almost soundless voice speaking a single word. Perhaps if he projected it, it would trigger a response. Pitching his voice in the same key and intensity he projected the word as best he could remember it.

And the voice began again.

Kworn quivered with excitement. Something outside the artifact was forcing it to speak. He was certain of it. As certain as he was that the artifact was recording himself and his offspring. But who—or what—was receiving the record? And why?

This could be a fascinating speculation, Kworn thought. But there would be time enough for that later. His immediate need was to get out. Already the food supply was running low, and his offspring was becoming enormous. He'd have to leave soon if he was ever going to. And he'd have to do something about his own growth. Already it was reaching dangerous levels. He was on the ragged edge of another reproduction, and he couldn't afford it.

Regretfully, he began moving the cornified cells of his mantle and his underlayer toward his inner surfaces, arranging them in a protective layer around his germ plasm and absorptive cells. There would be enough surface absorption to take care of his maintenance needs, and his body could retain its peak of cellular energy. Yet the desire to feed and bud was almost overpowering. His body screamed at him for denying it the right that food would give it, but Kworn resisted the demands of his flesh until the frantic cellular urges passed.

Beside him his offspring pulsed with physical sensation. Kworn envied it even as he pitied it. The poor mindless thing could be used as a means to the end of his escape, but it was useless for anything else. It was far too large, and far too stupid, to survive in the outside world. Kworn extruded a net of hair-like pseudopods and swept the tank in which they lay. It was featureless, save for a hole where the filament had not completely withdrawn when it had pulled him into this place. A few places in the wall had a different texture than the others, probably the sense organs of the recorder. He rippled with satisfaction. There was a grille of poison metal in the top of the tank through which flowed a steady current of warm air. It would be pleasant to investigate this further, Kworn thought, but there was no time. His offspring had seen to that.

He placed his eye on a thin pseudopod and thrust it through the hole in the wall of the tank. It was still night outside, but a faint line of brightness along the horizon indicated the coming of dawn. The artifact glittered icily beneath him, and he had a feeling of giddiness as he looked down the vertiginous drop to the disk below. The dark blotch of Caada's burned body was almost invisible against the faintly gleaming loom of the still-warm disk. Kworn shuddered. Caada hadn't deserved a death like that. Kworn looked down, estimating the chances with his new intelligence, and then slapped a thick communication fibril against his offspring's quivering flesh and hurled a projection at its recoiling mass.

Considering the fact that its cells were direct derivations of his own, Kworn thought grimly, it was surprising how hard it was to establish control. The youngster had developed a surprising amount of individuality in its few xals of free existence. He felt a surge of thankfulness to the old Ul Kworn as the youngster yielded to his firm projection. His precursor had always sought compliant germ plasm to produce what he had called "discipline and order." It was, in fact, weakness. It was detrimental to survival. But right now that weakness was essential.

Under the probing lash of his projection the infant extruded a thick mass of tissue that met and interlocked with a similar mass of his own. As soon as the contact firmed, Kworn began flowing toward his eye, which was still in the half-open hole in the side of the tank.

The outside cold struck his sense centers with spicules of ice as he flowed to the outside, clinging to his offspring's gradually extending pseudopod. Slowly he dropped below the cylinder. The infant was frantic. It disliked the cold and struggled to break free, but Kworn clung limpetlike to his offspring's flesh as it twisted and writhed in an effort to return to the warmth and comfort into which it was born.

"Let go!" his offspring screamed. "I don't like this place."

"In a moment," Kworn said as he turned the vague writhings into a swinging pendulum motion. "Help me move back and forth."

"I can't. I'm cold. Let me go!"

"Help me," Kworn ordered grimly, "or hang out here and freeze."

His offspring shuddered and twitched. The momentum of the swing increased. Kworn tightened his grip.

"You promised to let go!" his offspring wailed. "You prom—"

The infant's projection was cut off as Kworn loosed himself at the upward arc of the swing, spread his mantle and plummeted toward the ground. Fear swept through him as his body curved through the thin air, missing the edge of the disk and landing on the ground with a sense-jarring thud. Behind and above him up against the cylinder, the thick tendril of his offspring's flesh withdrew quickly from sight. For a moment the Ul Kworn's gaze remained riveted on the row of odd markings on the metal surface, and then he turned his attention to life.

There was no reason to waste the pain of regret upon that half sentient mass of tissue that was his offspring. The stupid flesh of his flesh would remain happy in the darkness with the dwindling food until its flesh grew great enough to touch the poison metal in the ceiling of the tank.

And then—

With a harsh projection of horror, the Ul Kworn moved, circling the artifact on Caada's vacated strip. And as he moved he concentrated energy into his high-level communication organs, and projected a warning of danger.

"Move!" he screamed. "Move forward for your lives!"

The line rippled. Reddish mantles unfolded as the Folk reacted. The nearest, shocked from estivation, were in motion even before they came to full awareness. Alarms like this weren't given without reason.

Varsi's reaction, Kworn noted, was faster than any of his fellows. The young Ul had some favorable self-preservation characteristics. He'd have to consider sharing some germ plasm with him at the next reproduction season, after all.

In a giant arc, the Folk pressed forward under the white glow of emerging dawn. Behind them the artifact began to project again in its strange tongue. But in mid-cry it stopped abruptly. And from it came a wail of mindless agony that tore at Kworn's mind with regret more bitter because nothing could be done about it.

His offspring had touched the poison metal.

Kworn turned his eye backward. The artifact was shaking on its broad base from the violence of his offspring's tortured writhings. As he watched, a brilliant burst of light flared from its top. Heat swept across the land, searing the lichens and a scattered few of the Folk too slow to escape. The giant structure burned with a light more brilliant than the sun and left behind a great cloud of white vapor that hung on the air like the menacing cloud of a samshin. Beneath the cloud the land was bare save for a few twisted pieces of smoking metal.

The roadblock was gone.

Kworn moved slowly forward, gleaning Caada's strip and half of his own, which he shared with Varsi.

He would need that young Ul in the future. It was well to place him under an obligation. The new thoughts and old memories weren't dying. They remained, and were focused upon the idea of living better than at this subsistence level. It should be possible to grow lichens, and breed a more prolific type of lichen feeder. Water channeled from the canals would stimulate lichen growth a thousandfold. And with a more abundant food supply, perhaps some of the Folk could be stimulated to think and apply ancient buried skills to circumvent Nature.

It was theoretically possible. The new breed would have to be like Varsi, tough, driving and selfishly independent. In time they might inherit the world. Civilization could arise again. It was not impossible.

His thoughts turned briefly back to the artifact. It still bothered him. He still knew far too little about it. It was a fascinating speculation to dream of what it might have been. At any rate, one thing was sure. It was not a structure of his race. If nothing else, those cabalistic markings on the side of the cylinder were utterly alien.

Thoughtfully he traced them in the sand. What did they mean?

James V. McConnell

Born in Okmulgee, Oklahoma, James V. McConnell (1925–   ) has become one of the world's most famous experimental psychologists, most noted perhaps for his experiments on cannibalistic memory transfer in flatworms.

After military service in the navy during World War II, he completed his B.A. at Louisiana State University, then obtained an M.A. (1954) and Ph.D. (1956) from the University of Texas. He was appointed to an instructorship at the University of Michigan at Ann Arbor (1956) and quickly rose to full professor (1963) as a result of prodigious research efforts that now total more than one hundred fifty professional papers.

A Fulbright Scholar (1954–55) and winner of a U.S. Department of Health, Education, and Welfare Research Career-Development Award (1963), he has received grants from the National Institute of Mental Health and the Atomic Energy Commission and acted as consultant to the U. S. Department of Defense, the Smithsonian Institution and the U. S. Department of Commerce.

Notable books include *Psychology* (1961), *A Manual of Psychological Experimentation on Planarians* (1965), *Psychology: The Human Science* (1978) and *Understanding Human Behavior* (1984).

Between 1953 and 1957, McConnell published nine science fiction stories. Most are very well written, and one, which follows below—the definitive worm's eye view of an experimental psychologist—is an acknowledged classic.

LEARNING THEORY

by James V. McConnell

I AM WRITING this because I presume He wants me to. Otherwise He would not have left paper and pencil handy for me to use. And I put the word *He* in capitals because it seems the only thing to do. If I am dead and in hell, then this is only proper. However, if I am merely a captive somewhere, then surely a little flattery won't hurt matters.

As I sit here in this small room and think about it, I am impressed most of all by the suddenness of the whole thing. At one moment I was out walking in the woods near my suburban home. The next thing I knew, here I was in a small, featureless room, naked as a jaybird, with only my powers of rationalization to stand betwen me and insanity. When the "change" was made (whatever the change was), I was not conscious of so much as a momentary flicker between walking in the woods and being here in this room. Whoever is responsible for all of this is to be complimented—either He has developed an instantaneous anesthetic or He has solved the problem of instantaneous transportation of matter. I would prefer to think it the former, for the latter leads to too much anxiety.

As I recall, I was immersed in the problem of how to teach my class in beginning psychology some of the more abstruse points of learning theory when the transition came. How far away life at the university seems at the moment: I must be forgiven if now I am much more concerned about where I am and how to get out of here than about how freshmen can be cajoled into understanding Hull or Tolman.

Problem 1: Where am I? For an answer, I can only describe this room. It is about twenty feet square, some twelve feet high, with no windows, but with what might be a door in the middle of one of the walls. Everything is of a uniform gray color, and the walls and ceiling emit a fairly pleasant achromatic light. The walls themselves are of some hard material that might be metal since it feels slightly cool to the touch. The floor is of a softer, rubbery material that yields a little when I walk on it. Also, it has a rather "tingly" feel to it, suggesting that it may be in constant vibration. It is somewhat warmer than the walls, which is all to the good since it appears I must sleep on the floor.

The only furniture in the room consists of what might be a table and what passes for a chair. They are not quite that, but they can be made to serve this purpose. On the table I found the paper and the pencil. No, let me correct myself. What I call paper is a good deal rougher and thicker than I am used to, and what I call a pencil is nothing more than a thin round stick of graphite which I have sharpened by rubbing one end of it on the table.

And that is the sum of my surroundings. I wish I knew what He has done with my clothes. The suit was an old one, but I am worried about the walking boots. I was very fond of those boots—they were quite expensive and I would hate to lose them.

The problem still remains to be answered, however, as to just where in the hell I am—if not hell itself!

Problem 2 is a knottier one: Why am I here? Were I subject to paranoid tendencies, I would doubtless come to the conclusion that my enemies had kidnapped me. Or perhaps that the Russians had taken such an interest in my research that they had spirited me away to some Siberian hideout and would soon appear to demand either cooperation or death. Sadly enough, I am too reality oriented. My research was highly interesting to me, and perhaps to a few other psychologists who like to dabble in esoteric problems of animal learning, but it was scarcely startling enough to warrant such attention as kidnapping.

So I am left as baffled as before. Where am I, and why? And who is He?

I have decided to forgo all attempts at keeping this diary according to "days" or "hours." Such units of time have no meaning in my present circumstances, for the light remains constant all the time I am awake. The human organism is not possessed of as neat an internal clock as some of the lower species. Far too many studies have shown that a human being who is isolated from all external stimulation soon loses his sense of time. So I will merely indicate breaks in the narrative and hope that He will understand that if He wasn't bright enough to leave me with my wristwatch, He couldn't expect me to keep an accurate record.

Nothing much has happened. I have slept, been fed and watered, and have emptied my bladder and bowels. The food was waiting on the table when I awoke last time. I must say that He has little of the gourmet in Him. Protein balls are not my idea of a feast royal. However, they will serve to keep body and soul together (presuming, of course, that they *are* together at the moment). But I must object to my source of liquid refreshment. The meal made me very thirsty, and I was in the process of cursing Him and everybody else when I noticed a small nipple that had appeared in the wall while I was asleep. At first I thought that perhaps Freud was right after all, and that my libido had taken over control of my imagery. Exprimentation convinced me, however, that the thing was real, and that it is my present source of water. If one sucks on the thing, it delivers a slightly cool and somewhat sweetish flow of liquid. But really, it's a most undignified procedure. It's bad enough to have to sit around all day in my birthday suit. But for a full professor to have to stand on his tiptoes and suck on an artificial nipple in order to obtain water is asking a little too much.

252

I'd complain to the management if only I knew to whom to complain!

Following eating and drinking, the call to nature became a little too strong to ignore. Now, I was adequately toilet-trained with indoor plumbing, and the absence of same is most annoying. However, there was nothing much to do but choose a corner of the room and make the best of a none-too-pleasant situation. (As a side-thought, I wonder if the choosing of a corner was in any way instinctive?) However, the upshot of the whole thing was my learning what is probably the purpose of the vibration of the floor. For the excreted material disappeared through the floor not too many minutes later. The process was a gradual one. Now I will be faced with all kinds of uncomfortable thoughts concerning what might possibly happen to me if I slept too long!

Perhaps this is to be expected, but I find myself becoming a little paranoid after all. In attempting to solve my Problem 2, why I am here, I have begun to wonder if perhaps some of my colleagues at the university are not using me as a subject in some kind of experiment. It would be just like McCleary to dream up some fantastic kind of "human-in-isolation" experiment and use me as a pilot observer. You would think that he'd have asked my permission first. However, perhaps it's important that the subject not know what's happening to him. If so, I have one happy thought to console me. If McCleary *is* responsible for this, he'll have to take over the teaching of my classes for the time being. And how he hates teaching learning theory to freshmen!

You know, this place seems dreadfully quiet to me.

Suddenly I have solved two of my problems. I know both where I am and who He is. And I bless the day that I got interested in the perception of motion.

I should say to begin with that the air in this room seems to have more than the usual concentration of dust particles. This didn't seem particularly noteworthy until I noticed that most of them seemed to pile up along the floor against one wall in particular. For a while I was sure that this was due to the ventilation system—perhaps there was an outgoing air duct there where this particular wall was joined to the floor. However, when I went over and put my hand to the floor there, I could feel no breeze whatsoever. Yet even as I held my hand along the dividing line between the wall and the floor, dust motes covered my hand with a thin coating. I tried this same experiment everywhere else in the room to no avail. This was the only spot where the phenomenon occurred, and it occured along the entire length of this one wall.

But if ventilation was not responsible for the phenomenon, what was? All at once there popped into my mind some calculations I had made when the rocket boys had first proposed a manned satellite station. Engineers are notoriously naive when it comes to the performance of a human being in most situations, and I remembered that the problem of the perception of the satellite's rotation seemingly had been ignored by the slipstick crowd. They had planned to rotate the doughnut-shaped satellite in order to substitute centrifugal force for the force of gravity. Thus the outer shell of the doughnut would appear to be "down" to anyone inside the thing. Apparently they had not realized that man is at least as sensitive to angular rotation as he is to variations in the pull of gravity. As I figured the problem then, if a man aboard the doughnut moved his head as much as three or four feet outward from the center of the doughnut, he would have become fairly dizzy! Rather annoying it would have been, too, to have been hit by a wave of nausea every time one sat down in a chair. Also, as I pondered the problem, it became apparent that dust particles and the like would probably show a tendency to move in a direction opposite to the direction of the rotation, and hence pile up against any wall or such that impeded their flight.

Using the behavior of the dust particles as a clue, I then climbed atop the table and leaped off. Sure enough, my head felt like a mule had kicked it by the time I landed on the floor. My hypothesis was confirmed.

So I am aboard a spaceship!

The thought is incredible, but in a strange way comforting. At least now I can postpone worrying about heaven and hell—and somehow I find the idea of being in a spaceship much more to the liking of a confirmed agnostic. I suppose I owe

McCleary an apology—I should have known he would never have put himself in a position where he would have to teach freshmen all about learning.

And, of course, I know who "He" is. Or rather, I know who He *isn't*, which is something else again. Surely, though I can no longer think of Him as being human. Whether I should be consoled at this or not, I have no way of telling.

I still have no notion of *why* I am here, however, nor why this alien chose to pick me of all people to pay a visit to His spaceship. What possible use could I be? Surely if He were interested in making contact with the human race, He would have spirited away a politician. After all, that's what politicians are for! Since there has been no effort made to communicate with me, however, I must reluctantly give up any cherished hopes that His purpose is that of making contact with *genus homo*.

Or perhaps He's a galactic scientist of some kind, a biologist of sorts, out gathering specimens. Now, that's a particularly nasty thought. What if He turned out to be a physiologist, interested in cutting me open eventually, to see what makes me tick? Will my innards be smeared over a glass slide for scores of youthful Hims to peer at under a microscope? Brrrr! I don't mind giving my life to science, but I'd rather do it a little at a time.

If you don't mind, I think I'll go do a little repressing for a while.

Good God! I should have known it! Destiny will play her little tricks, and all jokes have their cosmic angles. He is a *psychologist!* Had I given it due consideration, I would have realized that whenever you come across a new species, you worry about behavior first, physiology second. So I have received the ultimate insult—or the ultimate compliment. I don't know which. I have become a specimen for an alien psychologist!

This thought first occurred to me when I awoke after my latest sleep (which was filled, I must admit, with most frightening dreams). It was immediately obvious that something about the room had changed. Almost at once I noticed that one of the walls now had a lever of some kind protruding from it, and to one side of the lever, a small hole in the wall with a container beneath the hole. I wandered over to the lever, inspected it a few moments, then accidentally depressed the thing. At once there came a loud clicking noise, and a protein ball popped out of the hole and fell into the container.

For just a moment a frown crossed my brow. This seemed somehow so strangely familiar. Then, all at once, I burst into wild laughter. The room had been changed into a gigantic Skinner box! For years I had been studying animal learning by putting white rats in a Skinner box and following the changes in the rats' behavior. The rats had to learn to press the lever in order to get a pellet of food, which was delivered to them through just such an apparatus as is now affixed to the wall of my cell. And now, after all of these years, and after all of the learning studies I had done, to find myself trapped like a rat in a Skinner box! Perhaps this was hell after all, I told myself, and the Lord High Executioner's admonition to "let the punishment fit the crime" was being followed.

Frankly, this sudden turn of events has left me a little shaken.

I seem to be performing according to theory. It didn't take me long to discover that pressing the lever would give me food some of the time, while at other times all I got was the click and no protein ball. It appears that approximately every twelve hours the thing delivers me a random number of protein balls—the number has varied from five to fifteen so far. I never know ahead of time how many pellets—I mean protein balls— the apparatus will deliver, and it spews them out intermittently. Sometimes I have to press the lever a dozen times or so before it will give me anything, while at other times it gives me one ball for each press. Since I don't have a watch on me, I am never quite sure when the twelve hours have passed, so I stomp over to the lever and press it every few minutes when I think it's getting close to time to be fed. Just like my rats always did. And since the pellets are small and I never get enough of them, occasionally I find myself banging away on the lever with all the compulsion of a stupid animal. But I missed the feeding time once and almost starved to death (so it seemed) before the lever delivered food the next time. About the only consolation to my wounded pride is that at this rate of starvation, I'll lose my bay window in short order.

At least He doesn't seem to be fattening me up for the kill. Or maybe he just likes lean meat!

I have been promoted. Apparently He in his infinite alien wisdom has decided that I'm intelligent enough to handle the Skinner-type apparatus, so I've been promoted to solving a maze. Can you picture the irony of the situation? All of the classic learning theory methodology is practically being thrown in my face. If only I could communicate with Him! I don't mind being subjected to tests nearly as much as I mind being underestimated. Why, I can solve puzzles hundreds of times more complex than what He's throwing at me. But how can I tell Him?

As it turns out, the maze is much like our standard T-mazes, and it is not too difficult to learn. It's a rather long one, true, with some 23 choice points along the way. I spent the better part of half an hour wandering through the thing the first time I found myself in it. Surprisingly enough, I didn't realize the first time out what I was in, so I made no conscious attempt to memorize the correct turns. It wasn't until I reached the final turn and found food waiting for me that I recognized what I was expected to do. The next time through the maze my perform-ance was a good deal better, and I was able to turn in a perfect performance in not too long a time. However, it does not do my ego any good to realize that my own white rats could have learned the maze a little sooner than I did.

My "home cage," so to speak, still has the Skinner apparatus in it, but the lever delivers food only occasionally now. I still give it a whirl now and again, but since I'm getting a fairly good supply of food at the end of the maze each time, I don't pay the lever much attention.

Now that I am very sure of what is happening to me, quite naturally my thoughts have turned to how I can get out of this situation. Mazes I can solve without too much difficulty, but how to escape apparently is beyond my intellectual capacity.

But then, come to think of it, there was precious little chance for my own experimental animals to get out of my clutches. And assuming that I am unable to escape, what then? After He has finished putting me through as many paces as He wishes, where do we go from there? Will He treat me as I treated most of my nonhuman subjects—that is, will I get tossed into a jar containing chloroform? "Following the experiment, the animals were sacrificed," as we so euphemistically report in the scientific literature. This doesn't appeal to me much, as you can imagine. Or maybe if I seem particularly bright to Him, He may use me for breeding purposes, to establish a colony of His own. Now, that might have possibilities . . .

Oh, damn Freud anyhow!

And damn Him too! I had just gotten the maze well learned when He upped and changed things on me. I stumbled about like a bat in the sunlight for quite some time before I finally got to the goal box. I'm afraid my performance was pretty poor. What He did was just to reverse the whole maze so that it was a mirror image of what it used to be. Took me only two trials to discover the solution. Let Him figure that one out if He's so smart!

My performance on the maze reversal must have pleased Him, because now He's added a new complication. And again I suppose I could have predicted the next step if I had been thinking along the right direction. I woke up a few hours ago to find myself in a totally different room. There was nothing whatsoever in the room, but oppposite me were two doors in the wall—one door pure white, the other jet black. Between me and the doors was a deep pit filled with water. I didn't like the looks of the situation, for it occurred to me right away that He had devised a kind of jumping stand for me. I had to choose which of the doors was open and led to food. The other door would be locked. If I jumped at the wrong door, and found it locked, I'd fall in the water. I needed a bath, that was for sure, but I didn't relish getting it in this fashion.

While I stood there watching, I got the shock of my life. I mean it quite literally. The bastard had thought of everything.

When I used to run rats on jumping stands, to overcome their reluctance to jump, I used to shock them. He's following exactly the same pattern. The floor in this room is wired, but good. I howled and jumped about and showed all the usual anxiety behavior. It took me less than two seconds to come to my senses and make a flying leap at the white door, however.

You know something? That water is ice cold!

I have now, by my own calculations, solved no fewer than eighty-seven different problems on the jumping stand, and I'm getting sick and tired of it. Once I got angry and just pointed at the correct door—and got shocked for not going ahead and jumping. I shouted bloody murder, cursing Him at the top of my voice, telling Him if He didn't like my performance, He could damn well lump it. All He did, of course, was to increase the shock.

Frankly, I don't know how much longer I can put up with this. It's not that the work is difficult. If He were giving me half a chance to show my capabilities, I wouldn't mind it. I suppose I've contemplated a thousand different means of escaping, but none of them is worth mentioning. But if I don't get out of here soon, I shall go stark raving mad!

For almost an hour after it happened, I sat in this room and just wept. I realize that it is not the style in our culture for a grown man to weep, but there are times when cultural taboos must be forgotten. Again, had I thought much about the sort of experiments He must have had in mind, I most probably could have predicted the next step. Even so, I most likely would have repressed the knowledge.

One of the standard problems which any learning psychologist is interested in is this one—will an animal learn something if you fail to reward him for his performance? There are many theorists, such as Hull and Spence, who believe that reward (or "reinforcement," as they call it) is absolutely necessary for learning to occur. This is mere stuff and nonsense, as anyone with a grain of sense knows, but nonetheless the "reinforcement" theory has been dominant in the field for years

259

now. We fought a hard battle with Spence and Hull, and actually had them with their backs to the wall at one point, when suddenly they came up with the concept of "secondary reinforcement." That is, anything associated with a reward takes on the ability to act as a reward itself. For example, the mere sight of food would become a reward in and of itself—almost as much a reward, in fact, as is the eating of the food. The *sight* of the food, indeed! But nonetheless, it saved their theories for the moment.

For the past five years now, I have been trying to design an experiment that would show beyond a shadow of a doubt that the *sight* of a reward was not sufficient for learning to take place. And now look at what has happened to me!

I'm sure that He must lean toward Hull and Spence in His theorizing, for earlier today, when I found myself in the jumping stand room, instead of being rewarded with my usual protein balls when I made the correct jump, I . . . I'm sorry, but it is difficult to write about even now. For when I made the correct jump and the door opened and I started toward the food, I found it had been replaced with a photograph. A calendar photograph. You know the one. Her name, I think, is Monroe.

I sat on the floor and cried. For five whole years I have been attacking the validity of the secondary reinforcement theory, and now I find myself giving Him evidence that the theory is correct! For I cannot help "learning" which of the doors is the correct one to jump through. I refuse to stand on the apparatus and have the life shocked out of me, and I refuse to pick the wrong door all the time and get an icy bath time after time. It isn't fair! For He will doubtless put it all down to the fact that the mere *sight* of the photograph is functioning as a reward, and that I am learning the problems merely to be able to see Miss What's-her-name in her bare skin!

I can just see Him now, sitting somewhere else in this spaceship, gathering in all the data I am giving Him, plotting all kinds of learning curves, chortling to Himself just because I am confirming all of His pet theories. I just wish . . .

Almost an hour has gone by since I wrote the above section. It seems longer than that, but surely it's been only an hour. And I have spent the time deep in thought. For I have discovered a way out of this place, I think. The question is, dare I do it?

I was in the midst of writing that paragraph about His sitting and chortling and confirming His theories, when it suddenly struck me that theories are born of the equipment that one uses. This has probably been true throughout the history of all science, but perhaps most true of all in psychology. If Skinner had never invented his blasted box, if the maze and the jumping stand had not been developed, we probably would have entirely different theories of learning today than we now have. For if nothing else, the type of equipment that one uses drastically reduces the type of behavior that one's subjects can show, and one's theories have to account only for the type of behavior that appears in the laboratories.

It follows from this also that any two cultures that devise the same sort of experimental procedures will come up with almost identical theories.

Keeping all this in mind, it's not hard for me to believe that He is an ironclad reinforcement theorist, for He uses all of the various paraphernalia that they use, and uses it in exactly the same way.

My means of escape is therefore obvious. He expects from me confirmation of all His pet theories. Well, he won't get it any more! I know all of His theories backwards and forwards, and this means I know how to give Him results that will tear His theories right smack in half!

I can almost predict the results. What does any learning theorist do with an animal that won't behave properly, that refuses to give the results that are predicted? One gets rid of the beast, quite naturally. For one wishes to use only healthy, normal animals in one's work, and any animal that gives "unusual" results is removed from the study but quickly. After all, if it doesn't perform as expected, it must be sick, abnormal, or aberrant in one way or another . . .

There is no guarantee, of course, what method He will employ to dispose of my now annoying presence. Will He "sacrifice" me? Or will He just return me to the "permanent colony?" I cannot say. I know only that I will be free from what is now an intolerable situation.

Just wait until He looks at His results from now on!

FROM: Experimenter-in-Chief, Interstellar Labship PSYCH- 145

TO: Director, Bureau of Science

Thlan, my friend, this will be an informal missive. I will send the official report along later, but I wanted to give you my subjective impressions first.

The work with the newly discovered species is, for the moment, at a standstill. Things went exceedingly well at first. We picked what seemed to be a normal, healthy animal and smattered it into our standard test apparatus. I may have told you that this new species seemed quite identical to our usual laboratory animals, so we included a couple of the "toys" that our home animals seem so fond of—thin pieces of material made from wood pulp and a tiny stick of graphite. Imagine our surprise, and our pleasure, when this new specimen made exactly the same use of the materials as have all of our home colony specimens. Could it be that there are certain innate behavior patterns to be found throughout the universe in the lower species?

Well, I merely pose the question. The answer is of little importance to a learning theorist. Your friend Verpk keeps insisting that the use of these "toys" may have some deeper meaning to it, and that perhaps we should investigate further. At his insistence, then, I include with this informal missive the materials used by our first subject. In my opinion, Verpk is guilty of gross anthropomorphism, and I wish to have nothing further to do with the question. However, this behavior did give us hope that our newly discovered colony would yield subjects whose performances would be exactly in accordance with standard theory.

And, in truth, this is exactly what seemed to be the case. The animal solved the Bfian box problem in short order, yielding as beautiful data as I have ever seen. We then shifted it to maze, maze-reversal and jumping stand problems, and the results could not have confirmed our theories better had we rigged the data. However, when we switched the animal to secondary reinforcement problems, it seemed to undergo a strange sort of change. No longer was its performance up to par. In fact, at times it seemed to go quite berserk. For part of the experiment, it would perform superbly. But then, just as it seemed to be solving whatever problem we set it to, its behavior would subtly change into patterns that obviously could not come from a normal specimen. It got worse and worse, until its behavior departed radically from that which our theories predicted. Naturally, we knew then that something had happened to the animal, for our theories are based upon thousands of experiments with similar subjects, and hence our theories must be right. But our theories hold only for normal subjects, and for normal species, so it soon became apparent to us that we had stumbled upon some abnormal type of animal.

Upon due consideration, we returned the subject to its home colony. However, we also voted almost unanimously to request from you permission to take steps to destroy the complete colony. It is obviously of little scientific use to us, and stands as a potential danger that we must take adequate steps against. Since all colonies are under your protection, we therefore request permission to destroy it.

I must report, by the way, that Verpk's vote was the only one that was cast against this procedure. He has some silly notion that one should study behavior as one finds it. Frankly, I cannot understand why you have seen fit to saddle me with him on this expedition, but perhaps you have your own reasons.

Verpk's vote notwithstanding, however, the rest of us are of the considered opinion that this whole new colony must be destroyed, and quickly. For it is obviously diseased or some such—as reference to our theories has proven. And should it by some chance come in contact with our other colonies, and infect our other animals with whatever disease or aberration it has, we would never be able to predict their behavior again. I need not carry the argument further, I think.

May we have your permission to destroy the colony as soon as possible, then, so that we may search out yet other colonies and test our theories against other healthy animals? For it is only in this fashion that science progresses.

Respectfully yours,

Iowyy

James Tiptree, Jr.

Born in Chicago, Illinois, James Tiptree, Jr. (1915–   )
astounded the science fiction world for ten years with
powerful science fiction stories. Even more astounding was
the revelation in 1977 that Tiptree was in reality Alice
Hastings Bradley Sheldon, a Ph.D. in experimental psychology and only child of the famous explorers Herbert and
Mary Bradley.

A former artist (1925–1941), photo-intelligence officer
for the U. S. Army Air Force (1942–1946) and CIA em-
ployee (1952–1955), Sheldon turned to academics relatively late in life. She acquired her B.A. from American
University in 1959 and her doctorate from George Washington University in 1967.

Fear of losing her dissertation grant, ruining future em-
ployment opportunities with the CIA and damaging her
reputation with her colleagues in psychology caused her to
initially use the pen name. Ironically though, her dreams of
a career as research psychologist were ended by ill-health,
age and possibly ageism as well as sexism. But her dissertation on the responses of animals to novel stimuli in differ-
ing environments was nominated for best dissertation of
the year and has become recognized as a classic in the field.

So far, her science fiction consists of two novels and
nearly fifty shorter works. Twice she has won the Hugo
Award (1973, 1976) and three times the Nebula Award
(1973, 1976, 1977), including one award for the powerful
psychological study of alien love that follows.

LOVE IS THE PLAN
THE PLAN IS DEATH

by James Tiptree, Jr.

R EMEMBERING—
Do you hear, my little red? Hold me softly. The cold grows.

I remember:

—I am hugely black and hopeful, I bounce on six legs along the mountains in the new warm! . . . *Sing the changer, Sing the stranger! Will the changes change forever?* . . . All my hums have words now. Another change!

Eagerly I bound on sunward following the tiny thrill in the air. The forests have been shrinking again. Then I see. It is me! Me-Myself, MOGGADEET—I have grown bigger more in the winter cold! I astonish myself, Moggadeet-the-small!

Excitement, enticement shrilling from the sun-side of the world. I come! . . . The sun is changing again too. *Sun is walking in the night! Sun is walking back to Summer in the warming of the light!* . . . Warm is Me-Moggadeet Myself. Forget the bad-time winter.

Memory quakes me.

The Old One.

I stop, pluck up a tree. So much I wanted to ask the Old One. No time. Cold. Tree goes end over end down-cliff, I watch the fatclimbers tumble out. Not hungry.

The Old One warned me of the cold—I didn't believe him. I move on, grieving . . . *Old One told you, The cold, the cold will hold you. Chill cold! Kill cold. In the cold I killed you.*

But it's warm now, all different. I'm Moggadeet again.

I bound over a hill and see my brother Frim.

At first I don't know him. A big black old one! I think. And in the warm, we can speak!

I surge toward him, bashing trees. The big black is crouched over a ravine, peering down. Black back has shiny ripples like— It IS Frim! Frim-I-hunted-for, Frim-run-away! But he's so big now! Giant Frim! *A stranger, a changer—*

"Frim!"

He doesn't hear me; all his eye-turrets are under the trees. His end is sticking up oddlike, all atremble. What's he hunting?

"Frim! It's me, Moggadeet!"

But he only quivers his legs; I see his spurs pushing out. What a fool, Frim! I remind myself how timid he is, I try to move gently. When I get closer I'm astonished again. I'm bigger than he is now. *Changes!* I can see right over his shoulder into the ravine.

Hot yellow-green in there. A little glade all lit with sun. I bend my eyes to see what Frim is after and all astonishments blow up the world.

I see you.

I saw you.

I will always see you. Dancing in the green fire, my tiny red star! So bright! So small! So perfect! So fierce! I knew you, Oh yes, I knew you in that first instant, my dawnberry, my scarlet minikin. *Red!* A tiny baby red one, smaller than my smallest eye. And so brave!

The Old One said it. Red is the color of love.

I see you swat at a hopper twice your size, my eyes bulge as you leap after it and go rolling, shrilling *Lililee! Lilileee-ee!* in baby wrath. Oh my mighty hunter, you don't know someone is looking right into your tender little love-fur! Oh yes! Palest pink it is, just brushed with rose. My jaws spurt, the world flashes and reels.

And then Frim, poor fool, feels me behind him and rears up.

But what a Frim! His throat-sacs are ballooning purple-black, his plates are engorged like the Mother of the storm clouds! Glittering, rattling his spurs! His tail booms! "It's mine!" he bellows—I can hardly understand him. He jumps straight at me.

"Stop, Frim, stop!" I cry, dodging away bewildered. It's warm—how can Frim be wild, kill-wild?

"Brother Frim!" I call gently, soothingly. But something is badly wrong! My voice is bellowing too! Yes, in the warm and I want only to calm him, I am full of love—but the kill-roar is rushing through me, I too am swelling, rattling, booming! Invincible! To crush—to rend—

Oh, I am shamed.

I came to myself in the wreckage of Frim, Frim-pieces everywhere, myself is sodden with Frim. But I did not eat him! I did not! Should I take joy in that? Did I defy the Plan? But my throat was closed. Not because it was Frim but because it was darling you. *You!* Where are you? The glade is empty! Oh fearful fear, I have frightened you, you are run away! I forget Frim. I forget everything but you my heartmeat, my precious tiny red.

I smash trees, I uproot rocks, I tear the ravine open! Oh, where are you hiding? Suddenly I have a new fear: Has my wild search harmed you? I force myself calm. I begin questing, circling, ever wider over the trees, moving cloud-silent, thrusting my eyes and ears down into every glade. A new humming fills my throat. *Oooo, Oo-oo, Rum-a-looly-loo,* I moan. Hunting, hunting for you.

Once I glimpse a black bigness far away and I am suddenly up at my full height, roaring. Attack the black! Was it another brother? I would slay him, but the stranger is already vanishing. I roar again. No—*it roars me,* the new power of black. Yet deep inside, Myself-Moggadeet is watching, fearing. Attack the black—even in the warm? Is there no safety, are we truly like the fatclimbers? But at the same time it feels—Oh, right! Oh, good! Sweet is the Plan. I give myself up to seeking you, my new song longing *Oo-loo* and *Looly rum-a-loo-oo-loo.*

And you answered! You!

So tiny you, hidden under a leaf! Shrilling *Li! Li! Lililee!* Trilling, thrilling—half-mocking, already imperious. Oh, how I whirl, crash, try to look under all my feet, stop frozen in horror of squashing the *Lilili! Lee!* Rocking, longing, moaning Moggadeet.

And you came out, you did.

My adorable firemite, threatening ME!

When I see your littlest hunting claws upraised my whole gut melts, it floods me. I am all tender jelly. *Tender!* Oh, tender-fierce like a Mother, I think! Isn't that how a Mother feels? My jaws are sluicing juice that isn't hunger-juice—I am choking with fear of frighting you or bruising your tininess—I ache to grip and knead you, to eat you in one gulp, in a thousand nibbles—

Oh, the power of *red*—the Old One said it! Now I feel my special hands, my tender hands I always carry hidden—now they come swelling out, come pushing toward my head! What? What?

My secret hands begin to knead and roll the stuff that's dripping from my jaws.

Ah, that arouses you too, my redling, doesn't it?

Yes, yes, I feel—torture—I feel your shy excitement! How your body remembers even now our love-dawn, our very first moments of Moggadeet-Leely. Before I knew You-Yourself, before you knew Me. It began then, my heartlet, our love-knowing began in that very first instant when your Moggadeet stared down at you like a monster bursting. I saw how new you were, how helpless!

Yes, even while I loomed over you marveling—even while my secret hands drew and spun your fate—even then it came to me in pity that long ago, last year when I was a child, I saw other little red ones among my brothers, before our Mother drove them away. I was only a foolish baby then; I didn't understand. I thought they'd grown strange and silly in their redness and Mother did well to turn them out. Oh stupid Moggadeet!

269

But now I saw *you*, my flamelet—I understood! You were only that day cast out by your Mother. Never had you felt the terrors of a night alone in the world; you couldn't imagine that such a monster as Frim was hunting you. Oh my ruby nestling, my baby red! Never, I vowed it, never would I leave you—and have I not kept that vow? Never! I, Moggadeet, *I would be your Mother.*

Great is the Plan, but I was greater!

All I learned of hunting in my lonely year, to drift like the air, to leap, to grip so delicately—all these learnings became for you! Not to bruise the smallest portion of your bright body. Oh yes! I captured you whole in all your tiny perfection, though you sizzled and spat and fought me like the sunspark you are. And then—

And then—

I began to—Oh, terror! Delight-shame! How can I speak such a beautiful secret?—the Plan took me as a Mother guides her child and with my special hands I began to—

I began to bind you up!

Oh yes! Oh yes! My special hands that had no use now all unfurled and engorged and alive, never stopping the working in the strong juice of my jaws—they began to *bind* you, passing over and around and beneath you, every moment piercing me with fear and joy. I wound among your darling little limbs, into your inmost delicate recesses, gently swathing and soothing you, winding and binding until you became a shining jewel. Mine!

—But you responded. I know that now. We know! Oh yes, in your fierce struggles, shyly you helped me, always at the end each strand fell sweetly into place ... *Winding you, binding you, loving Leelyloo!* ... How our bodies moved in our first weaving song! I feel it even now, I melt with excitement! How I wove the silk about you, tying each tiny limb, making you perfectly helpless. How fearlessly you gazed up at me, your terrifying captor! You! You were never frightened, as I'm not frightened now. Isn't it strange, my loveling? This sweetness that floods our bodies when we yield to the Plan. Great is the Plan! Fear it, fight it—but hold the sweetness yet.

Sweetly began our lovetime, when first I became your new true Mother, never to cast you out. How I fed you and caressed and cossetted and fondled you! What a responsibility it is to be a Mother. Anxiously I carried you furled in my secret arms, savagely I drove off all intruders, even the harmless banlings in the grass, in fear every moment that you were stifled or crushed!

And all the warm nights long, how I cared for your helpless little body, carefully releasing each infant limb, flexing and stretching it, cleaning every scarlet morsel of you with my giant tongue, nibbling your baby claws with my terrible teeth, reveling in your baby hum, pretending to devour you while you shrieked with glee, *Li! Lilili! Love-lili, Leelylee!* But the greatest joy of all—

We spoke!

We spoke together, we two! We communed, we shared, we poured ourselves one into the other. Love, how we stammered and stumbled at the first, you in your strange Mother-tongue and I in mine! How we blended our singing wordlessly and then with words, until more and more we came to see with each other's eyes, to hear, to taste, to feel the world of each other, until I became Leelyloo and you became Moggadeet, until finally we became together a new thing, Moggadeet-Leely, Lilliloo-Mogga, Lili-Mogglooly-deet!

Oh, love, are we the first? Have others loved with their whole selves? Oh sad thinking, that lovers before us have left no trace. Remember us! Will you remember, my adored, though Moggadeet has spoiled everything and the cold grows? If only I could hear you speak once more, my red, my innocent one. You are remembering, your body tells me you remember even now. Softly, hold me softly yet. Hear your Moggadeet!

You told me how it was being you, yourself, tiny-redling Lilliloo. Of your Mother, your dreams, your baby joys and fears. And I told you mine, and all my learnings in the world since the day when my own Mother—

Hear me, my heartmate! Time runs away.

—On the last day of my childhood my Mother called us all under her.

271

"Sons! S-son-n-nss!" Why did her dear voice creak so?

My brothers came in slowly, fearfully from the summer green. But I, small Moggadeet, I climb eagerly up under the great arch of her body, seeking the golden Mother-fur. Right into her warm cave I come, where her Mother-eyes are glowing, the cave that sheltered us so strongly all our lives, as I shelter you, my dawnflower.

I long to touch her, to hear her speak and sing to us again. Her Mother-fur troubles me, it is tattered and drab. Shyly I press against one of her huge food-glands. It feels dry, but a glow sparks deep in her Mother-eye.

"Mother," I whisper. "It's me, Moggadeet!"

"SONNNNNS!" Her voice rumbles through her armor. My big brothers huddle by her legs, peering back at the sunlight. They look so funny, shedding, half gold, half black.

"I'm afraid!" whimpers my brother Frim nearby. Like me Frim still has his gold baby fur. Mother is speaking again but her voice booms so I can hardly understand.

"WINNN-TER! WINTER, I SAY! AFTER THE WARM COMES BEFORE THE COLD WINTER. THE COLD WIN-TER BEFORE THE WARM COMES AGAIN, COMES . . ."

Frim whimpers louder; I cuff him. What's wrong, why is her loving voice so hoarse and strange now? She always hummed us so tenderly, we nestled in her warm Mother-fur sucking the lovely Mother-juices, rocking to her steady walking-song. *Ee mooly-mooly, Ee-mooly-mooly,* while far below the earth rolled by. Oh, yes, and how we held our breaths and squealed when she began her mighty hunting-hum! *Tann! Tann! Dir! Dir! Dir Hataan! HATONN!* How we clung in the thrilling climax when she plunged upon her prey and we heard the crunching, the tearing, the gurgling in her body that meant soon her food-glands would be richly full.

Suddenly I see a black streak down below—a big brother is running away! Mother's booming voice breaks off. Her great body tenses, her plates clash. Mother roars!

Running, screaming down below! I burrow up into her fur, am flung about as she leaps.

"OUT! GO OUT!" she bellows. Her terrible hunting-limbs crash down, she roars without words, shuddering, jolting.

When I dare to peek out I see the others all have fled. All except one!

A black body is lying under Mother's claws. It's my brother Sesso—yes! But Mother is tearing him, is eating him! I watch in horror—Sesso she cared for so proudly, so tenderly! I sob, I bury my head in her fur. But the beautiful fur is coming loose in my hands, her golden Mother-fur is dying! I cling desperately, trying not to hear the crunches, the gulps and gurgling. The world is ending, all is terrible, terrible.

And yet, my fireberry, even then I almost understood. Great is the Plan!

Presently Mother stops feeding and begins to move. The rocky ground jolts by far below. Her stride is not smooth but jerks me, even her deep hum is strange. *On! On! Alone! Ever alone. And on!* The rumbling ceases. Silence. Mother is resting.

"Mother!" I whisper. "Mother, it's Moggadeet. I'm here!"

Her stomach plates contract, a belch reverberates in her vaults.

"Go," she groans. "Go. Too late. Mother no more."

"I don't want to leave you. Why must I go? Mother!" I wail, "Speak to me!" I keen my baby hum, *Deet! Deet! Tikki-takka! Deet!* hoping Mother will answer, crooning deep, *Brum! Brumm! Brumaloo-brum!* Now I see one huge Mother-eye glowing faintly but she only makes a grating sound.

"Too late. No more . . . The winter, I say. I did speak. Before the winter, go. Go."

"Tell me about Outside, Mother," I plead.

Another groan or cough nearly shakes me from my perch. But when she speaks again her voice sounds gentler.

"Talk?" she grumbles, "Talk, talk, talk. You are a strange son. Talk, like your Father."

"What's that, Mother? What's a Father?"

She belches again. "Always talk. The winters grow, he said. Oh, yes. Tell them the winters grow. So I did. Late. Winter, I spoke you. Cold!" Her voice booms. "No more! Too late." Outside I hear her armor rattle and clank.

"Mother, speak to me!"

"Go. Go-o-o!"

Her belly-plates clash around me. I jump for another nest of fur but it comes loose in my grip. Wailing, I save myself by hanging to one of her great walking limbs. It is rigid, thrumming like rock.

"GO!" she roars.

Her Mother-eyes are shriveling, dead! I panic, scramble down, everything is vibrating, resonating around me. Mother is holding back a storm of rage!

I leap for the ground, I rush diving into a crevice, I wiggle and burrow under the fearful bellowing and clanging that rains on me from above. Into the rocks I go with the hunting claws of Mother crashing behind me.

Oh, my redling, my little tenderling! Never have you known such a night. Those dreadful hours hiding from the monster that had been my loving Mother!

I saw her once more, yes. When dawn came I clambered up a ledge and peered through the mist. It was warm then, the mists were warm. I knew what Mothers looked like; the sudden glimpses of huge horned dark shapes before our own Mother hooted us under her . . . Oh yes, and then would come Mother's earth-shaking challenge and the strange Mother's answering roar, and we'd cling tight, feeling her surge of kill-fury, buffeted, deafened, battered while our Mother charged and struck. And once while our Mother fed I peeped out and saw a strange baby squealing in the remnants on the ground below . . .

But now it was my own dear Mother I saw lurching away through the mists, that great rusty-gray hulk so horned and bossed that only her hunting-eyes showed above her armor, swiveling mindlessly, questing for anything that moved. She crashed her way across the mountains and as she went she thrummed a new harsh song. *Cold! Cold! Ice and Lone. Ice! And cold! And end.* I never saw her again.

When the sun rose I saw that the gold fur was peeling from my shiny black. All by itself my hunting-limb flashed out and knocked a hopper right into my jaws.

You see, my berry, how much larger and stronger I was than you when Mother sent us away? That is also the Plan. For you were not yet born! I had to live on while the warm turned to cold and while the winter passed to warm again before you would be waiting. I had to grow and learn. To *learn*, my Lilliloo! That is important. Only we black ones have a time to learn—the Old One said it.

Such small learnings at first! To drink the flat water-stuff without choking, to catch the shiny flying things that bite and to watch the storm clouds and the moving of the sun. And the nights, and the soft things that moved on the trees. And the bushes that kept shrinking, shrinking—only it was me, Moggadeet, growing larger! Oh yes! And the day when I could knock down a fatclimber from its vine!

But all these learnings were easy—the Plan in my body guided me. It guides me now, Lilliloo, even now it would give me peace and joy if I yielded to it. But I will not! I will remember to the end, I will speak to the end!

I will speak the big learnings. How I saw—though I was so busy catching and eating more, more, always more—I saw all things were changing, changing. *Changers!* The bushes changed their buds to berries, the fatclimbers changed their colors, even the sun changed, and the hills. And I saw all things were together with others of their kind but only me, Moggadeet. I was alone. Oh, so alone!

I went marching through the valleys in my shiny new black, humming my new song *Turra-tarra! Tarra Tan!* Once I glimpsed my brother Frim and I called him, but he ran like the wind. Away, alone! And when I went to the next valley I found the trees all mashed down. And in the distance I saw a black one like me—only many times as big! Huge! Almost as big as a Mother, sleek and glossy-new. I would have called but he reared up and saw me and roared so terribly that I too fled like the wind to empty mountains. Alone.

And so I learned, my redling, how we are alone even though my heart was full of love. And I wandered, puzzling and eating ever more and more. I saw the Trails; they meant nothing to me then. But I began to learn the important thing.

The cold.

You know it, my little red. How in the warm days I am me, Myself-Moggadeet. Ever-growing, ever-learning. In the warm we think, we speak. We love! We make our own Plan, Oh, did we not, my lovemate?

But in the cold, in the night—for the nights were growing colder—in the cold night I was—what?—Not Moggadeet. Not Moggadeet-thinking. Not Me-Myself. Only Something-that-lives, acts without thought. Helpless-Moggadeet. In the cold is only the Plan. I almost thought it.

And then one day the night-chill lingered and lingered and the sun was hidden in the mists. And I found myself going up the Trails.

The Trails are a part of the Plan too, my redling.

The Trails are of winter. There we must go all of us, we blacks. When the cold grows stronger the Plan calls us upward, upward, we begin to drift up the Trails, up along the ridges to the cold, the night-side of the mountains. Up beyond the forests where the trees grow scant and turn to stony deadwood.

So the Plan drew me and I followed, only half-aware. Sometimes I came into warmer sunlight where I could stop and feed and try to think, but the cold fogs rose again and I went on, on and up. I began to catch sight of others like me far along the mountain-flank, moving steadily up. They didn't rear or roar when they saw me. I didn't call to them. Each one alone we climbed on toward the Caves, unthinking, blind. And so I would have gone too.

But then the great thing happened.

—Oh no, my Lililoo! Not the *greatest*. The greatest of all is you, will always be you. My precious sunmite, my red love-baby! Don't be angry, no, no, my sharing one. Hold me softly. I must say our big learning. Hear your Moggadeet, hear and remember!

In the sun's last warm I found him, the Old One. A terrible sight! So maimed and damaged, parts rotting and gone. I stared, thinking him dead. Suddenly his head rolled feebly and a croak came out.

"Young . . . one?" An eye opened in his festering head, a flyer pecked at it. "Young one . . . wait!"

And I understood him! Oh, with love—

No, no, my redling! Gently! Gently hear your Moggadeet. We *spoke*, the Old One and I! Old to young, we shared. I think it cannot happen.

"No old ones," he creaked. "Never to speak . . . we blacks. Never. It is not . . . the Plan. Only me . . . I wait . . ."

"Plan" I ask, half-knowing. "What is the Plan?"

"A beauty," he whispers. "In the warm, a beauty in the air . . . I followed . . . but another black one saw me and we fought . . . and I was damaged, but still the Plan made me follow until I was crushed and torn and dead . . . But I lived! And the Plan let me go and I crawled here . . . to wait . . . to share . . . but—"

His head sags. Quickly I snatch a flyer from the air and push it to his torn jaws.

"Old One! What is the Plan?"

He swallows painfully, his one eye holding mine.

"In us," he says thickly, stronger now. "In us, moving us in all things necessary for the life. You have seen. When the baby is golden the Mother cherishes it all winter long. But when it turns red or black she drives it away. Was it not so?"

"Yes, but—"

"That's the Plan! Always the Plan. Gold is the color of Mother-care but black is the color of rage. Attack the black! Black is to kill. Even a Mother, even her own baby, she cannot defy the Plan. Hear me, young one!"

"I hear. I have seen," I answer. "But what is red?"

"*Red!*" He groans. "Red is the color of love."

"No!" I say, stupid Moggadeet! "I know love. Love is gold."

The Old One's eyes turns from me. "Love," he sighs. "When the beauty comes in the air, you will see . . ." He falls silent there together in the last misty sunwarm. Dimly on the slopes I can see other black ones like myself drifting steadily upward on their own Trails among the stone-tree heaps, into the icy mists.

"Old One! Where do we go?"

"You go to the Caves of Winter. That is the Plan."

"Winter, yes. The cold. Mother told us. And after the cold winter comes the warm. I remember. The winter will pass, won't it? Why did she say, the winters grow? Teach me, Old One. What is a Father?"

"Fa-ther? A word I don't know. But wait—" His mangled head turns to me. "*The winters grow?* Your mother said this?

Oh cold! Oh lonely," he groans. "A big learning she gave you. This learning I fear to think."

His eye rolls, glaring. I am frightened inside.

"Look around, young one. These stony deadwoods. Dead shells of trees that grow in the warm valleys. Why are they here? The cold has killed them. No living tree grows here now. Think, young one!"

I look, and true! It is a warm forest killed to stone.

"Once it was warm here. Once it was like the valleys. But the cold has grown stronger. The winter grows. Do you see? *And the warm grows less and less.*"

"But the warm is life! The warm is Me-Myself!"

"Yes. In the warm we think, we learn. In the cold is only the Plan. In the cold we are blind . . . Waiting here, I thought, was there a time when it was warm here once? Did we come here, we blacks, in the warm to speak, to share? Oh young one, a fearful thinking. Does our time of learning grow shorter, shorter? Where will it end? Will the winters grow until we can learn nothing but only live blindly in the Plan, like the silly fatclimbers who sing but do not speak?"

His words fill me with cold fear. Such a terrible learning! I feel anger.

"No! We will not! We must—we must hold the warm!"

"Hold the warm?" He twists painfully to stare at me. "Hold the warm . . . A great thinking. Yes. But how? How? Soon it will be too cold to think, even here!"

"The warm will come again," I tell him. "Then we must learn a way to hold it, you and I!"

His head lolls.

"No . . . When the warm comes I will not be here . . . and you will be too busy for thinking, young one."

"I will help you! I will carry you to the Caves—"

"In the Caves," he gasps, "In each Cave there are two black ones like yourself. One is living, waiting mindless for the winter to pass . . . And while he waits, he eats. He eats the other, that is how he lives. That is the Plan. As you will eat me, my youngling."

"No!" I cry in horror. "I will never harm you!"

278

"When the cold comes you will see," he whispers. "Great is the Plan!"

"No! You are wrong! I will break the Plan," I shout. A cold wind is blowing from the summit; the sun dies.

"Never will I harm you," I bellow. "You are wrong to say so!"

My scaleplates are rising, my tail begins to pound. Through the mists I hear his gasps.

I recall dragging a heavy black thing to my Cave.

Chill cold, kill cold . . . In the cold I killed you.

Leelyloo. He did not resist.

Great is the Plan. He accepted all, perhaps he even felt a strange joy, as I feel it now. In the Plan is joy. But if the Plan is wrong? *The winters grow.* Do the fatclimbers have their Plan too?

Oh, a hard thinking! How we tried, my redling, my joy. All the long warm days I explained it to you, over and over. How the winter would come and change us if we did not hold the warm. You understood! You share, you understand me now, my precious flame—though you can't speak I feel your sharing love. Softly . . .

Oh yes, we made our preparations, our own Plan. Even in the highest heat we made our Plan against the cold. Have other lovers done so? How I searched, carrying you my cherry bud; I crossed whole mountain ranges, following the sun until we found this warmest of warm valleys on the sunward side. Surely the cold would be weak here, I thought. How could they reach us here, the cold fogs, the icy winds that froze my inner Me and drew me up the Trails into the dead Caves of winter?

This time I would defy!

This time I have *you.*

"Don't take me there, my Moggadeet!" You begged, fearful of the strangeness. "Don't take me to the cold!"

"Never, my Leeliloo! Never, I vow it. Am I not your Mother, little redness?"

"But you will change! The cold will make you forget. Is it not the Plan?"

"We will break the Plan, Lili. See you are growing larger, heavier, my fireberry—and always more beautiful! Soon I will

279

not be able to carry you so easily, I could never carry you to the cold Trails. And I will never leave you!"

"But you are so big, Moggadeet! When the change comes you will forget and drag me to the cold."

"Never! Your Moggadeet has a deeper Plan! When the mists start I will take you to the farthest, warmest cranny of this cave, and there I will spin a wall so you can never never be pulled out. And I will never never leave you. Even the Plan cannot draw Moggadeet from Leelyloo!"

"But you will have to go hunting for food and the cold will take you then! You will forget me and follow the cold love of winter and leave me there to die! Perhaps that is the Plan!"

"Oh no, my precious, my redling! Don't grieve, don't cry! Hear your Moggadeet's Plan! From now on I'll hunt twice as hard. I'll fill this cave to the top, my fat little blushbud, I will fill it with food now so I can stay by you all the winter through!"

And so I did, didn't I my Lilli? Silly Moggadeet, how I hunted, how I brought lizards, hoppers, fatclimbers and ban-lings by the score. What a fool! For of course they rotted, there in the heat, and the heaps turned green and slimy—but still tasting good, eh, my berry? —so that we had to eat them then, gorging ourselves like babies. And how you grew!

Oh, beautiful you became, my jewel of redness—so bursting fat and shiny-full, but still my tiny one, my sunspark. Each night after I fed you I would part the silk, fondling your head, your eyes, your tender ears, trembling with excitement for the delicious moment when I would release your first scarlet limb to caress and exercise it and press it to my pulsing throat-sacs. Sometimes I would unbind two together for the sheer joy of seeing you move. And each night it took longer, each morning I had to make more silk to bind you up. How proud I was, my Leely, Lilliloo!

That was when my greatest thinking came.

As I was weaving you so tenderly into your shining cocoon, my joyberry, I thought, why not bind up living fatclimbers? Pen them alive so their flesh will stay sweet and they will serve us through the winter!

That was a great thinking, Lilliloo, and I did this, and it was good. Fatclimbers in plenty I walled in a little tunnel, and many, many other things as well, while the sun walked back toward winter and the shadows grew and grew. Fatclimbers and banlings and all tasty creatures and even—Oh, clever Moggadeet!—all manner of leaves and bark and stuffs for them to eat! Oh, we had broken the Plan for sure now!

"We have broken the Plan for sure, my Lilli-red. The fatclimbers are eating the twigs and bark, the banlings are eating juice from the wood, the great runners are munching grass, and we will eat them all!"

"Oh, Moggadeet, you are brave! Do you think we can really break the Plan? I am frightened! Give me a banling, I think it grows cold."

"You have eaten fifteen banlings, my minikin!" I teased you. "How fat you grow! Let me look at you again; yes, you must let your Moggadeet caress you while you eat. Ah, how adorable you are!"

And of course—Oh, you remember how it began then, our deepest love. For when I uncovered you one night with the first hint of cold in the air, I saw that you had changed.

Shall I say it? Your secret fur. Your *Mother-fur.*

Always I had cleaned you there tenderly, but without difficulty to restrain myself. But on this night when I parted the silk strands with my huge hunting claws, what new delights met my eyes! No longer pink and pale but fiery red! *Red!* Scarlet blaze like the reddest sunrise, gold-tipped! And swollen, curling, dewy—Oh! Commanding me to expose you, all of you. Oh, how your tender eyes melted me, and your breath musky-sweet and your limbs warm and heavy in my grasp!

Wildly I ripped away the last strands, dazed with bliss as you slowly stretched your whole blazing redness before my eyes. I knew then—*we* knew!—that the love we felt before was only a beginning. My hunting-limbs fell at my sides and my special hands, my weaving hands grew, filled with new, almost painful life. I could not speak, my throat-sacs filling, filling! And my love-hands rose up by themselves, pressing ecstatically, while my eyes bent closer, closer to your glorious *red!*

But suddenly the Me-Myself, Moggadeet awoke! I jumped back!

"Lilli! What's happening to us?"

"Oh, Moggadeet, I love you! Don't go away!"

"What is it, Leelyloo? Is it the Plan?"

"I don't care! Moggadeet, don't you love me?"

"I fear! I fear to harm you! You are so tiny. I am your Mother."

"No, Moggadeet, look! I am as big as you are. Don't be afraid."

I drew back—Oh, hard, hard!—and tried to look calmly.

"True, my redling, you have grown. But your limbs are so new, so tender. Oh, I can't look!"

Averting my eyes I began to spin a screen of silk, to shut away your maddening redness.

"We must wait, Lilliloo. We must go on as before. I don't know what this strange urging means; I fear it will bring you harm."

"Yes, Moggadeet. We will wait."

And so we waited. Oh, yes. Each night it grew more hard. We tried to be as before, to be happy, Leely-Moggadeet. Each night as I caressed your glowing limbs that seemed to offer themselves to me, as I swathed and unswathed them in turn, the urge rose in me hotter, more strong. To unveil you wholly! To look again upon your whole body!

"Oh yes, my darling, I feel—unbearable—how you remember with me those last days of our simple love.

Colder . . . colder. Mornings when I went to harvest the fatclimbers there was a whiteness on their fur and the banlings ceased to move. The sun sank ever lower, paler, and the cold mists hung above us, reaching down. Soon I dared not leave the cave. I stayed all day by your silken wall, humming Motherlike, *Brum-a-loo, Mooly-mooly . . . Lilliloo, Love Leely . . .* Strong Moggadeet!

"We'll wait, fireling. We will not yield to the Plan! . . . Aren't we happier than all others, here with our love in our warm cave?"

"Oh yes, Moggadeet."

"I'm Myself now. I am strong. I'll make my own Plan. I will not look at you until . . . until the warm, until the Sun comes back."

"Yes, Moggadeet . . . Moggadeet? My limbs are cramped."

"Oh, my precious, wait—see, I am opening the silk very carefully, I will not look—I won't—"

"Moggadeet, don't you love me?"

"Leelyloo! Oh, my glorious one! I fear, I fear—"

"Look, Moggadeet! See how big I am, how strong!"

"Oh, redling, my hands—my hands—what are they doing to you?"

For with my special hands I was pressing, pressing the hot juices from my throat-sacs and tenderly, tenderly parting your sweet Mother-fur and *placing my gift within your secret places*. And as I did this our eyes entwined and our limbs made a wreath.

"My darling, do I hurt you?"

"Oh no, Moggadeet! Oh, no!"

Oh, my adored one, those last days of our love!

Outside the world grew colder yet, and the fatclimbers ceased to eat and the banlings lay still and began to stink. But still we held the warmth deep in our cave and still I fed my beloved on the last of our food. And every night our new ritual of love became more free, richer, though I compelled myself to hide all but a portion of your sweet body. But each dawn it grew hard and harder for me to replace the silken bonds around your limbs.

"Moggadeet! Why do you not bind me? I am afraid!"

"A moment, Lilli, a moment. I must caress you just once more."

"I'm afraid, Moggadeet! Cease now and bind me!"

"But why, my lovekin? Why must I hide you? Is this not some foolish part of the Plan?"

"I don't know, I feel so strange, Moggadeet, I—I'm changing."

"You grow more glorious every moment, my Lilli, my own. Let me look at you! It is wrong to bind you away!"

"No, Moggadeet! No!"

But I would not listen, would I? Oh foolish Moggadeet-who-thought-to-be-your-Mother. Great is the Plan!

I did not listen, I did not bind you up. No! I ripped them away, the strong silk strands. Mad with love I slashed them all at once, rushing from one limb to the next, until all your glorious body lay exposed. At last—I saw you whole!

Oh, Lilliloo, greatest of Mothers.

It was not I who was your Mother. You were mine.

Shining and bossed you lay, your armor newly grown, your mighty hunting limbs thicker than my head! What I had created. You! A Supermother, a Mother such as none have ever seen!

Stupefied with delight, I gazed.

And your huge hunting limb came out and seized me.

Great is the Plan. I felt only joy as your jaws took me.

As I feel it now.

And so we end, my Lilliloo, my redling, for your babies are swelling through your Mother-fur and your Moggadeet can speak no longer. I am nearly devoured. The cold grows, it grows, and your Mother-eyes are growing, glowing. Soon you will be alone with our children and the warm will come again.

Will you remember, my heartmate? Will you remember and tell them?

Tell them of the cold, Leelyloo. Tell them of our love.

Tell them . . . *the winters grow.*

Chad Oliver

Born in Cincinnati, Ohio, Chad (wick) Oliver (1928–   )
was still an undergraduate when he sold his first science
fiction story.

After finishing a B.A. (1951) and M.A. (1952) at the University of Texas at Austin, he completed course work for his
Ph.D. in anthropology (1961) at the University of California
at Los Angeles, returning to Austin in 1955 to serve as a
faculty member while working on his dissertation. With
the exception of some visiting professorships, it is there
that he has remained, becoming department chairperson in
1967 and full professor in 1968.

In addition to research papers, he has written four nonfiction books: *Mists of Dawn*, a juvenile, (1954); *Ecology and
Cultural Continuity as Contributing Factors in the Social
Organization of the Plains Indians* (1962); *Cultural Anthropology: The Discovery of Humanity* (1980); and *The
Kamba of Kenya* (1980).

A western novel *(The Wolf is My Brother,* 1967) brought
him a Golden Spur Award from the Western Writers of
America. But almost all the rest of his fiction is science
fiction. That includes five novels and approximately forty
shorter works. Particularly worthwhile are the vastly underrated *The Winds of Time* (1957), "Of Course" (1954),
"The Mother of Necessity" (1955), "Didn't He Ramble"
(1957) and "King of the Hill" (1972). For this collection we
have chosen a story about the origins of man, one that
seems to demand (How about it, Chad?) a couple of follow-ups.

TRANSFUSION

by Chad Oliver

THE MACHINE STOPPED.

There was no sound at all now, and the green light on the control panel blinked like a mocking eye. With the easy precision born of long routine, Ben Hazard did what had to be done. He did it automatically, without real interest, for there was no longer any hope.

He punched a figure into the recorder: 377.

He computed the year, using the Gottwald-Hazard Correlation, and added that to the record: 254,000 B.C.

He completed the form with the name of the site: Choukoutien.

Then, with a lack of anticipation that eloquently reminded him that this was the three hundred seventy-seventh check instead of the first, Ben Hazard took a long preliminary look through the viewer. He saw nothing that interested him.

Careful as always before leaving the Bucket, he punched in the usual datum: VIEWER SCAN NEGATIVE.....

He unlocked the hatch at the top of the Bucket and climbed out of the metallic gray sphere. It was not raining, for a change, and the sun was warm and golden in a clean blue sky.

Ben Hazard stretched his tired muscles and rested his eyes on the fresh green of the tangled plants that grew along the banks of the lazy stream to his right. The grass in the little meadow looked cool and inviting, and there were birds singing in the trees. He was impressed as always by how little this corner of the world had changed in fifty years. It was very much as it had been a thousand years ago, or two thousand, or three. . . .

It was just a small corner of nowhere, lost in the mists of time, waiting for the gray sheets of ice to come again.

It was just a little stream, bubbling along and minding its own business, and a lonely limestone hill scarred with the dark staring eyes of rock shelters and cave entrances.

There was nothing different about it.

It took Man to change things in a hurry, and Man wasn't home.

That was the problem.

Ben took the six wide-angle photographs of the terrain that he always took. There were no animals within camera range this trip. He clambered through the thick brown brush at the base of the limestone hill and climbed up the rough rocks to the cave entrance. It was still open, and he knew its location by heart.

He well remembered the thrill he had felt the first time he had entered this cave. His heart had hammered in his chest and his throat had been so dry that he couldn't swallow. His mind had been ablaze with memories and hopes and fears, and it had been the most exciting moment of his life.

Now, only the fear remained—and it was a new kind of fear, the fear of what he *wouldn't* find.

His light blazed ahead of him as he picked his way along the winding passage of the cave. He disturbed a cloud of indignant bats, but there was no other sign of life. He reached the central cavern, dark and hushed and hidden under the earth, and flashed his light around carefully.

There was nothing new.

He recognized the familiar bones of wolf, bear, tiger and camel. He photographed them again, and did manage to find the remains of an ostrich that he had not seen before. He took two pictures of that.

He spent half an hour poking around in the cavern, checking all of the meticulously recorded sites, and then made his way back to the sunlit entrance.

The despair welled up in him, greater than before. Bad news, even when it is expected, is hard to take when it is confirmed. And there was no longer any real doubt.

Man wasn't home.

Ben Hazard wasn't puzzled any longer. He was scared and worried. He couldn't pass the buck to anyone else this time. He had come back to see for himself, and he had seen.

Imagine a man who built a superb computer, a computer that could finally answer the toughest problems in his field. Suppose the ultimate in computers, and the ultimate in coded tapes; a machine—however hypothetical—that was never wrong. Just for kicks, suppose that the man feeds in an easy one: *What is two plus three?*

If the computer answers *six*, then the man is in trouble. Of course, the machine might be multiplying rather than adding—

But if the computer answers *zero* or *insufficient data*, what then?

Ben Hazard slowly walked back to the Bucket, climbed inside, and locked the hatch.

He filed his films under the proper code number.

He pushed in the familiar datum: FIELD RECONNAISSANCE NEGATIVE.

He sat down before the control board and got ready.

He was completely alone in the small metallic sphere; he could see every inch of it. He *knew* he was alone. And yet, as he had before, he had the odd impression that there was someone with him, someone looking over his shoulder. . . .

Ben Hazard had never been one to vault into the saddle and gallop off in all directions. He was a trained scientist, schooled to patience. He did not understand the soundless voice that kept whispering in his mind: *Hurry, hurry, hurry—*

"Boy," he said aloud, "you've been in solitary too long."

He pulled himself together and reached for the controls. He was determined to run out the string—twenty-three checks to go now—but he already knew the answer.

Man wasn't home.

When Ben Hazard returned to his original year of departure, which was 1982, he stepped out of the Bucket at New Mexico Station—for the machine, of necessity, moved in space as well as time. As a matter of fact, the spatial movement of the Bucket was one of the things that made it tough to do an intensive periodic survey of any single spot on the Earth's surface; it was hard to hold the Bucket on target.

According to his own reckoning, and in terms of psychological time, he had spent some forty days in his check of Choukoutien in the Middle Pleistocene. Viewed from the other end at New Mexico Station, he had been gone only five days.

The first man he saw was the big M.P. corporal.

"I'll need your prints and papers, sir," the M.P. said.

"Damnit, Ames." Ben handed over the papers and stuck his thumbs in the scanner. "Don't you know me by now?"

"Orders, sir."

Ben managed a tired smile. After all, the military implications of time travel were staggering, and care was essential. If you could move back in time only a few years and see what the other side had done, then you could counter their plans in the present. Since the old tribal squabbles were still going full blast, Gottwald had had to pull a million strings in order to get his hands on some of the available Buckets.

"Sorry, Ames. You look pretty good to me after a month or so of old camel bones."

"Nice to have you back, Dr. Hazard," the M.P. said neutrally.

After he had been duly identified as Benjamin Wright Hazard, professor of anthropology at Harvard and senior scientist on the Joint Smithsonian-Harvard-Berkeley Temporal Research Project, he was allowed to proceed. Ben crossed the crowded floor of the room they called Grand Central Station and paused a moment to see how the chimps were getting along.

There were two of them, Charles Darwin and Cleopatra, in separate cages. The apes had been the first time travelers, and were still used occasionally in testing new Buckets. Cleopatra scratched herself and hooted what might have been a greeting, but Charles Darwin was busy with a problem. He was trying to fit two sticks together so he could knock down a banana that was hanging just out of reach. He was obviously irritated, but he was no quitter.

"I know just how you feel, Charles," Ben said.

Charles Darwin pursed his mobile lips and redoubled his efforts.

What they won't do for one lousy banana.

Ben looked around for Nate York, who was working with the chimps, and spotted him talking to a technician and keeping track of his experiment out of the corner of his eye. Ben waved and went on to the elevator.

He rode up to the fourth floor and walked into Ed Stone's office. Ed was seated at his desk and he looked very industrious as he studied the dry white skull in front of him. The skull, however, was just a paper weight; Ed had used it for years.

He stood up, grinned, and stuck out his hand. "Sure glad you're back, Ben. Any luck?"

Ben shook hands and straddled a chair. He pulled out his pipe, filled it from a battered red can, and lit it gratefully. It felt good to be back with Ed. A man doesn't find too many other men he can really talk to in his lifetime, and Ed was definitely Number One. Since they were old friends, they spoke a private language.

"He was out to lunch," Ben said.

"For twenty thousand years?"

"Sinanthropus has always been famous for his dietary eccentricities."

Ed nodded to show that he caught the rather specialized joke—Sinanthropus had been a cannibal—and he leaned forward, his elbows on the desk. "You satisfied now?"

"Absolutely."

"No margin for error?" Ed insisted.

"None. I didn't really doubt Thompson's report, but I wanted to make certain. Sinanthropus isn't there. Period."

"That tears it then. We're up the creek for sure."

"Without a paddle."

"Without even a canoe." Ben puffed on his pipe. "Blast it, Ed, where *are* they?"

"You tell me. Since you left, Gottwald and I have gotten exactly nowhere. The way it looks right now, man hasn't got any ancestors—and that's crazy."

It's more than crazy, Ben thought. It's frightening. When you stop to think about it, man is a lot more than just an individual. Through his children, he extends on into the future. Through his ancestors, he stretches back far into the past. It is immortality of a sort. And when you chop off one end—

"I'm scared," he said. "I don't mind admitting it. There's an answer somewhere, and we've got to find it."

"I know how you feel, Ben. If this thing means what it seems to mean, then all science is just so much hot air. There's no cause and effect, no evidence, no reason. Man isn't what he thinks he is at all. We're just frightened animals sitting in a cave gaping at the darkness outside. Don't think I don't feel it, too. But what are we going to *do*?"

Ben stood up and knocked out his pipe. "Right now, I'm going home and hit the sack; I'm dead. Then the three of us— you and I and Gottwald—are going to sit down and hash this thing out. Then we'll at least know where we are."

"Will we?"

"We'd better."

He walked to the elevator and rode down to the ground floor of New Mexico Station. He had to identify himself twice more before he finally emerged into the glare of the desert sunlight. The situation struck him as the height of irony: here they were worried about spies and fancy feuds, when all the time—

What?

He climbed into his car and started for home. The summer day was bright and hot, but he felt as though he were driving down an endless tunnel of darkness, an infinite black cave to nowhere.

The voice whispered in his brain: *Hurry, hurry*—

His home was a lonely one, lonely with a special kind of emptiness. All his homes seemed deserted now that Anne was gone, but he liked this one better than most.

It was built of adobe with heavy exposed roof beams, cool in the summer and warm in winter. The Mexican tile floor was artfully broken up by lovely Navaho rugs—the rare Two Gray Hills kind in subdued and intricate grays and blacks and whites. He had brought many of his books with him from Boston and their familiar jackets lined the walls.

Ben was used to loneliness, but memories died hard. The plane crash that had taken Anne from him had left an emptiness in his heart. Sometimes, late in the evening, he thought he heard her footsteps in the kitchen. Often, when the telephone rang, he waited for her to answer it.

Fifteen years of marriage are hard to forget.

Ben took a hot shower, shaved, and cooked himself a steak from the freezer. Then he poured a healthy jolt of scotch over two ice cubes and sat down in the big armchair, propping his feet on the padded bench. He was still tired, but he felt more like a human being.

His eyes wandered to his books. There was usually something relaxing about old books and long-read titles, something reassuring. It had always been that way for him, but not any longer.

The titles jeered at him: *Mankind So Far, Up from the Ape, History of the Primates, Fossil Men, The Story of Man, Human Origins, The Fossil Evidence for Human Evolution, History of the Vertebrates* . . .

Little man, what now?

"We seem to have made a slight mistake, as the chemist remarked when his lab blew up," Ben said aloud.

Yes, but where could they have gone wrong?

Take Sinanthropus, for example. The remains of forty different Sinanthropus individuals had been excavated from the site of Choukoutien in China by Black and Weidenreich, two excellent men. There was plenty of material and it had been thoroughly studied. Scientists knew when Sinanthropus had lived in the Middle Pleistocene, where he lived, and how he lived. They even had the hearths where he cooked his food, the tools he used, the animals he killed. They knew what he looked like. They knew how he was related to his cousin, Pithecanthropus Erectus, and to modern men. There was a cast of his skull in every anthropology museum in the world, a picture of him in every textbook.

There was nothing mysterious about Sam Sinanthropus. He was one of the regulars.

Ben and Gottwald had nailed the date to the wall at 250,000 B.C. After Thompson's incredible report, Ben himself had gone back in time to search for Sinanthropus. Just to make certain, he had checked through twenty thousand years.

Nobody home.

Sinanthropus wasn't there.

That was bad enough.

But *all* the early human and prehuman fossils were missing.

There *were* no men back in the Pleistocene.

No Australopithecus, no Pithecanthropus, no Neanderthal, no nothing.

It was impossible.

At first, Ben had figured that there must be an error somewhere in the dating of the fossils. After all, a geologist's casual "Middle Pleistocene" isn't much of a target, and radiocarbon dating was no good that far back. But the Gottwald-Hazard Correlation had removed that possibility.

The fossil men simply were not there.

They had disappeared. Or they had never been there. Or—

Ben got up and poured himself another drink. He needed it.

When the Winfield-Homans equations had cracked the time barrier and Ben had been invited by old Franz Gottwald to take part in the Temporal Research Project, Ben had leaped at the opportunity. It was a scientist's dream come true.

He could actually go back and *see* the long-vanished ancestors of the human species. He could listen to them talk, watch their kids, see them make their tools, hear their songs. No more sweating with a few broken bones. No more puzzling over flint artifacts. No more digging in ancient firepits.

He had felt like a man about to sit down to a Gargantuan feast.

Unhappily, it had been the cook's night out. There was nothing to eat.

Every scientist knows in his heart that his best theories are only educated guesses. There is a special Hall of Fame reserved for thundering blunders: the flat Earth, the medical humors, the unicorn.

Yes, and don't forget Piltdown Man.

Every scientist expects to revise his theories in the light of new knowledge. That's what science means. But he doesn't expect to find out that it's *all* wrong. He doesn't expect his Manhattan Project to show conclusively that uranium doesn't actually exist.

Ben finished his drink. He leaned back and closed his eyes. There had to be an answer somewhere—or some-when. *Had* to be. A world of total ignorance is a world of terror; anything can happen.

Where was Man?

And why?

He went to bed and dreamed of darkness and ancient fears. He dreamed that he lived in a strange and alien world, a world of fire and blackness and living shadows—

When he woke up the next morning, he wasn't at all sure that he had been dreaming.

Among them, an impartial observer would have agreed, the three men in the conference room at New Mexico Station knew just about all there was to know concerning early forms of man. At the moment, in Ben's opinion, they might as well have been the supreme experts on the Ptolemaic theory of epicycles.

They were three very different men.

Ben Hazard was tall and lean and craggy-featured, as though the winds of life had weathered him down to the tough, naked rock that would yield no further. His blue eyes had an ageless quality about them, the agelessness of deep seas and high mountains, but they retained an alert and restless curiosity that had changed little from the eyes of an Ohio farm boy who had long ago wondered at the magic of the rain and filled his father's old cigar boxes with strange stones that carried the imprints of plants and shells from the dawn of time.

Ed Stone looked like part of what he was: a Texan, burned by the sun, his narrow gray eyes quiet and steady. He was not a big man, and his soft speech and deliberate movements gave him a deceptive air of lassitude. Ed was an easy man to underestimate; he wasted no time on frills or pretense, but there was a razor-sharp brain in his skull. He was younger than Ben, not yet forty, but Ben trusted his judgment more than he did his own.

Franz Gottwald, old only in years, was more than a man now; he was an institution. They called him the dean of American anthropology, but not to his white-bearded face; Franz had small respect for deans. They stood when he walked into meetings, and Franz took it as his due—he had earned it, but it concerned him no more than the make of the car he drove. Ben and Ed had both studied under Franz, and they still deferred to him, but the relationship was a warm one. Franz had been born in Germany—he never spoke about his life before he had come to the United States at the age of thirty—and his voice was still flavored by a slight accent that generations of graduate students had tried to mimic without success. He was the Grand Old Man.

"Well?" asked Dr. Gottwald when Ben had finished his report. "What is the next step, gentlemen?"

Ed Stone tapped on the polished table with a yellow pencil that showed distinct traces of gnawing. "We've got to accept the facts and go on from there. We know what the situation is, and we think that we haven't made any whopping mistakes. In a nutshell, man has vanished from his own past. What we need is an explanation, and the way to get it is to find some relatively sane hypothesis that we can *test*, not just kick around. Agreed?"

"Very scientific, Edward," Gottwald said, stroking his neat white beard.

"Okay," Ben said. "Let's work from what we know. Those skeletons *were* in place in Africa, in China, in Europe, in Java—they had to be there because that's where they were originally dug up. The bones are real, I've held them in my hands, and they're still in place in the museums. No amount of twaddle about alternate time-tracks and congruent universes is going to change that. Furthermore, unless Franz and I are the prize dopes of all time, the dating of those fossils is accurate in terms of geology and the associated flora and fauna and whatnot. The Buckets work; there's no question about that. So why can't we find the men who left the skeletons, or even the bones themselves in their original sites?"

"That's a question with only one possible answer," Ed said.

"Check. Paradoxes aside—and there are no paradoxes if you have enough accurate information—the facts have to speak for themselves. *We don't find them because they are not there.* Next question: Where the devil are they?"

Ed leaned forward, chewing on his pencil. "If we forget about their geological context, none of those fossils are more than a few hundred years old. I mean, that's when they were found. Even Neanderthal only goes back to around 1856 or thereabouts. Science itself is an amazingly recent phenomenon. So—"

"You mean Piltdown?" Gottwald suggested, smiling.

"Maybe."

Ben filled his pipe and lit it. "I've thought about that, too. I guess all of us have. If one fossil man was a fake, why not all of them? But it won't hold water, and you know it. For one thing, it would have required a worldwide conspiracy, which is nonsense. For another—sheer manpower aside—the knowledge that would have been required to fake all those fossils simply did not exist at the time they were discovered. Piltdown wouldn't have lasted five minutes with fluorine dating and decent X rays, and no one can sell me on the idea that men like Weidenreich and Von Koenigswald and Dart were fakers. Anyhow, that idea would leave us with a problem tougher than the one we're trying to solve—where did man come from if he had no past, no ancestors? I vote we exorcise that particular ghost."

"Keep going," Gottwald said.

Ed took it up. "Facts, Ben. Leave the theories for later. If neither the bones nor the men were present back in the Pleistocene where they belong, but the bones were present to be discovered later, then they *have* to appear somewhere in between. Our problem right now is *when.*"

Ben took his pipe out of his mouth and gestured with it, excited now. "We can handle that one. Damnit, *all* of our data can't be haywire. Look: for most of his presumed existence, close to a million years, man was a rare animal—all the bones of the fossil men ever discovered wouldn't fill up this room we're sitting in; all the crucial ones would fit in a broom closet. Okay? But by Neolithic times, with agricultural villages, there were men everywhere, even here in the New World. That record is clear. So those fossils *had* to be in place by around eight thousand years ago. All we have to do—"

"Is to work back the other way," Ed finished, standing up. "By God, that's it! We can send teams back through history, checking at short intervals, until we *see* how it started. As long as the bones are where they should be, fine. When they disappear—and they have to disappear, because we know they're not there earlier—we'll reverse our field and check it hour by hour if necessary. Then we'll know what happened. After that, we can kick the theories around until we're green in the face."

"It'll work," Ben said, feeling like a man walking out of a heavy fog. "It won't be easy, but it can be done. Only—"

"Only what?" Gottwald asked.

"Only I wonder what we'll find. I'm a little afraid of what we're going to see."

"One thing sure," Ed said.

"Yes?"

"This old world of ours will never be the same. Too bad—I kind of liked it the way it was."

Gottwald nodded, stroking his beard.

For months, Ben Hazard virtually lived within the whitewashed walls of New Mexico Station. He felt oddly like a man fighting a rattlesnake with his fists at some busy intersection, while all about him people hurried by without a glance, intent on their own affairs.

What went on in New Mexico Station was, of course, classified information. In Ben's opinion, this meant that there had been a ludicrous reversion to the techniques of magic. Facts were stamped with the sacred symbol of CLASSIFIED, thereby presumably robbing them of their power. Nevertheless, the world outside didn't know what the score was, and probably didn't care, while inside the station—

History flickered by, a wonderful and terrible film.

Man was its hero and its villain—but for how long?

The teams went back, careful to do nothing and to touch nothing. The teams left Grand Central, and pushed back, probing, searching. . . .

Back past the Roman Legions and the temples of Athens, back beyond the pyramids of Egypt and the marvels of Ur, back through the sunbaked villages of the first farmers, back into the dark shadows of prehistory—

And the teams found nothing.

At every site they could reach without revealing their presence, the bones of the early men were right where they should have been, waiting patiently to be unearthed.

Back past 8,000 B.C.

Back past 10,000.

Back past 15,000—

And then, when the teams reached 25,000 B.C., it happened. Quite suddenly, in regions as far removed from one another as France and Java, the bones disappeared.

And not just the bones.

Man himself was gone.

The world, in some ways, was as it had been—or was to be. The gray waves still tossed on the mighty seas, the forests were cool and green under clean blue skies, the sparkling sheets of snow and ice still gleamed beneath a golden sun.

The Earth was the same, but it was a strangely empty world without men. A desolate and somehow fearful world, hushed by long silences and stroked coldly by the restless winds. . . .

"That's it," Ben said. "Whatever it was, we know when it happened—somewhere between 23,000 and 25,000 at the end of the Upper Paleolithic. I'm going back there."

"*We're* going back there," Ed corrected him. "If I sit this one out I'll be ready for the giggle factory."

Ben smiled, not trying to hide his relief. "I think I could use some company this trip."

"It's a funny feeling, Ben."

"Yes." Ben Hazard glanced toward the waiting Buckets. "I've seen a lot of things in my life, but I never thought I'd see the Beginning."

* * *

The machine stopped and the green light winked.

Ed checked the viewer while Ben punched data into the recorder.

"Nothing yet," Ed said. "It's raining."

"Swell." Ben unlocked the hatch and the two men climbed out. The sky above them was cold and gray. An icy rain was pouring down from heavy, low-hanging clouds. There was no thunder. Apart from the steady hiss of the rain, France in the year 24,571 B.C. was as silent as a tomb. "Let's get this thing covered up."

They hauled out the plastic cover, camouflaged to blend with the landscape, and draped it over the metallic gray sphere. They had been checking for eighteen days without results, but they were taking no chances.

They crossed the narrow valley through sheets of rain, their boots sinking into the soaked ground with every step. They climbed up the rocks to the gaping black hole of the cave entrance and worked their way in under the rock ledge, out of the rain. They switched on their lights, got down on their hands and knees, and went over every inch of the dry area just back of the rock overhang.

Nothing.

The gray rain pelted the hillside and became a torrent of water that splashed out over the cave entrance in a hissing silver waterfall. It was a little warmer in the cave, but dark and singularly uninviting.

"Here we go again," Ed muttered. "I know this blasted cave better than my own backyard."

"I'd like to see that backyard of yours about now. We could smoke up some chickens in the barbecue pit and sample some of Betty's tequila sours."

"Right now I'd just settle for the tequila. If we can't figure this thing out any other way we might just as well start looking in the old bottle."

"Heigh-ho," Ben sighed, staring at the waiting cave. "Enter one dwarf and one gnome, while thousands cheer."

"I don't hear a thing."

Ed took the lead and they picked and crawled their way back through the narrow passages of the cave, their lights throwing grotesque black shadows that danced eerily on the spires and pillars of ancient, dripping stone. Ben sensed the weight of the great rocks above him and his chest felt constricted. It was hard to breathe, hard to keep going.

"Whatever I am in my next incarnation," he said, "I hope it isn't a mole."

"You won't even make the mammals," Ed assured him.

They came out into a long, twisted vault. It was deep in the cave, far from the hidden skies and insulated from the pounding of the rain. They flashed their lights over the walls, across the dry gray ceiling, into the ageless silence.

Nothing.

No cave paintings.

It was as though man had never been, and never was to be.

"I'm beginning to wonder whether *I'm* real," Ed said.

"Wait a minute." Ben turned back toward the cave entrance, his body rigid. "Did you hear something?"

Ed held his breath and listened. "Yeah. There it is again."

It was faint and remote as it came to them in the subterranean vault, but there was no mistaking it.

A sound of thunder, powerful beyond belief.

Steady, now.

Coming closer.

And there had been no thunder in that cold, hissing rain. . . .

"Come on." Ben ran across the cavern and got down on his hands and knees to crawl back through the twisting passage that led to the world outside. "There's something out there."

"What is it?"

Ben didn't stop. He clawed at the rocks until his hands were bloody. "I think the lunch hour's over," he panted. "I think Man's coming home."

Like two frightened savages, they crouched in the cave entrance and looked out across the rain-swept valley. The solid stone vibrated under their feet and the cold gray sky was shattered by blasting roars.

One thing was certain: that was no natural thunder.

"We've got to get out of here," Ben yelled. "We've got to hide before—"

"Where? The Bucket?"

"That's the best bet. It's almost invisible in this rain, and we can see through the viewer."

"Right. Run for it."

They scrambled down among the slick rocks and ran across the wet grass and mud of the valley floor. It was cold and the rain pelted their faces in icy gray sheets. The deafening roar grew even louder, falling down from the leaden sky.

Fumbling in their haste, they jerked up a corner of the plastic cover so that the viewer could operate. Then they squirmed and wriggled under the plastic, dropped through the hatch, and sealed the lock. They dripped all over the sphere but there was no time to bother about it. Even inside the Bucket they could feel the ocean of sound around them.

Ben cut in the recorder. "Start the cameras."

"Done."

"Hang on—"

The shattering roar reached an ear-splitting crescendo. Suddenly, there was something to see.

Light.

Searing white flame stabbing down from the gray skies.

They saw it: Gargantuan, lovely, huge beyond reason.

Before their eyes, like a vast metal fish from an unknown and terrible sea, the spaceship landed in the rain-soaked valley of Paleolithic France.

The long silence came again.

Fists clenched, Ben Hazard watched the Creation.

The great ship towered in the rain, so enormous that it was hard to imagine that it had ever moved. It might have been there always, but it was totally alien, out of place in its setting of hills and earth and sodden grasses.

Circular ports opened in the vast ship like half a hundred awakening eyes. Bright warm yellow light splashed out through the rain. Men—strangely dressed in dark, close-fitting tunics—floated out of the ship and down to the ground on columns of the yellow light.

The men were human, no different physically from Ben or Ed.

Equipment of some sort drifted down the shafts of light: strange spider-legged machines, self-propelled crates that

301

gleamed in the light, shielded stands that might have been for maps or charts, metallic robots that were twice the size of a man.

The yellow light deflected the rain—Ben could see water dripping down the yellow columns as though solid tubes had been punched through the air—and the rain was also diverted from the men and their equipment.

The men from the ship moved quickly. They fanned out and went to work with the precision of trained specialists who knew exactly what they were doing.

Incredible as it was, Ben thought that he knew what they were doing too.

The spider-legged machines stayed on the valley floor, pulsing. Most of the men, together with three of the robots and the bulk of the self-propelled crates, made their way up to the cave Ben and Ed had just left and vanished inside.

"Want to bet on what's in those crates?" Ben whispered.

"Haven't the faintest idea, but two bits says you spell it b-o-n-e-s."

The great ship waited, the streams of yellow light still spilling out into the rain. Five men pored over the shielded stands, looking for all the world like engineers surveying a site. Others worked over the spider-legged machines, setting up tubes of the yellow light that ran from the machines to the rocky hills. Two of the robots, as far as Ben could see, were simply stacking rocks into piles.

After three hours, when it was already growing dark, the men came back out of the cave. The robots and the crates were reloaded through the ship's ports and the uniformed men boarded the ship again.

Night fell. Ben stretched to ease his cramped muscles, but he didn't take his eyes from the viewer for a second.

The rain died down to a gentle patter and then stopped entirely. The overcast lifted and slender white clouds sailed through the wind-swept sky. The moon rose, fat and silver, its radiance dimming the burning stars.

The impossible ship, towering so complacently beneath the moon of Earth, was a skyscraper of light. It literally hummed with activity. Ben would have given a lot to know what was going on inside that ship, but there was no way to find out.

The pulsing spider-legged machines clicked and buzzed in the cold of the valley night. Rocks were conveyed along tubes of the yellow light to the machines, which were stamping something out by the hundreds of thousands. Something. . . .

Artifacts?

The long, uncanny night ended. Ben and Ed watched in utter fascination, their fears almost forgotten, sleep never even considered.

Dawn streaked the eastern sky, touching the clouds with fingers of rose and gold. A light breeze rustled the wet, heavy grasses. Water still dripped from the rocks.

The uniformed men came back out of the ship, riding the columns of yellow light. The robots gathered up some immense logs and stacked them near the mouth of the cave. They treated the wood with some substance to dry it, then ignited a blazing fire.

Squads of men moved over the valley floor, erasing all traces of their presence. One of them got quite close to the Bucket and Ben felt a sudden numbing chill. What would happen if they were seen? He was no longer worried about himself. But what about all the men who were to live on the Earth? Or—

The squad moved away.

Just as the red sun lifted behind the hills, while the log fire still blazed by the cave, the ship landed the last of its strange cargo.

Human beings.

Ben felt the sweat grow clammy in the palms of his hands.

They floated down the shafts of yellow light, shepherded by the uniformed men. There were one hundred of them by actual count, fifty men and fifty women. There were no children. They were a tall, robust people, dressed in animal skins. They shivered in the cold and seemed dazed and uncomprehending. They had to be led by the hand, and several had to be carried by the robots.

The uniformed men took them across the wet valley, a safe distance away from the ship. They huddled together like

303

sheep, clasping one another in sexless innocence. Their eyes turned from the fire to the ship, understanding neither.

It was a scene beyond age; it had always been. There were the rows of uniformed men, standing rigidly at attention. And there were the clustered people in animal skins, waiting without hope, without regret.

An officer—Ben thought of him that way, though his uniform was no different from the others—stepped forward and made what seemed to be a speech. At any rate, he talked for a long time—nearly an hour. It was clear that the dazed people did not understand a word of what he was saying, and that, too, was older than time.

It's a ceremony, Ben thought. *It must be some kind of ritual. I hadn't expected that.*

When it was over, the officer stood for a long minute looking at the huddle of people. Ben tried to read his expression in the viewer, but it was impossible. It might have been regret. It might have been hope. It might have been only curiosity.

Then, at a signal, the uniformed men turned and abandoned the others. They walked back to their waiting ship and the columns of yellow light took them inside. The ports closed.

Ten minutes later, the ship came to life.

White flame flared beneath its jets and the earth trembled. The terrible roar came again. The people who had been left behind fell to the ground, covering their ears with their hands. The great ship lifted slowly into the blue sky, then faster and faster—

It was gone, and only the sound remained.

In time, that, too, was gone.

Ben watched his own ancestors with an almost hypnotic fascination. They did not move.

Get up, get up—

The skin-clad people stood up shakily after what seemed to be hours. They stared blankly at one another. As though driven by some vague instinct that spoke through their shock, they turned and looked at the blazing fire that burned by the mouth of the cave.

Slowly, one by one, they pulled themselves over the rocks to the fire. They stood before it, seeking a warmth they could not understand.

The sun climbed higher, flooding the rain-clean world with golden light.

The people stood for a long time watching the fire burn down. They did nothing and said nothing.

Hurry, hurry. The voice spoke again in Ben's brain. He shook his head. Was he thinking about those dazed people out there, or was someone thinking about *him*?

Gradually, some of them seemed to recover their senses. They began to move about purposefully—still slowly, still uncertainly. One man picked up a fresh log and threw it on the fire. Another crouched down and fingered a chipped piece of flint he found on a rock. Two women stepped behind the fire and started into the dark cave.

Ben turned away from the viewer, his unshaven face haggard. "Meet Cro-Magnon," he said, waving his hand.

Ed lit a cigarette, his first in eighteen hours. His hand was shaking. "Meet everybody, you mean. Those jokers planted the other boys—Neanderthal and whatnot—back in the cave before they landed the living ones."

"We came out of that ship too, Ed."

"I know, but where did the *ship* come from? And why?"

Ben took a last long look at the people huddled around the fire. He didn't feel like talking. He was too tired to think. None of it made any sense.

What kind of people could *do* a thing like that?

"Let's go home," Ed said quietly.

They went out and removed the plastic cover, and then set the controls for New Mexico Station in a world that was no longer their own.

Old Franz Gottwald sat behind his desk. His white suit was freshly pressed and his hair was neatly combed. He stroked his beard in the old familiar gesture, and only the gleam in his eyes revealed the excitement within him.

305

"It has always been my belief, gentlemen, that there is no substitute for solid thinking based on verified facts. There is a time for action and there is a time for thought. I need hardly remind you that action without thought is pointless; it is the act of an animal, the contraction of an earthworm. We have the facts we need. You have been back for three days, but the thinking is yet to be done."

"We've been beating our brains out," Ben protested.

"That may be, Ben, but a man can beat his brains out with a club. It is not thinking."

"*You* try thinking," Ed said, grinding out a cigarette.

Gottwald smiled. "You are too old to have your thinking done for you, Edward. I have given you all I can give. It is your turn now."

Ben sat back in his chair and lit his pipe. He took his time doing it, trying to clear his mind. He had to forget those frightened people huddled around a fire, had to forget the emotions he had felt when the great ship had left them behind. Gottwald was right, as always.

The time had come for thought.

"Okay," he said. "We all know the facts. Where do we go from here?"

"I would suggest to you, gentlemen, that we will get no answers until we begin to ask the right questions. That is elementary, if I may borrow from Mr. Holmes."

"You want questions?" Ed laughed shortly. "Here's one, and it's a dilly. There's a hole in all this big enough to drive the American Anthropological Association through in a fleet of trucks. What about the apes?"

Ben nodded. "You quoted Conan Doyle, Franz, so I'll borrow a line from another Englishman—Darwin's pal Huxley, 'Bone for bone, organ for organ, man's body is repeated in the body of the ape.' Hell, we all know that. There are differences, sure, but the apes are closer to men than they are to monkeys. If man didn't evolve on Earth—"

"You've answered your own question, Ben."

"Of course!" Ed fished out another cigarette. "If man didn't evolve on Earth, then neither did the apes. That ship—or some ship—brought them both. But that's impossible."

"Impossible?" Franz asked.

"Maybe not," Ben said slowly. "After all, there are only four living genera of apes—two in Africa and two in Asia. We could even leave out the gibbon; he's a pretty primitive customer. It *could* have been done."

"Not for all the primates," Ed insisted. "Not for all the monkeys and lemurs and tarsiers, not for all the fossil primate bones. It would have made Noah's Ark look like a rowboat."

"I would venture the suggestion that your image is not very apt," Gottwald said. "That ship *was* big enough to make any of our ships look like rowboats."

"Never mind," Ben said, determined not to get sidetracked. "It doesn't matter. Let's assume that the apes were seeded, just as the men were. The other primates could have evolved here without outside interference, just as the other animals did. That isn't the real problem."

"I wonder," Ed said. "Could that ship have come out of *time* as well as space? After all, if we have time travel they must have it. They could do anything—"

"Bunk," Gottwald snorted. "Don't let yourself get carried away, Edward. Anything is *not* possible. A scientific law is a scientific law, no matter who is working with it, or where, or when. We know from the Winfield-Homans Equations that it is impossible to go back into time and alter it in any way, just as it is impossible go to into the future that does not yet exist. There are no paradoxes in time travel. Let's not make this thing harder than it is by charging off into all the blind alleys we can think of. Ben was on the right track. What is the real problem here?"

Ben sighed. He saw the problem all too clearly. "It boils down to this, I think. *Why* did they plant those fossils—and probably the apes too? I can think of fifty reasons why they might have seeded men like themselves on a barren planet— population pressure and so forth—but why go to all the trouble of planting a false evolutionary picture for them to dig up later?"

"Maybe it isn't false," Ed said slowly.

Franz Gottwald smiled. "Now you're *thinking*, Edward."

307

"Sorry, Ed. I don't follow you. You saw them plant those bones. If that isn't a prime example of salting a site, then what the devil is it?"

"Don't shoot, pal. I was trying to say that the fossils could have been planted and *still* tell a true story. Maybe I'm just an old codger set in his ways, but I can't believe that human evolution is a myth. And there's a clincher, Ben: Why bother with the apes if there is no relationship?"

"I still don't see—"

"He means," Gottwald said patiently, "that the fossil sequence is a true one—*someplace else.*"

Ed nodded. "Exactly. The evolutionary series is the genuine article, but man developed on their world rather than on ours. When they seeded men on Earth, they also provided them with a kind of history book—if they could read it."

Ben chewed on his pipe. It made sense, to the extent that anything made sense any more. "I'll buy that. But where does it leave us?"

"Still up that well-known creek. Every answer we get just leads back to the same old question. *Why* did they leave us a history book?"

"Answer that one," Gottwald said, "and you win the gold cigar."

Ben got to his feet. His head felt as though it were stuffed with dusty cotton.

"Where are you going?"

"I'm going fishing. As long as I'm up the creek I might as well do something useful. I'll see you later."

"I hope you catch something," Ed said.

"So do I," Ben Hazard said grimly.

The car hummed sleepily across the monotonous flatlands of New Mexico, passed through the gently rolling country that rested the eye, and climbed into the cool mountains where the pines grew tall and the grass was a thick dark green in the meadows.

Ben loved the mountains. The happiest times of his life had been spent up next to the sky, where the air was crisp and the streams ran clear. He needed the mountains, and he always returned to them when the pressure was too much to bear.

He turned off the main road and jolted over a gravel trail; paved roads and good fishing were mutually exclusive, like cities and sanity. He noted with approval that the clouds were draping the mountain peaks, shadowing the land below. When the sun was too bright the fish could see a man coming.

He took a deep breath, savoring the tonic of the air.

Relax, that's the ticket.

He checked to see that no interloper had discovered his favorite stretch of water, then parked his car by the side of Mill Creek, a gliding stream of crystal-clean water that tumbled icily out of the mountains and snaked its lazy way through the long green valley. He grinned like a kid with his first cane pole.

Ben pulled on his waders, assembled his rod with practiced skill, and tied on his two pet flies—a Gray Hackle Yellow and a Royal Coachman. He hung his net over one shoulder and his trout basket over the other, lit his pipe and waded out into the cold water of Mill Creek.

He felt wonderful. He hooked a nice brook trout within five minutes. He felt the knots and the tensions flow out of him like melting snow, and that was the first step.

He *had* to relax. There was no other way.

Consider the plight of a baseball player in a bad slump. He gives it all he has, tries twice as hard as usual, but everything he does backfires. His hits don't fall in, he misses the easy grounders. He lies awake at night and worries.

"Relax, Mac," his manager tells him. "All you gotta do is *relax*. Take it easy."

Sure, but how?

It was the same with a tough scientific problem. Ben had long ago discovered that persistent and orderly logic could take him only so far. There came a time when no amount of forced thinking would get the job done.

The fresh insights and the new slants seldom came to him when he went after them, no matter how hard he tried. In fact, the more he sweated over a problem the more stubbornly recalcitrant his mind became. The big ideas, and the good ones, came to him in a flash of almost intuitive understanding. The trick was to let the conscious mind get out of the way, let the message get through—

In Ben's case, go fishing.

It took him two hours, seven trout and part of a banana to get the answer he sought.

He had taken a long, cool drink from the stream, cleaned his fish, and was sitting down on a rock to eat the lunch he had packed when the idea came.

He had peeled a banana and taken one bite of it when his mind was triggered by a single, innocuous word:

Banana.

Not just any old banana, of course. A specific one, used for a specific purpose.

Remember?

Charles Darwin and Cleopatra, two chimpanzees in their cages. Charles Darwin pushing his ape brain to the limit to fit two sticks together. Why?

To get a banana.

One lousy banana.

That was well enough, but there was more. Darwin might get his banana, and that was all he cared about. But who had placed the sticks in the cage, who had supplied the banana?

And why?

That was an easy one. It was so simple a child could have figured it out. Someone had given Charles Darwin two sticks and a banana for just one reason: to see whether or not he could solve the problem.

In a nutshell, a scientific experiment.

Now, consider another Charles Darwin, another problem.

Or consider Ben Hazard.

What is the toughest problem a man can tackle? Howells pointed it out many years ago. Of all the animals, man is the only one who wonders where he has come from and where he is going. All the other questions are petty compared to that one. It pushes the human brain to the limit. . . .

Ben stood up, his lunch forgotten.

It was all so obvious.

Men had been seeded on the Earth, and a problem had been planted with them—a real problem, one capable of yielding to a true solution. A dazed huddle of human beings had been abandoned by a fire in the mouth of a cave, lost in the morning of a strange new world. Then they had been left strictly alone; there was no evidence that they had been helped in any way since that time.

Why?

To see what they could do.

To see how long it would take them to solve the problem.

In a nutshell, a scientific experiment.

Ben picked up his rod and started back toward the car.

There was one more thing, one more inevitable characteristic of a scientific experiment. No scientist merely sets up his experiment and then goes off and forgets about it, even if he is the absolute ultimate in absentminded professors.

No.

He has to stick around to see how it all comes out. He has to observe, take notes.

It was monstrous.

The whole history of man on Earth. . . .

Ben climbed into his car, started the engine.

There's more. Face up to it.

Suppose that you had set up a fantastic planetary experiment with human beings. Suppose that you—or one of your descendants, for human generations are slow—came back to check on your experiment. What would you do, what would you be?

A garage mechanic?

A shoe salesman?

A pool room shark?

Hardly. You'd have to be in a position to know what was going on. You'd have to work in a field where you could find out the score.

In a word, you'd be an anthropologist.

There's still more. Take it to the end of the line.

Now, suppose that man on Earth cracked the time barrier. Suppose a Temporal Research Project was set up. Wouldn't you be in on it, right at the top?

Sure.

You wouldn't miss it for anything.

Well, who would fit the description? It couldn't be Ed; Ben had known him most of his life, known his folks and his wife and his kids, visited the Texas town that had been his home.

It wasn't Ben.

That left Franz Gottwald.

Franz, who had come from Germany and never talked about his past. Franz, with the strangely alien accent. Franz, who had no family. Franz, who had contributed nothing to the project but shrewd, prodding questions. . . .

Franz.

The Grand Old Man.

Ben drove with his hands clenched on the wheel and his lips pressed into a thin, hard line. Night had fallen by the time he got out of the mountains, and he drove across an enchanted desert beneath the magic of the stars. The headlights of his car lanced into the night, stabbing, stabbing—

He passed the great New Mexico rocket base, from which men had hurled their missiles to the moon and beyond. There had been talk of a manned shot to Mars. . . .

How far would the experimenters let them go?

Ben lit a cigarette, not wanting to fool with his pipe in the car. He was filled with a cold anger he had never known before.

He had solved the problem.

Very well.

It was time to collect his banana.

It was after midnight when Ben got home.

He stuck his fish in the freezer, took a shower and sat down in his comfortable armchair to collect his thoughts. He promptly discovered yet another fundamental truth about human beings: when they get tired enough, they sleep.

He woke up with a start and looked at his watch. It was five o'clock in the morning.

Ben shaved and was surprised to find that he was hungry. He cooked himself some bacon and scrambled eggs, drank three cups of instant coffee and felt ready for anything.

Even Franz.

He got into his car and drove through the still-sleeping town to Gottwald's house. It looked safe and familiar in the pale morning light. As a matter of fact, it looked a lot like his own house, since both had been supplied by the government.

That, he thought, was a laugh.

The government had given *Gottwald* a house to live in.

He got out of his car, walked up to the door, and rang the bell. Franz never got to the office before nine, and his car was still in the garage.

His ring was greeted by total silence.

He tried again. holding his finger on the bell. He rang it long enough to wake the dead.

No answer.

Ben tried the door. It was unlocked. He took a deep breath and stepped inside. The house was neat and clean. The familiar books were on the shelves in the living room. It was like stepping into his own home.

"Franz! It's me, Ben."

No answer.

Ben strode over to the bedroom, opened the door and looked inside. The bed was tidily made, and Franz wasn't in it. Ben walked through the whole house, even peering inside the closets, before he was satisfied.

Franz wasn't home.

Fine. A Scientist keeps records, doesn't he?

Ben proceeded to ransack the house. He looked in dresser drawers, on closet shelves, even in the refrigerator. He found nothing unusual. Then he tried the obvious.

He opened Gottwald's desk and looked inside.

The first thing he saw was a letter addressed to himself. There it was, a white envelope with his name typed on it: *Dr. Benjamin Wright Hazard.*

Not to be opened until Christmas?

Ben took the letter, ripped it open, and took out a single sheet of paper. He started to read it, then groped for a chair and sat down.

The letter was neatly typed. It said:

> *My Dear Ben:*
> *I have always believed that a scientist must be capable of making predictions. This is not always an easy matter when you are dealing with human beings, but I have known you for a long, long time.*
> *Obviously, you are searching my home, or you would*

*not be reading this note. Obviously, if you are searching
my home, you know part of the truth.*

*If you would like to know the rest of the story, the
procedure is simple. Look behind the picture of the
sand-painting in my bedroom. You will find a button
there. Press the button for exactly five seconds. Then
walk out into my patio and stand directly in front of the
barbecue pit.*

Trust me, Ben. I am not a cannibal.

The letter was signed with Gottwald's scrawled signature.

Ben got up and walked into the bedroom. He looked behind
the picture that was hanging over the dresser. There was a
small red button.

Press the button for exactly five seconds.

And then—what?

Ben replaced the picture. The whole thing was a trifle too
reminiscent of a feebleminded practical joke. Press the button
and get a shock. Press the button and get squirted with water.
Press the button and blow up the house—

No. That was absurd.

Wasn't it?

He hesitated. He could call Ed, but then Ed would insist on
coming over right away—and Ed had a wife and kids. He could
call the police, but the story he had to tell would have sounded
absolutely balmy. He had no proof.

He went back to Gottwald's desk, found some paper, and
typed a letter. He outlined the theory he had formed and wrote
down exactly what he was going to do. He put the letter into an
envelope, addressed the envelope to Ed, stamped it, and went
outside and dropped it in the mailbox on the corner.

He went back into the house.

This time he did not hesitate—not for a second.

He punched the button behind the picture for exactly five
seconds. Nothing happened. He went out into the patio and
stood directly in front of the barbecue pit.

The wall around the patio hid the outside world, but the blue
sky overhead was the same as ever. He saw nothing, heard
nothing.

"Snipe hunt," he said aloud.

Then, with breathtaking suddenness, something *did* happen.

There was an abrupt stillness in the air, a total cessation of sound. It was as though invisible glass walls had slipped silently into place and sealed off the world around him.

There was no perceptible transition. One moment the cone of yellow light was not there, and the next it was. It surrounded him: taut, living, seething with an energy that prickled his skin.

He knew that yellow light.

He had seen it once before, in the dawn of time. . . .

Ben held his breath; he couldn't help it. He felt strangely weightless, buoyant, a cork in a nameless sea—

His feet left the ground.

"Good God," Ben said.

He was lifted into the yellow light, absorbed in it. He could see perfectly, and it didn't help his stomach any. He could see the town below him—there was Gottwald's patio, the barbecue pit, the adobe house. He began to regret the bacon and eggs he had eaten.

He forced himself to breathe again. The air was warm and tasteless. He rose into the sky, fighting down panic.

Think of it as an elevator. It's just a way of getting from one place to another. I can see out, but of course nothing is visible from the outside.

But then how did I see the yellow light before?

This must be different. They couldn't risk being seen—

Relax!

But he kept going higher, and faster.

The Earth was far away.

It was an uncanny feeling—not exactly unpleasant, but he didn't care for the view. It was like falling through the sky. It was impossible to avoid the idea that he was falling, that he was going to hit something. . . .

The blue of the sky faded into black, and he saw the stars.

Where am I going, where are they taking me?

There!

Look up, look up—

There it was, at the end of the tunnel of yellow light.

315

It blotted out the stars.

It was huge even against the immense backdrop of space itself. It stunned his mind with its size, but he recognized it.

It was the same ship that had landed the first men on Earth.

Dark now, dark and vast and lonely—but the same ship.

The shaft of yellow light pulled him inside; there was no air lock. As suddenly as it had come, the light was gone.

Ben stumbled and almost fell. The gravity seemed normal, but the light had supported him for so long that it took his legs a moment to adjust themselves.

He stood in a cool green room. It was utterly silent.

Ben swallowed hard.

He crossed the room to a metal door. The door opened before he reached it. There was only blackness beyond, blackness and the total silence of the dead.

Ben Hazard tried to fight down the numbing conviction that the ship was empty.

There is an almost palpable air of desolation about long deserted things, about empty houses and derelict ships and crumbling ruins. There is a special kind of silence about a place that has once known life and knows it no longer. There is a type of death that hovers over things that have not been *used* for a long, long time.

That was the way the ship felt.

Ben could see only the small green room in which he stood and the corridor of darkness outside the door. It could have been only a tiny fraction of the great ship, only one room in the vast city in the sky. But he *knew* that the men who had once lived in the ship were gone. He knew it with a certainty that his mind could not question.

It was a ghost ship.

He knew it was.

That was why his heart almost stopped when he heard the footsteps moving toward him through the silence.

Heavy steps.

Metallic steps.

Ben backed away from the door. He tried to close it but it would not shut. He saw a white light coming at him through the dark tunnel. The light was higher than a man—

Metallic steps?

Ben got a grip on himself and waited. *You fool, you knew they had robots. You saw them. Robots don't die, do they? Do they kill?*

He saw it now, saw its outline behind the light. Twice the size of a man, its metal body gleaming.

It had no face.

The robot filled the doorway and stopped. Ben could hear it now: a soft whirring noise that somehow reminded him of distant winds. He told himself that it was just a machine, just an animated hunk of metal, and his mind accepted the analysis. But it is one thing to know what a robot is, and it is quite another to find yourself in the same room with one.

"Well?" Ben said. He had to say something.

The robot was evidently under no such compulsion. it said nothing and did nothing. It simply stood there.

After a long, uncomfortable minute, the robot turned around and walked into the dark corridor, its light flashing ahead of it. It took four steps, stopped, and looked back over its shoulder.

There was just one thing to do, and one way to go.

Ben nodded and stepped through the doorway after the robot.

He followed the giant metallic figure along what seemed to be miles of featureless passageways. Ben heard no voices, saw no lights, met no living things.

He felt no fear now; he was beyond that. He knew that he was in a state of shock where nothing could get through to him, nothing could hurt him. He felt only a kind of sadness, the sadness a man knows when he walks through the tunnels of a pyramid or passes a graveyard on a lonely night.

The ship that men had built was so vast, so silent, so empty.

A door opened ahead of them.

Light spilled out into the corridor.

Ben followed the robot into a large, comfortable room. The room was old, old and worn, but it was alive. It was warm and vital and human because there were two people in it. Ben had never before been quite so glad to see anyone.

One of the persons was an elderly woman he had never met before.

The other was Franz Gottwald.

317

"Hello, Ben, he said, smiling. "I don't believe you know my wife."

Ben wasn't sure whether he was coming into a nightmare or coming out of one, but his manners were automatic.

"I'm very pleased to meet you," he said, and meant it.

The room had a subtle strangeness about it that once more reminded Ben of a dream. It was not merely the expected strangeness of design of a new kind of room, a room lost in the lonely miles of a silent spaceship; it was an out-of-phase oddness that at first he could not identify.

Then he caught it. There were alien things in the room: furniture that was planned for human beings but produced by a totally different culture pattern, carvings that were grotesque to his eyes, rugs that glowed in curiously wrong figures. But there were also familiar, everyday items from the world he knew: a prosaic reading lamp, a coffeepot bubbling on a table, some potted plants, a framed painting by Covarrubias. The mixture was a trifle jarring, but it did have a reassuring air of homeliness.

How strange the mind is. At a time like this, it concentrates on a room.

"Sit down, sit down," Franz said. "Coffee?"

"Thank you." Ben tried a chair and found it comfortable.

The woman he persisted in thinking of as Mrs. Gottwald—though that was certainly not her actual name—poured a cup and handed it to him. Her lined, delicate face seemed radiant with happiness, but there were tears in her eyes.

"I speak the language too a little," she said hesitantly. "We are so proud of you, so happy—"

Ben took a sip of the coffee to cover his embarrassment. He didn't know what he had expected, but certainly not *this*.

"Don't say anything more, Arnin," Franz said sharply. "We must be very careful."

"That robot of yours," Ben said. "Couldn't you send him out for oiling or something?"

Franz nodded. "I forgot how weird he must seem to you. Please forgive me. I would have greeted you myself, but I am growing old and it is a long walk." He spoke to the robot in a language Ben had never heard, and the robot left the room.

Ben relaxed a little. "You two up here all alone?"

An inane question. But what can I do, what can I say?

Old Franz seated himself next to Ben. He still wore his white suit. He seemed tired, more tired than Ben had ever seen him, but there was a kind of hope in his eyes, a hope that was almost a prayer.

"Ben," he said slowly, "It is hard for me to talk to you—now. I can imagine how you must feel after what you have been through. But you must trust me a little longer. Just forget where you are, Ben—a spaceship is just a ship. Imagine that we are back at the station, imagine that we are talking as we have talked so many times before. You must think clearly. This is important, my boy, more important than you can know. I want you to tell me what you have discovered—I want to know what led you here. Omit nothing, and choose your words with care. Be as specific and precise as you can. Will you do this one last thing for me? When you have finished, I think I will be able to answer all your questions."

Ben had to smile. *Be as specific and precise as you can.* How many times had he heard Franz use that very phrase on examinations?

He reached for his pipe. For a moment he had a wild, irrational fear that he had forgotten it—that would have been the last straw, somehow—but it was there. He filled it and lit it gratefully.

"It's your party, Franz. I'll tell you what I know."

"Proceed, Ben—and be careful."

Mrs. Gottwald—Arnin—sat very still, waiting.

The ship was terribly silent around them.

Ben took his time and told Franz what he knew and what he believed. He left nothing out and made no attempt to soften his words.

When he was finished, Gottwald's wife was crying openly.

Franz, amazingly, looked like a man who had suddenly been relieved of a sentence of death.

"Well?" Ben asked.

Gottwald stood up and stroked his white beard. "You must think I am some kind of a monster," he said, smiling.

Ben shrugged. "I don't know."

319

Mrs. Gottwald dried her eyes. "Tell him," she said. "You can tell him now."

Gottwald nodded. "I am proud of you, Ben, very proud."

"I was right?"

"You were right in the only thing that matters. The fossils *were* a test, and you have passed that test with flying colors. Of course, you had some help from Edward—"

"I'll give him part of the banana."

Gottwald's smile vanished. "Yes. Yes, I daresay you will. But I am vain enough to want to clear up one slight error in your reconstruction. I do not care for the role of monster, and mad scientists have always seemed rather dull to me."

"The truth is the truth."

"A redundancy, Ben. But never mind. I must tell you that what has happened on Earth was *not* a mere scientific experiment. I must also tell you that I am not only a scientist who has come back, as you put it, to see how the chimpanzees are doing. In fact, I didn't come back at all. We—my people—never left. I was born right here in this ship, in orbit around the Earth. It has always been here."

"For twenty-five thousand years?"

"For twenty-five thousand years."

"But what have you been doing?"

"We've been waiting for you, Ben. You almost did not get here in time. My wife and I are the only ones left."

"Waiting for *me*? But—"

Gottwald held up his hand. "No, not this way. I can show you better than I can tell you. If my people had lived—my other people, I should say, for I have lived on the Earth most of my life—there would have been an impressive ceremony. That can never be now. But I can show you the history lesson we prepared. Will you come with me? It is not far."

The old man turned and walked toward the door, his wife leaning on his arm.

"So long," she whispered. "We have waited so long."

Ben got up and followed them into the corridor.

In a large assembly room filled with empty seats, somewhere in the great deserted ship, Ben saw the history of Man.

It was more than a film, although a screen was used. Ben lived the history, felt it, was a part of it.

It was not a story of what King Glotz did to King Goop; the proud names of conventional history fade into insignificance when the perspective is broad enough. It was a story of Man, of all men.

It was Gottwald's story—and Ben's.

Ben lived it.

Millions of years ago, on a world that circled a sun so far away that the astronomers of Earth had no name for it and not even a number, a new animal called Man appeared. His evolution had been a freakish thing, a million-to-one shot, and it was not likely to be repeated.

Man, the first animal to substitute cultural growth for physical change, was an immediate success. His tools and his weapons grew ever more efficient. On his home world, Man was a patient animal—but he was Man.

He was restless, curious. One world could not hold him. He built his first primitive spaceships and set out to explore the great dark sea around him. He established colonies and bases on a few of the worlds of his star system. He looked outward, out along the infinite corridors of the universe, and it was not in him to stop.

He tinkered and worked and experimented.

He found the faster-than-light drive.

He pushed on through the terrible emptiness of interstellar space. He touched strange worlds and stranger suns—

And he found that Man was not alone.

There were ships greater than his, and Beings—

Man discovered the Enemy.

It was not a case of misunderstanding, not a failure of diplomacy, not an accident born of fear or greed or stupidity. Man was a civilized animal. He was careful, reasonable, prepared to do whatever was ethically right.

He had no chance.

The Enemy—pounced. That was the only word for it. They were hunters, destroyers, killers. They were motivated by a savage hunger for destruction that Man had never known. They took many shapes, many forms.

Ben saw them.

He saw them rip ships apart, gut them with an utter ferocity that was beyond understanding. He saw them tear human beings to shreds, and eat them, and worse—

The Beings were more different from Man than the fish that swim in the sea, and yet. . . .

Ben recognized them. He knew them.

They were there, all of them.

Literally, the Beings of nightmares.

The monsters that had troubled the dark sleeps of Earth, the things that crawled through myths, the Enemy who lived in the black side of the mind. The dragons, the serpents, the faces carved on masks, the Beings shaped on stones dug up in rotting jungles—

The Enemy.

We on Earth have not completely forgotten. We remember, despite the shocks that cleansed our minds. We remember, we remember. We have seen them in the darkness that lives always beyond the fires, we have heard them in the thunder that booms in the long, long night.

We remember.

It was not a war. A war, after all, is a specific kind of contest with rules of a sort. There were no rules. It was not a drive for conquest, not an attempt at exploitation. It was something new, something totally alien.

It was destruction.

It was extermination.

It was a fight between two different kinds of life, as senseless as a bolt of lightning that forked into the massive body of a screaming dinosaur.

Man wasn't ready.

He fell back, fighting where he could.

The Enemy followed.

Whether he liked it or not, Man was in a fight to the finish.

He fought for his life. He pushed himself to the utmost, tried everything he could think of, fought with everything he had. He exhausted his ingenuity. The Enemy countered his every move.

There was a limit.

Man could not go on.

Ben leaned forward, his fists clenched on his chair. He was a product of his culture. He read the books, saw the tri-di plays. He expected a happy ending.

There wasn't one.

Man lost.

He was utterly routed.

He had time for one last throw of the dice, one last desperate try for survival. He did his best.

He worked out the Plan.

It wasn't enough to run away, to find a remote planet and hide. It wasn't enough just to gain time.

Man faced the facts. He had met the Enemy and he had lost. He had tried everything he knew, and it hadn't been good enough. One day, no matter how far he ran, he would meet the Enemy again.

What could he do?

Man lives by his culture, his way of life. The potential for any culture is great but it is not limitless. Culture has a way of putting blinders on its bearers; it leads them down certain paths and ignores others. Technological complexity is fine, but it is impotent without the one necessary ingredient:

Ideas.

Man needed new ideas, radically new concepts.

He needed a whole new way of thinking.

Transplanting the existing culture would not do the job. It would simply go on producing variants of the ideas that had already been tried.

Man didn't need transplanting.

He needed a transfusion, a transfusion of ideas.

He needed a brand-new culture with fresh solutions to old problems.

There is only one way to get a really different culture pattern: grow it from scratch.

Sow the seeds and get out.

Man put the Plan into effect.

With the last of his resources, he outfitted four fugitive ships and sent them out into the wastes of the seas between the stars.

"We don't know what happened to the other three ships," Franz Gottwald said quietly when the projection was over. "No ship knew the destination of any other ship. They went in different directions, each searching for remote, hidden worlds that might become new homes for men. There is no way of knowing what became of the others; I think it highly unlikely that any of them survived."

"Then Earth is all there is?"

"That is what we believe, Ben—we have to go ahead on that assumption. You know most of the rest of the story. This ship slipped through the Enemy and found Earth. We landed human beings who were so conditioned that they could remember little or nothing, for they had to begin all over again. We planted the fossils and the apes as a test, just as you supposed."

"But why? There was no need for such a stunt—"

Gottwald smiled. "It wasn't a stunt, my boy. It was the key to everything. You see, we had to warn the men of Earth about what they had to face. More than that, once their cultures had developed along their own lines, we had to share what we had with them. I need hardly remind you that this ship is tech- nologically many thousands of years ahead of anything the Earth has produced. But we couldn't turn the ship over to them until we were *certain* they were ready. You don't give atomic bombs to babies. The men of Earth had to *prove* that they could handle the toughest problem we could dream up. You solved it, Ben."

"I didn't do it alone."

"No, of course not. I can tell you now that my people—my other people—never did invent time travel. That was a totally unexpected means of tackling the problem; we never could have done it. It is the most hopeful thing that has happened."

"But what became of the men and women who stayed here on the ship?"

Franz shook his head. "Twenty-five thousand years is a long, long time, Ben. We were a defeated people. We worked hard; we were not idle. For one thing, we prepared dictionaries for every major language on Earth so that all the data in our libraries will be available to you. But man does not live well inside a ship. Each generation we became fewer; children were very scarce."

"It's like the old enigma of the cities, isn't it?"

"Exactly. No city in human history has ever reproduced its population. Urban births are always lower than rural ones. All cities have always drawn their personnel from the surrounding countryside. The ship was sealed up; we had no rural areas. It was only a matter of time before we were all gone. My wife and I were the last ones, Ben—and we had no children."

"We were so afraid," Mrs. Gottwald said. "So afraid that you would not come before it was too late."

"What would you have done?"

Franz shrugged wearily. "That is one decision I was spared. I did cheat a little, my boy. I was careful to give you no help, but I did plant some projectors near you that kept you stirred up. They broadcast frequencies that . . . ah . . . stimulate the mind, keep it in a state of urgency. Perhaps you noticed them?"

Ben nodded. He remembered the voice that spoke in his skull:

Hurry, hurry—

"Franz, what will happen now?"

Gottwald stroked his beard, his eyes very tired. "I can't tell you that. I don't know the answer. I have studied the men of Earth for most of my life, and I still don't know. You are a tough people, Ben, tougher than we ever were. You have fought many battles, and your history is a proud one. But I cannot read the future. I have done my best, and the rest is up to you."

"It's a terrible responsibility."

"Yes, for you and for others like you it will be a crushing burden. But it will be a long fight; we will not live to see more than the beginning of it. It will take centuries for the men of Earth to learn all that is in this ship. It's an odd thing, Ben—I have never seen the Enemy face to face. You will probably never see them. But what we do now will determine whether mankind lives or dies."

"It's too much for one man."

"Yes." Gottwald smiled, remembering. "It is."

"I don't know where to begin."

"We will wait for Edward—he will be here tomorrow, unless I don't know him at all—and then the three of us will sit down together for one last time. We will think it out. I am very tired,

325

Ben; my wife and I have lived past our time. It is hard to be old, and to have no children. I always thought of you and Edward as my sons; I hope you do not find this too maudlin."

Ben searched for words and couldn't find any.

Franz put his arm around his wife. "Sometimes, when the job was too big for me, when I felt myself giving up, I would walk up into the old control room of this ship. My wife and I have stood there many times. Would you like to see it?"

"I need it, Franz."

"Yes. So do I. Come along."

They walked for what seemed to be miles through the dark passages of the empty ship, then rode a series of elevators up to the control room.

Franz switched on the lights.

"The ship is not dead, you know," he said. "It is only the people who are gone. The computers still maintain the ship's orbit, and the defensive screens still make it invulnerable to detection—you wouldn't have seen it if you had not been coming up the light tube, and there is no way the ship can be tracked from Earth. What do you think of the control room?"

Ben stared at it. It was a large chamber, acres in extent, but it was strangely empty. There were panels of switches and a few small machines, but the control room was mostly empty space.

"It's not what I expected," he said, hiding his disappointment.

Franz smiled. "When machinery is efficient you don't need a lot of it. There is no need for flashing lights and sparks of electricity. What you see here gets the job done."

Ben felt a sudden depression. He had badly needed a lift, and he didn't see it here. "If you'll forgive me for saying so, Franz, it isn't very inspiring. It suppose it is different for you—"

Gottwald answered him by throwing a switch.

Two immense screens flared into life, covering the whole front of the control room.

Ben caught his breath.

One of the screens showed the globe of the Earth far below, blue and green and necklaced with silver clouds.

The other showed the stars.

The stars were alive, so close he could almost touch them with his hand. They burned like radiant beacons in the cold sea of space. They whispered to him, called to him—

Ben knew then that the men of Earth had remembered something more than monsters and nightmares, something more than the fears and terrors that crept through the great dark night.

Not all the dreams had been nightmares.

Through all the years and all the sorrows, Man had never forgotten.

I remember, I remember.

I have seen you through all the centuries of nights. I have looked up to see you, I have lifted my head to pray, I have known wonder—

I remember.

Ben looked again at the sleeping Earth.

He sensed that Old Franz and his wife had drawn back into the shadows.

He stood up straight, squaring his shoulders.

Then Ben Hazard turned once more and looked out into the blazing heritage of the stars.

I remember, I remember—

It has been long, but you, too, have not forgotten.

Wait for us.

We'll be back.

Morton Klass

One of a pair of science fiction writing professorial brothers, Morton Klass (1927–   ) was born in Brooklyn, New York.

While Philip (William Tenn) preferred English, his younger brother liked anthropology, acquiring a B.A. from Brooklyn College (1955) and a Ph.D. from Columbia University (1959). After teaching at Bennington College for awhile (1959–1964), Morton returned to New York City, working first at Columbia University and then at Barnard College where he has been a full professor since 1969.

In addition to numerous research papers, he has authored or co-authored four academic books: *East Indians in Trinidad: A Study of Cultural Persistence* (1961), *The Kinds of Mankind: An Introduction to Race and Racism* (1971), *From Field to Factory: Community Structure and Industrialization in West Bengal* (1978) and *Caste: The Emergence of the South Asian Social System* (1980). For his work he has been named a fellow of the American Anthropological Association, the American Council of Learned Societies and the Social Science Research Council.

One of just a few science fiction stories he has written, the following work can best be described as a NeanderTHAL tale.

IN THE BEGINNING

by Morton Klass

IN WHICH IT is considered whether the smartest of all forms of life is necessarily the wisest of all.

Homo sapiens—Means: "Man Who Understands." A vertebrate mammal, primate order, hominid family. After the disappearance of the preceding species, Neanderthalensis, Sapiens became the only extant species of man on Earth. Gradually increasing in numbers, Sapiens eventually populated the entire planet, with tremendous technological developments and intricate cultural variations marking . . .

Professor Philo Putnam was in no mood to argue about the existence of a soul. Anyone who'd seen his face an hour earlier, as he surveyed the charred remains of his pet brontosaurus, could have told the delegates of the Anti-Resurrection League they were making a bad mistake in barging into the professor's office.

"Putnam!" Mrs. Featherby roared, coming straight to the point. She elbowed the biology department's prim secretary, Miss Kalish out of the way and advanced on the professor's desk like an irritated Mark IV tank. The horse-faced gentleman and the hatchet-faced lady pressed close behind her.

"Mrs. Featherby," Professor Putnam acknowledged wearily. He rose to his feet, less out of politeness than because it is easier to swing a desk lamp in a standing position.

The A-RL's guiding light in Connecticut slammed her pudgy hands down on his desk and stared up at him accusingly.

"I've just been reliably informed that you're going ahead with the monster. I . . . we've come here for an immediate denial!"

Professor Putnam glanced regretfully at the desk lamp. "To which, ah . . . *monster* . . . are you referring?" he asked cautiously.

"*You* know!" Miss Hassom piped shrilly from behind the protecting bulk of her chairlady. "That so-called prehistoric man. Ne-nean—"

"Neanderthal Man," Dr. Trine supplied, in his resonant baritone. "It is not enough, apparently, that you must question the decisions of heaven, and return to the unwilling face of Earth those poor creatures which had been eternally banned from it. No, you needs must add insult to injury, profanity to desecration! Constructing an obscene, shambling caricature of the most noble creation—"

"It won't have a soul!" Mrs. Featherby interjected. She resented having the floor taken away from her by subordinates. "It will be a soulless, inhuman Frankenstein monster—threatening the lives of women and children."

That was when the professor lost his precarious grip on his temper.

"What do you propose to do about it?" he demanded savagely, thrusting his reddening face dangerously close to Mrs. Featherby's. He pointed at the floor. "Down in the laboratory we have eight Neanderthal fetuses in tanks. You want to run down and smash the tanks? Somebody tossed a hand grenade in the brontosaurus pen this morning. Why not blow up the whole college? Or you could wait till after they're completed and put ground glass in their food. It worked with our prize eohippus last month—"

331

"How dare you!" Mrs. Featherby shrieked. "The idea! Accusing the Anti-Resurrection League of engaging in lawless, criminal activities!"

She whirled to face the cringing Miss Hassom. "I warned them!" she said angrily. "I *warned* the membership! I told them Professor Putnam wouldn't listen to reason! Why, he was the man who started all this filthy resurrection business in the first place! Is it likely he'd listen to reason? Take steps without consulting him, I said. But *no*! I was overruled!"

Miss Hassom hung her head.

"Surely, Professor," Dr. Trine suggested smoothly, "you didn't mean what you said. The A-RL is composed solely of responsible citizens, honestly concerned about this terrible problem. But we in no way condone acts of violence. An apology from you, I am sure, would be sufficient to—"

"I'll apologize for nothing!" Professor Putnam slammed his fist down on his desk. "Your organization claims to be opposed to mob action, but everything you write in your newspapers or say over the radio is calculated to inflame idiots into burning us at the stake! If you're not aware of what you're doing, you're bigger fools than even I think—"

"There's no point to our listening to any more of this drivel." Mrs. Featherby turned and marched to the door, and her cohorts fell in behind her. She paused with her hand on the knob for a parting broadside.

"If I were you, Professor Putnam, I would start emptying my desk drawers. I'll guarantee you won't be occupying this office by tomorrow morning!"

Dr. Trine, the last one out, closed the door gently behind him.

Putnam sank back into his chair and ran a shaking hand over his eyes. "If you were I, madam," he muttered somberly, "I'd throw myself to the tyrannosauri."

"Can . . . can she do it, Professor?" Miss Kalish asked timidly from the far corner of the office.

"Do what?" Professor Putnam stared at her sharply. "Oh . . . have me fired? I don't know. Probably. They say a third of the board of trustees are members of the A-RL."

He shrugged and stood up. "I'm not going to worry about that now. It's bound to happen, sooner or later. What's more important is that the Neanderthalenses should achieve completion today. I want to be there—"

He started for the door, then hesitated. "Would you care to come along, Miss Kalish? I don't have to tell you what this means to me. Besides, that won't be a pleasant phone to answer for the next few days."

Miss Kalish stared down at the floor, absently smoothing a crease in her severe skirt. "I . . ." She hesitated. "Please don't be angry, Professor Putnam, but . . . what Dr. Trine said—" She raised her head suddenly and took a deep breath. "Will . . . will they really be shambling, horrible-looking creatures?"

Professor Philo Putnam ran a hand through his stiff gray hair. "Miss Kalish," he said, with gentle reproach, "I'm not angry, but I am surprised at you. You're not a biologist, of course, but you've been my secretary since I became head of the department. Surely in fifteen years you've learned *something* about what I'm doing—"

"That's not fair, Professor!" Miss Kalish interrupted heatedly. "I guess I know as much about some things as half your graduate students! Didn't I type the final manuscript of your paper on artificial uteri? Why, I stayed up with you all night when you were waiting for your first chick embryo to hatch out of its tank. And I never said anything when you started resurrecting fossils—and you should have heard how my mother carried on! But this is different—"

"There's nothing different about it! If I can take an Appelbaum chromosome print from a bone cell of a stegosaurus fossil and transfer it to a crocodile zygote, what's different about changing the gene pattern of a chimpanzee zygote to that of a Neanderthal? Both the method and the result are the same. In one case you end up with an infant stegosaurus, in the other—"

Miss Kalish gestured impatiently. "That's not what I'm talking about at all, Professor! The thing is, I've seen some pretty awful things come slithering out of your tanks, and I've never turned a hair." She gulped and looked ill. "But if you start fooling around with . . . with *human* babies, or something like them, and they come out looking like what that Dr. Trine said, and grow up to be shambling beasts—well, I just don't want to go down to your old laboratory!"

Turning away from him, she burst into tears.

Philo Putnam clucked sympathetically. He walked over to her and put his arm around her shoulders. It was the first time in all their fifteen years together that they'd had any sort of intimate contact, and it disturbed them both considerably. Miss Kalish stiffened and stopped crying, and Professor Putnam dropped his arm awkwardly. Privately, the professor was astonished to realize that it was also the first time in fifteen years he was aware of his secretary as a female. He thought back. Well, make it thirteen.

"The . . . ah . . . nine-month-old fetus, Miss Kalish," he said, clearing his throat uncomfortably, "is never prepossessing, I'm afraid. But I'm sure you've seen preserved specimens from time to time without being unduly upset. The ones in the laboratory are alive, of course, which shouldn't bother you. There are practically no differences between them and other human infants. I'll guarantee that a month after completion they'll be sufficiently attractive to provoke the usual feminine gurgles."

He raised a hand to forestall a threatened interruption. "As for what they'll look like when they reach maturity," he went on, "that's one of the reasons we're doing this experiment. We know about Neanderthal's bone structure and whatever else we can infer from that. But we don't even know whether he was hirsute or hairless. If our specimens run true to form, they'll be about five feet tall, give or take a few inches, with receding brows and chins, long arms and slightly bent legs. That may not sound very handsome to you, but then, you're not a lady Neanderthal."

Professor Putnam smiled hopefully at his secretary. "Now, Miss Kalish—would you care to come down to the laboratory?"

"Why, certainly. Thank you—Professor," Miss Kalish said demurely, and started for the door. Moving swiftly, Professor Putnam managed to get to it in time to hold it open for her.

There were only two men in the laboratory when they arrived, but the large room seemed surprisingly crowded. This was not caused, of course, by the presence of Oscar Felzen, Professor Putnam's senior lab assistant. Undergraduate rumor had it that Felzen actually slept in the laboratory at night, tucked on a slab alongside of the department's skeleton. Certainly, the thin, retiring, Felzen was as much a part of the laboratory as the cages of pterodactyl chicks and the piercing odor of formaldehyde.

But the heavyset man in the blue pinstripe suit, who paced restlessly in front of the bank of tanks, on the other hand, definitely did not belong in a laboratory. President D. Abernathy Grosvenor belonged where indeed he felt most at home— on a temporary grandstand at one end of the football field, introducing a nervous lieutenant governor to row on row of cap-and-gowned students and doting parents.

"Ah! Professor Putnam—here you are at last!" President Grosvenor announced, as the biologist and his secretary entered. Hesitating uneasily for a moment, he went on: "Your assistant has been showing me around"—Felzen stared at him, astonished— "and I must say it has been most informative. Fine laboratory. Good work. Wish I had more time to wander about and see all the magnificent things you fellows are doing. Unfortunately, running a university is a full-time job. Have to forget about what I'd like to do, and concentrate instead on all those unpleasant, but absolutely necessary details of administration that only I—"

President Grosvenor took a deep breath. It was obvious he had arrived at the crux of his visit.

"Matter of fact, that reminds me of what I came to see you about, professor." He shook his head mournfully. "Really, Professor, you should have been more diplomatic with Mrs. Featherby and her committee. I did my best to explain to them that you're a scientist—temperamental, deeply engrossed in your work—and all that, but I'm afraid they were too enraged. If only you'd bear in mind that since the horrors of the Atomic War, hatred of scientists . . . well, Mrs. Featherby said something about taking the matter up with one of the trustees, and stormed out. When nobody answered in your office, I came here. I must say you took your time getting here, incidentally—"

"I didn't come directly," Professor Putnam said, breaking in, his face growing almost as red as Miss Kalish's had become. "My secretary and I . . . uh . . . had some matters to discuss. But I am sorry I lost my temper with that insufferable committee. If I had known they were going to land on your neck—Just the same," he added heatedly. "what was I to do? Basically, they won't be satisfied until I agree to forget about this experiment entirely. And then they'll be after us to stop doing other things. Eventually, I'll be reduced to breeding new strains of geraniums, or something equally innocuous. Are you willing to go along with that, President Grosvenor? Shall I tell Felzen to start dismantling the equipment?"

President Grosvenor raised his hand dramatically. "Please, Professor! As long as I am president of this university, no group and no individual—no matter how powerful—shall interfere with scientific freedom! You have my word!"

He paused and scratched his chin absently. "On the other hand, it must be admitted that this little . . . ah . . . contretemps, comes at an awkward time. And the trustees, when awakened, can be exceedingly difficult to deal with. Would it not be the better part of valor to . . . say . . . postpone this experiment for a little while, Professor? I'm sure there must be tremendous areas of prehistoric life which you haven't studied as yet. I'd say, forget about Neanderthal and restore some other creature. When you come right down to it, you know, Neanderthal *was* just an animal, and surely it's ridiculous to get so hot and bothered over it."

Professor Philo Putnam frowned. "Neanderthal man," he said carefully, "was *not* an animal—not in the sense you're using the word, anyway. He was a human being, of a different species, perhaps, but nevertheless a human."

The president waved a deprecatory hand. "Please, Professor!" he admonished. "For the purposes of this discussion, there's no point in being rigidly technical. The creature may have been approximately human, but so is a gorilla. Neanderthal was a subman, with only the most rudimentary capacity to think, to create, or to do anything else that we term human. Surely you'll concede that?"

Philo Putnam strode over to his workbench and picked up a large rock. He turned, and President Grosvenor retreated a step in sudden alarm. Exhibiting the rock, the professor demanded, "Do you know what this is, President Grosvenor? You probably don't, so I'll tell you. It's an Acheulian flint hand-ax—maybe three hundred thousand years old, or older. Neanderthal man made it, and an anthropologist friend of mine presented it to me about a year ago. I haven't been able to get it out of my mind. Shall I tell you why?"

Oscar Felzen and Miss Kalish, both intrigued, nodded their heads, but the professor was staring at Grosvenor.

In a soft voice, he went on: "It's a crude, unprepossessing weapon. Compared to a nuclear fission bomb, the thing is pathetic, and it certainly wouldn't stand a chance against a rifle. As a matter of fact, it couldn't even compete with the arrows of our Cro-Magnon ancestors. But if you look at it from another angle, what a tremendous thing it is!"

He held it up in both hands, turning it slowly. "I'm not talking about the chipping technique, though I understand it represents magnificent craftsmanship. Forget about this specimen, and think back to the first one that was ever made. There had to be a first one, you know. And there was a man who made it. Before him, stretching all the way back to the beginning, you've got an unbroken line of creatures who could use their pseudopods, their teeth, or their claws. Monkeylike animals, who could wave a dead branch and throw a rock or a coconut. Later apes might even have carried a favorite rock or branch around with them. But this . . . this *man* . . . selected a lump of flint and worked on it until he had something which fitted his hand comfortably if he held it at one end. He fashioned the other end into a rough point, useful for cracking a bison's skull."

He waved the hand-ax at his listeners. "Note that word, 'useful.' What he made was a tool, the first one ever seen on this planet! After him, you get makers of bigger and better, more varied and more complex tools, but he made the first one! Every inventor after him merely added to the list, but worked with tools which had already been invented. More important, they worked with the knowledge that tools existed. But the man who first conceived of a tool as such, who created the first one—what a mind he must have had! I wonder how many brilliant men who came after him would have had that much genius? Da Vinci, maybe . . . possibly Einstein? Certainly not the man who merely constructed the first wheel! And you call such a man subhuman?"

With a sudden surge of emotion, Professor Putnam snorted and shrugged his shoulders.

President Grosvenor cleared his throat uncertainly. "Very interesting theory, Professor, though a bit fanciful, I suspect. This entire discussion has nothing to do with the matter at hand, but since we've been carried along this far, I'd like to point out an obvious weakness in your argument. I'm a student of history and political science—not the laboratory sciences—and what stands out to me is not Neanderthal's mechanical abilities, however great they may or may not have been. You pointed out yourself that he went down under Cro-Magnon's arrows. Pragmatically, then, he was inferior. He could not stand the acid test of survival. He was supplanted by a superior human—"

"Superior! Certainly! But superior *how*?" Putnam spat the words out angrily. "Superior as a savage—as a killer—as a beast! You talked about my being fanciful . . . now I will get fanciful! Think about Neanderthal; the first rational, creative creature on Earth—which he was—with his tools, his art, his religion and culture. Suppose he was a peaceful, basically civilized creature, painfully working out the first formless beginnings of civilization. Then along comes our ancestors—noble savages, perfect savages! They acquire his knowledge, improve upon it in a typically savage way—to construct better instruments of destruction—and so destroy the actually superior Neanderthal, as they did every other creature who ever got in their way!"

"But nevertheless—Cro-Magnon did win out. You've got to admit that's *some* indication of superiority!"

Professor Putnam shrugged again. "If I did, I'd have to admit the inherent superiority of every shark that ever chewed up a swimming man. It's the superiority of the beast in its natural

habitat. If my thesis is correct, Cro-Magnon was a better savage. Certainly his record as a civilized creature isn't very much
to boast about—"

"But this is all idiotic!" President Grosvenor shouted. "We're
wasting time arguing about a lot of thorough-going nonsense.
What matters is, will you or will you not discontinue your
present experiment? That's what the board of trustees will ask
me in a little while, and I've come here for your assurance that
you will!"

Philo Putnam took a deep breath. Before answering, he
glanced at the worried faces of Oscar Felzen and Miss Kalish.
He smiled at them, briefly, and walked absently over to the
bank of tanks.

Staring down through the transparent top of the nearest tank,
he said, "I'm very sorry, President Grosvenor, but it's out of the
question. I don't want to be unreasonable, or cause you embarrassment, but when I work at something I do it because that's
the next thing for me to do. I can't quit and do something else
simply because at this moment there's nothing else *for* me to
do. Everything else has either been done already, or has to wait
until I assimilate the results of this experiment. I might just as
well quit."

"Don't you realize, Putnam, that you'll have to do exactly
that if you don't back down? I'd protect you if I could, but I
can't! The A-RL is too powerful, and they're out to get you this
time. If only you'd— What's wrong, man?"

Professor Putnam was staring down into the tank with
mounting excitement. After consulting the instrument panel
on the wall above, he whirled and stared about the laboratory
wildly for a moment.

"Miss Kalish!" he shouted, his voice cracking like a whip.
"Open that cabinet on the wall over there. You'll find layettes
and baskets for eight babies—set them up in a row on that
bench. Make sure we have everything we need and that it's all
sterile. *Move,* woman!"

With a muffled gasp, his secretary bounded across the floor.
The professor switched his attention to Felzen. "Better get the
incubators going, Oscar—we may need them. And do some-

thing about the temperature of the lab—it's freezing!"

Putnam trotted in the direction of the tank on the far end of the bank. The open-mouthed president caught at his arm as the biologist went by.

"Look here, Professor!" President Grosvenor protested. "I don't know what's going on, but we've got an important matter to settle. The board of trustees—"

"Blast the board of trustees!" Philo Putnam exploded. "And let go of my arm! Don't you understand? Can't you see the red lights are on over the tanks? Completion is about to take place!"

"That's all very well," President Grosvenor said firmly, "but the fact remains that your position in this university is in jeopardy. I refuse to leave until you give me a direct statement."

The professor's face reddened. Then he took a deep breath and held it for a long moment. When he spoke, his voice was surprisingly calm.

"Tell the trustees—and the Anti-Resurrection League—that as long as I am in charge of my laboratory I alone will decide what experiments I am going to conduct. If you and the others decide to knuckle under to the A-RL, that's your business, not mine. Do anything you like—put Mrs. Featherby in charge of the biology department—but right now, get out of my laboratory and stay out of it as long as it's mine! I've got work to do!"

His voice rose dangerously on the last words, and the president released him and stepped back.

"You're being very foolish, Putnam—very foolish. I'll do what I can, but"—he paused at the door—"if I were you—"

"I know! I *know*! I've already emptied my desk drawers! Now get out!"

Before the sound of the door slamming had died away, Professor Putnam was bending over the last uterine tank in the bank, crooning softly and happily to himself.

It was Miss Kalish who timidly proposed coffee about two hours later. Two hours of continually checking over preparations, peering at dials and gauges, and making careful notes of fetal movements, had thoroughly exhausted all three. Professor

Putnam nodded glumly, and with a relieved sigh, Oscar Felzen had started a pot of coffee going on the lab hot plate.

"How much longer will it be, Professor Putnam?" Miss Kalish asked, puncturing a can of condensed milk.

The professor shrugged. "Hard to say. Human births take anywhere from one to eighteen hours. The tanks are set to respond to the needs of the individual fetus, so for all I know we may be here all night." He smiled benevolently at his secretary. "No need for you to stay, Miss Kalish. Go home, if you like."

Miss Kalish shook her head emphatically. "Certainly not! I mean—if it's all right with you, I'd like to stay. Since my mother died, I can stay out as long as I like."

Her eyes brightened, and she chuckled softly. "This is so much like old times. Remember how we all sat around drinking coffee and waiting for that chick to hatch? It never did, did it, Professor Putnam?"

The professor cleared his throat. "No, I'm afraid it never did. The next one did, though. Ah . . . call me Philo, ah . . . Leona. I doubt if I'll be a professor much longer in any case."

"You might have been, if you'd only kept your head with the president," Oscar Felzen grumbled, as he poured coffee all around. "Anyway, you didn't mean all those things you said to him, did you? About Neanderthal having been a superior race, and modern man his inferior. That's hardly scientific—"

"I know, Oscar—you're right. I went too far. About Neanderthalis, anyhow. I'll admit *that* part may have been vague theorizing, but I'll stand behind anything I said about the species that supplanted him."

"What's wrong with us?" Miss Kalish demanded.

Professor Putnam shrugged and sipped his coffee. He made a face and added another spoonful of sugar. "With us? As individuals, maybe nothing—maybe a lot—I don't know. But as a species we've got plenty to be ashamed of. Oh, we build things and erect cities, but everybody knows that's only supposed to be the beginning. Once we actually get a civilization started, what always happens? What happened to Babylon, Greece, Samarkand, Chichen-Itza, and all the others? Either they're torn

up by their own internal stresses and strains, or howling con-
quistadores come along and smash everything."

He took a long swig of coffee. His secretary seized the opportunity deftly. "But you can't blame that on the individual!
People don't want to fight or break things or kill. If a whole
society goes crazy, how can you blame the poor man or
woman—"

"Who else can you blame? Who makes up the society?
What's a mob?"

"There have been some people who didn't go along with the
others," Felzen pointed out.

Professor Putnam nodded violently. "Certainly! And what
happens to them? Anytime a Socrates or a Michael Servetus
opens his mouth, the crowd—the mass of individuals present—rips him to pieces. Face the facts! The human race is
intelligent enough to know what civilization is, to draw up the
blueprints and start constructing it—but we can't live in it!
Not stable enough, as far as I can see. As I said, fine savages—
fit for caves and nothing else. Take the present time. The twentieth century has only another twenty-five years to go, and if
you look back over—"

He stopped abruptly as the door opened.

President D. Abernathy Grosvenor entered, looking considerably uncomfortable. He was followed by Mrs. Featherby, who
looked thoroughly triumphant.

Philo Putnam shoved away his coffee cup and stood up.

"Ah . . . Professor Putnam," President Grosvenor began. "I
fear I have unpleasant news—"

"He means you're through!" Mrs. Featherby put in.
"Finished!"

Putnam ignored her carefully. "I have a contract, you know,
President Grosvenor," he pointed out.

The president's face became even more miserable. "Of
course, we're really asking you to hand in your resignation.
After all—if you're not wanted . . . what I mean is, there's no
point—"

Professor Putnam nodded. "You're right. Don't worry about
my resignation—you'll get it. But in return for my contract

I want a week of complete freedom to wind up my experiments, plus the right to take any specimens I want with me. Agreed?

President Grosvenor seemed immensely relieved. "Certainly, Professor! And if there's anything else—"

"Yes. Get another secretary for the biology department. Miss Kalish and I are planning to get married, and she'll be leaving with me."

"I'm leaving too," Oscar Felzen said moodily, pouring himself another cup of coffee."

Philo Putnam smiled approvingly. "Good! You'll come with us, too, then—" He caught sight of Mrs. Featherby and his smile froze. "This is still my laboratory for another week, President Grosvenor, so get *her* out of it before I—"

"Did you hear him?" Mrs. Featherby bellowed indignantly, as the president hurriedly bundled her through the door.

"Absolutely abominable. Mrs. Featherby. Thoroughly reprehensible." He directed a last what-can-I-do-it's-my-job glance at Professor Putnam, and closed the door behind them.

There was a moment of silence.

"Where do we go from here, Professor?" Oscar Felzen asked gloomily.

Philo Putnam chuckled and snapped his fingers. "To my farm in Southern California, of course! You and I will raise the Neanderthalenses and continue with our experiments. Miss Kalish . . . Leona, I mean—" He turned to her with sudden concern. "You are coming with us, aren't you? What I said about us getting married—you will, won't you?"

Miss Kalish blushed and lowered her eyes. "Of course, Philo," she said softly. Then she raised her eyes again as a thought struck her. "*What* farm?"

Putnam threw back his head and laughed. "I've seen this coming for years," he told them, snapping his fingers again. "Been preparing for this ever since the first physicist was lynched. I've got a hundred acres of land in a practically unpopulated area. There's a well on it, though, and a good house, electricity and a fine lab. Plus my Proto-minks—"

"Professor! Look!" Oscar Felzen cried, pointing excitedly.

"The green light is blinking over the first tank! The fetus is completed!"

Pausing only to whip on sterile gloves and a mask, Professor Putnam hurried over to the tank. Carefully, he lifted up the transparent top and put it aside. While the other two held their breaths, he reached in and lifted out the tiny, wrinkled occupant.

The baby gasped, wriggled in his arms, and began to whimper.

"I've done it!" the professor crowed. "What man has destroyed, man can re-create! And with the money we'll make from the Proto-minks—"

"What Proto-minks?" Miss Kalish demanded.

Professor Putnam chuckled. "Remember the mink from the glacial epoch, Oscar? The one that didn't seem to be of any scientific significance?"

Oscar nodded vaguely, removing a baby from the fourth tank. "I think so. But didn't we destroy them all?"

"All except two. I raised them on my farm. It turns out the adult Proto-mink has a fur that's superior to any living animal's. Makes sable and chinchilla look ratty. Stands to reason, you know. Comparatively speaking, we're living in an almost tropical climate. For real fur-bearing creatures, you can't beat a glacial—"

"But—what are you going to do with them?" his wife-to-be asked.

"Market the fur, of course! If nothing else, it'll keep us in food and lab equipment. With luck, we'll be completely independent economically."

Oscar Felzen appeared dubious. "It sounds a little farfetched, Professor. After all, none of us have any real business experience—"

"I hate to be told I can't do something," Professor Putnam told him irritably. "They told Appelbaum he'd never take a chromosome print which would reproduce the molecular structure of the gene, and then they told my old professor, Morelli, that he'd never find chromosomes in a fossil bone cell. Some of them even said there *were* no cells in a fossil bone! But he did it, and I transformed them successfully to a living zygote!"

Felzen shrugged, grinning. "Okay. So there are no limits to what the human mind can do. But what happens to your argument about the inferiority of Homo sapiens?"

Frowning, Professor Putnam emptied the last tank. "I don't know. Maybe that's why this experiment was so important to me. All of these experiments, in fact. We're finally reversing the age-old destruction, bringing back all the creatures we've so wantonly destroyed."

He handed the squalling infant over to Miss Kalish. "Don't misunderstand me, Oscar. It's not last month's ichthyosaurus that matters, or Neanderthalis here. They're meaningless. But if from this work man learns to live with himself as well as with the other creatures around him, then humanity is on its way!"

The first Neanderthal baby woke up and began to cry lustily.

> *. . . his comparatively brief tenure. Though surprisingly ingenious, Sapiens was emotionally unstable. Throughout his thirty thousand years on Earth, he made unceasing attempts to destroy both his own and all other species. To his credit, however, is the fact that, just before Sapiens' last—and successful—attempt at self-destruction, he reintroduced to Earth the more stable Homo Neanderthalensis II (q.v.) who was able to survive Sapiens' final cataclysm, thereby inheriting the planet and Sol's eventual position in the galactic . . .*
> —*Encyclopedia Galactica*

Suzette Haden Elgin

Born in Louisiana, Missouri, Suzette Haden Elgin (1936–
) has enjoyed scientific success as a professor of linguistics and artistic success as a musician, poet and writer.

After initially attending the University of Chicago, she obtained her B.A. degree in French and English from California State University, Chico (1967), then went on to complete an M.A. (1970) and a Ph.D. (1973) in linguistics at the University of California, San Diego. She specialized in Amerindian languages such as Navajo, Kumeyaay and Hopi, teaching at San Diego State University as an associate professor of linguistics from 1972 to 1980. Now a professor emeritus, she lives in Arkansas, directing the Ozark Center for Language Studies and concentrating on her writing.

In addition to a number of research papers, she has authored or co-authored several books about linguistics, rhetoric, and communication, including *A Guide to Transformational Grammar: History, Theory, and Practice* (1973), *What is Linguistics?* (1979), and *The Gentle Art of Self-Defense* (1980).

Elgin began her literary career as a poet, winning the University of Chicago's Academy of American Poets Award in 1955 and a Eugene Saxon Memorial Trust fellowship in poetry from Harpers in 1958. But since the 1970s she has written six science fiction novels and about a dozen shorter works. In the story below (which concludes *At the Seventh Level*, 1972) we see several of her major interests at work.

MODULATION IN ALL THINGS

by Suzette Haden Elgin

1.

THE YOUNG MAN in the student tunic motioned the emissary to be seated on a low wooden bench against the wall. The bench was the only furnishing the room contained except an altar in the center and a high case of ancient books.

"Please be seated," he said, "and when the Poet Jacinth has ended her meditation I will come and take you to her."

"You are allowed to speak to me in prose?" marveled the emissary.

"Certain Poets serving in the function of communicators between the Temple of Poetry and the people are excused from the vow of verse-speaking while on duty, citizen," murmured the student.

"Very good. And you'll go with me to see this . . . this Poet?"

"Yes, citizen."

"The Light be praised," said the emissary with satisfaction. "I wasn't happy about going by myself."

348

The student nodded to show his understanding. "One's first interview with the Poet Jacinth is not an experience to be taken lightly."

"Do you know her well?"

"I? Certainly not! She is female, and not of my household."

The emissary stared at the floor. "I see," he said. "I am sorry to have offended you, young citizen."

"It's perfectly understandable," said the student gravely. "There are no traditions available to our people for dealing with a poet of the Seventh Level who happens, the Light alone knows why, to be female."

"It hardly seems possible, even after all these years."

"And yet," said the student, "she has given our temple the finest poems of this age. The Light does not err, you see."

"She is expecting me, of course?" asked the emissary.

The student frowned and studied his fingernails. "There was a messenger from the council this morning," he said. "However, the Poet Jacinth has been in meditation since before dawn; there has been no opportunity for the messenger to communicate with her."

"What! You mean to tell me, man, that I must see her without any advance preparation whatsoever? Surely *she* is allowed to speak only verse?"

"Correct, Citizen ban-Dan."

"Then how am I—how are we to communicate?"

"I would suggest that you instruct the Poet Jacinth merely to listen, citizen. That would be less complicated."

"What," breathed the emissary, "are they trying to do to me? What are they trying to *do*?"

The student chuckled softly. "Apparently," he said with a sly casualness, "the council acted rather hastily on this question."

He was gone before the hot words that leaped to the emissary's lips could be spoken, and it was thoroughly apparent that Citizen ban-Dan's elaborate costume and impressive title had not impressed the student in the least. It was, of course, quite possible that the youth was the son of a wealthy family and accustomed to elaborate dress and ceremony. One could not tell with students, since they must all dress alike until graduation, regardless of their rank or the circumstances of their households.

There was therefore nothing left to do but wait and hope that he would do and say the right thing, and that the Poet Jacinth would see him soon, before he died of the heat.

The student erred, though, mused Citizen Arafiel ban-Dan, emissary extraordinary of the Legislative Council of the planet of Abba. The council had not acted hastily. The formal carrying out of the decision had perhaps been rather abrupt, but it had required three days of angry debate in the Council Hall before all the members had been convinced that it was really necessary—or for that matter, seemly—to disturb the Poet Jacinth with this problem.

Some of the elder members had been almost apoplectic with rage at the very idea. Indeed, the member from the Sector of the Lion, a conservative and wealthy sector inhabited mostly by the old and sedate families of Abba's very rich, had threatened to retire from the council if the others persisted in their intention.

"I say it is blasphemous!" he had shouted, his old voice trembling but still powerful. "Never in the history of Abba, never once in ten thousand years, has a female been involved in matters of government—that is the first thing! And even if the Poet Jacinth were not a female, even if that did not enter into this, the very idea, the very concept, of approaching a poet of the Seventh Level, a holy being dedicated to a life of meditation and sacred composition, and asking that poet to assist in a ... a translation! Gentlemen, my gorge rises at the thought! On two counts, this whole plan is both blasphemous and obscene, and I will take the Sector of the Lion out of Abba if necessary before I will see it implemented by this council!"

The emissary chuckled, remembering the old man's thunder and fire, ringing through the hall and all being duly noted by the robosecs on their aluminum pedestals. Nothing bothered *them*, of course, except noises that interfered with the performances of their duty.

It had been far from easy to persuade the old man—and many others who, though perhaps less dramatically vocal, sided with him on the question. It *was* a tricky problem, an unheard-of problem, with no precedent to follow, and a planet with ten thousand years of recorded history is accustomed to a heavy backlog of precedent.

Fortunately, they had had a powerful weapon on their side. The elder member from the Sector of the Lion was a wealthy man, and it was his credit disk that was being hurt by the situation that they wanted the Poet Jacinth to solve for them. Had it been anything else he would never have given in.

They had shown him the figures, patiently repeating, until he at last grasped the size of the sum that it was costing the planet of Abba—and the taxpayers of Abba, including himself as one of the heaviest-paying of those taxpayers—to provide the ten planet-colonies of Abba with enough edible protein to maintain their populations. They had reminded him, also, of the inevitable tragedy that faced Abba if the planet-colonies could not be made more economical to operate, to provide living space for the ever-growing population that threatened to swamp the home planet. They had shown him the bill that resulted from attempting to ship food out from Earth, the agricultural planet two galaxies away. And they had waved under his nose, finally, all the incredible advantages of that ubiquitous plant from the distant world X513, the *ithu* plant that was 93 percent edible protein, and that would grow anywhere, anywhere at all.

The old man had gasped and stuttered and spluttered, but in the end he had given in and the rest with him.

And now here he sat, emissary of the August Council, all decked out in title and finery to cover the trembling man beneath, all alone with the task of justifying all this to the holy woman.

The emissary sighed a mighty sigh. He was not a devout man. Religion, he felt, was a necessity, since it kept the females busy and out of trouble, and since it provided the Three Galaxies with those very useful people, the Maklunites, with their insane dedication to service and self-sacrifice. It was not for men, however, particularly busy men like himself. It was only at moments like this that he felt its lack. He gave the altar across from him an uneasy look, wondering, and then put the unworthy thought from his mind. After all, this was but a female he was to deal with.

When at last he was allowed to enter the garden of the Trance Cloister he found the Poet Jacinth sitting on a boulder underneath a small waterfall, waiting for him to speak. He stood before her, miserable, torn between his proper knowledge of the proper attitude to take when speaking with a female and the proper attitude to take when speaking with a poet—never mind a poet of the Seventh Level!—and she had smiled at him and nodded pleasantly and put him at ease with a casual couplet on the weather, and he had simply thrown tradition to the winds, since it failed him here, and begun to speak.

"I come to you today on a strange errand, my lady Poet," he began. "It would perhaps be easier for both of us if you would hear me out before you speak."

She nodded, her lovely face solemn and attentive, leaning forward slightly to hear him better. It was most flattering. She reminded him of one of the youngest and most delightful of his concubines, and he warmed slightly to his task.

"You will know, of course," he said, "of the ten planet-colonies maintained by Abba. They are planet surrogates, of course, artificial asteroids except for three that were once this planet's moons. On all of these ten planets, Poet Jacinth, there is a very serious problem, and it is the opinion of the council that only you can help us find its solution."

She frowned, the perfect brows drawing together charmingly over her dark eyes, but she had remained silent as he had asked her to do. It crossed his mind that she was after all only a young female, and a virgin, and that it was not going so badly.

The emissary relaxed, and if he had been watching Jacinth he would have seen a smile tug at the corners of her mouth, but he was staring at the blossoms of the gaza trees and trying to keep his mind on the seriousness of his mission, and he did not notice the poet's lack of respect.

"You see," he went on, "the living space on these ten colony planets is desperately needed by our people. The crowding in our cities in such that, given the culture of our people, we cannot continue to support our population. You understand, of course, that the extended household of the family, with women's quarters and parks and garden, could not lend itself to blocks of buildings hundreds of stories high?"

She nodded charmingly.

"We must then send colonists, pioneers, to the new planets. And it is quite true that people, particularly the young people, and most particularly those young people who have not managed to win a place in any of the professions except that of Service, are eager and willing to go as colonists.

"Unfortunately, most unfortunately, however, the colonies are not succeeding." A gaza blossom, a great green star covered with white pollen, fell onto his robe, and he brushed it off impatiently.

"Where was I?"

To his great pleasure, the poet clapped her hands softly, and immediately a student appeared with a tray of teas and wine, giving him a moment to collect himself.

"Ah, yes," he said, as the student poured their drinks, "the colonies are failing. They are failing because on not one of the ten planets within the practical reach of our starships can any of the protein plants, which we know of, be successfully cultivated. This leaves us with three choices. One, we can send edible protein, grown on Abba, to the colonies; this we are now doing, but we are no longer able to bear the drain on our own resources. Two, we can send protein from Earth, at an incredible and unendurable cost; this would not help much longer even if we could afford it, since almost all of Earth is now given over to fruits and vegetables. Third, protein synthesis can be instituted by the colonists themselves. This, too, is being done, but with the best facilities available to our scientists, it has been impossible to devise any sort of synthetic protein that can be eaten with pleasure over any long period of time. The colonists rebel against the diet, they find it tasteless and boring, and the eventual result, if they force themselves to eat it for the sake of the colony, is an epidemic of psychosomatic stomach difficulties—all in their heads, certainly, but quite as destructive to their health as genuine organic disease. We have been at our wit's ends, my lady Poet—until we learned, two years ago, of the existence of a protein plant that is both good to eat and economical to grow, and that can be grown on the ten colonies . . . or anywhere else, for that matter."

He glanced at his ring, saw with horror that there was little time left before the compulsory Hour of Meditation. He would have to get through the rest of it in a rush.

"This plant," he said, "comes from the world X513, whose inhabitants are known as the Serpent People. We need only establish communication with them, only learn how trade may be discussed! It is that simple—and this we have not been able to do. The greatest linguists of Abba have put two years of work into the attempt to learn this language, and they have failed. In every conversational attempt made so far, the Serpent People have left after only a few sentences, obviously deeply offended in some way, and it has only been with great difficulty that we have managed to obtain their consent to one more meeting, two months away, at the Intergalactic Trade Fair. They do not come to the trade fair ordinarily ... they are a curious, proud people, apparently quite self-sufficient on their world, not at all anxious to engage in any social or business activity. We do not understand them, and they either do not understand us or do not care to try."

She was nodding gravely, her eyes lowered, one hand idly playing in the falling water behind her.

"Poet Jacinth," he said earnestly, "the future of the colonies—and therefore the future of this planet—depends upon you. You are the greatest expert in language and the use of language that we have. There is no one else we can turn to now to determine how the language of the Serpent People can be used successfully. It is for this reason alone that we have interrupted your solitude and your meditation. We hope that you will appreciate the gravity of the situation. We hope you will forgive us."

He had come to an end at last, and he realized, ashamed, that he was trembling and covered with perspiration. There he stood in his almost-royal garments, he, a male of the profession of government, trembling like a frightened child before a slender little female in a red linen shift. It had been too much for him; never in his lifetime had he so exposed himself before a female, not even before his mother. He *had* bolted then, as he had wanted to do at the beginning, thrusting into her hands the packet of language tapes and the translations of the experts, and had almost run for the exit gate. There had been no time for her to speak, nor would he have waited to hear her if there had. His only concern was to escape, to get out of his borrowed finery and into his own clothing, and to spend at least half an evening in the company of his most humble and unintelligent concubine. He did not even know if he had succeeded or failed in his mission, nor did he care; he had done all that he could do.

2.

Jacinth went over the data for the third time, wonderingly. The linguists, all poets of the Fourth Level, had done what appeared to her to be an excellent job. They had taken standard tapes beamed from X513, submitted them to computer analysis in the ordinary way, and seemingly had produced all the needed information. And yet it had not sufficed for communication.

Methodically she went over it again, one infopacket at a time. The answer had to be in there somewhere.

They had isolated and catalogued the consonant phonemes first. M, B, V, TH, Z, L, R, NG. Only eight? Two nasals, two liquids, two fricative and two stops. That wasn't much to make a language of, eight consonant phonemes. And only eight vowels as well, three nasals plus the standard five, A, E, I, O, U. A sixteen-phoneme system did not offer much complexity of sound, unless it was a tonal system, and the computer had ruled that out. It was a nontonal.

Morphemes appeared to be all of one syllable, all simple in construction. It looked like a language constructed by a child, or an extremely language-naive adult. It was curious that it should have offered difficulty at all, much less that it had stumped the best of their linguists for two years.

The Poet Jacinth wished, not for the first time, that she had someone to talk to. As a fully invested poet, however, she was required to speak only in verse, and it did very badly for general discussion. Plus, she was not allowed to speak to females, lest she give them unseemly ideas of aspiring to the profession themselves. And males did not care to talk to her because of the conflict between the attitude of paternal tolerance due her as a female and the attitude of humble reverence due her as a poet.

She sighed and went to the corner of the room where her com-system console stood, and punched the key for a ser-vorobot. When it appeared she requested a small computer and a linguistics program tape.

She attached the computer hookup to her com-system, folded her slim legs under her, and sank down at the keyboard to work.

REVIEW LINGUISTICS PROGRAM, she tapped out.

In a moment the computer clicked and its side panel flashed the single word COMPLETED.

She then inserted the tapes prepared by the linguists for the language of X513, instructing the computer to indicate deviations from the basic information on the first tape. While the computer hummed its way through the task, she examined once again the threedy image of a citizen of X513 that had been included with the data, marveling at the beauty of the being whose picture glowed in her hand.

She inserted the threedy side in her com-system and punched the project button, and at once the image was projected life-size in the center of the room for her examination.

These were a very beautiful people, if the specimen whose image she saw before her was any example. It stood perhaps eight feet high, if "stood" was the proper word to use, since the Serpent People resembled a serpent more than any other creature with which Jacinth was familiar, and their manner of "standing" was much that of the king cobra of Earth. How much length might be involved in the coiled body she could not judge, but eight feet was held upright. The entire body was transparent, except for what she assumed was the head, and appeared to be made of strung beads of translucent crystal, caught together at the top and twisted into a rope. Alternate strands of the "beads" were in shades of deep-green and blue, the others were without color, and the whole meshed at the top in a sphere of opaque beads that must house the being's brain and whatever structures it might use for speech.

She studied it silently, knowing very well how deeply she might be in error in her analysis even of its physical structure. Perhaps the seeming "head" was really the creature's foot, or its stomach, or its sexual organs. Perhaps it was not one being but

356

a colony, each strand representing a unique individual, all joined in some communal life-system. There was as yet no way of knowing, since no citizen of X513 had ever been examined by the doctors of Abba, or of any other planet so far as was known.

Behind her the computer clicked again to signal completion of the review. She turned off the slide and went to examine the side panel. It said NO DEVIATIONS.

Very well, then. Her instinct had found no flaws in the analysis. Her computer agreed with her instinct. Therefore there *were* no flaws in the analysis, the translations of the language were as correct as could be asked, the representations of the sounds on the tapes were adequate, and no portion of the system violated the base theory of universal linguistics. Nonetheless, it had not been possible to speak to the Serpent People.

The Poet Jacinth smiled; it was a stimulating problem.

Somewhere in all of this there had to be the reason, the single explanatory factor that was being overlooked.

She left everything as it was so that she might return to it when she chose, deactivating the servorobots that would otherwise have put everything away for her, and went out into the garden.

Sitting on her favorite stone, the soft sound of falling water on her back, she closed her eyes and performed the ritual seventeen breaths, allowing all consciousness of her surroundings to leave her. When her relaxation of consciousness was complete, all that was left to her of physical awareness was the sensation that both the light and the water flowed through her being as freely as through the air, and she waited, patient and poised. Somewhere, there was something that she almost knew, something that she almost realized, something that was familiar about the language and about the problem, something that she remembered, almost. . . . She let the time pass, unaware, and waited.

And then she had it. She allowed her consciousness to return to her gently, becoming aware of the garden about her, noticing that it had grown almost dark and the air in the garden had turned cold and heavy with pale-green dew. There would be people upset about her.

She rose quickly and went into her room, gathered up the materials and reactivated the servorobots, and then she began to dictate, ignoring the soft bell that called her to eat. She would eat when she had finished with this, after she was sure that she had captured all that she must say, before she became in any way confused. She began to dictate to the com-system, watching with pleasure the intricate pattern of its dancing lights as it wrote down her words:

TO THE COUNCIL OF ABBA:

When first I read the letters that you sent me
(and I am honored that you asked my help,
for in the service of this spinning world
lies my whole happiness and my satisfaction)
there came to me a sense that I had known,
somewhere before, a problem of this kind,
a feeling that I once solved just such a problem,
as a child, perhaps? Certainly long ago.
And so I went at once into my garden
and let the Light direct me to your aid.

Then I remembered what I had forgotten.
I was a child, a small and noisy female,
spending my days in the courts of my lady mother,
and there had been summoned to the household
 banharihn
a student of poetry, ranking at Third Level,
whose single function was to teach us all to sing,
and some were to learn to play the singing strings.
And so . . .

The members of the council were hushed as it came to an end. It was, somehow, blasphemous that a female should write so well; it was humiliating that she should solve a problem that had baffled the greatest of their linguists; it was embarrassing that the solution should have been so—once pointed out—overpoweringly obvious.

Emissary ban-Dan stepped to the center of the council chamber and cleared his throat.

358

"Is it clear to all the members," he asked, "just what the Poet Jacinth is telling us? I should like to add that her conclusions have, of course, already been checked by the linguists and she is quite correct. There should be no further problem in our communicating—after a fashion—with the people of X513."

"But how is it possible," demanded a member, "how is it possible to speak such a language?"

The emissary tried to think of some tactful way to put his answer, but there didn't seem to be one.

"You are familiar with the colorful birds of Old Earth. . . . the parrots?" he asked courteously.

"Yes," snapped the member, "not that I see how that is relevant."

"It is quite, quite relevant. You see, actually we *cannot* speak the language of X513. As members of the human race, our human capacity for language does not allow us to do so, any more than the parrots can speak Abban or Panglish or any other human language. However—again, like the parrots—we can learn to mimic, and, after a fashion, to communicate. At least to the extent of trade, which is all that we really need, you know."

Several members were on their feet now, demanding the floor. The chairman recognized one, who demanded, his voice shaking, if Citizen ban-Dan was insinuating that these people of X513 were superior in intelligence to humans and that we were in effect too *stupid* to speak their language?

"Citizens," said ban-Dan worriedly, hoping the information the linguists had given him would get him through this without disaster, "I have said nothing of the kind. I said to you that their language equipment was *different*. Superiority has nothing to do with it. What reason has there been to believe that an alien race, totally nonhuman, would share the language equipment of humans? What sort of pompous, insular idea is that?"

The council was silent, and the emissary drew a deep breath and went on.

"I cannot imagine it, myself," he admitted. "But it is nonetheless true that the people of X513—who, by the way, resent being called 'Serpent People' since they are neither serpents nor people—the people of X513 speak their language with no diffi-

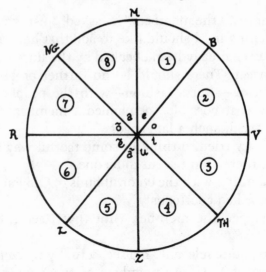

culty whatsoever. Their infants speak it flawlessly by the age
of three or so, just as do your Abban children. Certainly we of
Abba shall not be able to speak it, however, without the aid of
some sort of mechanical device."

There was still no comment, and he smiled to himself and
went on. "I have here a set of threedies for projection prepared
by the linguists. They have been hastily put together and are
somewhat rough; I think, though, that they will make everything clear. In fact, I probably need show only the first."

He lifted his hand and on all sides of the council chamber a
single image was projected. It was a huge circle, divided into
eight equal segments, like the ancient dessert called a pie. At
the center point of each segment there was a single vowel
symbol; at the boundary between each segment, on the outside
rim, there was a single consonant; and each segment was
numbered.

"This is the whole solution, gentlemen," said the emissary
quietly. "There are, as you can see, only sixteen sound segments in the entire language.

"What the Poet Jacinth remembered was an incident from
her childhood. A music teacher had been brought to instruct
the women of her household. He had explained to them the
manner of playing and singing a simple folk-song in the key of

A. Then he showed them how to play the same song in the key of E, and again in the key of C. The Poet Jacinth remembered her amazement and her disbelief; it seemed to her at that time that it could not be true that the same song, with the same words and tune, could be played in two different keys. And what struck her even more forcibly was that the same song, played in two different keys at the same time, created an unholy discord. She was so concerned about all this that it was necessary for the music teacher to explain to her the theory of keys and modulations, something that bored the other females of the household to such an extent that the child was punished for her curiosity.

"Citizens, this is a language that modulates; the analogy with music is exact and precise."

The emissary glanced at his notes, hoping that he would not become as confused in reading aloud the example given him by the linguists as he had become in reading it to himself.

"Refer to the projected chart, if you please," he said. "Now, a given segment, say the syllable represented by the letters MEB—see them there, E at the point of the segment, and M and B at the boundaries—this syllable 'meb' meaning roughly 'table for eating,' will transpose in another environment. For instance, if one says to a servant, 'Set the table for dinner,' the syllable must be rendered VITH, using the letters of the third segment of the circle, the one reserved for speaking to someone of lower status. If, on the other hand, one calls a beloved friend to join one at the table, the word must be pronounced MEB, using segment one of the wheel of letters. In an emergency, if the table was on fire, for example, the word would become THUZ, using segment four. If the table were a work of art, it would be referred to as a LER, using segment six, which is reserved for art and ritual.

"And so it goes, you see—there was nothing wrong with the translations of the words as prepared by our linguists, it's just that the 'word,' for the people of X513, is not a stable unit. It changes constantly, depending upon the social situation, the status of the speakers and the like."

"Ah, yes," said the senior member from the Sector of the Fish. "Now I begin to see. Let us say that one of our linguists heard a citizen of X513 referring to a necklace as a BLUB when speaking to an assistant. That would be the proper term for addressing someone of inferior position. Then when our linguist attempted to compliment the X513 person on the fine workmanship of the BLUB he would have addressed *him* as an inferior! No wonder they were offended."

"But surely," commented the member from the Sector of the Panther-Ram, his beard quivering with indignation, "surely they should have been aware that one could make unintentional errors in a language of such incredible intricacy!"

"Why?" asked the emissary. "They have no difficulty with their language, nor do they see it as one of incredible intricacy. They had no difficulty avoiding making errors in *our* language, apparently, either—why should they expect us to make errors in theirs?"

"It's utterly incredible," said the president of the council, wearily. "You realize, I am sure, that the only way we will be able to speak this language is with the help of a computer; certainly we could not follow the modulations quickly enough without such help."

There was an embarrassed murmur through the council chamber and, to his horror, the emissary heard mutterings in the back about the feasibility of applying the same principle to Abban in order to allow a modulation of the language that would be suitable for speech with females. As if life were not complicated enough!

"What we *can* do," the president went on, oblivious to the absurdities in the back of the room, "is have the linguists and computers compose for us an opening speech to be addressed to the people of X513 at the Intergalactic Trade Fair. This must be a speech that will unambiguously explain our linguistic situation to him. This is most important, since presumably once he understands what the problem is he will be more tolerant of our subsequent errors. And," he concluded, "we will have our protein source for the colonies. This is a great day for Abba, citizens, and one to be long remembered."

Emissary ban-Dan raised his staff of office, requesting permission to speak, and the president nodded gravely.

"Citizen President," said ban-Dan, "what about the Poet Jacinth?"

"What about her? What do you mean?"

"Well, you realize what she has done—she has single-handedly solved the major problem of the future existence of ten planets. It is not as if the people of X513 would have been willing to discuss matters in the intergalactic gesture language, you know. The situation was *really* desperate, and it was the Poet Jacinth who came to our rescue. It seems to me that she should have some sort of reward, some recognition."

"She is a female, citizen."

"But—"

"She has been signally honored, after all, in being allowed to participate in an activity of our government, something no female has ever done before."

"But—"

"No doubt our own linguists, had they had sufficient time, would have reached the solution without her assistance."

"But, Eminent Citizen, I still feel—"

The president leaned from his chair and shook a warning finger at the emissary.

"Modulation—that is, *moderation*—in all things, young man! Moderation in all things!"

And he rang the gong to dismiss the council.

Mario A. Pei

One of the world's greatest linguists, Mario A. Pei (1901–1978) was born in Rome, Italy. He entered the U.S. in 1908 and became a naturalized citizen in 1925.

After finishing his A.B. from City College (1925) and his Ph.D. from Columbia University (1932), he accepted a professorship in Romance philology at Columbia University (1937), remaining there—with several interruptions for visiting professorships and World War II—until his retirement in 1970.

He authored or co-authored approximately thirty-five nonfiction books, mostly on language and linguistics. Some examples are *The World's Chief Languages* (1946), *French Precursors of the Chanson de Roland* (1948), *The Story of Language* (1949), *The Story of the English Language* (1967), *Invitation to Linguistics: A Basic Introduction to the Science of Language* (1965), *The Story of Latin and the Romance Languages* (1976) and *Weasel Words: The Art of Saying What You Don't Mean* (1978).

His awards and honors include the Freedom Foundation's George Washington Honor Medal (1957), the Italian Republic's Cavaliere Ufficiale Order of Merit (1958) and Unico Club's Oscar Award for Literature.

His fiction includes a werewolf novel (*The Sparrows of Paris,* 1958), and several fantasies and a couple of science fiction tales included in *Tales of the Natural and Supernatural* (1971). The work we have chosen is, we think, his most dialectical romp.

THE BONES OF CHARLEMAGNE

by *Mario A. Pei*

T HE GERMAN MAID stood poised over me inquiringly with the percolator. *"Mehr Kaffee?"* she asked invitingly.

"Danke, nein," I said; then, turning to my host, "Freddy," I said firmly, "I have only two days left, and I want to visit Aachen."

"But why Aachen?" inquired my friend. "There's nothing much there. It was the first town we took when we came into Germany, and it got pretty badly shot up. It's been rebuilt some, but most of it is still in ruins. The Rathaus, the towers, the cathedral and the Hochmünster are still a mess."

"Yes, zat ees so," interjected pretty French-born Mrs. Irish. "I came through eet when I was coming here to join my husband. Lots of rueens and rubble!"

"I have my reasons," I said darkly, fingering my Kümmel glass. "Can't we go there tomorrow?"

"Well, it's a one-hundred-fifty-mile drive. If we leave at six A.M. we'll be there by ten. But look—"

"But me no buts!" I said with finality. "It's Aachen!" And I drained the glass.

Freddy Irish shrugged his shoulders in the inimitable way he had acquired during his long European sojourn as head of the army's educational program.

"Okay! Aachen it is! But I can think of dozens of places you'd rather visit. There's Cologne, for instance, and Koblenz, if you want a Rhine city. Or Heidelberg. That's practically untouched, you know. We could even go up to Mainz and visit your old friend Professor Lerch. Here, let me give you some more Kümmel!"

I deliberately withdrew my glass. "Shall I be ready to start at six?" I asked.

"*Comme vous voulez, mon vieux!*" murmured the head of the education program resignedly.

"You know, I won't be able to go weez you," spoke up pretty Mrs. Irish. "Tomorrow is ze day when I must address ze Frankfurt Ladies' Society for Democratic Action. I geeve zem a talk on ze status of women in a free society."

I already knew that. That was why I had waited until the last two days of my stay. I wanted no one but Irish to be with me on my pilgrimage. He, a former student of mine, would understand, but no one else would.

"*Quel dommage!*" I said hypocritically, but with inward rejoicing. "We shall miss you so! But we'll be back by nine for another of your delicious dinners."

The next morning, as we sped along the half-deserted autobahn into the British zone, with the pale spring sun on our backs and the hilly Rhine country fleeting by, Irish brought up the subject again, just as I expected.

"Tell me, Pei," he asked, without taking his eyes off the curving, green-bordered ribbon of the road, "Why are we going to Aachen?"

"Couldn't you figure it out for yourself last night?" I replied, "I couldn't talk before your wife, the children and the maid. They would have laughed and blabbed all over the post."

"That much I did figure out," said Irish, swerving to the right

367

to allow a military jeep to pass. "Has it something to do with Charlemagne?"

"Of course!" I replied.

"Well, what do you expect to see? The cathedral is a shambles. The Hungarian Chapel is still standing. The bones are there, in their golden shrine. The Germans took them out when we were shelling the city, and hid them in the hills. Then they were brought back and restored to their resting place. That is all."

"How about the documents in the archives?"

"Don't be silly! You know everything was moved under Charlemagne's successors. There are neither archives nor documents in Aachen, outside of the municipal ones in the Grashaus. All you'll find will be an ornate shrine and a few disjointed bones. It is worth while your going there just to see them?"

I put on my best lecturing voice, the one with which I held my classes enthralled. "Friend Irish," I boomed, "Charlemagne was Christendom's greatest and mightiest emperor. He it was who welded the Western world into a powerful empire capable of withstanding the pressure of the Moors on the south and the heathen Slavs on the east. He brought the light of culture back into eighth- and ninth-century France and Germany. If his work had been allowed to stand, we would have today a unified Western Europe, instead of a lineup of weak nations that we have to defend from Russian communism!"

"But above all—" Irish broke in with a grin.

"You know?" I said in feigned surprise.

"Sure! Don't you remember I took the course with you? And even though you're skeptical, I *have* read all your books on the subject. I can give the lecture almost as well as you can."

I relaxed on the cushions of the Buick and half closed my eyes.

"All right!" I challenged. "Let's hear you do it!"

"Above all," Irish orated with an air of professorial profundity, "Charlemagne was responsible for the emergence of the French language. Shortly after the beginning of his reign, he was shocked at the way his French subjects spoke their ancestral Latin, which in the course of centuries of ignorance had turned into a barbarous jargon. So, in the year 787, he ordered the priests and bishops of his French realms to use good, grammatical Latin in their sermons. It turned out that the people couldn't understand the good Latin. There was widespread dissatisfaction, because in those days church sermons took the place of radio, television, the movies, the theater and the nightclub. Charlemagne's edict struck at the heart of the country's religious and social life. But it took Charlemagne a long time to realize this. The noble experiment went on for over thirty years before it dawned upon the noble emperor that the people really weren't speaking Latin any more. Then, in 813, he made a right-about face, reversed his earlier decree, and ordered the sermons to be preached not in Latin, but in the rustic Romance tongue, in other words, French. So French became semiofficial, and after a few years people began even to write it. How good is that?"

"It's good, but watch the road. You almost sideswiped that car we just passed."

"I know just how you feel about it," Irish said soothingly. "You've spent so many years poring over those musty old documents of the eighth and ninth centuries that you almost live in that period. You feel you know Charlemagne and his court by heart. Now you want to go and make his personal acquaintance."

"It isn't only that," I answered. "There's a whole mystery to be solved. Just what were the people in the French part of Charlemagne's realms speaking before he started his reform, and while the reform was in progress? Were they already speaking the sort of French we read in the Oaths of Strasbourg, or was it still broken-down Latin? You know the arguments we've had in our linguistic societies. Some people think the French were speaking French back in the fifth century; others think they spoke some form or other of Latin until Charlemagne's reform gave it its death blow."

"But—" Irish tried to interrupt. I went right on. "Our real trouble is that they didn't make phonograph recordings in those days, so we can never have absolute proof. If we could only get hold of one of the people of that period, and question him as we do a native when we want to find out about some American Indian dialect—"

369

Freddy's tone was bantering. "So what do you propose to do by going to Aachen? Interrogate the emperor's bones?"

"Not quite," I replied thoughtfully. "But there may be some old documents lying around, some old inscriptions, something that has been overlooked. After all, Aachen was Charlemagne's capital, you know."

Irish laughed. "If anything had been there, do you think it would have escaped the notice of those nineteenth-century German philologists? Those weasels could ferret out anything in sight and out of sight. They even created a few things that weren't there to start with."

"Just the same, I want to take one good look for myself. Do you mind?"

"Of course not! But you don't mind if I kid you a bit, do you? I won't give you away at the post, but this is the way it's going to sound in the *New York Times* headlines: 'Astounding Discovery Made by American Linguist! University Professor Rends Veil of Mystery from Language of the Dark Ages! Conclusive Proof Offered That Eighth-Century Frenchmen Spoke French!'"

I had to laugh. "And nine hundred ninety-nine people out of one thousand will say, 'Well, what's so strange about that?'"

But Freddy was not to be denied. "But the professional journals will carry the real story. Quote: 'The controversy as to the origin of the French language is ended forever. A document, unmistakably written in French, and antedating the 842 A.D. Oaths of Strasbourg by at least fifty years, was discovered last month in the sarcophagus of Charlemagne at Aachen, where it had lain undetected through twelve centuries and at least as many major wars. The discoverer, a professor at—'"

He rambled on and on, gesticulating with one hand and waxing more enthusiastic as he warmed up to his own tale. I listened to him out of my left ear, half amused, while I looked over the fleeting countryside, the green, rolling West German meadows, the orderly cows nibbling at the grass in the fields, the neat, slow-flowing streams that wound their gentle course toward the Rhine. A few more cars were moving on the autobahn now, many military jeeps among them. Here and there, set well back from the four-lane highway, stood clumps of trim houses, with pointed gables and eaves, some of them still pockmarked by war. Groups of farmers and laborers moved through the fields, some still wearing portions of the field-gray uniform of the defeated German army.

"Aachen lies over that hill," Freddy interrupted his imaginary newspaper account to inform me. "We leave the highway at the next turn. Look, you can see the eighth-century spire of the cathedral—what's left of it!"

I'll never know just what happened at the autobahn exit. Perhaps Irish, carried away by his journalistic enthusiasm, was driving too fast as he swung off the main highway. Perhaps the hay wagon had no right to be standing at an autobahn exit. The fact is we both saw it where it stood, surrounded by a group of gesticulating German farmers with pitchforks. But we saw it too late, and there was too little room in the narrow exit to avoid it. Freddy tried to swing out to the left while the farmers yelled and scattered. But he swung too far. There were trees along the exit, great, ancient oaks and elms. We crashed into one of them. I felt a sickening blow on the head, things like fiery cartwheels spun around in front of my eyes. Then I blacked out.

I came to a few minutes later. I half opened my eyes, but the sunlight hurt them, and I closed them again. I became conscious of a gentle, swaying motion. My head ached and throbbed. People were talking around me, in low tones. Half-consciously, I tried to listen to what they were saying. But it was no use. Their voices were low, and the few words that reached my ears were strange. What kind of a German dialect could this be? "Ostarmanoth"; "trohtîn"; "nidarstîg"; "ziu tuot ir?"

The gently swaying motion continued. It was rhythmical and soothing. I put my hand up to my head, and found it heavily bandaged in coarse cloth. What had happened to Freddy, I wondered. Had he been killed?

Then I heard his voice, speaking in irate but precise German. "Where the devil are you taking us? Why don't you phone for a field ambulance? We've got to get him to a hospital—fast! Do you want him to bleed to death?"

In my half-stupor, I grinned a sickly grin. *He* at least wasn't hurt! And my own condition couldn't be too bad, or I wouldn't be listening.

Then came a reply, in the same strange language as before, but this time in a clear, loud voice. The only thing that kept me from sitting bolt upright was my physical condition. It sounded like no modern German dialect, but rather like Old Franconian, the tongue of the Germanic portion of Charlemagne's medieval realm, a language I had studied, but had never heard spoken save by Edwin Roedder, my professor of Old High German. As far as I could make it out, the man was telling Freddy to keep quiet and mind his own business; they were doing everything for me that could be done; and why did he have to speak in such a strange jargon, anyway?

This time I opened my eyes. I was on a stretcher, borne on the shoulders of four men. The two in front were big, strapping fellows. But how strangely they were dressed! They had on close-fitting, short gray tunics, with leather belts, knee-length trousers, leggings fastened by bands, and sandals with straps. On their heads they wore round metal helmets, beneath which cascaded billows of tawny blond hair, caught in braids like little girls' pigtails, which dangled over their shoulders. They had flowing beards and drooping mustaches.

I cautiously rolled my eyes, without moving my throbbing head. Beside my litter strode several other men, similarly attired. But slung around their necks were small round shields, and in their hands they held wicked-looking short spears, which they used as walking sticks. Then I noticed that they, as well as my bearers, had short swords in scabbards that swung from their leather girdles.

"Freddy!" I called out weakly.

He came running up to me. He seemed shaken, but unhurt. "Who the devil are these fellows?" I asked. "Where are they taking us?"

"That's what I've been trying to find out," he replied with a puzzled expression. "I sort of passed out when we crashed. When I came to, you were lying on the grass in a pool of blood, with a big gash in your head, and they were swarming all around us."

"They don't look like the farmers you almost ran into."

"No, they don't! And look at the way they're dressed! They look like characters out of *Götterdämmerung!* They could be members of the Nazi underground! And the gosh-awful dialect they use! I've never run into it before, and I've been around these parts often enough! Why, I can hardly understand them or make them understand me!"

"Freddy," I said weakly, "you know what that dialect sounds like?"

He shook his head.

"Old Franconian!"

He looked at me strangely. "Isn't that what they spoke in Charlemagne's time?"

"Yes," I said simply.

"But look, that's been extinct for the last ten centuries! Are you feeling all right?"

I thought it wise to change the subject. "Who bandaged my head?" I inquired.

"Why, they did! I kept telling them to send for a doctor, but I couldn't seem to make them understand. They gave you first aid, but it was pretty rough stuff. No disinfectant, no gauze, no cotton; just an old dirty piece of linen around your head. I hope they get you to a doctor soon! I don't recognize my Germans at all! They're always so efficient and up-to-date and clean!"

"These fellows must be from the backwoods," I remarked.

"What backwoods? This is the most thickly settled part of Germany!"

"Talk to them again, Freddy," I requested. My head throbbed, but with something more than pain.

"Where are you taking my friend and me?" Irish obediently inquired in his most grammatical German of one of my bearers.

The man looked at him as though he hadn't quite understood. Irish repeated his question, very slowly and distinctly.

This time the stretcher-bearer laughed. "Listen, fellows!" he called out to his mates. "The foreigner wants to know where we are taking him. Why, to Lord Egginhard's castle, of course! Where else could we take you?"

They all laughed, while a chill ran up and down my spine. There was absolutely no mistaking the language this time. It

373

was indeed Old Middle Franconian, a tongue that had lain dead
for ten centuries!

I must have dozed off again after that. My next recollection
is of finding myself borne through a long, low-vaulted corridor,
with small barred windows, into a great, gloomy hall, with a
vaulted ceiling supported by massive columns, a long wooden
table in the center, a huge open fireplace at the end, in which
were roaring logs. Wooden, backless benches along the sides of
the table were practically the only other furniture in the place.
The floor was strewn with rushes, and a few gnawed bones
among the rushes bore witness to the presence of dogs. There
were only two small, paneless windows in the great hall, but
torches set in sconces along the wall cast a fitful light mixed
with fleeting shadows upon trophies of war and the chase that
lined the sides of the room—skulls of oxen and stag antlers,
panoplies of round shields, swords and battle-axes, tattered
banners with ancient devices.

My bearers set down my litter on the cold stone floor, and
one of their number marched up the length of the table to the
fireplace, where sat on a strangely shaped chair a middle-aged
gentleman with a thick, graying beard, clad in a long white
tunic. They confabulated for a while in low tones, while Irish
and the rest of the men who had brought us in stood in silence,
shuffling their feet uneasily. Then the middle-aged gentleman
rose from his seat and advanced to where I lay. I noticed that he
was rather small in stature, and slow and deliberate in his
movements.

"Welcome, foreigners!" he said. The language was the same
as that of our bearers, but the tone was soothing and pleasant.
"My retainers tell me you suffered an accident on your way
here. We of Charlemagne's court lead simple lives, in the fear of
God. But what we have is always at the pilgrim's bidding. You
are pilgrims to the Holy Land, are you not?"

"Well, not exactly!" Irish replied in his prim, modern German. "You see, we are Americans, and—"

"Oh, Armoricans!" exclaimed our host, interrupting him.
"Doubly welcome, then! In my childhood I spent a year in
Armorica, and well do I recall how kind was the treatment I

received at the hands of your countrymen of the Breton March! Count Roland, of blessed memory, he who died like a hero at Roncevaux protecting our emperor's retreat full thirty years ago"—the kindly voice of our host grew sad and slightly querulous—"was my host at his castle in Brittany. What a man! What a hero! Had he but lived, our noble emperor would be richer today by thirty provinces, for he conquered him one a year! But, fair sirs, I forget my duties as host! As Armoricans, you no doubt have difficulty with our rough Franconian tongue. Let us speak Latin instead."

Latin! My philologist's heart bounded up within my breast. Crazy and incredible as this whole adventure seemed, I was determined to make the most of it. Providence had somehow managed to put me back into Charlemagne's time. Now I would know, beyond the shadow of a doubt, what the language of Charlemagne's French provinces was! Of course Egginhard would still call it Latin! But now I would hear it, record it indelibly in my mind, carry it back with me to my own twentieth-century world, to my own linguistic societies of America, spread the word to language scholars the world over that the mystery of the birth of the French language had at last been solved!

"By all means!" I cried out in my best Latin from where I lay. "*Latine loquamur!* Let us speak Latin!"

The Lord Egginhard turned a smiling countenance to me. "Ah, my friend, I see that you will recover fast! My own physician shall attend you! Meanwhile, a cup of wine to restore your strength!"

My face fell. I had expected the good Lord Egginhard to speak in the transitional tongue of Charlemagne's French provinces. Instead, he used good, straight, Ciceronian Latin, such as might be envied by many a modern priest!

"But this is not the language of the people in Armorica!" I stammered back weakly.

Egginhard smiled. "Come, come, my friend! You know well that no man of distinction speaks *that* any more, even in your western Frankish lands! Ever since our good Lord Charlemagne issued his edict of Nantes, in which he ordered the church sermons to be given in good grammatical Latin, everybody who is anybody in the lands of Roman speech has learned his Latin. Only unlettered boors and peasants continue to use the rustic tongue. Here around the capital city of Aquisgranum the language of the people is German, and none of us know or remember the vulgar tongue of the Roman lands. But we of the court all pride ourselves on our Latin, learned in the schools of Alcuin of York. Here, drain this cup!"

The strong Rhine wine must have gone to my head, for after a few seconds everything began to swim before my eyes, including the long, graying beard of the good Lord Egginhard.

When I woke up I found myself lying in a small chamber, on a short, narrow, uncomfortable bed. The sunlight streamed in through a small round window, and so did a chilly breeze. I got up to close the window, but there was no pane. Then I remembered. Of course not! No glass windows in the early ninth century, save in churches. Only wooden shutters, which were removed in the spring and put on again in the fall.

I looked around. There was my uncomfortable medieval bed, fitted with hard pillows and coarse woolen blankets, and hemmed in by draperies, a straight-backed chair, over which my clothes were neatly folded, a capacious night-vase, and something faintly resembling a chest of drawers. The cool breeze from the window reminded me that I was stark naked, and I shiveringly hurried to get on some clothes. My twentieth-century eyes roved around for an instant in search of a bathroom door. Of course, I should have known better. There was only one door to the room, a heavy, oaken, iron-studded affair, leading to the corridor outside, no doubt. As I looked at it, it creaked on its hinges and swung open. A towering retainer stood in the doorway, filling it with his bulk.

"My lord Egginhard requests the honor of your company at mass, in the chapel," he said in Franconian. He eyed me suspiciously, as if to say: "I suspect you are a heathen. Come along, or else—"

"Some water?" I countered.

"To drink? Not before holy communion!"

"No, to wash!"

He looked at me strangely, then shrugged his shoulders and

marched off without another word. Soon he was back with a bucket of water. He stood in the doorway, motionless, with folded arms, while I performed my ablutions. I felt almost certain he wanted to make sure I didn't drink before communion.

As I washed I felt the stubble on my chin. My razor, with all other personal belongings, was in my suitcase in the baggage compartment of Freddy's Buick. But what did it matter? Everybody in the ninth century wore a full beard!

When I was ready, my bodyguard escorted me through drafty corridors and down winding staircases to the chapel of the palace. There I found Freddy waiting in the midst of a few dozen retainers.

"Listen!" he said to me. "You're a Catholic, but I'm an Episcopalian—low! What am I supposed to do?"

"Just watch me and do everything I do!" I whispered back. "Don't worry about forms. It's the same God! You don't want these people to take you for a Moslem or a heretic, do you?"

"No, I guess it wouldn't be safe!" he said.

At this moment Egginhard arrived, accompanied by several other men of evident rank and three ladies clad in long, blue tunics with wide, flowing, embroidered sleeves. One, in particular, drew my attention. She was young, blonde, blue-eyed, and very attractive. I noticed that she wore around the neck a fitted band that hung gracefully in front of her tunic, and a rich silver girdle with a long pendant hanging down in front from a lowered waistline. Her flowing golden hair was partly concealed by a small, circular veil held in place by a gold circlet.

Egginhard and his retinue bowed courteously to us, and we bowed back. Then the priest and his acolytes entered from the sacristy, and we all knelt down on the cold stone floor.

This was one time when I felt grateful that my church is a conservative institution. The service did not differ greatly from the twentieth-century one to which I was accustomed. We all received communion, including Irish.

When we had filed out of the chapel and back into the great hall, Egginhard made the presentations. Among the gentlemen were the captain of his guard, a ruffianly-looking fellow who had lost one eye battling with the Moors of Spain, and had never bothered to replace it; Egginhard's scribe, Helmegaudus; two of his friends who had come visiting from Trier; and a young nephew who had just won his knightly spurs fighting the Slavs. The ladies were Emma, Egginhard's wife; Bertherada, the wife of one of his friends; and Giselda, sister of the young knight and Egginhard's niece. She blushed prettily on being introduced to the strangers from Armorica.

Irish, I discovered, had given our names in Latin the night before, after I had passed out. Fredericus Hibernicus and Marius Peius did not sound too strange to our hosts. But Egginhard wanted to know if Hibernicus, as the name implied, had his family roots in the distant island of Hibernia, and if Marius was of Roman origin. Both questions were truthfully answered in the affirmative, and I was further able to add that I was a native of Rome, but had moved off to "Armorica" at a very tender age. This availed me admiring glances from the ladies, particularly Giselda, and it was my turn to blush.

The long table literally groaned under platters of food and beakers of wine, and we all sat down in merry mood, Egginhard at the head, then his honored guests from Armorica, then the ladies and gentlemen of his household, then the retainers and servants. In the light of the numerous company set to partake of Egginhard's bounty, the food and drink did not seem so overflowing as it had looked at first glance, but there was certainly plenty for all.

The white-robed host called upon the chaplain to say grace, then seized a large round wheaten loaf, cut it into pieces with a knife, and passed the pieces down the table. Everyone fell to with a good appetite, including the strangers from Armorica. There was wild boar and venison, a kid roasted whole on the spit, boiled cabbage and turnips, fragrant bread, and abundant, sparkling Rhine wine.

"Don't you miss our morning coffee?" asked Irish from across the table.

"Coffee? What is that?" quickly asked Giselda, seated on my left.

I looked down into her lovely, upturned, inquiring face, her large blue eyes staring up into mine. For an instant I forgot about the purpose of my mission, even my strange surroundings.

"It's a beverage we have in Armorica," I replied gaily. "We use it especially at the morning meal, in place of wine. Some drink it straight, others sweeten it and mix it with milk or cream."

"How strange!" she mused. "Does it grow on vines, like grapes?"

"No, it comes from the berry of a shrub that grows in South Armorica. But the shrub originally comes from Africa."

"From Africa!" Her blue eyes widened with fear. "Then it must have been brought in by the Moors!"

"Yes, that is exactly what happened," I replied, anticipating history by a few centuries.

She picked up daintily, between her thumb and forefinger, a large slice of venison that a servant had put on our joint platter and began to nibble at it.

"Do tell me more about Armorica!" she begged.

"It's a great country," I replied, "with vast cities, tall edifices, and lots of noise and movement."

"Surely," she answered, with a faint smile of unbelief, "your cities are no larger than our Aquisgranum, and your edifices no taller than our lovely basilica of the Blessed Mother of God! And as for noise and movement, our marketplace is thronged with hundreds of people six days of the week!"

I thought of the New York subway, Times Square and the Empire State Building, and held my peace.

"And do all men dress like you two in Armorica?" my lovely interviewer continued.

I nodded. "More or less."

"What strange garb! Your *bracae* are so long! They reach all the way down to your ankles. How do you keep them from getting caught in the brambles when you are out walking or riding? And what are these peculiar fastenings?" She fingered one of the buttons on my coat. "How do you get them on and off?"

I showed her. She was delighted, and began playing with my buttons and buttonholes like a child that has found a new toy. I looked down at the lovely golden hair that cascaded over her shoulders, and sighed.

The sigh was an emotional release, and brought me back to earth. I had a job to do! Perhaps she could help me.

"Fair Lady Giselda," I inquired craftily. "Have you ever been to the Roman-speaking portions of our Lord Charlemagne's empire?"

"Yes," she replied, leaving my buttons alone and looking up into my face with her innocent blue eyes. "When I was child of six, we went in the emperor's retinue to his castle at Laon."

"And did you learn anything of the language there? I mean the tongue of the serfs and servants, not the language of the palace."

"Yes, indeed! I spoke it quite fluently then. But I've forgotten it since. But why do you ask? Of what importance can be the tongue of serfs and stable-grooms?"

I ignored her question and pursued my course relentlessly. "Do you recall whether it differed much from the Latin we are speaking?"

"Not too much, to be sure, but there were differences. But—"

"Can you tell me some of the differences?"

She drew up, a little haughtily. "Sir Marius, are you trifling with me? Why do you seek from me what you already know?"

I bit my lip. As an Armorican, I was certainly supposed to know the language of Charlemagne's western provinces.

"I wanted to see whether the language of Laon differs from that of Armorica," I lied, somewhat lamely. Then, before she had a chance to open her pretty mouth, I pressed on: "Don't you recall any words or phrases from Laon?"

She shook her head. "No, I don't. But—"

"Let's take a word or two, at random. I'll give you the word, and you try to remember how they said it in Laon. All right?"

"All right!" she laughed.

"Amata?" I said.

Now I swear I meant no offense. I was carried away by my subject. *Amata* happens to be the feminine past participle of *amo,* "to love," and means "beloved." But it is also a key word in the transformation from Latin to French. All I wanted to know was whether the people of Laon still said *amata* or had already shifted to Old French *amede.*

But Giselda took it personally. She suddenly dropped her eyes from mine, blushing furiously.

"Sir Marius!" she said in a low voice. "Are you not presuming upon our hospitality?"

I was taken aback and sat speechless, the blood mounting to my own face. Luckily, Uncle Egginhard came to my rescue.

"Sir Marius, and you, Sir Fredericus," he addressed us from the head of the table. "As soon as you are finished, we ride to the emperor's palace. Our good Lord Charlemagne has heard of your coming, and wishes to see his two Armorican subjects who travel to the Holy Land. Are you ready?"

I scrambled to my feet over the seat, glad to be relieved of my embarrassment.

"We are ready, my lord, when you are!" I replied, bowing to my host.

The company broke up, somewhat noisily. While the men-at-arms went about the business of preparing our mounts, I turned to the Lady Giselda, who had remained seated. "Forgive me!" I said simply.

She raised her beautiful eyes to mine, while the lovely blush overspread once more her soft cheeks. She did not speak, but in her eyes I read forgiveness and, perhaps, something akin to gratitude.

I turned away abruptly and sought Irish, who had engaged Giselda's brother in a lengthy and somewhat confused conversation, of which I caught the tail end.

"But these things you tell me are unbelievable!" the young knight was saying heatedly, almost angrily. "Weapons that can strike and kill men half a league away! Forsooth! Our best archers can only shoot their shafts a few hundred yards! And catapults that can batter down entire cities with all their inhabitants! And men flying like birds through the air! Sir Fredericus, either you lie, or you describe the inventions of the arch-adversary of mankind! Mind how you speak of these things, lest you be accused of communing with witches and warlocks!"

Irish was about to reply just as heatedly, but I intervened. "Do not heed my friend, Sir Hubertus, I pray you; he often lets his fancy run away with him when he is in his cups!"

Since this was obviously the case, the young knight muttered something to himself and went off to talk with his sister.

I took Irish by the arm and led him aside. "Come on, fellow, pull yourself together!" I whispered to him. "For heaven's sake, don't drink too much, and don't make any wrong moves! We're in the ninth century, you know!"

Irish gave himself a shake. "Guess you're right! I'd better keep my mouth shut! But tell me, what the devil do you make of all this?"

I held out my hands in a helpless gesture. "I don't know. Maybe it's a dream. Maybe it's a miracle."

"Maybe we're both dead, killed in that car crash," suggested Irish. "The next world is supposed to be timeless, so why not be put back into any old period?"

I shook my head. "No, this just doesn't seem to jibe with all the accounts we have of the hereafter. This life we're leading here is far too material to be either heaven, hell or purgatory. We eat, we drink, we sleep—"

"Yes," interrupted Irish, "We even make love. Wait until your wife hears about you and the Lady Giselda! I was watching you from across the table, even while I talked nonsense to her brother. That lady is smitten with you, make no mistake about it!"

I felt myself flushing at this reminder of my normal existence. "Don't talk nonsense!" I said impatiently. "I know I'm married!"

"Sort of nice, though, to get back into the early ninth century, where your twentieth-century obligations can't reach you, isn't it?" he persisted, with something resembling a knowing leer.

"Listen, Freddy, forget it!" I said, nettled. "You can have all the ninth-century ladies you want out of this trip. So far as I'm concerned, I can't figure out all the angles, but there's one thing I *am* going to get out of it, and that's some information about the language they spoke in Charlemagne's France!"

"And how far have you gotten? Did the Lady Giselda enlighten you?" Irish asked with a grin.

"No, worse luck! She's forgotten it, and speaks nothing but Franconian and Latin. But we're going to the fountainhead of all knowledge on the subject right now!"

"You mean Charlemagne?"

"Who else? He put in the language reform about twenty-five years ago, didn't he? Or should we say twelve centuries ago? At any rate, he must know why he did it, what sort of language it was that got on his delicate imperial nerves when he heard it spoken in his French provinces!"

"Wish you luck!" said Irish. "But remember, a bird in the hand is worth two in the bush!"

I wanted to ask him what he meant by this familiar quotation that sounded like a wisecrack, but we were told that our mounts were ready.

We filed out into the castle courtyard, where finely caparisoned horses awaited us. Luckily we both knew how to ride, despite the automobile age from which we hailed. The ladies rode side-saddle, and I found myself paired off with Giselda once more as we rode out beneath the raised portcullis and over the moat drawbridge into the open country beyond.

The sun was bright, the air fresh and invigorating, and I stared around me curiously. As I gazed back at the castle from which we had issued it looked gray, grim and forbidding, with its massive stone walls, crenellated battlements and squat, ugly towers. The road was little more than a dusty footpath. But the countryside was glorious. In the sparkling air there was no sign of the murk and smog that usually mar industrialized modern West Germany. Around the castle lay cultivated fields and vineyards, but beyond stretched vast, dense green forests of ancient oaks and elms. Beyond the forests could be seen a spire, rising in the distance, the spire of Charlemagne's own cathedral in the heart of his capital city of Aquisgranum, or Aix, or Aachen, according to the language and historical period you prefer.

My spirits rose buoyantly. Several of my numerous years seemed to have been lifted from my shoulders since I had severed connections with my own century. I felt strong, youthful, vigorous, cantering on my big roan horse, as I had not felt in many a year driving an automobile. Something inspired me to lift my voice in song, and I did. It was something I had heard on the Arthur Godfrey program, a lilting drinking song sung by the male quartet, which had a French refrain: *"Vive l'amour! Vive la compagnie!"* Perhaps I was guided in my choice by a desire to see whether anyone in the party showed any signs of recognition of the words. But they did not, though they listened to me admiringly enough. When I was through, Egginhard shouted back over his shoulder: "Well done, Sir Marius! You are a bard as well as a knight and a pilgrim!" Then he broke out himself into a dreary Franconian chant in which he was joined by the others.

Giselda had listened raptly. "What strange music, Sir Marius!" she exclaimed. "But pray tell me, what was the tongue in which you sang? Some of the words sounded slightly familiar."

I beamed at her. "Which ones?" I inquired eagerly.

"The ones toward the end. *Vive l'amour!* Does that mean what I think it means?"

"*Vivat amor!*" I translated into Latin for her. "Long live love!"

She blushed again and sighed. "Do the men in Armorica think and speak of nothing but love?" she asked. "Here in our German lands, their sole thoughts are of war and the chase."

"Not at all!" I hastened to assure her. "It is a common complaint among the women of Armorica that their men think and talk only of commerce, and that talk of love is left to the foreigners who come to our midst."

"But you, Sir Marius, are different!"

"I am not a native Armorican, you see, my lady. I was born a Roman. In the country of my birth both men and women think, talk and sing of love."

"Love—and learning!" she turned aside the point of my verbal sword with the easy grace of a skilled fencer. "You must be quite a man of learning, Sir Marius, as well as a bard and a . . ." She paused, at a loss for a word, and blushed once more.

"Wolf?" I suggested.

She looked at me strangely, and I mentally bit my tongue. Of course the word did not carry the same connotation in the ninth century that it does today!

"I would not jest about such matters, Sir Marius!" she said seriously. "The retainers swear there are werewolves in these forests we are about to enter. They commune with the devils, and devour hapless travelers who are caught in the woods when darkness descends. Perhaps that is where you get your lore!"

I hastened to retrieve my prestige. "But what in the world makes you think I am a man of learning?" I inquired.

"The questions you ask, Sir Marius. Your curiosity about matters of speech. Only clerics and monks are interested in such matters, and—" she faltered, then in a low voice continued—"and wizards, those who cast spells with strange tongues, and strange glances! Why, I will wager that you even know how to read and write!"

"That indeed I do!" I replied, laughing easily. "But I assure you, fair lady, I am no sorcerer. Else would I have knelt at mass by your side, and partaken of holy communion?"

The argument was cogent, and the cloud lifted from the face of my lovely riding partner. To clinch the matter, I continued, "And as for reading and writing, your own Uncle Egginhard is a renowned scholar. How is he progressing with his history of our emperor's life?"

The Lady Giselda gave a visible start and looked at me with something akin to horror, while she drew her horse away from mine.

"So! You know about that? A most carefully guarded secret, known to no one in these realms save the emperor, my uncle and me. And you, an utter stranger, know it? Will you still deny you are a sorcerer?"

She spurred her horse from my side, and galloped off to join her uncle at the head of the party. Irish, who had been riding behind, fell in with me.

"Now see what you've gone and done!" he bantered. "You scared the lady off! What was the topic of your engrossing conversation? Did you threaten to kidnap her off into the future so that she went away from you in a huff?"

I shook my head. "Worse than that! I referred to her uncle's biography of Charlemagne! It's common property where we come from, but here it seems to be a deeply guarded secret. So now we're sorcerers! We know too much!"

Irish laughed. "Funny that it should have happened to you after you had warned me!" he exclaimed. "What's the matter? Didn't your ninth-century chronicles inform you that the job was done on the QT?"

"No, they did not!" I replied shortly. "Nowhere in Egginhard's *Life of Charlemagne* is it mentioned that the writing

Mario A. Pei

was done in secret. But still I should have known! Egginhard
didn't bring it out till after Charlemagne's death!"

"Well, stop worrying!" said Irish. "The most they can do to
us is burn us at the stake, and then we'll probably wake up and
find ourselves in a twentieth-century German hospital!"

I shook my head angrily. "Not before I've found out what I
want to find out!" I said.

For a time, our ride through the dark forest was uneventful.
Giselda actually came back and engaged me in conversation
again. But this time both of us were on our guard. She asked me
some rather pointed questions about Armorica, and I parried
them to the best of my ability. I wondered if she had passed on
her suspicions to her uncle. But his attitude toward us seemed
unchanged. At one point he fell back and joined in our conversation, but with such dignity and charm that I began to feel
reassured. Either Giselda had not spoken or she had not been
believed.

One further incident befell us, however, before we got out of
the forest and onto the green plain that lies before Aachen. Sir
Hubertus and one of Egginhard's friends, riding ahead of us,
jestingly made a wager as to which of them could first reach a
certain giant elm a quarter of a league away on the straight
road. As they started off at a gallop, my big roan horse, which
had behaved perfectly all morning, suddenly took the bit between his teeth and joined in the race. I tried to rein him in,
but without success. As we swept ahead, I failed to notice a
low-lying branch extending over the path from a tree by the
roadside. I struck my injured head against it, and was thrown.
As I lay dazed and half-conscious on the ground, the first one to
reach my side was the Lady Giselda. She jumped from her
horse, knelt beside me, and raised my head in her arms. I
looked up into her blue eyes, and saw them filled with concern, tenderness and perhaps something more. *"Liebling!"* she
exclaimed in Franconian, and again, in Latin: *"Amatus!"* Then,
for the second time in two short days, I passed out.

I came to in a room quite similar to the one in which I had
awakened in the morning. But this time I was partly clad, and
there were people about me, hovering solicitously—Irish,

386

Egginhard, Sir Hubertus, Giselda and an old white-clad gentleman who was strange to me. He, apparently, had just finished bandaging my head again.

"There!" he said, with an air of deep satisfaction. "He is regaining his senses. I think he will be all right for the audience with the emperor. The injury is not serious. Come, young sir, drink this potion!"

"Where are we?" I weakly asked Irish after draining the strong, sweetish liquid in the proffered cup.

"In the emperor's palace," he replied. "You passed out cold after you hit that tree, and we had to bring you into the city slung over a horse, like a bag of flour. You don't know what you missed! What a city! I'd never have dreamed a medieval town could be so beautiful! And this palace we're in! What splendor! They must have plundered all of Europe, Asia and Africa to collect the stuff they have in here!"

The others were looking at us strangely.

"What is he saying, my love?" inquired Giselda, bending over me and kissing me square on the mouth with her lovely, luscious, unrouged lips.

Startled, I drew back. "Did I hurt your poor head, beloved?" asked Giselda with affectionate concern, smoothing my pillow.

"Seems you're stuck, my friend!" said Irish in a tone of sympathy. "Did your chronicles tell you that in this medieval Germanic world the women picked their men instead of vice versa?"

I shook my head. "No! And furthermore, I don't believe it!"

Egginhard broke into our conversation. "The emperor is awaiting us in the throne room, Sir Marius. If you feel equal to it, we shall go there. Your friend and your affianced will support you. It is not far."

My affianced! I felt like telling him that I already had a perfectly good wife back in the twentieth century, and that bigamy was bigamy in any part or period of the Christian world. Then I recalled the ease with which Merovingian and Carolingian rulers, including Charlemagne himself, got rid of their wives when another took their fancy, and judged it best to hold my peace for a time. Anyway, I was too weak to argue.

We got under way, with Irish supporting me on the left and Giselda on the right. Her lithe young body felt supple, pliant and vigorous, and I found it a pleasure to rest most of my weight against her shoulder.

Down a wide marble staircase we went, with Egginhard leading the procession, and through spacious chambers where our footsteps were deadened by thick Oriental rugs, and gurgling fountains played in the center.

"Behold!" said our guide, turning to me. "These chambers are completely outfitted with the gifts sent to our beloved emperor by the Caliph of Baghdad, Haroun-al-Raschid. Would that the Saracens of Spain were as enlightened and touched by God's grace as is that noble Moslem ruler! He and our emperor call each other brother!"

We passed into a vast antechamber adorned with the more familiar Germanic trappings, banners and panoplies and hunting trophies. Fierce-visaged men-at-arms loitered about, brandishing menacing-looking halberds.

"Pray, announce us to the emperor," Egginhard addressed the captain of the guards.

Beyond a wide open portal we could catch a glimpse of an inner chamber, with mosaic floors and richly attired noblemen standing about the entrance.

There was a flourish of trumpets. "The Lord Egginhard, minister of public works and councillor of the emperor!" announced a herald. "The Lord Hubertus, his nephew! The Lady Giselda, his niece! The Lord Fredericus Hibernicus, of Armorica! The Lord Marius Peius, also of Armorica, affianced of the Lady Giselda!"

"So!" I thought to myself. "The good news has leaked out! This is going to be hard to explain when the time comes!"

But there was nothing to be done. We were ushered into the throne room.

It was indeed a sight to behold, something like a cross between the Rotunda of the Columbia Law Memorial Library, the Sistine Chapel, and the lobby of Radio City Music Hall. A vast, circular chamber, with colored mosaic floors, a great open dome overhead through which the sunlight streamed in, walls lost to view behind the forest of marble and alabaster columns that lined the sides of the great hall. Somewhere above us, but unseen, were musicians, playing soft, majestic music on strange medieval instruments. In the center, but set well back from the entrance, was a great raised dais of azure and gold cloth, studded with silver stars. Upon this, a mighty throne, fashioned of gold and marble, on which sat a tall, robust, white-bearded, long-haired man of venerable and noble aspect, who wore over his linen shirt and breeches a long, white, silk-fringed tunic and a blue mantle with a gold buckle. A sword with golden hilt and belt was fastened to his side. On his hoary head was set a great golden crown, studded with gems, and in his hands he bore a golden scepter and a globe of crystal and gold, surmounted by a cross. He peered intently in our direction with his large, lively eyes as we advanced slowly toward him. Beside him, seated on lower and smaller thrones, were at least a dozen men and women, some very young, others fairly on in years. Recalling my genealogy, I had no difficulty in identifying them as Charlemagne's children by his three wives and numerous concubines.

"Come forward, my friend, come forward!" exclaimed the monarch in a voice that was not loud, but rich and pleasant. "Present your guests from my province of Armorica, that I may welcome them to our capital city!"

Egginhard halted before the throne and bowed low. We followed suit, to the best of our ability.

"Forgive my friend Sir Marius Peius, my Lord!" said Egginhard. "He has suffered two unfortunate accidents on his way here, and has risen from his bed only at your bidding. And behold his companion, the noble Armorican knight Fredericus Hibernicus."

"Welcome, my loyal subjects, welcome indeed! What news do you bring us from our well-beloved province of Armorica, twice beloved because it was once the home of my fair nephew Count Roland, who held the pass at Roncevaux against the savage Basques?"

"My Lord Charlemagne," replied Irish, "things go fairly well in Armorica. Trade is good, and were it not for the excessive taxation under which the population groans, there would be widespread happiness and prosperity."

"Indeed, Sir Fredericus!" exclaimed the emperor. "Do my tax gatherers then not observe the moderation with which I charged them? I shall have the matter looked into, and if I find that any of them have transgressed my orders, I shall have them beheaded. And how goes the war?"

"We do not dignify it by that name, Your Majesty," said Irish. "We simply call it a police action. But it has cost us plenty of men and money, and there is no end in sight."

"Yes, those Breton tribesmen are fierce and difficult to control," replied Charlemagne. "But we have confidence in the ability of our loyal Armorican armies to stamp out the rebellion and restore order."

They were talking at cross-purposes, and I trembled lest Freddy should put his foot into it. Despite my feeling of faintness and dizziness, I spoke up.

"Your reform of the language goes on apace, my lord," I said. "You see in us two fruits of your wise policy. We, who have grown up since your edict of Nantes, speak only good Latin."

Charlemagne laughed. "Indeed, Sir Marius! I am happy to get that report from you. I had heard otherwise. Some of my *missi dominici* have informed me that among the mass of the population the language is going from bad to worse, and there are a few among my scholars who suggest that I withdraw the reform and permit the rustic tongue to be again used in the church sermons."

"That were a pity, my lord," I said quickly. "Now that we of the nobility, at least, speak nothing but good grammatical Latin, the work should be kept up. If I may presume to ask a question, sire, how did that rustic language sound in the days before the edict?"

Charlemagne laughed again. "In truth, Sir Marius, I never knew it. My own ancestral tongue is, as you know, Franconian, and in the days of my youth here at Aquisgranum my good father King Pepin had me taught Latin because, he said, that was the language of our western realms. But after my accession to the throne, I had the surprise of my life when I sojourned at Laon and discovered that the serfs and scullions and stableboys could hardly understand me, or I them. So I decided to bring the tongue of Rome back to them, with the help of God's church."

Perhaps my face betrayed my disappointment, for Charlemagne quickly added: "But if you are curious, I have one here at my court who surely can enlighten you. He is my own nephew Nithardus, one of our youthful scholars. He is a young man of strange, almost revolutionary ideas. Just fancy! He claims that the rustic tongue will someday become the language of all of our western realms, and that it will even be written! I should indeed like to see him, or anyone else, attempt to write that barbarous jargon!"

I was speechless with joy. Nithardus! The man who thirty years later was to compose the Oaths of Strasbourg, earliest known document of French! Could I but consult him!

"Could I talk to this—Nithardus?" I gulped.

"Why, assuredly! Adaltrud, tell the captain of the guard to fetch me Nithardus!"

The lady thus addressed was a young woman of rare beauty with flashing dark eyes and raven locks that escaped rebelliously from beneath the circular veil on her head. I remembered that she was one of Charlemagne's daughters by one of his later concubines.

"Lord and father!" demurely replied the damsel. "Have you forgotten that you yourself sent out Nithardus a month ago to your western realms, with instructions to bring you back a report on the progress of the reform?"

"Ah, indeed! That is true!" exclaimed the emperor. "But no matter! He will be back in a week, and surely you, Sir Marius, and you, Sir Fredericus, will tarry here with us at least until then. Tonight we dine together in my great dining hall. Egginhard, see that your friends are made comfortable in our palace."

The audience was at an end. We bowed and withdrew from the imperial presence. Frustration and hope were having a tug-of-war within me as I stepped over the threshold of the throne room, supported by Irish and Giselda.

The evening meal in Charlemagne's great banquet hall was a

391

repetition, on a vaster and more elaborate scale, of what we had had in the morning.

Instead of simple, backless wooden benches, there were high-backed chairs with armrests. The table was far more sumptuously set, and it literally groaned under a wealth of both strange and familiar viands. Menservants brought in roast peacocks and pheasants, a whole wild boar roasted on the spit and flanked by suckling pigs, stuffed pigeons and haunches of venison, strange pies and pastries, platters of exotic fruits. Seated at the long board were countless knights and ladies of the court in brocaded silken garments, two sharing a plate, with knives as the sole tableware. The wine flowed in profusion—heady, sparkling Rhine and Moselle vintages, the precursors of the later Riesling and Liebfraumilch. The silver goblets were no sooner emptied than they were refilled, and no sooner refilled than they were emptied.

The great emperor, white-clad, white-bearded and benign, sat on a raised throne at the head of the table. Below him sat his many sons and daughters, in order of descending age, then came his honored guests, then the noblemen and noblewomen of his court. I found myself seated by the right side of his youngest daughter, the raven-haired Adaltrud, with my bride-to-be Giselda on my own right, as was fitting and proper. Egginhard, Irish and Hubertus were on the other side of the table, but somewhat below us, and out of earshot. My position, between a blonde and a brunette beauty, was enviable, and I made up my mind to enjoy it and let the morrow take care of itself.

"Tonight I feel as though I were in heaven!" I said, addressing both my fair companions at once.

Adaltrud looked at me archly with her flashing dark eyes. "Indeed, Sir Marius! And how may that be?"

"I have an angel on either side of me!"

Adaltrud laughed merrily, throwing back her head so that her black locks danced on her shoulders, and displaying to my advantage the lovely whiteness of her throat and neck. Giselda laughed, too, but her laugh sounded slightly hollow. Ever since the seating arrangement had been announced, something had seemed to be preying on her mind.

"Sir Marius, you are indeed a flatterer!" exclaimed Adaltrud, eyeing me coyly. "Are all the knights like you, back in Armorica?"

"I am not qualified to pass judgment on my peers, my lady," I replied modestly. "But in Rome, where I was born—"

"Yes," interrupted Giselda, bitingly. "In Rome, they are all lovers, or monks, or scholars—or sorcerers!"

"Or all of these combined," quickly replied Adaltrud. "Save perhaps the second. Let us rejoice, Giselda, that Sir Marius is at least not a monk!"

"There are times when I almost wish he were!" replied my blonde affianced uncompromisingly.

The conversation was taking an alarming turn. The thought of the unhappy Abelard flashed through my mind. But that, I reasoned, was still a couple of centuries in the future.

"My lady Adaltrud," I said quickly, to change the subject. "Have you spoken often with this young scholar Nithardus, whom your royal father mentioned earlier today?"

"Indeed I have, Sir Marius," replied the damsel. Then she added, tantalizingly, "He and I have often discoursed about this matter of my father's linguistic reform."

"Ah!" My interest was aroused. "And has he enlightened you on the state of the popular tongue in our western provinces?"

"Forsooth, Sir Marius!" the princess laughed. "I need no enlightenment! I have spent years in the nunnery at Laon, and I speak the language of the western peasants as easily as my own Franconian, or this Latin that we speak now!"

The wave of joy that surged through me made me quite oblivious of the impatient tapping of Giselda's foot on my right. But she would not be denied.

"Beloved!" she said, and her tone belied her word. "The emperor is signaling for you to join him!"

A glance at the head of the table showed me that hers was unfortunately not a ruse. Charlemagne was beckoning to me. I could have wished him in his twentieth-century sarcophagus, but it would have done no good. In the ninth century, when an emperor beckons to you, you go!

"My lady, Adaltrud," I said, rising from my seat and bowing to both my fair partners. "I must speak to you again of this matter, if you will permit."

"It will be doubly a pleasure, my lord!" replied the maiden, looking at me with obvious meaning. Giselda looked daggers at both of us.

Charlemagne had me sit on a stool by his side and began plying me with endless questions on the state of affairs in Armorica. These I answered skilfully enough with an effort of the will and the imagination. But my mind kept wandering from time to time up to Adaltrud and the mine of precious information she could turn out to be. There would be danger in questioning her, a twofold danger. On the one hand, I knew enough from history about the loose morals of all of Charlemagne's daughters to realize that if I had caught her fancy, I would not get my information for nothing, and one complication could easily lead to another. On the other hand, Giselda had made no secret of her fierce jealousy, and she, too, in her blonde, blue-eyed way, could prove dangerous. But the true scholar defies all peril when knowledge in his chosen field is to be gained. I must interview the Lady Adaltrud at all costs. . . .

She herself offered the opportunity. I had been conversing with the emperor for half an hour when she rose from her place and came toward us.

"Lord and father," she said with a graceful bow, "have I your permission to take Sir Marius off to the throne room? I wish to show him the inscription on the slab of lapis lazuli that the emperor of Constantinople sent you, and see if his interpretation agrees with that of Nithardus."

"I do not recollect the inscription, my daughter," said the benign monarch, "but you may have Sir Marius. See that you bring him back safe and sound. I would speak with him again ere we retire."

Adaltrud took me gently by the hand and led me away, her bewitching eyes beckoning invitingly to me. I glanced back to where Giselda sat. Her face was frozen into a livid mask of jealous anger. She looked for all the world like an irate Val-kyrie. A cold chill ran up and down my spine, and I shuddered.

"Follow me, my lord!" said Adaltrud as we stepped over the threshold of the banquet room into the dimly lighted corridor beyond.

"This is not the way to the throne room," I ventured.

"No, of course not!" she laughed, giving my hand a playful squeeze. "I am taking you to my own chamber, where we can talk at ease of the things that interest us!"

"Such as?" I asked.

"Why, the language of our western provinces, to be sure!" she replied with feigned innocence. "How could we discuss that in the din of the banquet hall, with that beautiful blue-eyed watchdog on your right nudging you and stamping on the floor?"

"Look, my lady!" I said with some alarm. "Could we not meet somewhere in the morning, say in the palace garden, and have our talk?"

"Sir Marius," she replied, halting for an instant to look up into my eyes, but retaining her grip on my hand. "Some here in this court say I have strange, hidden powers. I can read your thoughts. I know for a fact that the subject of our western tongue is with you not a mere interest, but an obsession. Is it not so?"

I had to admit that it was.

"Therefore, there is no time like the present to discuss it, and give you the knowledge you seek. Tomorrow—who knows where we may be tomorrow?"

With these strangely prophetic words, she resumed her advance along the corridor, and I followed.

"Besides," she went on, "there are other things to talk about once your curiosity is appeased. There are things I should like to know—and experience!" She came closer to me, so that I could feel the warmth of her slender young body through the silken garments. "Are you afraid to be alone with me, Sir Marius?" She pouted coquettishly. "You, a Roman and an Armorican, born in a country where all men are lovers and raised in one where all men are exploiters?"

I had been tempted to break away from the blandishments of this ninth-century Circe and run back to the banquet hall and the comparative protection of Charlemagne, Irish, even Giselda. But her words nettled me. Who was this obscure, illegitimate daughter of a ninth-century ruler to cast aspersions upon my manhood?

"Let's go!" I said shortly.

She smiled a self-satisfied smile, grasped my hand more firmly and advanced swiftly down the dim corridor and up a winding, drafty staircase, then along another corridor till we halted before a massive, iron-studded door. She opened it wide and gestured gracefully to me.

"Come in, Sir Marius! Welcome to my chamber!"

Like the spider and the fly, I thought as I crossed the threshold.

Milady's chamber was quite unlike the others I had seen. Illuminated by soft tapers set in wall sconces, it was hung with silken draperies, while the floor was covered with thick Eastern rugs, a gift of Haroun-al-Raschid, no doubt. A faint, pleasant perfume pervaded the air. Small panoplies of arms hung on the walls, interspersed with beautifully carved stone images of saints. In one corner, under a blue silken canopy, was a low, wide, comfortable-looking bed, with damask pillows and coverlets. Soft divans occupied the other corners, and to one of these Adaltrud led me.

"Pray be seated, Sir Marius. A cup of wine?"

She took a curiously shaped flagon from a low table and filled two silver goblets.

"To your health—and to a warmer and more intimate friendship between us!" she said, looking straight into my eyes as she invitingly proffered a cup.

We drank in silence, then she sat by my side, very close to me.

"Now tell me," she said, resting her head on the back of the divan and half closing her eyes. "What do you want to know—and why?"

I gazed at her intently. This illegitimate child of the great emperor was ravishingly beautiful—lithe as a panther, exquisitely molded, with milk-white skin that set off the brunette loveliness of her hair and eyes. Young, too. She could not be past twenty-five. Why did she have to pick on me, a man approaching his fifties? Then I recalled that medieval standards of manly beauty ran to middle age and graying hair rather than to the callow ebullience of youth. All to the good—save that I had a purpose to fulfill.

I drew as far away from fair Adaltrud as I dared. "My desires are very simple, my lady," I began in extremely businesslike fashion. "For reasons of my own, I am interested in obtaining a clear, unbiased, eyewitness account of the popular language of our western provinces. It's as simple as all that!"

Adaltrud's laugh was silvery and full throated. "Sir Marius, you are a gay dog indeed! Why do you seek information about the language of our western provinces, when you yourself claim to hail from them? If it is true that you come to us from Armorica," she stressed the *if* significantly, "Then what can I tell you that you don't already know?"

I saw there was no use lying to this shrewd young enchantress. "My lady," I replied slowly, "perhaps I do not come from Armorica, Perhaps I have come to you, quite by accident, from another world, a world that you know nothing of because it still lies far off into the future."

I paused. She looked at me expectantly. "Pray go on, Sir Marius!" she said, half seriously, half mockingly.

"My lady," I blurted out desperately, resolved to make a clean breast of it. "I come from over one thousand years hence, from a country whose existence is as yet unsuspected. In the world that I have left, and to which I hope to return, there is widespread ignorance and curiosity about certain things that happened in what to us is the past. In my own particular sphere, we want to know precisely how the Latin we are speaking turned into another tongue, which we call French. The crucial point in our investigation is your historical period, your father's reform and its effects upon the language of the masses. It is imperative that I find out precisely what the present status of the western tongue is, and report it back to my fellow scholars in the twentieth century. Do I make myself clear?"

She looked at me tauntingly. "Indeed you do, Sir Marius! In the course of my brief span of years, I have seen and heard of

397

many subterfuges whereby both men and women sought to obtain their ends, which in the end were almost always identical. Many such schemings could have been dispensed with, by a mere statement of purpose, a mere 'I desire you! Will you be mine?', which would have saved time and heartaches. But never have I heard so ingenious a subterfuge as yours, Sir Marius of Rome and Armorica! In order to win me, you devise trips into the unknowable future, weird studies into languages that interest no one, strange, diabolical stories! It is all so unnecessary, so utterly superfluous, Sir Marius!"

She edged closer to me as she spoke. Suddenly, she flung her shapely arms about my neck, and planted her hot, luscious lips squarely upon mine.

At that very moment, the door of the chamber was flung open. In the doorway, tall, implacably lovely, her blue eyes ablaze with fury, stood the Lady Giselda, my affianced.

She advanced slowly to where we sat, while Adaltrud and I remained frozen in our one-sided embrace.

"You, Adaltrud, I know!" exclaimed my blonde betrothed, in a voice low-pitched with anger. "I know you as everyone in this court knows you, for the harlot that you are. But this time, Adaltrud, you have met your match! What this man says is true! He is no ordinary mortal, no lover for a day, whom you can steal from another woman, suck dry, then throw away! He is a fiend, a werewolf, an enchanter from another world, whose mere glance inflames women with passion and desire! Beware, Adaltrud, lest your soul be forfeit to the adversary of mankind, whose minion this creature is!"

I shook myself free from Adaltrud's encircling arms and sprang forward. Giselda retreated before me, making the sign of the cross. *"Vade retro, Satanas!"* she exclaimed.

"Giselda!" I cried out. "Please listen to me! I assure you—"

"I will not listen to your blandishments, fiend!" she replied, backing to the wall. "Rather will I treat you as all emissaries of the devil must be treated!"

She swung around and seized a battle-ax from a panoply. "You go to your infernal master, fiend!" she cried, advancing upon me and swinging the weapon.

"Giselda! Please!" I shouted. "Don't do it! I have a wife back where I come from!"

"A wife!" she snapped. "Probably an entire bevy of witches and she-devils! Enchanter, you have cast your last spell!"

The battle-ax rose and descended. I could not parry it. With a sickening thud it came down on my poor, much mistreated head. For the third time everything spun around before my eyes and went black. As I sank into nothingness, it seemed to me I felt Adaltrud's warm arms seizing me, supporting me, bearing me off.

Again there was that gently swaying, faintly soothing motion that I had experienced on the litter that bore me to Egginhard's castle. I was sick! The sunlight hurt my eyes, even though they were closed.

"*Ja*, he will be all right for the trip!" I heard. The voice was Egginhard's but the words were in modern German.

"You are quite sure, *Herr Doktor?*" It was Freddy's voice.

I opened my eyes with an effort. God, I was sick! I was on a moving litter. But this time it was carried by four men in white intern's uniforms.

I looked around. Giselda and Adaltrud were walking beside my litter, one on the right, the other on the left. But now they wore nurses' uniforms instead of their ninth-century trappings.

"Freddy!" I called out weakly.

He came running up. "Good! The doctor said you'd regain consciousness before we got you on the plane! How are you feeling?"

"Plane? What plane?" I asked.

"You suffered a slight head injury when we crashed," he explained. "And you've been unconscious for two days. But they performed a little operation on you at the Aachen hospital, and you'll be quite all right. The real trouble is, you've got a broken leg. It's set in a plaster cast, but it will be two months before you can walk. I wired your wife suggesting we keep you here. She said she'd rather take care of you herself if we could ship you back to New York by plane. So by plane you're going! Sorry, old man! It was all my fault! I should have driven more carefully!"

"How about—them?" I pointed to Adaltrud and Giselda.

"They are Fräulein Altmeister and Fräulein Koch, the two *Krankenschwester* who took care of you in the hospital. Fine girls. They gave you the best of care. Good looking, too!"

"Yes, I know!" I said somewhat ruefully. "And that man you were speaking to a moment ago?"

"That was Dr. Wilhelm Meyer of the Aachen hospital. He operated on you. Wonderful doctor. Old school, you know. Still wears a venerable gray beard, like they used to in the old days. But he certainly fixed you up!"

The litter was being carried up the gangplank of the big army plane.

"You'll be at LaGuardia field by tomorrow morning," said Irish. "Your wife will be there with an ambulance, and she'll take you right home. Sorry you never got to see the bones of Charlemagne. Maybe next trip!"

Within ten minutes the last good-byes were said and the big machine was off. Lying comfortably on a bed, with a stewardess hovering over me, I looked through the window at the sun-drenched field beneath. There were Adaltrud and Giselda and Irish and Egginhard, waving good-bye. Far off to the left rose the twin towers of the Rathaus, very much the worse for wear. The wrecked eighth-century spire of the cathedral stood up in the air like a pointing finger that has been suddenly chopped off. I thought I could even discern the ruins of the lovely Hochmünster, with its ancient marble and granite columns. There, buried somewhere in the old Hungarian chapel, reposed the bones of Charlemagne, in their ornate shrine. They had guarded their secret well from the twentieth-century intruder who had sought to pierce it!